ns
The Sum of His Worth

Also by Ron Argo

Year of the Monkey
Baby Love
The Courage to Kill

The Sum of His Worth

Ron Argo

Cliff Edge Publishing
Cortaro, Arizona

Hardcover edition © 2011, 2013 by Ronald Argo
Digital e-book edition © 2013 by Ron Argo

This book is a work of fiction. Except for some historical figures all names, characters, places and incidents are either the product of the author's imagination or are used fictitiously.

All rights reserved including the right of reproduction in whole or in part in any form.

Cliff Edge Publishing
PO Box 450
Cortaro, AZ 85652-0450

Library of Congress Cataloging-in-Publication Data

Argo, Ronald.
  The sum of his worth / Ron Argo.
     pages cm
  ISBN 978-0-9894035-7-3 (alk. paper)
  1. Teenage boys--Fiction. 2. African Americans--Civil rights--Alabama--Anniston--History--20th century--Fiction. 3. Anniston (Ala.)--Race relations--Fiction. 4. Civil rights workers--Crimes against--Alabama--Anniston--History--20th century--Fiction. 5. Crimes aboard buses--Alabama--Anniston--History--20th century--Fiction. 6. Ku Klux Klan (1915-)--Alabama--History--Fiction. I. Title.

PS3551.R418S86 2013
813'.54--dc23

2013027130

Cover Design © 2103 by Renato Prete
Visit the author's website at www.ronargo.com
Visit the publisher's website at www.cliffedgepublishing.com

In memory of Dr. W. H. West

This book is dedicated to the civil rights workers who were beaten and jailed in Alabama and Mississippi during the summer of the Freedom Rides, 1961; to "Little Joe" Postiglione, who took the photographs published in the *Anniston* (AL) *Star* of the bus burning in that city; and to the Birmingham Civil Rights Institute for its continued good work toward racial equality in the state of Alabama and throughout the United States of America; and to my beautiful friend Herman Stinson, another victim of senseless suicide.

Acknowledgements

Since I grew up during the 1960s in an Alabama town that Woodstock closely resembled—Anniston—I pulled from my own experiences and memories much of the body of this story, and it was easy enough to gather other data from archives. What *was* difficult, I'll tell you, was getting into the trenches with those memories and realities to put together the story, a pit bull's bite into the psyche coming to terms today with the hate and prejudices that were my environment back then. But I got it done and I have people to thank for helping me along, not necessarily in order of this listing. I want to thank John Postiglione for opening up his heart and his father's photo and FBI files, the hard evidence that nailed the soul of racism that occurred on Mother's Day in 1961. I want to thank my childhood friend Kit Downing whose remarkable memory of the '50s and natural ease took me back to those days, and to Charlotte Downing, thanks for you gracious hospitality. Thanks to my best friend growing up, Jimmy Ledbetter, for being there for me and being himself. Thanks to the local people who, in 2011, sponsored the 50th anniversary of the bus burning in Anniston and who dignified the event by bringing together some of the surviving Klansmen and injured bus riders. I want to thank Fred Shuttlesworth and Hank Thomas and Genevieve Hughes who suffered so much emotional and physical harm but never quit. A special thanks goes to Ann Skains, a Southern friend, for her righteous clarity and support. For her enduring toleration and support I wish to thank my wife Mary Anderson, and particularly my daughter Lisa Argo whose enthusiasm for me during this project helped get me through some rough writing times.

Summary, 1958

We'd come out to the woods three hours ago to shoot our rifles and drink some beer. Now we were out of both but still hanging around. Cause who wanted to get back to the concrete oven of Woodstock? Out here, deep in the woods and in the midnight cool, it felt like you were floating in space or something, like you could be riding that sliver of cold moon I kept seeing pass across the tips of pines.

Still, we should've been gone because our lives were about to change.

The chiggers wouldn't give up, but that was nothing. For me, anyway. Herman, he swatted at them like crazy, mumbling profanities like they'd get the message and vamoose. The only thing that got me was pine sap. I hated the stuff with a passion. And wouldn't you know it, it just so happened right then—probably cause I was thinking about it—that I leaned off a tree and felt it sticking to the soft underside of my arm, the worst place it could get on you. Almost.

"Shit, man, let's go," I said. "I'm ready to go." Pine sap could find me on a church pew, anywhere.

"Just a minute. What's the big hurry?" Herman was still looking for the phantom possum he had missed but claimed emphatically he hit. We never heard it fall and a possum is a heavy, clumsy animal that makes a lot of noise, even if it comes down wounded instead of falling deadweight through the branches. Besides, it was too dense that far up to see much of anything, except every now and then that arch of cool white moon.

If it hadn't been for his stubbornness we wouldn't have been there when it happened, though I wasn't going to put the blame square on Herman. It takes two to tango. I told him to at least turn the damn radio off so the critters would quieten down.

I popped a stick match under my thumbnail and breathed in its acrid phosphorus odor, a smell like—I don't know—that smells; comforting. I turned the match upside down to see how long it'd take the flame to reach my fingers and then how long I could hold on. Two blinks of the eye, that was it before I tossed it to the mossy ground, shaking the heat off my hand.

"Look, bean brain," I said, striking another match, trying it again, "I gotta get up early. I got an appointment."

He stared at the match like a damn moth then turned off the portable. He wasn't buying the appointment thing, though. His eyes narrowed. "Appointment for what? Shit, what kinda 'pointment you got? And lay off the matches, somebody might spot us."

I didn't have to answer. My only appointment was with Vicki and you sure couldn't call that an appointment. A rendezvous maybe, after her parents went to work. I wasn't going to tell Herman that, though, cause he would just start advising me what to do with her, like I'd never been with a girl before. By the time you were fourteen years old, like both of us were, you had sure better been with a girl already. But I had to admit Herman knew what he was talking about when it came to girls. He was a real lover boy, had this James Dean/Dean Martin way of talking to girls that sent them. They swarmed him at every party we went to together. I hated him for it. Girls rubbed themselves all over Herman, sticking their fingers in his greasy curly locks and parting their wet lips, just waiting till he got ready to plant one on them. He usually did. But Herman's flaw was he fell in love and then he hit hard when it came to an end. I still couldn't figure why they would get their hands greasy in his hair. It was disgusting. He oiled it with Brylcreem and applied Vaseline to the ducktail when he chose to have one and sometimes used his sister's rose oil on his Elvis sideburns. Me, I used Butch Wax because I wanted my flattop standing up like brush bristles.

"You missed, let's go." I was getting aggravated with him now. I wanted to get home so I could scrub the pine sap off my arm and get to sleep. "You probably hit a house a mile away and they've called the cops on us. They'll be here anytime now, you want that?"

"I heard him fall. He's around here somewheres."

It wasn't doing any good arguing with a bullhead like Herman Brown. I just shook my head and dropped the subject.

We'd used up the five bullets we each had hours ago. That was about to become important because we might have been able to help that poor man with a couple of shots in the air.

"Shh, listen," I said in a low voice. "Hear it?"

"Yeah … You think it's the cops?"

Right then a light began to flicker through the timber, getting brighter, like the ghostly figure in my mind's eye of the headless horseman barreling toward you through the woods in the Sleepy Hollow story. That's how fast the light was coming on. Too fast for us to even run, so we stood thin behind separate trees to dodge the wavering flashes of light casting shadows into the woods beyond us.

Then voices, growing loud and angry. They were working their way right toward us.

I didn't know what to do. Maybe we should run, I thought, but then Herman put a finger to his lips, calmly, telling me without words to stay put and wait it out. The mob wasn't twenty feet from us when they stopped in the small clearing where moments earlier I'd seen the moon and we could hear them breathing hard and spitting and cursing. Someone moaned.

I peeked into the glare of their flashlights, then quickly jerked back behind the tree and stood tall, making myself even skinnier. I tried it again, looking with one eye. They were gathered in a tight circle around someone I couldn't see. Maybe there were ten or twelve men. They wore their white robes but didn't have on the pointy hoods. I guess the formality out here in the woods wasn't important at this final stage. I knew a little about the KKK, since I'd lived in Alabama all my life. But it was the first time I'd ever seen them in a gathering, doing it.

I heard a rough voice saying, "... is it, you sonofabitchin' nigger faggot—" and then another one bellowed something deep I couldn't quite figure out, something like "... not in God's kingdom!—" or "... no home in God's kingdom!—" Something like that, but either way managing to get God in there, like they had His blessing for what they were doing. Then the Klansman's voice got lost in the surge of the forest and other ghastly sounds that hurt me to hear, the unforgettable sound of wood smashing against flesh.

I saw the faces of most of the men but didn't recognize any of them. But there were two boys in the crowd that I did know. One was from school, Sugarman Cole, a smart but dangerous hood. The other boy, Leon Legget, was a redneck punk who didn't even go to school but hung out with some of Lamar Junior's delinquents. I'd seen him around. His daddy and uncles owned gas stations on the west side that served only whites. Made sure everybody knew it with signs saying, "Whites Only," hanging right over the pumps so you couldn't miss the message. Everybody knew they were high-up Klansmen, even when they were too mean and hot-tempered to be on the white citizen's council or even accepted into the state KKK confederation.

I couldn't see the Negro but I saw the rope go up and over a branch. It wouldn't be long now.

Oh God, I thought, *he's going to die, a man's really going to die!* I tried to swallow a lump in my throat but it didn't budge. I just held it. I looked at Herman again. He was mesmerized. Then he glanced my way, his opaque eyes wide and fearful. All of a sudden I had to pee something fierce; I thought I was going to puke, too. I'd never been so scared.

I looked away, up to the treetops and focused on the black sky where you could see some stars in the small window of blackness. I thought about the depth of that void, of how many planets there were beyond my vision and if there might have been creatures like us on those planets in those faraway solar systems who might be looking down on me, on us, and if right then they might be in the middle of some anarchy or cruel, unfair behavior too, like this angry mob. The wonderment of it kept me from puking but not from being sick over them hanging that poor guy.

They did it fast.

He hadn't gotten to say anything because they'd already stuffed his mouth with something and put a hood on his head to cover up his bulbous eyes. Those terrible sounds came from two-by-fours, hard blows to his head and upper body. I got a quick glimpse of him between men. He didn't take long to slump, thank God. I don't think he knew when he got hung.

I glanced again at Herman and saw that he was going to collapse. The tears running down his face glistened in the glow of lights. He was trying hard not to gasp and he managed to send the gasps through his nose, making muffled, strangled sputtering noises, which weren't too loud. I looked pleadingly at him, hoping I could show him how important it was right then not to lose control. He didn't look back at me again, I think out of shame because he was crying and he didn't want me to see what a sissy he was. But I didn't think that at all. Herman was too crazy to be a sissy.

I think seeing him whimper saved me from breaking down. I had never seen anything so grisly ever before. I was pretty sure Herman hadn't either.

Then all of a sudden, in an act of harebrained idiocy, Herman balked. He pushed off from his tree like he was starting a hundred-meter race. *Oh, shit!* I thought. There was nothing for me to do but take off too.

He was easy to keep in sight with his flashlight beam jumping around trees like illuminated monkeys. The mob had to see it too. I wanted to shout, "Keep the light to the ground, you moron." I looked behind me and saw them coming, their lights wavering all around like the woods was on fire. The mob started screaming at us.

A hoarse voice rang out, "Hey, hold up ... Don't you motherfuckers run on us, you know what's good for you. You hear me? Hey, goddamnit!" The voice sputtered and vibrated from the man running.

I knew what was good for us and it sure wasn't stopping, giving up. Maybe the threat in that voice motivated both of us to speed up cause we were getting ahead of the main body. The two boys stayed closer behind us. I knew how fast Sugarman Cole could run; I'd run against him in gym playing basketball, and he was fast.

Thicker woods slowed us down. Tree limbs dropped lower and the ground growth and vines grabbed at our ankles. It also slowed down our pursuers. They must not have had guns, since I didn't hear any cock and no shots.

I made a decision to split off from Herman, thinking we stood a better chance that way because it might give us an edge when they slowed down a little deciding who would go after which one of us. All I needed was a few steps lead and I could climb a tree and get out of sight. I could climb fast as lightning.

There was no way to signal Herman; he was barrel-assing ahead. Considering how much shorter he was than me, he could run like hell. I split off when we hit an oak grove. Oaks spread out and left open space and I could get through with less light. They were easier to climb, too, plus you didn't get sapped, like you did from pines.

I cut the flashlight and humped as quietly as I could and listened hard for footsteps, since I didn't see light behind me. Somehow a low oak branch reached out and got me under the nose and I lost my footing and dropped my gun. I went down too. My eyes watered from the pain but I didn't need to see anyway, only to listen, and I still heard nothing close by, although I saw fragments of weak lights and heard noises from the mob a distance away. But I didn't dare turn the flashlight on to find my rifle since I knew one of the boys was on my tail.

I discovered something in that instant about myself that I hadn't ever thought about before and probably wouldn't have wanted to ever think about. Even if I'd had bullets left, I wasn't going to shoot a person. Even the kind of murdering useless, redneck punks that were chasing me. All it took to learn that was to imagine what it would be like to fire a bullet into someone. I left the thought behind and climbed.

I could make out the form of the tree that'd knocked me down and grabbed hold of its limbs and didn't stop till I had laid thirty or forty feet under me. Then I stopped to listen again. My heart went like a hummingbird's; I couldn't seem to get air and I thought I was going to fall. I braced myself between limbs in case I got too dizzy to hold on. I may even have blacked out for a moment because there was no sound in my ears or light in my eyes for that long.

Then I heard something. Then I saw lights below me and my gut started churning. I grew so scared saliva dripped off my lip but my throat was too dry to swallow. I hugged what was left of the core of the oak and tried to think of something that would put me somewhere else—on the white beaches of Panama City or in my uncle's boat on the Coosa casting for surface bass.

There was rustling below. I waited and didn't breathe. A voice that sounded like Sugarman Cole's shouted, "You better keep your mouth shut, shitass. I got your gun. We'll get you."

The rest of that summer I hid in my room with the shade down and listened to my portable and watched the oscillating fan blow around the blistering air. I didn't come out except to eat chili beans and crackers and deliver my papers, then eat supper and maybe watch TV shows with Mother till her toes stopped fidgeting. I didn't think they had caught Herman since there was no word he was dead, but he never called. I was mad as hell at him for taking off like that when they would have never known we were there if he could've just stuck it out. I wouldn't have this terrible death warrant hanging over me now and I would still have the .22 my grandfather gave me when I was seven.

Summer, the next year

CHAPTER 1

Somehow I made it the whole way through ninth grade, both of us did, me and Herman, without telling a soul about the lynching and without the KKK sneaking around our windows late at night, grabbing us. I cooled to Herman for a while but finally forgave him. It helped that he gave me three of his sister's Elvis singles I didn't have. The Klan never found Herman's gun or his portable, thank God. He told me he waited a week after it happened then he went back there and somehow found both those things. What balls! There's no way I'd have gone back. He said he found no trace of the man's body; they'd left nothing behind.

We seemed to be out of danger, as long as neither of us got loose lips. So I tried to put that whole episode to rest and just hoped Herman would never become a Klansman and turn on me.

Anyway, I still had other problems. Compared to the Ku Klux Klan ever on my mind, it didn't seem like much of an issue that I was about to start high school without a girlfriend. But it was. Everybody had a girlfriend by the time high school rolled around; it was expected. I had made two girlfriends in the summer but complications had sprung up. Now it looked like I might lose both of them.

That wasn't my only concern on the verge of high school. Gerald Henry would be waiting to fight me the first day of school. Gerald Henry led a westside gang. Last week I was riding my bike by the pool hall on West Tenth Street when his gang blocked me at the alley and he came up and popped me on the nose. He got some blood but not much. Gerald Henry was half a foot shorter than me, shorter even than Herman, and he had to look up to tell me he was too busy to mess with me at the moment but would see me behind the school yard and rearrange my face then. I thought about thanking him for letting me off till later but that would probably have provoked him as sarcasm. Never mind what I was doing on the west side.

I still had three weeks to go; time to learn how to fight from my Negro friend who was a boxer, work on my tan, and with some luck settle things with at least one of those girls.

It was Wednesday and on Wednesdays the newspaper was thin and easy to fold, which made it easier to sling from the street. So I finished my route before three o'clock and pedaled fast to Scarborough Drug Store where I could sit at the fountain for a while in the air conditioning. I ate a packet of peanut butter crackers and sucked down a frosty chocolate shake while thumbing through a Superman comic book off the rack. I scoffed down the crackers faster than you could say Jiminy Cricket and grabbed another packet so I could get away with paying for only one. The soda jerk would get wise if you did it too often, so I only did it about once a week.

A man waiting at the pharmacy watched me and knew what I'd done; I know because he cracked a grin. But he didn't care; he was making hurry-up gestures to the pharmacist, a pall of worry on his face. I got interested in him. He wore tennis clothes; everything on him was bright white, from the visor on his head to his unscuffed tennis shoes. He was tall and had big white teeth, which stood out to me more than his dazzling brightness. He caught me staring and I managed to return a crooked grin.

"How you doin'?" I said, stupidly.

"There's a dog in the alley that someone must have hit." He said it in a confidential way. I liked that he would confide in me, a stranger, a kid. "I'm getting some stuff to clean him up."

"Can I see?"

"He's a mess."

I ran out the side door and saw the blood trail that led from the sidewalk out front. It meandered down the alley where the drips disappeared in the bushes at the back of the building. I pushed back the bushes and there was the dog. A mutt, not much to look at. It didn't have a lot of color, mostly spotted gray with some white on the chest and a rusty brown front leg. A lot of red on his underside, but that was blood. I figured he had crawled into the shrubs to die out of sight. Dogs will do that whereas cats, when they finally die, just croak on the spot. You saw them all around, but hardly ever did you see a dead dog lying in the street or grass. The mutt breathed hard, in quick gasps. He was bleeding something fierce from somewhere underneath; I didn't want to look. He yelped trying to wag his tail, which made me cringe and feel just awful.

The tall man appeared. "You can occupy him while I treat him, okay?"

I didn't want to touch the bloody thing. When he rolled him, you could see guts and white bone. But I got down close to the wet nose and rubbed it with my own nose. The dog was real friendly. I rubbed him behind the ears and he propped his head on my knee. He seemed to have tears in his eyes, but that could've just been from all the blue there. He tried to lick me in the face. I let him.

The man knew what he was doing. He worked fast. I cringed again watching him stick a needle into the wound and start sewing up the big gashes in the dog's stomach underneath the ribs and on its hip. Took him only about ten minutes. Maybe fifteen.

"You think his back's broken?" I asked. "I mean he had to crawl, prob'ly to die … Poor ole thing."

"Most likely multiple fractures. I'll take her in for X-rays and treatment. What's your name?"

The question caught me off guard. "Uh, Sonny. What's yours?"

"I'm Joe. Nice to meet you, Sonny. I better get going to the vet with our friend Pearl here."

"Pearl? Oh, I get it," I said, flustered that he'd made fun of my accent saying 'poor ole thing.'

He cradled the dog in his arms, getting matted blood all over his white tennis clothes, and he wore a collared shirt with the arrow logo on the chest, which meant it was expensive. I followed him around to the street where his car was parked, a brand-new looking T-Bird convertible. Yeah! It was the most beautiful car I'd ever seen, solid white with slick white leather seats trimmed in red and big white sidewall tires. He started to put the dog in the passenger seat.

"Wait a second," I said. "Let me put some newspapers down first."

He nodded and I spread a handful of leftover newspapers on the white seat. He gently put the dog in. There was no way that mutt was going to make it. Her head slumped and she didn't move a muscle. I thought the dog was either asleep or already dead.

"Thanks for your help, Sonny."

"Sure," I said and watched him drive away fast, those salved '56 cams rumbling and echoing off the asphalt.

Chapter 2

I didn't think much about the mangy dog after that or the guy that tried to save it. It had surely died and what benefit was there in going around thinking about dogs dying? None. When the thought of dying came up any more, I would think about the man they lynched. So I sure wasn't going to mope over some dead mutt, especially since my thoughts were all on Vicki and Susie. Big problems there.

After meeting the girls, I had gone to both of their houses and real quick discovered they lived on the same street, same block even, one on each corner of the west side of Calhoun Street. Vicki lived in the apartments on the north end at the city limit sign by the edge of the woods and Susie's little house was at the other end next to a four-way stop intersection where people going by could easily see someone waiting at the door, on both the front porch and the back of the house. Someone like me.

The block wasn't the longest in town either, with only four houses separating Susie's bungalow and Vicki's apartment building. Out of all the girls at the pool I could have gone after—and there were always a ton of them at the start of summer—I had to pick two neighbors who were also good friends. But there was nothing I could do about it. That was just the way it turned out. You might call it fate and that I was destined to fail with both girls, but I didn't believe in that sort of thing.

I'd met Vicki June third, the first day after school let out and the first day the swimming pool in Wells Park opened for the summer. It was jammed, making it easy to accidentally bump into her under water. I got her name and number helping her up the ladder. When Vicki didn't show up after a couple more days, I met Susie.

It took them a long time to figure it out. That was two weeks ago. The phone rang a lot till Mother finally told them not to call again. She didn't minced her words. We shared a party line and Mother wasn't keen on other people picking up to listen in on the smutty conversations her sons had with their girlfriends. It aggravated her something awful having to share the phone with who knows what strangers. But there was no way she could afford a private line, a widow with three sons, secretary at the First Baptist Church of Woodstock bringing in a puny $55 a week and that was it. There wasn't a pension or any inheritance fund from our dead-and-buried father. He didn't have a life insurance policy, no Social Security or veteran's benefits of any kind even though Pops had been in the war. At least we *had* a phone.

That I had girlfriends at the same time living on the same block tells you something about me, that I'm either not too bright or a little bit crazy. I think deep down I must have wanted them to discover I was a two-timer just to see what would happen. The challenge of having to win back one or the other or both when they caught me could've been what thrilled me, not the deceit. A half-wit would know they'd find out. But I wasn't thrilled, if that's the word, when they actually did figure me out.

I tried to make up with Vicki first for reasons that are easy to understand. Vicki won the bikini contest at the county fair that spring. When I came over in the morning she would have on the very bikini she won the contest in and, seeing me coming up the walk, play peek-a-boo at the front door. We discussed what we would both wear on the phone the night before. I always had to not wear a shirt. Shoes were okay, but she didn't want me wearing underwear or a T-shirt, just my cuffed blue denims. If it happened to be raining in the morning, I'd wait till I was on her tiny porch to take off my shirt before I rang the chimes.

Vicki gave me the blue balls more than once in that pink bikini, but what I liked her in best was her mother's see-through negligee. I just didn't like the stiff hospital bra she wore underneath it, so stiff you couldn't even feel anything through it. Walking up to her screened door, I would catch a glimpse of her outline through the negligee, throwing her hip out or thrusting the pointy brassiere, teasing me.

It was always great *near-sex* with Vicki cause I could never consummate with her. I could not stay hard when it came time. While she writhed in bed, teasing me more, I hid behind the bedroom door trying to get the rubber on and my dick just would shrink to nothing. Panic closed all possibilities to actually get it in her, and oh I wanted to so bad. But sure enough, soon as I left her house I would get a throbbing boner and have to hurry home to do something about it before the blue balls set in. I probably should have just stopped at Susie's house; the only reason I didn't was because that would be a really snaky thing to do. I still thought about it, though.

The next morning I laid in bed four hours working up the courage to call Vicki; it was a crisp sunny morning without dew and that had brought out the early songbirds in the lone crabapple tree outside my window. She hung up on me without a word. When I didn't call her right back the phone rang and it was her.

"You shithead bastard," she said in a voice that wasn't loud. I felt the urge immediately. I pictured her in the negligee, screen door wide open awaiting me—without that puritanical nurse bra!

"I'm sorry, I was going to tell you all about it yesterday. But since you found out I …"

I just couldn't finish the sentence, it was such a crummy attempt at apologizing. I guess after her harsh words I'd already started to think about Susie.

"We're through," she said, sounding serious. "I don't want to ever see you again."

"What did I do, Vicki?" I couldn't help it. But I wanted Vicki to spell it out so I could see if she was mad about Susie or that I just couldn't do it with her.

"You know what you did, Sonny. You shithead. You fartface—"

"C'mon, Vicki … I got an idea. Why don't I come over and take you to the pool? At eleven. I'll buy you an Orange Crush, maybe some M&Ms."

She was silent a moment, then, "What if I wanted a Milky Way? You don't even know what I like! How are you going to take me, on that wobbly bike? Don't make me laugh."

She hung up. And she didn't call back this time.

Susie was rounder than Vicki but had exotic eyes and smooth, tanned skin. Her language was a lot nicer, too. I called her up but her little brother, Sir Stevie, said she wouldn't talk to me and that I better never call again or she would sic Phil on me. Phil? Did she already had a new boyfriend? Or maybe she had had this Phil guy for a boyfriend already, just like I had Vicki. And he was probably one of those bull-necked creeps on Lamar Junior High's wresting team. Varsity. Just my luck.

I went for a bike ride and took Jody, our cocker, in the basket so he wouldn't have to run while I thought over my options. It didn't take long to realize I had no options because I no longer had either girlfriend. It put me in a frustrating bind, cause now I was free to run with my friends but I didn't want to go to the drive-in with a carload of boys on Friday night and get drunk and end up having to fight whichever Gerald Henry, or now Phil, cruised through looking for trouble. If you were with a girl you usually didn't have to fight. Fighting didn't appeal to me at all. That's why I didn't run in a gang, like my brother Stuart.

The rest of the summer was a drag. The sweltering heat and humidity slowed everything to a crawl. Bugs came out that I'd never seen before, like nits and gnats and no-see-ems but bigger, almost as large as mosquitoes but you couldn't hear them coming. Then, zap, ouch, you had another welt on your neck or leg or face or midriff if you were a girl. I slept late and ate canned hash and toast and went to the municipal pool in the mornings and got myself a Milky Way out of the vending machine, when I didn't even like Milky Ways. I swam a long time, mostly underwater where it was peaceful, then did my route in the afternoon.

Neither one of my brothers were there to get on my nerves. My little brother, Bag-a-bones, was at Boy Scout camp in New Mexico, going to Carlsbad Caverns. Which had been paid for by our church, the lucky twerp. He didn't do anything to get sponsored; he had only joined the Scouts after Thanksgiving last year. It could have been me going if they hadn't kicked me out of the troop. I didn't protest; I hated the Scout leader anyway, a straight-laced Baptist proctor and pallbearer who didn't even smoke. He caught me puffing a cigarette in the basement hallway of the church once, where nobody ever went. Except him that one time.

The other reason Scout Master Crammer had me kicked out, though he never gave it as an official reason, was somebody unknown told him about me and Herman spying on this buxom waitress in her bedroom window as she undressed for a shower, or got dressed after her shower. After the shower was sexier cause she was still wet and she would massage her tits drying them. And that's why we spied on her, the tits. I hoped it wasn't Herman who told him; that would be awful disappointing to find out.

Anyway, Mother and Pops had named Bag-a-bones "Chance" on the certificate, but me and Stuart nicknamed him Bag-a-bones because he was a praying mantis, a grasshopper with the same long neck and eggy Adam's apple of Ichabod Crane, which he disgustingly bobbed from chin to collarbone when he got excited. So I only had my older brother to dodge and I was usually gone before he even got up.

Only one good thing happened that August, that summer. On Saturday the fifteenth, Mother and I signed the papers at 11:16 a.m. and I got my first motorbike, a Moped. It had pedals, like a bicycle, but it was no bicycle. It had power. It could climb hills.

Mother was reluctant but it was easy enough for me to talk her into co-signing. I could tell she was trying to be positive by saying she thought I'd learn something about the value of money, which I guess I did. But that motorbike was my ticket to independence. The Moped came from Sears, Roebucks & Co. and cost $99. My payments were $12.89 a month for a year, including the insurance they made us take out. You didn't have to have a driver's license for a pedaled motorized vehicle, I guess, cause they sold it to me. If I collected every penny owed me from my customers every month, I could pocket around $30, so I had no problem paying those monthly notes.

My route was a two-mile haul from the newspaper plant straight uphill. The twelve hundred block of East Tenth was so steep you couldn't pedal up it on a bicycle. Even pushing my Flyer got my legs burning and sometimes both legs would cramp up. I especially dreaded those two miles on Thursday afternoons and Sunday mornings when a hundred papers could weigh upwards to a hundred-fifty or more pounds. I sweated a lot of dog slobber before throwing the first paper. For three years I hauled papers on the Flyer, getting up while my brothers slept on those pitch black Sunday mornings when you could see the cold wind throwing the streetlight hard against the brick apartment walls. Waking up in a rain or sometimes snow made it real hard to crawl out of the covers at three a.m. Those were miserable times. But I did it. Not like Stuart who couldn't take the work and turned over the route to me after only a year, not even that, ten-and-a-half months.

But on my new Moped, getting to the *Star* building and then to my route was fun. I could get almost forty-five miles per hour out of that baby on downward-sloped streets, its little piston whining and buzzing like a hummingbird's wings. Forty-five-miles-per-hour was a lot faster than I could pedal the Flyer downhill. Even when it rained I didn't mind too much; on Sunday mornings, with all the extra weight, I cranked it to the max and got a flying start up that steep block on Tenth. If the light turned red on me, I'd just go through it; the cops and nobody else were ever out that early. I pedaled in a blur to get the Moped up and over the crest. Or, if there was a reason I was delayed at the light or just lazy, I could go three blocks around and wouldn't have to pedal much. On weekdays I sailed through the route tossing papers right and left. On the Moped, I could usually finish the whole route in about eighteen to twenty minutes. Which gave me time to get back to the pool and cool off. I could have hauled Vicki over there, given her a thrill.

The motorbike may have made my job easier and gotten me around to see my friends, but the scooter didn't turn any girl's eyes when I wheeled up to the pool and slowly circled the fence to see who was there. It didn't take long for it to sink into my simple brain that the little bike was no Harley. One afternoon in late August I talked to a girlfriend of Susie's who would still talk to me and she tried to keep a straight face asking if I wanted to race against her brother, who rode a Harley, in a cross-country, and then to insult me further, "Can you make it go without pedaling off?" I burned rubber just to show her. But the stinger was in me.

I drove up Vicki and Susie's street and bleated the horn the length of the block, not caring that they knew it was me. I talked myself into believing that in their private thoughts they were wondering which one I was beeping at. But neither came outside when I went by.

The rest of the summer I ran the Moped and let the wind hit my face as hard as it could. All I wanted to do was go faster, feel harder wind. I wanted a Harley.

But I was going into high school riding that silly pedal scooter and destined to remain a virgin.

Chapter 3

A few days before school rolled around I scouted around and found just the place to hide my ride, in a cluster of red maple behind Curly's Auto Body Shop a block from Woodstock High. It was a shortcut kids would take sometimes to get to the football-and-track field. So there was no reason to be furtive about going in and out of the woods there.

    That first day I was nervous for all kinds of reasons and not the least for the fight I was expecting to have with Gerald Henry. I wore a new plaid shirt Mother bought that was stiff and ugly so I didn't mind getting blood on it. When I pulled up to Curly's, I cut the engine and pedaled around back and into the woods. Around seven-thirty I sauntered back out into the clearing, book satchel under arm like I'd just come out of my shortcut to school. It was quiet. I looked around and didn't see anyone. Then I heard a snigger from the other side of the body shop. I kept walking but there came more snickering so I turned and saw the punk Gerald Henry leaning on the side of the shop, his head lowered to show off his jelly roll. Same gang of four with him as at the pool hall earlier that summer. The other four laid back a little. A cigarette hung from Gerald Henry's contorted lips. Both his arms drooped; his thumbs were stuck in his pants pockets. The bastard was waiting just like he said. And I wondered, *How the hell he know I was here?*

He looked like a kindergartner in the fold of the heftier punks, all wearing dark leather jackets so everybody would know they were a gang. Leather jackets. They didn't care if it would be a hundred degrees today with a hundred percent humidity. The West Side Bozos, I decided they should call themselves. My brother Stuart called them the Dinkleberries. Stuart said his gang was going to mix it up with them sometime, maybe rumble.

"What's going on in the woods, hotshot?" he said in a girlish deadpan and leaned off the corrugated wall. The auto shop was an old quonset, probably disposed of by the army after World War I. It wasn't open for business yet though I figured some of the grimy mechanics were inside smoking cigarettes and sipping Cokes, maybe a snort of shine to get them going. Gerald Henry was probably a pal of theirs.

My satchel was stuffed with pencils and notebook paper and Superman and a Green Lantern comic book in case I got bored in one of the classes, algebra or history or social studies or English composition, any one of those. "Had to hide my weeds, you know. Don't wanna get caught, not the first day." My tone was conspiratorial, a little confessional.

He wasn't buying it. "You don't fuckin smoke. What's in the bag?"

"Hell yeah, I do, Lucky Strike…"

It sounded like he didn't even remember socking me that day. I damn well remembered.

"You know, stuff. School shit." I opened up the satchel and showed him so he wouldn't have to jerk it out of my hand. I was getting a little nervous and felt like I was sweating. I was working myself into getting ready.

"Wait here," he said suddenly, to me or his boys or both. He didn't throw the satchel to the ground, which amazed me. He just dropped it and dashed into the maple grove.

I grinned at the four punks, all of them meaner than him by far.

In a minute he reappeared wearing a shiteating grin that told me he had found the Moped. I tried to keep a straight face. He looked at me, evenly at first, then shook his head and started to laugh. It was pathetic.

I would have rather let him hit me square in the mouth twice than have him find the Moped. He kept laughing as his boys disappeared two at a time behind the trees to see what was so funny.

Then the look on his pale face turned pitiful, as if he knew that anyone riding a Moped had probably never made it with a girl and really didn't smoke and I think he lost interest. What was to gain pounding a sissy with a Moped.

Making things worse, I was pretty sure I was ready for him—though not the beefy idiots he had backing him up. I had secretly at night been working out over at Harvey Nixon's house on the punching bag in his back yard and paying close attention to his instructions on how to swipe away blows to the head and body. Harvey was a professional boxer and he was a Negro, so he knew what he was talking about.

But Gerald Henry just laughed, him and the four punks in his gang, and walked off. Just like that. It left me humiliated and fuming.

And then I had to go face the first day of high school in my purple plaid shirt with that crappy disposition.

Chapter 4

On Saturday I woke screaming in pain. It came from somewhere in my jaw. Stuart rolled over and buried his head under his pillow. I kept screaming till Mother shoved open the door.

"What is it? What's wrong?"

"I don't know but it's killing me. I felt it in the night but forgot about it. Ohh …"

Stuart rolled over with a smirk on his sleepy face and said, "You gotta tell her more than that, bonehead. And stop hollerin', I'm trying to sleep."

"You leave your brother alone, mister. He's hurting, can't you see?" Mother said, making me feel a little better. "Sonny, is it your tooth?"

"Yeah, yeah! That must be it."

She touched me on the jaw and I screamed bloody murder. Stuart got out of bed and I swear he had a boner. How could that be when I was dying, when Mother was in the room? He left in his drawers, at least covering the bulge and keeping his back toward our mother.

She told me to get dressed then ran out of the room and in a shake she was back with an icepack she made out of ice cubes in an apron that had been tied around itself to hold in the ice.

"Here, put this on your jaw. I'll call a dentist."

"Not Dr. McMahon, please! I hate him."

"He's your dentist, Sonny. Have some sense!"

I tried to dress and hold the ice against my face at the same time. Impossible. I put the icepack down and slipped into jeans and a T-shirt cause it was supposed to be a hot one today.

The ice helped when I held it on my jaw, numbed it, but right away started hurting again when I took it off, so I kept it there until nearly all the ice cubes had melted down my T-shirt. No breakfast for me, no way. I couldn't even think of food.

In the kitchen, Mother was on the phone, sounding desperate and panicky. I took a sip of cold grapefruit juice cause that's all there was to drink. It set fire to a network of nerves in that side of my face. Screaming again, I spit it out. I figured out that the worse pain was on the back jaw on my right side, maybe on top. The pain shot all the way around my head to the other ear.

In a minute she said, "C'mon, let's go. Now!"

In the Chevy she said, "Your dentist doesn't work weekends. He can't see you before Tuesday. I told them thanks a lot. We've only been going to him since you were five."

"Good. Good for you, Mother. So where are we going?" It hurt to talk but I did it.

"Someone who'll see you, that's who."

Whenever I saw Dr. McMahon, one of those long rubber bands or something else on his drill would break and I'd have to sit there and wait till he could get it going again. By then the deadener had half worn off and he had to give me another shot or tell me to grip the arms. "We're just about done, young feller," he'd say and I'd brace myself. After seeing him I couldn't chew even soft foods for days, for sure no chocolate chunks.

Mother added, "Stuart complains about Dr. McMahon also. The one I found who'll see you, Dr. Peach, sounds real nice. He doesn't handle emergencies either, but said don't you worry, just bring the boy in. He's coming to meet us right away, too."

"Peach?" I said. "Weird name."

"Don't make fun of people's names," she admonished.

"I'm not! I just said—" I didn't finish cause it would just start an argument. Plus it hurt.

This Dr. Peach was in a single-story medical building on 10th Street, only about five minutes from home. We walked down a hallway and found the door to his office standing open with the lights on like a regular workday. A tall man in a green smock and some kind of green, alien-looking cap appeared from the back to greet us. He had a big smile and big teeth. "Come on in, put him in here."

He led me into a torture room and I took a seat. I still had an icepack attached and wasn't hurting much, just some throbbing.

He slipped on these thick glasses that made his eyes huge. A tan line ran across his forehead just under the hairline. He gave me a strange kind of look, like he was real pleased to see me and then went to work with his depressor and some other shiny instrument. He seemed familiar somehow.

"It looks abscessed, Mrs.—uh, I'm sorry, I've forgotten your name."

"That's alright, Doctor. I'm Olivia Poe and this is Sonny."

"Yes, Sonny. Of course. Well, we'll need to deaden you up a little, Sonny. Is that alright? Looks like you've seen dentists before."

"Ah, I 'ave," I mumbled.

"So you wouldn't be allergic to Novocain … Mrs. Poe?"

"No sir, he's not," Mother said.

Mother said she'd wait in the other room. It gave her the nerves seeing her sons get worked on.

"If you like you'll find a soft drink in the small refrigerator in my office, back that way. Go ahead and make yourself comfortable. This shouldn't take long. Sonny has a pretty normal jaw line, good strong bones. He'll be fine."

"It's his little brother that has the perfect teeth," Mother said unnecessarily, showing off, I guess. "Chance never had a filling and he's eleven now, thank the Lord. But not my other boys. We never get to go on a vacation just because of the dental bills—"

"Alright, Mother!" I said.

"Well, thank you, Doctor, I will have a soda."

He didn't have to do any drilling. But I would have bet his equipment was in good shape. Everything sparkled in that room. He seemed more than competent; he was totally confident and had sure hands. Dr. Peach wrestled out a molar embedded way at the back of my upper jaw. It wasn't an easy tooth to even reach, much less to pull—"Extract," as he said. It hadn't even broken through the gum yet. He had to cut and use some forceps that looked so scary I closed my eyes when they went into my mouth. But I never felt pain, only some pressure from his strong hands, and it took some strength to work that tooth out. Old Dr. McMahon didn't have that kind of strength. Since I had to go to the dentist a lot, I was really glad to have someone who knew what he was doing.

After he finished, Mother hemmed and hawed and started to beg for low payments cause she just didn't have a dime.

Dr. Peach said, "Sit down a minute," and we all sat in the waiting room chairs. He kept on the ugly green surgeon hat that covered up everything on his head except the round of his face.

He crossed his legs then rubbed his chin as if trying to figure out the right payment plan for Mother.

"Mrs. Poe," he said, and his voice turned serious. He leaned forward as if to make sure she would hear him. "If you don't mind my asking, do you have a husband?"

Mother looked at her lap. I thought she might break down, which was going to embarrass the hell out of me.

He added, "You said you have other children?"

"Two. Boys. All of them are boys."

"That's got to be rough on a mom. My parents also had three boys, I can sympathize."

She did break down.

"Come on, Mother," I said. "I can pay. Could we make payments, is that alright?" My voice was all twisted up and my words came out in a garble around my fat tongue and thick lip. But I thought he understood.

He didn't respond. He kept talking to Mother.

"I'm sorry, Mrs. Poe. I didn't mean to upset you. Listen, I am not going to charge you for today. Call it a token of my esteem for you, for having to endure raising all those rascals by yourself." He gave her this enormous smile, like he was actually glad to help out.

After Mother thanked him profusely, embarrassing the crap out of me even more, we got out of there.

She kept saying on the way home, "What a gentleman that Dr. Peach is." She was beside herself with wonderment, like he was some kind of savior. But I kind of thought the same about him, when you think about it. It probably even ruined his Saturday plans and he didn't say anything.

Aside from all the gratefulness, there was one less tooth in my head to give me trouble, and that afternoon I threw my papers as usual with only occasional little stabs of pain.

Chapter 5

On a bright day a couple weeks later I ran into Joe, the guy who rescued the dog. I was throwing papers on Broadmore Terrace when he drove by in that fantastic white T-Bird. I only glimpsed the car but I knew it was him cause there weren't that many '56 T-Birds in Woodstock and also cause he honked.

Broadmore was a wide straight street separated by a grassy median where the broad limbs of magnolias stretched across both lanes. Those were old trees. The street ran down the middle of my paper route and divided my good customers on the south, those who never cried about paying on time, with the delinquents to the north where there were some apartments and duplexes, the ones who enjoyed telling me to come next Saturday to collect, and then not being there when I went back. Sometimes it would take three months before I could make them cough up.

The T-Bird was headed the other direction. Then I saw it coming back. I pulled to the median curb, cut the little two-stroke motor. He stopped in the street beside me. He had the top off and his hair lay back off his forehead where the wind had plastered it like a Talladega stock car racer. There was a tan line on his forehead, probably from where he'd worn the visor all summer playing tennis.

"Sonny, hello. This your route?" he asked. My paper bag was half full and hanging tight around my neck.

"Part of it. Starts up on Tenth at Bush, over to Edgemont and down to Fifth. Sort of a big square."

"Pretty big area. How many papers do you deliver?"

"A hun'rd five right now. Summer it goes down."

He laughed. "You looked like the Red Baron flying off that hill. A new motorbike?"

"Yeah," I said dully. I had thought I was over being embarrassed for riding the pedal bike. "My mother had to sign," I added just as dully.

I couldn't help staring at his convertible with its slick Thunderbird lines, the whitewalls circling those shiny chrome spoke wheels. Even the steering wheel was half chrome. He got my attention. "You like the Bird, huh? Want to take a ride?"

"Sure!"

"You want to finish your paper route first?"

"It can wait."

"Go ahead and finish," he said. "I live in the next block back up, on the other side. Brick house. I'll be outside."

"Hey, that's just a block off my route. I coulda been your paperboy."

He nodded. "By the way, how's that jaw of yours feeling? Any discomfort?"

"Huh?" I said. My brain hopped on it: I remembered the big smile on the dentist's face, the familiarity of it. The tan line on his forehead, same as Joe's. They were one and the same, Joe and Dr. Peach. "Oh, uh, it's great—" I stammered.

He chuckled. "It's alright, Sonny. How would you recognize me in those greens? I wasn't sure it was you either—people's looks change when they're in pain. I wasn't sure until your mother said your name. So count us even. See you in a bit."

Great, I thought, pretty dumb of me. But it was pretty neat, too. I knew he was a bighearted guy when he helped that pitiful dog. It was nice they were the same people, him and the dentist. And I liked the Red Baron image. I just decided from now on that's what I'd call the Moped.

After finishing the route, I puttered up to where his car was parked on a brick driveway just off the street. The top was still off. Good. Convertibles were tons more fun to ride in, with the wind and all. To be fair, I didn't know that from experience since I had never ridden in a convertible. But you can figure.

He waved and went back to watering a flowerbed in front of a hedge that went across the front of the house. The land his house was on took up a lot of the block. Ivy climbed up the walls on both floors and around tall shuttered windows. There were lots of trees, walnut and ash and of course pine, some looking old as those magnolias on the street, practically hiding the house. Neighboring houses were there but you couldn't see them for all the trees.

I jumped the curb on the Moped, the Red Baron, and biked up the walkway to the steps and hiked the scooter onto its stand. I pitched one of the leftover newspapers up the stairs to the front door, in case he didn't subscribe.

A dog came running toward me, its stubby tail wagging.

"Hey! It's alive."

"As you can see, she pulled through. Pearl, come on, girl," he called to the mutt, "you remember Sonny. You better, he helped save your mangy hide."

He laughed a full, rich laugh. Pearl wagged her short tail just like she understood what he said and she came up to me wanting to get patted. The watery blue eyes seemed brighter than before; they could hypnotize you.

"You figure out what kind she is?"

"Cow dog. Australian. They're bred for herding sheep and cattle," he said. "I can't offer her sheep but I don't think it much matters. She'll herd anything, honeybees, birds, ants, people, you name it. Mind if Pearl comes along? She loves to bite the wind."

"Naw," I said. "I'm glad she's alive. She won't jump out, will she?"

He grinned. "Hasn't yet. I could never locate an owner. So, Pearl's stuck with me."

I looked around the Good Samaritan's big yard. "Yeah, a real shame for her."

"You ready?"

We drove the length of Broadmore Terrace, the Thunderbird plunging in and out of magnolia shadows like a bird through clouds, and turned north onto Bush Street past block after block of nice houses till they turned to trailers and on out past the army base on the Tallulah Highway, all the way over winding blacktops into the national forest. It was a sweet, smooth ride, the wind hardly noticeable.

"You want to step it up?"

"Hell yeah," I said, and when we hit a straightaway he got us up to a hundred miles an hour in a blink. It was great. The needle of the half-circle speedometer pointed to the sky, way short of the "160" it said it could do.

"Will it go that fast?" I asked, now against wind that teared up my eyes. He wore sunglasses.

"She's a high-performance three-twelve, but I've never had her over a hundred or so. Just never had the nerve." He grinned and showed a row of white teeth. "Are you a daredevil?"

"You bet," I screamed, "always have been."

Pearl stood on my lap, grabbing wind with her teeth, trying to herd it up.

"Then you can help me get my nerve up."

"Go faster? When? Now?"

That night at supper I said to Mother, "Guess what?" I was bursting to tell somebody I'd ridden in a T-Bird.

She was tired. She usually got tired on weeknights after having to make us supper. Tonight, she made salmon patties again. From a can of course, not a fresh fish. They were always from the can. I hated salmon patties but I would eat them anyway because it was that or nothing.

"I met this guy and went for a ride in his '56 T-Bird. Has a high-performance engine. What a car!" I said it generally, if smugly, to the table, but I was really saying it for Stuart's benefit cause I wanted to rouse him.

Bag-a-bones was playing basketball at the Y.

I didn't expect Mother to blow up at me.

"'This guy?' What do you mean?" she asked before she blew up. "Is he a boy from school?"

"Nah, he's grown."

Then she blew up. "Sonny, never, I mean don't you *ever* get in a car with a strange man. Who is this man?"

It really threw me.

Stuart smirked. "He's a queer, right?"

"You hush up that talk," Mother told him sternly, then after a moment added, "You can just be excused, mister." She kept her fork pointed at him, waiting for him to leave the table but he didn't move. He just went on eating. Stuart thought he was too big to mind Mother anymore. She waited and when he didn't go she turned back to me, her puffy face and big eyes settling down some.

I stopped teasing cause it threw me what Stuart said. "He *wasn't* a stranger, Mother. It's Dr. Peach. He has a T-Bird. You do remember him, don't you, the dentist who gave you three-hundred-dollars' worth of dental service—for *free*? And Stuart, you go to hell, turdbreath."

"Alright, Sonny. Same goes for you, don't talk like that to your brother. Especially at the dinner table."

"Yes, Mother," I said obediently, just to piss off Stuart.

"I didn't tell you about the dog he saved last summer, did I?" I added. "It's an Australian sheep dog, a rare and important breed. That's when I first met Dr. Peach. I didn't recognize him at the dentist's office. He didn't recognize me, either."

Stuart sighed sarcastically, then laughed out loud. "Think Jody's rare and important?"

He meant our short legged cocker spaniel with the tangled dirty blond locks, the dog that never looked at the sky, the dog that peed on the carpet at any strange noise.

I tried to kick Stuart but there was a big post in the way. "What of it?" I said, like a lamebrain—I tended to get tongue-tied trying to defend myself against Stuart.

I had always been jealous of him. Some of his friends had cars and they made it a point to tell me there was no way I was going to tag along. Now I thought maybe he was just a little jealous of *me*, getting to ride in a Thunderbird, 1956, the coolest of the three years they made them.

"I've already decided," Mother said, "he will be all you boys' regular dentist from now on. That Dr. Peach is a fine gentleman."

"A good dentist, too," I added. "I don't think Stuart should see him, though. He might get molested."

Stuart lunged at me from across the round table. He grabbed my throat and squeezed. Hard. I stuck his arm with my fork. Maybe I drew blood, but it was enough to make him turn loose.

"That's it, boys! Get up from the table. I mean now!"

We did; we knew the tone in her voice meant business. I waited till Stuart left the kitchen and then I got my books out of the living room, where Mother would fall asleep watching TV, and went back and sat in the kitchen nook for the next three hours, till the house grew quiet.

Chapter 6

At school the next morning I racked the Red Baron in the "Bikes Only" area behind the woodshop, where the big rides were, the Harleys, a couple of really sharp twin-cylinder Indians. Let them laugh, I didn't care anymore. Maybe I did a little, cause I didn't get there early. I got there late. The bell rang before I dismounted, which meant I was tardy. Up to now, I'd escaped Mr. Smiley, the vice principal and the guy in charge of discipline, and I sure wasn't looking forward to ever having to see him. He was big with big arms and he swung hard, they said. His two-foot paddle had a hole the size of a silver dollar in the end that supposedly left a huge circular blister on your butt or leg or wherever it landed cause he was known to be so mad when he swung it could land anywhere. The more blisters you got depended on the charges against you. I had seen him roaming the corridors, slapping the paddle on his pant leg, teasing students as he looked for someone doing something wrong, like sticking gum on their locker door.

Now I had to go to the principal's office to get a pass, but I didn't have to see Mr. Smiley, not the first time.

We had nine minutes between classes. High school was great that way, getting let loose for nine whole minutes between classes and having different teachers, so if you didn't like one you might really like the next teacher and have something to look forward to. You had time to talk about girls or a test or how shitty a teacher was. I liked getting to school on time cause my first period class was English and Miss West made it fun.

After first period I had gym. So did Stuart and sometimes we'd run into each other and walk there together. Even though I was still pissed over his stupid comment about Dr. Peach last night, I needed to tell him something.

I fell in behind him in the corridor. I watched him for a minute. He walked in a slump, slow-footed, dragging himself down the hallway like he'd lost his girlfriend and was as alone as a guy could ever be, nowhere to go but the Heartbreak Hotel. I wasn't depressed before but looking at my older brother almost made me want to cry. It was very sudden. I saw him in a way I'd never thought of Stuart before, seeing him as a little kid who'd been whipped by a tough life even before he had time to get going. And in a way that was true of the boy who hadn't asked for the role of man of the family. But my sudden despair was probably because of what I wanted to talk to him about.

I'd heard a rumor that brought the lynching rushing back into my thoughts. It had now been over a year, but as I caught up to Stuart and said hey to him, I suddenly felt this strong urge to tell him about it. I had to pinch my leg inside my pants till I grimaced to keep from it. I knew the pinch would remind me that Herman and I had vowed on our lives never to mention that night, not even to our families. The urge didn't pass easily, but it passed.

I spoke low-keyed so other kids wouldn't hear. "I hear Sugarman Cole's gonna beat your ass."

"When," he said matter-of-factly, like he already knew and knew why, like he knew all about it when I felt certain he didn't know jack shit.

"Do what?" I said in a singsong.

"Do Wayne—"

"Doberman!" I yelled quick, before he could.

We bandied that little take on the Sgt. Bilko character when what we were talking about was other worldly, making no sense, or just seemed absurd. I guess it sounded silly, but that was me and Stuart.

Having to fight Sugarman Cole was not absurd; it was pretty scary. He was big and fast and I had seen how hard he could swing a club when he used one on that Negro they hung. It was almost like he frothed at the mouth doing it. Where do you get that much hate, and why? It appeared in my nightmares sometimes, just like it happened, happening all over again. The blows from sticks smashing his skull even though you couldn't see the damage with a cloth over his head. The sound told you. And then Sugarman's face, bigger than life, grinning down on me before he shoots me with my own rifle. I didn't know where he got the nickname, but there was nothing sweet about Sugarman Cole.

"You don't want to fight him, Stuart," I said nervously, squeezing flesh inside my pocket.

Stuart got cocky on me. "It's nothing for you to worry about, shit-for-brains."

"Then fuck off."

I looked at his bare arm to see if I'd punctured his skin last night and, yep, there was a big blue bruise and a couple tiny holes in the middle of it. I felt immediately sorry. He should've put ointment or something on it.

Stuart wouldn't let me get a locker on the same row as him, so I followed him over to his locker. I was still scared for him. I could tell by his picked-up pace he was giving some thought to what I'd said, and he might have been a little nervous even if he would never admit it. At least to me, his punk little brother.

"Look here," I said out of earshot of some boys changing into "Rams Gym" T-shirts, "I meant to tell you last night but I forgot after you pissed me off. Got any idea why he's after you?"

Stuart turned his head a little but only enough to let me know he'd heard me. He was like that, carrying around some kind of stupid pride that I couldn't ever figure out. He said, "Not a clue."

Did I mention he was also cheap on words, like he had to pay a fee for using them? "I know it's not over a girl, cause you don't have a girlfriend. Do you, shithead?"

I tightened my gut, ready for his fist, but he didn't lay it on me. He looked straight at me. "Who says?"

"What?"

"About Sugar."

"'Sugar?' You call him *Sugar?*" He gave me his usual look of disgust. I said, "I don't know. I just overheard it. But he means business. You don't want to fuck around with him, Stuart."

"I'll give him a couple beers."

I felt my face get warm. Stuart was talking about beers from our beer brewing operation, which was his and mine, fifty-fifty. Any outside distribution he had to clear with me and vice versa, even one bottle. I thought about it before I said anything because if a beer or two would get Sugarman Cole off his back, then it was worth it. But Stuart couldn't just up and decide solo who got our beer. So I got stern with him, as a good business partner ought to. "Over my dead body."

He gave me that superior smirk and swung open his locker door to dismiss me.

We had already produced one batch of about two cases of pretty good brew with not too much junk in it and had a second crop going now, calling it "Poe's Suds," after our last name, brewing it right under Mother's nose and her never suspecting a thing. Somebody before us had left a broken icebox in the furnace room which we had access to through a door attached to our terrace apartment. The refrigerator still closed pretty tight even though its door lock was busted, but it kept a constant temperature of one degree plus or minus 68 inside. You needed that for proper fermentation. We had two cases sitting in that refrigerator just about ready. Stuart and I planned to sell this batch to the booze-loving members of his gang. With my split I had planned to get a gold cross necklace for Vicki or a silver cross necklace for Susie. But I guess I didn't have to worry about that anymore; I could spend my share on a back tire and a clutch cable for the Baron. I could start saving up for a Harley.

Whenever I had to threaten Stuart about anything, it would be over the beer. All I had to do was mention one of the members of his gang, or rather the gang member's old man. I knew both son and father. The boy was Nookie Grimes, who was my friend till Stuart stole him from me last year. After they spent a night in jail together down in Panama

City for vagrancy, Stuart invited Nookie in with the Dukes. And that finished off what friendship me and Nookie might have ever had.

Nookie's old man was a drop-down drunk who Stuart knew would have raided our operation in a second if he'd known about it. The old man fought in the Battle of the Bulge and had never really come back from there and was always desperate for a drink. I'd be over to see Nookie and the old man would corner me away from Nookie's mother, give me some change to go get him two little bottles of vanilla extract, tell me to hide it in my underwear so the ole lady wouldn't find it when she searched me, which she was bound to do soon as I stepped back into the house from the mission. She found the bottles on me once, in my socks, but that was the last time. I was true to the old man, I think, because he had fought and killed in combat and it had screwed him up royally, with him drinking vanilla extract and Bay Rum aftershave. I guess his wife was messed up too, but her battles had only been with demons of her own invention, not real enemies.

Everybody was leaving the locker room for the practice field and I hadn't even changed yet. I couldn't afford to go to the vice principal's office for a second time in the same day, less than an hour apart.

"I gotta get dressed," I said, still standing there like an idiot watching Stuart dress. "Okay," I conceded, "offer him a beer. But if you have to fight him, I could get Herman and Junior Pound and maybe Ledbelly and me to cover your back in case he brings somebody along. I sure hope he don't, that he'll take the beer."

I wanted to tell him what I'd seen Sugarman do that night so he would know that he might show up with a bunch of Klansmen or their slimy sons, like Leon Legget, because as far as I knew, Sugarman Cole didn't belong to any gang. He was a free-floating independent; as far as I knew he didn't even have a mother cause I couldn't imagine it.

Stuart looked interested but there was no way he would ask his kid brother for help. "It's a free country," he said with a shrug and sat on the bench to tie his Keds. If he hadn't been my brother, Stuart would've been just another punk in my book who I wouldn't give so much as the time of day.

It turned into a long school day with this business about a fight unresolved. I still didn't know what it was about or when it was going to happen, maybe today or maybe when this new batch of beer finished brewing, which ought to be in six days according to our chart. Not only was I distracted in just about every class and couldn't answer the teachers' questions when they fingered me, but I could only round up one of the boys, Ledbelly, who agreed to help in case Stuart needed it.

"But only if you really, really need me," he said, skittishly. Ledbelly wasn't a fighter. The other two, Herman and Junior Pound were, but both were absent from school today.

It shouldn't have bothered me anyway; Stuart had the Dukes, they could back him or even help him. They could do what gangs did, stand together against conflict. Except the Dukes weren't really a hood gang, not like Gerald Henry's West Side Bozos. They were more like the Dukes of Earl, only interested in drinking beer and throwing parties, trying to pick up girls.

Ledbelly had been my friend since first grade and we'd been in Scouts together and all that. He lived off Sunset Drive up in the Woodlands above the country club where houses were scattered around on cleared-out hillsides with treetop views down to the golf course's fairways. He was rich. I was rich when we got to be friends at Blessed Sacrament, the private elementary school I attended my first five school years, counting kindergarten. Then Pops had his accident and we went broke so I switched to regular school. I loved staying over Friday nights at his house cause we had pepperoni and sausage pizzas that his mother would order and have delivered. I never had a delivered pizza at home after Pops croaked.

Ledbelly and I would sneak out late at night and go coon hunting with his hounds. He had about four of them. Once we got a family of coons treed that we couldn't get to with our sacks. I said, "Let's shoot at 'em, get 'em moving." His dogs were barking like crazy, making enough racket that I thought the forest marshals would come out and run us in. They didn't, but Ledbelly wasn't going to let me shoot either. He started climbing the tree, an old loblolly pine that could've gone up a hundred-fifty feet, so high you couldn't see the top of it in the daylight, much less using a flashlight. He disappeared up there and all I could see was a beam of light shoot through the branches every now and then. He could've been kidnapped by a space ship that high up. He made no noise and said nothing and after about an hour I was getting cold and bored. His dogs even stopped baying and decided to lay down at the base of the tree and wait, devoted hounds that they were. I reckoned the only thing for me to do was start climbing myself. I didn't take my rifle or the coon bag since I was only going after Ledbelly. Sap was getting all over my clothes and hands. The stuff's worse than a skeeter attack when you're sweaty; pine sap seemed to spot me like it was alive and liked my smell. About thirty or forty feet up I heard some rustling that didn't sound human. I couldn't tell you how I knew it wasn't human, except that when I shined my light behind me, I saw it wasn't human. It was a huge tree cat and it was madder than hell. It hissed and arched its back with the hair sticking straight up just like a regular barn cat when it was cornered and ready to fight to the death. The flashlight got bumped out of my hand in my rush to back away onto another limb. I couldn't see all of its body for the branches but I saw its yellow eyes in the weak moonlight and its long tail switching about three feet out on both sides of its body. I bet it weighed more than a hundred pounds; it was a cougar or maybe even a panther. My first thought was that it killed Ledbelly, but I would have heard him scream or he would've dropped. Belly was still up there, hiding from the big cat. Maybe it had eaten the coons. Maybe it had its own family and was just protecting them, only trying to scare off intruders.

Ledbelly jumped down right in front of me, slick as a cat himself. "Make yourself big as you can," he whispered. "It's a real panther and we need to catch it."

"You're crazier than shit, Belly. You'll have to shoot him or he'll kill us!"

I moved to another branch with my arms held out, swelling my chest and spreading shoulders as wide as they'd go. So did Ledbelly and we both breathed loud, sort of imitating the big cat's hiss. It was a miracle. The panther backed away with those yellow eyes right on us. Then it jumped up to another limb and climbed skyward. He was fast as greased lightning. Ledbelly still had his flashlight trained on the beast and kept it on him till he completely disappeared up there in the far reaches of outer space. He didn't take a shot at it and I was glad about that, despite what I'd said. And the cat was too fast for him to throw his bag. I was glad about that too. Cause how would you bring in a hundred-pound cat ripping through a cloth bag? We moved pretty fast getting down the tree. I had sap all over me and his mother was not happy with either one of us.

Ledbelly said when he was up there he never found a coon. He thought they must have jumped onto another tree or that it might have been a family of cougars or bobcats we'd heard.

Nobody ever believed us about the black panther. The teachers I told in eighth grade all laughed and said, irreverently, *Oh, you are just so-o lucky to be alive.* So did other people, my cousins who lived in Birmingham. They didn't even bother to laugh. But my science teacher, Mrs. Tolbert, said she had heard of black panthers in these parts. I know she was serious cause she didn't pat my head or even smirk. Ledbelly and I stopped telling the story cause we were tired of getting ridiculed.

The thing that impressed me was how fearless Ledbelly had been thirty feet up in that pine tree facing off a big mad cat like that. He had proved himself and that was why I included him in the after-school posse to help Stuart, if needed.

Before we reached the football practice field to do our calisthenics and sprints, I told Stuart, "You got permission to give him two beers, if you have to."

Chapter 7

I had now been in high school long enough to know it wasn't what it was cracked up to be. For one thing, I hadn't figured you'd be forced to take algebra in tenth grade, and I didn't know how hard it would be. I asked Mother couldn't she do something to get me out of it, but she just sighed and squeezed out this sympathetic look, the one she used when she didn't want to be bothered but with just enough attention that she wouldn't feel guilty for ignoring her middle son either. I hated it when she used that look. I remembered back to sixth grade, when she first invented it. Probably would remember it when I was seventy-five. I'd finished safety patrol and jumped on my bike going to show off for some girl and my tires slipped in the gravel. My face hit the asphalt and it put a hole in my cheek. Nothing real serious, but boy did it bleed. It scared the hell out of me and I hurried home, knowing Mother had stayed home sick that day. I felt weak walking into her bedroom holding this gross bloody hand towel someone gave me tight against my face. Her bedroom was dark and smelled like a sick room. Her eyes were puffy and red when I woke her up, but she did nothing but give me a sad smile and pat my head and rolled over without saying a word. I was bleeding to death and all she could do was pat me on the head, like I was a dog.

I wasn't going to get any help from her with my algebra problem. But Dr. Peach said he knew algebra. I saw him the Saturday after Mother refused to get me out of the class. I puttered by after my route to see if he might be there and, if I played my cards right, maybe go for a car ride. He was setting up to wash the Bird in the front yard. I said hey and grabbed a rag out of the bucket and went at it with him. Then he wanted to wax it so I went along with that too, and didn't complain when it took more than an hour, putting it on then rubbing like heck to get it off. He wanted to know how high school was going and I told him okay except for algebra.

"That's a tough one." He looked worried, not sympathetic like Mother, and said he couldn't help me today but come by his office after I finished my route next Wednesday, his afternoon off, and he would show me some tricks to help me learn how to study the subject.

The 10th Street Medical Building was a block down from Scarborough Drug Store where I usually stopped after throwing papers anyway.

"What time do you usually finish your route?" he asked.

About three-thirty or four on school days, I told him. He said he had some lab work to do and would do that till I showed up. He thanked me for helping with the car and gave me three bucks.

Those first three days of the week I paid close attention in algebra class and worked hard on the assignments so I wouldn't look so dumb when I took the algebra problems to him. I studied so hard that I got it and when I went to his office on Wednesday, I worked out that day's problems by myself. All he had to do was give me some advice, which was, "Just don't get behind, even with one assignment, one problem."

He showed his big choppers. I wondered why it was that dentists always had perfect teeth, or, say, that police chiefs like ours had bulldogs that looked just like them. He said, "Keep up with the class work and you won't have any problem with algebra. Says me."

"Okay, if you say so. That's what I'll do."

"That a promise?" He was grinning, but serious, I could tell.

"Yeah, I guess. Promise."

He asked if I had any more homework and I said, yeah, some English, and he said get on it, that he would be busy in the lab for a while longer. I spread my paper out and went to work. His private office was a great place to study. There were no windows and it was quiet. Maybe because it was Wednesday afternoon and none of his patients were in his torture rooms moaning and groaning. I sat in his chair, the highback swivel behind the desk. There was also a narrow couch against the hallway wall and a chair across from the desk, I guess for people who had to consult with him. Citations and diplomas took up the wall behind the desk. The big one in the middle of the others read, University of Alabama School of Dentistry, 1949, with a lot of signatures. Behind the glass in another frame was part of a football jersey, with number "87" on it and in smaller red letters "Bama," stitched above it. The Crimson Tide. Wow. Next to the jersey there was a narrow gold-gilded frame with a scripted quote: *True non-violence is mightier than the mightiest violence—Mahatma Gandhi* … How, I wondered, did this fit in with being a dentist and playing football for Alabama?

It would probably be intimidating for the patient to sit across from the doctor with all those impressive diplomas and plaques staring at you while you try to listen to tooth advice without your eyes wandering up over his head to read them. But when I looked at the plaques, Chamber of Commerce, Optimists, an Outstanding Achievement award from the mayor and the city of Woodstock, I only thought how great it would be if I could earn a fat diploma some day. Be somebody. I wasn't intimidated around Dr. Peach; he was way too cool to make me feel that way.

There was a big blotter on the desk of a world map under clear plastic. The map was tucked under flaps at the corners; it didn't include the states of Alaska and Hawaii, both of which were ratified as states this year, Hawaii just last month. Learned that in History. I daydreamed of going to a couple of the places on the map, Istanbul or Saigon or Tasmania maybe—no, not Tasmania, Morocco, mysterious and exotic Morocco.

I was finishing up with the quiz when Dr. Peach came in and sat in the client's chair. I had one more question that took half a second, then I stuffed the paper in my notebook. "Finished."

"Excellent. And you're satisfied it's correct?"

"You bet."

"Then maybe we can go up the street, get a shake?"

"Sure."

It was a sunny and warm and bright afternoon. Dr. Peach stood more than a foot taller than me and I was tall for my age. On the way he asked if I had a girlfriend. I couldn't answer that, so I hemmed and hawed and asked him, "Do you?"

He responded with a robust laugh. "I've thought about it, but it wouldn't do for me," he said, like he was half serious and half teasing. He didn't keep me in suspense for long. "Jeanne might not cotton to that idea," he said.

"Jeanne?"

"My fiancée."

"Oh," I said. "That's nice. Great."

"Jeanne goes to Auburn. She comes up whenever she can get away—when she finishes her algebra." He grinned.

"So, do you?" he asked again.

"Yeah. No. Maybe, it's hard to say," I said, squirming. "I'm going to try Susie again, I think."

He looked at me quizzically, still with the wry grin, as we walked through the front doors of Scarborough's into the blasting air conditioning. "Sounds like it might be a little complicated. But don't tell me anything about your Susie. I might just be sympathetic toward her."

"Huh?"

"Well," he offered, "if she turns you down—again, I'm guessing—then I would have to turn *un*sympathetic toward her, since I'd have to put myself on your side."

"Oh. Well, she's a nice girl—Yeah, I know, all the girls say she's sweet, which is just another way of saying she's a dog which ought to be the very first reason to stay away. But I like her anyway."

"Then I like her, too. Even if she is sweet."

"Thanks, Doctor. Then I'll try to see her again."

"Why don't you call me Joe? No need for us to be formal. Unless of course you need another tooth yanked. Do you?"

"Okay, Doctor Joe. Joe. That was the first time. I've never had a tooth pulled before. Wait a minute, except that time I strung one to the doorknob. Wasn't fun."

He made that painful-looking grimace that I noticed before, where he stretched his lips apart and twisted up his whole lower face. "Ouch," he said. "Should *never* do that."

"I won't, not anymore."

I got home just before suppertime and went into the kitchen where Mother was boiling potatoes and frying up some okra. I smelled the sweet scent of buttermilk cornbread in the oven and realized I was starving. When Mother turned her back I jabbed a fork in a ring of okra, but she turned on me like a wasp and popped my hand with the greasy fork she used to flip the okra pieces.

"Get on out of here," she said without humor.

In ten minutes she hollered that supper was ready. She was fast and I appreciated that about her, especially when you had such appetizing aromas swirling around the house.

We had our suppers in the kitchen nook. That way she didn't have far from the stove to our plates and could sit down herself much faster than if we ate all our meals in the dining room. We saved the dining room for Sunday breakfasts and holidays or when Uncle Tommy or our grandmother came over. It was rare when you could get Goodla over since she still worked—collecting tickets at the Roxy Theater downtown—and was always too tired to make the drive, which was out of her way.

Chance got there in time to eat. He brought home his cheerful face saying that his team advanced to the semis, clobbering the Ravens by eighteen points. "Yeah, and I scored twenty, eight out of eight from the line."

I was happy that the Wolves advanced, but that didn't help keep me from still being disgusted watching him eat; he went at it like a pig goes for slop. There would not be enough food for all of us, so Stuart wasn't going to get anything tonight since he wasn't here. I know it would have been decent if I called and told him that. But the hell with him; he'd get by, probably steal something from Kroger.

Afterwards I sat at the little desk in our bedroom and wrote in my new personal journal something to the effect did I think Dr. Peach, or Doctor Joe, which was the name I decided to use when writing, that maybe he wanted to be like a father figure to me since I didn't have one anymore. Just to help me out; he liked helping people out—even dogs—I could see that, and I was a poor kid. And I sure lacked direction, even if I now had all this independence. Or maybe that was what *I* wanted from him. But now I was pulling from Freud, who would've said I better be careful with any self-psychoanalyzing, cause I would probably be wrong. But I wrote that down anyway cause that was all I could think up.

After Pops's accident, Mother went to work. But even if she'd had the time to help get us involved with school and plan for our futures, it wouldn't have mattered because she had no control over us, at least Stuart and me. Me and Stuart could run rings around her and we weren't about to mind her. I mean, what was she going to do, come in the middle of the night and hack her sons to pieces with an ax? Stuart led the way with Mother since he was the oldest and the meanest. He usually just stared her down. But sometimes he would hit her. He wouldn't shout at her, he wouldn't say a word, just BAM, pop her with his open hand and walk out. I felt real sorry for her when he did that. But I guess she was used to being hit. She said Pops used to hit her when he was drunk.

Mother could be a real sweet person but she was always tired. She'd come in and have to pick things up then get supper ready before she could even sit down. She had to do the dishes, too, since we ran after eating. She could usually snag Bag-a-bones to help her clear the table, but that was because he was eleven, too little to fight back when she came at him. He wouldn't sass her either, too chicken. But, to be fair, Bag-a-bones had to sleep in Mother's bed, so probably that's why he helped with the table and held off badmouthing her. But he wouldn't be eleven forever. He was already as tall as me and he was definitely going to be the tallest one of the bunch, like our father. Pops was six-feet five-inches and real skinny, like Bag-a-bones.

Come Saturdays she wanted us up and busy. Our beds needed making, our clothes had to be washed and ironed, there were floors to sweep, stores to go to, a hundred things to do and none of them fun. I just hated Saturday mornings when Mother got on her warpath. It was one of the times she wasn't sweet.

She was a farmer's daughter and I guess Papa and Miss Stella didn't really pass on much to her in the way of preparing her for the world, much less preparing her to prepare her future kids for their own future world, although Mother had gone to Birmingham College of Business for a year till she discovered Pops. But she told me that she didn't know what else to do with herself coming off the farm. I guess she wanted to prepare herself, she just didn't have enough time before she and Pops got hitched. She didn't talk much about him but she said Pops hadn't been ready for family life either. I tried to pick up as many snippets as I could of his wayward ways but it didn't come easy from my tight-lipped mother. It was the dark side of him that caused the accident, she said.

But all that didn't really matter when Pops was alive. He was a good provider. Pops owned one restaurant on the east side, a sit-down diner called Buddy's Cafe, and two others across Mason on the west side, a burger joint with car hops called the Hitchin Post and Pop's Ice Cream Parlor, and he made plenty of money that he never saved, I guess. We had lived in a two-story brick house on Sunset Drive in the Woodlands and Stuart and I were forced to go to Blessed Sacrament. Gussy came every day. Gussy did everything but wipe our butts. It was a big loss that I took hard when Mother had to let Gussy go. She had this trick she'd do while ironing. She got these big eyes and said, "Watch this, Sonny boy, you and your brother there," (she called me "Sonny boy" but never called Stuart by his name that I can remember and I always wondered why but never asked) and she would take a puff off her Camel then drink half a bottle of RC Cola, recite the alphabet, then blow out smoke and grin like the Cheshire cat. It amazed me, so later on when I took up smoking Kent's, I'd do it to impress girls. Of course I realized then it didn't take much breath to say the alphabet and that most of that smoke stayed in your lungs. It didn't seem to impress them much, either, so I stopped doing the trick. I still missed Gussy.

Back then we spent a lot of summers at the cabin of my Uncle Tommy's on the Coosa. Lots of fishing and swimming and skiing on the muddy water. Mother said life was good then, and what I remember was pretty good. But I could count my memories that included Pops with one hand if a finger had gotten cut off by a lawn mower.

I didn't hate my father when he died, which happened the day before July Fourth, in the year of our Lord, as they say, 1953. I was ten, Stuart was eleven, Chance was six. Stuart took it real hard because he was now expected to be the head of the house. He was about as ready for that job as I was. He immediately hated Pops for leaving him in charge; I suppose if I was Stuart I would too, but I had no feeling at all about his death. To me it was simply a fact. But as time went on I learned to hate Pops too. Every year it got worse. What I hated was his not being there to help Mother. I could see her lose more of her good humor trying to raise three boys on fifty-five dollars a week. She never got a raise that she told us about. I especially noticed the change every year when The Fourth rolled around, the anniversary of the accident. I made a note in my journal right then while I was thinking about it on how much she had changed every year at that time, her disposition growing sourer and less lively. I added a P.S. to be sure to notice again next July even though that was a long way off and I probably wouldn't look that far back in the journal.

That night rolled on. Stuart still hadn't come home; maybe he finally got caught stealing from the grocery store, but nobody called. I worked on my algebra and read a Wonder Woman comic and didn't talk to Stuart when he came into the room cause I was in bed nearly asleep.

Chapter 8

On Halloween night Herman Brown and I decided we'd be blood brothers. And we weren't even drunk, not yet. We stole his sister's shaver, the kind with a single-edged razor. It was easier to hold onto when you had a shaky hand than the double-sided razors in Herman's retractable. His family all had thick black hair and it needed shaving a lot more often than light hair like mine. The slice didn't hurt; we did it on the tops of our forearms. I sliced into his arm gently, hesitating only a second. He grinned, as if to say, That ain't nothing, and then he cut into mine, which was a deeper cut than his. I should've known, like swapping licks, you should never go first. We faced each other with our arms pressed together like the welded arms of Siamese twins. Brandy was our witness. Then we sealed the oath with a live cigarette laid on the Siamese arms down from where the blood had collected. That one did hurt, but I wasn't the one who jerked his arm away first. Herman made his little sister wipe up after us.

After we cleaned up Herman asked his old man if he could use the car. His dad didn't give him any crap at all, just, "Be careful that suicide knob don't whip back on you, Hermie." A '49 Olds fastback. You get in that baby and shut the doors and it was like closing a vault door behind you, heavy and quiet as a tomb in there. First thing, Herman puts the radio on WUSA, a damn country station. When Burl Ives came on, I turned it to a rock 'n' roll station. His old man had put in a stick shift on the floorboard with this oversized skull-head knob that kept vibrating loose and the cherry pink brodie knob on the steering wheel. The brodie knob was on the bottom when the tires were lined straight. There was a big metal visor covering half the windshield outside. Herman screeched the tires pulling away.

"You keep doing that and he won't let you borrow the car anymore," I said. Herman drove like a maniac most of the time, when he didn't even have a license yet.

"So you know where this place is, right?" he said, totally ignoring my advice.

"Yeah, drive toward the tracks."

It was good and dark when we crossed the westside tracks into Ash Town. Harvey Nixon had showed me where I could get some moonshine when I rode out here with him once in the drugstore delivery truck. He finally let me ride when I kept begging him but only when it was dark, never in the day when you could see inside the cab. I did it just so I could ride with a Negro. I thought I was the cat's meow, though I wasn't about to tell anyone, not Stuart or Herman, nobody except maybe Doctor Joe. Harvey said this man made the shine in his bathtub and he'd scoop you out a pint for a dollar-and-a-half.

There were no streetlights in Ash Town. The city didn't put light out here cause they didn't want the Negroes coming out at night; I guess they figured black people were up to no good coming out after dark. Like they were vampires or something. Harvey had pointed the house out to me but they looked pretty much the same up and down the streets. Some had shiny two-tone awnings on the windows and right now a few glowing Halloween pumpkins on the porches. Most of the places didn't turn on their porch lights. Still, I found 712 D St. pretty easy using my flashlight to read numbers on the porches. The flaking clapboard siding looked like it had gone through the Dust Bowl and screens weren't on some of the windows. They must have had a lot of flies in the summertime. Some of the houses used towels or sheets for curtains.

Herman parked right out front.

"C'mon," I said a couple of times cause he didn't seem to want to step onto the porch.

I knocked and said, "Hey, I'm Harvey Nixon's friend, Sonny."

I saw a tall, shiny black man in overalls inside the door, just standing there with no expression; his humorless face could've been permanently glued with that expression or it could've been a Halloween mask. But then his eyes shifted to the street behind us. The bulbous eyes came back to use and he nodded and stepped aside, and Herman and I went on in. I could tell what they'd had for supper from the smell, hush puppies and turnips or mustards and potatoes that had been boiled. I had never liked boiled potatoes cause they tasted like lightning bugs smelled. I liked them either fried or mashed with gravy.

"How you boys doin' tonight?" the man said a little tentatively. His name was supposed to be Jesse. I wanted only the clear white lightning—I didn't like the smoky charcoal stuff cause you couldn't see the bugs and rocks and maybe shards of glass in it. You might down something bad on accident. "712, right there, theys got your white stuff," Harvey had told me, pointing out the house that night he let me ride along. The open look on his big face had no deceit in it. "Name's Jesse," he'd said. "He a family man so if you goes there, look out you don' stare at nobody too long. Ain't polite."

We followed the tall man into the bathroom. Eyes watched us from the living room and a bedroom, little eyes, too. They all seemed exaggerated, bright orbs floating in black space, as focused as police flashlights in your car window. I smiled at the little eyes, not wanting them to be frightened of me and Herman. Their fixed stares didn't say if they were frightened or not. I'm not the enemy, I wanted to say. I don't think I was staring at them but I went ahead and stopped looking.

A cardboard packing box under the sink held some upright pint bottles nudged together. Jesse got a bottle out and handed it to me and I handed it to Herman without shaking it up to check its clarity. I could see it was milky, not clear, but neither was it the charred amber color. Jesse didn't make his moonshine in the bathtub, either. There was no equipment in the bathroom, just an empty claw footed tub with a dirt ring and a little mold on the walls around it, where those little-eyed kids took their bathes. He could have made it somewhere else, maybe on the screened porch out back, but I didn't see any reason to ask him.

We took a swig before we left to show Jesse and the watchful eyes that we trusted he hadn't sold us lye. And that maybe we could handle the stuff like grownups. It doesn't make you cough but you can't breathe and your eyes tear up and your throat burns like hell for two minutes. And you had better tilt the bottle gently or else the muck rushes into your mouth. When it's almost empty you have to use your teeth as a strainer. Then I pulled out two dollars and paid Jesse that amount and we got out of there.

Herman burned a half-circle of rubber making a U-turn. I cringed. "Goddamnit, you shithead! Don't do that."

He managed to get us out of Ash Town and back to 4th Street without the cops on our butts and sped east till we crossed the tracks to Mason and only then did he slow down. He worked the lights up Freeman Street to the Halloween party Herman said was at one of his ex-girlfriend's house.

"You've got no business going to an old girlfriend's party," I told him. "It could get us in trouble, mark my word."

It would be like me going to Vicki's party and seeing her with her new boyfriend, Raul or Reginald or whatever the hell he was called; it was just going to make Herman feel rotten and maybe piss off her new boyfriend.

"Screw it," he said, and he sounded defensive. "There'll be other girls there; I don't even have to see her." I still didn't like it.

Our bottle was about half gone when we changed into our Halloween outfits. We changed on the sidewalk with the meat wagon's doors open for privacy. Herman in a tweed sport's jacket and large-collared yellow shirt topped off with a blue ascot. Snazzy. Or better still, dandy. It was something Tony Curtis would wear to a Sinatra party at his Palm Springs digs. But not at Halloween. Herman's dark eyes twinkled like Tony's and his natural curly locks was slicked back just like Tony's, too, but Herman added a ducktail that Tony Curtis would never wear, which is probably what started the fight; you don't wear a ducktail unless you were a punk looking for trouble. "Comb it out," I pleaded with him before we headed in.

"Tony wears a tail," he said, sounding more defensive now. As we entered the house, he slicked the hair back with his hands.

It was a nice-looking brick house set below street level and surrounded by woods.

I said, "Well, try to be nice. Can you do that, huh? Just stay out of trouble."

"Trouble? My middle name is mis-er-ee," he twanged in a weak attempt at King Creole.

I was decked out as a high priest. I knew this boy whose uncle was Catholic and had something to do with Saint Michael's and for a pack of Kent's he "borrowed" a black clerical with a white-collar tab and a work cassock for me. It would have been worth three packs of cigarettes as it turned out. Usually, the girls went straight for Herman. He was the cute one, Mr. Hollywood, Mr. Tony Curtis. Right now he looked like Elvis, a little, with those wormy lips and double dimples. I didn't have dimples but girls would often mention "bedroom eyes—ohh yeah, daddy." Vicki, for one.

But tonight, in my priest's collar, it was me they flocked after, wanting forgiveness and penance and everlasting salvation in the kingdom of God Almighty. I tried to bestow godly virtues on every girl who sought me out. I blessed them with the holy water from a leftover vanilla extract bottle hanging from my neck, just a drop on the forehead hairline of every girl that I blessed and forgave. Some of them had to beg and I considered carefully their fates, but in the end I gave in and took their sweet faces in my hand and sprinkled the holy water on to their foreheads, anointing them, forgiving them the sins they might have in the future. I thought it would have been nice to have a bigger bottle of holy water so I could actually wet their face and then try to kiss their wet lips, kinda slip one in real fast while they were in their trance under my spell. Next time, I would do that, bring a bigger bottle, a pint-sized syrup bottle with a ring on the neck for easier dispensing.

Neither one of our costumes were very Halloweenish, no Frankenstein or Wolf Man, mummy or Martian with antennae. You probably wouldn't even call them costumes. But I thought we were too old to dress up like goblins or mice. Girls could get away with that till they were practically adults, but their costumes were clever and damn sexy. Like Herman's ex-girlfriend's. She wore skimpy kitty-cat see-through black lace tights with white puffballs in the right places just to tease your eyes, like a cat teasing the mouse under its paw. Every guy was after her to twist or mash or tame her with a slow dance. Even Herman. That was his mistake.

We left the bottle of shine on the backseat floorboard along with the Coke for when one of us wanted to come out for a snort.

I heard the row soon as I came back from my booster shot. A college boy didn't like it that Herman wanted to dance with the ex-girlfriend, now this boy's girlfriend, I figured. Or it might have been another girl Herman danced with and the boy was just jealous of him for no reason other than the girls swarmed him. That was the rumor getting to me, that the college boy was jealous of a high schooler. A real hotshot, this guy. I learned he went to Talladega State. Being short made Herman easy pickings for any guy bigger than him, only they didn't know about his temper. His good looks got him in trouble sometimes over things that had nothing to do with a girl. I finally quit practice boxing with Herman because it riled him when I landed a glove on his face or even his midsection, any punch that made him look bad and me look good. It was only practice and I didn't even swing hard but all I had to do was land one and he would get in this hot zone and come at me for blood. I had to throw off the gloves and run before he would calm down.

I saw this one happening before it happened. She was holding on to Herman's arm. He slid her arm off when the guy started shouting at him—"Hey, pretty boy. Yeah you, armpit, where're you think you're going? Talk to me, cutie pie! … I'll bust your ass." Herman showed his patent smile with the dimples and just walked away with his head bowed. Good for him, I thought.

The irate college boy was acting mad as hell for some reason; maybe he was flunking his very first quarter cause he didn't study. He went to parties instead. He could've had a Freudian inferiority complex because girls didn't jump quick enough to suit him or they didn't jump at all, although I thought he looked good enough if he'd only get rid of that bad attitude. I watched him follow Herman outside, kicking him in the butt all the way up the steps to the '49 Olds, shouting nasty stuff at him. Stuff I don't think I could have taken. Herman never turned around. He just kept his head down and kept moving with this guy kicking him in the ass and everybody watching. I ran to the car ahead of him and got behind the wheel so we could make our getaway. But it didn't go that way. Herman reached the car just behind me. He moved calmly, even rhythmically, which was unlike him. I thought, *Oh shit, watch out college boy.*

He reached inside the back door and stepped back to the street curb with the Coke bottle in his hand. He broke the neck off on the curb and stabbed it into the guy's face. Not just once. He hit him maybe three times before the college boy knew what had happened. Then the freshman fell backwards, stumbling on the curb. He sat there stunned, looking at his blood-slick hands. Then he started wailing and flailing, falling in the shrubs.

It was pandemonium. Girls ran around in circles screaming. Boys didn't know what to do. They just stood around gawking at all the blood spitting and spewing from the boy's face. Herman vanished into the night. I got the injured boy into Herman's old man's fastback, in the back seat with one of his buddies to hold him down, and shagged-ass to find a hospital. Someone, a woman I thought, shouted there was a hospital on Seventeenth, east. I looked in the rearview. He was slinging blood all over Herman's old man's beige interior.

"Goddamnit! Cover your face and sit back!" I hollered. "Don't move around, you'll bleed more."

It was a long night for that boy and for me. I would hear later he had to have over fifty stitches and his face was fractured in three places where the bottle struck bone. He was lucky he didn't lose an eye, or both eyes. I left him and his buddy at Emergency and drove fast back to my house and got a bucket of soapy water and a bunch of towels and tried to clean up the car before the blood dried any harder. I got most of it out. The college kid's mother called me the next evening to thank me for getting him to the hospital so fast. She said, "This was a lesson Richard needed." Never mind how the boy's mother got my phone number; I never even found out.

Later that night, around two in the morning, Herman showed up with leaves stuck to the dried blood on him. He tapped on my bedroom window where the crabapple branch scraped the screen. "Psst, Sonny, you there? Damnit, I can't see you in there, let me in."

I was going to have to put up with a lot from Herman Brown because now he was my blood brother.

Chapter 9

I was over at Scarborough's one afternoon having my chocolate shake and noticed Harvey Nixon near the pharmacy window. I nodded and went over to say hello. I wanted to tell him that the white lightning he turned me on to wasn't too bad except it could make you mean and that Jesse didn't actually make it in his bathtub. But of course I wasn't going to say that here.

"Hey, Harvey, how's it going? You making another delivery today?" I didn't think he worked after four-thirty on Tuesdays.

He looked around to see who was watching us. The soda jerk, maybe. No one else. He was fidgety.

"I's got my boy wid me. Out in the truck, lookin to find me a den'ist."

"Your boy hurting?"

"Yeah, he hurtin."

"Who you going to?"

"Tried that Dr. McMahon, but he don' take no colored. They's one down by Ash but he on vacation right now. Vacation! My boy, he gots to see *somebody*."

"Yeah, you don't want to see Dr. McMahon anyway. You know Dr. Peach, just down the street in the 10th Street Medical Building? I betcha he'd see your boy. You want me to call his office?"

"You think that'd be okay?"

"He's my dentist. I reckon he would take you in if he's still there."

Harvey nodded and I asked the woman behind the counter by the front window if I could borrow the store phone. She looked suspicious, looking from me to Harvey Nixon. She knew Harvey; he'd been driving the drug store truck as long as I remembered. She still looked skeptical, but finally said, "Well, I suppose. It ain't long distance, is it?"

"Thanks," I said. "It's one block away."

I got Gloria, his assistant. "Dr. Peach's office, may I help you?"

"Gloria? This is Sonny Poe, is Dr. Peach still there?"

"He's with his last patient, Sonny. It important?"

"Kinda. This kid I know's got a bad toothache. You think he might could see him, I mean today? Would you tell him it's my friend Harvey's boy?"

"Just a sec, Sonny, be right back."

In a minute she said, "Sonny? Yes, bring him on in."

"Thanks, Gloria, bye."

"This Dr. Peach," Harvey said, "he know my boy colored, don' he?"

"Yeah," I said, but I wasn't sure Doctor Joe would remember who Harvey was. "C'mon, let's get over there."

I paid my tab of sixty-nine cents. Shakes had just gone up to fifty cents and I had one packet of peanut butter crackers. It was getting too expensive to come in every day and still get my fifteen-cents of chocolate before my route. Maybe I'd start getting a soda instead of a shake; a fountain Coke cost a dime.

Outside, I looked in the truck cab at a little figure with a big baseball cap that hardly reached the edge of the window. I didn't recognize the team logo on the cap since it was from the Negro League, the "ABC" of the Atlanta Black Crackers. Was that still a team? I wondered. I looked under the hat brim and saw a little boy's miserable face.

"I'll see you down there, Harvey. It's room 107."

"Thanks, Sonny boy, thank you."

We all went through the swinging front glass doors together and marched quickly down the hall. The few people in the hallway frowned at the three of us, turning back around to frown some more and shake their heads.

Doctor Joe stood in the doorway between the torture rooms and the waiting room, wearing that green smock and a broad white smile that I should have recognized the day I came here for treatment. It was a patent smile, his and only his. I now would recognize it anywhere anytime, I felt sure.

"Okay, son," he said, bending at the waist and putting his hands on his knees like he was in a huddle to get the next play. "You got yourself a sore tooth, do you?"

The boy nodded silently. You couldn't see his face for the bill of his cap.

Harvey Nixon said, "I sho do preciate you seeing him, Doctor. Sho do. It just started hurtin him this mo'nin."

Doctor Joe kept his eye on the boy. "So you've been hurting all day, then? Did you get to school at all?"

"He come home bout noon."

"Well, come on in here and let's get rid of the hurt, okay, son?"

The boy nodded again but still looked miserable. Doctor Joe asked us to wait and he'd report in one minute what the problem was.

And he did. "It's just a cavity that needed fixing a couple of months back. Too much taffy, Mr. Nixon. Gotta watch that."

"That boy tell you that, Doctor?"

Doctor Joe nodded almost contentedly. "Tell his mamma he will need to brush more often—help keep the decay down. He'll be okay. Let me just fill it and he'll be ready to get out of here. They always are anxious for that."

Sitting in the empty waiting room, emptier because Gloria had also gone for the day, I thanked Harvey for showing me where I could buy some cheap shine. Otherwise, you have to pay five bucks for a pint of bonded at the backdoor of the Revis Hotel. "It was pretty good stuff, too," I said. "Thanks."

I didn't see any need to tell him it might have helped get this trouble-making kid fifty stitches in his face. Maybe the shine didn't cause the fight but I'd bet it contributed.

Doctor Joe brought the boy out in about fifteen minutes. He didn't look miserable now; he grinned lopsided from the dead lip but the grin restored his sweet-looking face. Doctor Joe sat down next to Harvey and crossed his legs, putting on a little more serious expression.

"Mr. Nixon, have you seen an orthodontist or dentist about the protrusion in your son's upper teeth?"

"No-suh, I ain't. You mean them buckteeth?"

"They could be straightened pretty easily. He would have a lot less complications later on with his bite and all you would need is for him to wear a retainer for a length of time. It shouldn't be too expensive and it would do wonders for his smile. Which lights up his face."

"It sho' do that, lights me up too. But I know what it cost and we just ain't gots the money to fix them teeth."

"Let me take a mold. I can put together a retainer for him and I'll charge you just what it cost for materials. It won't be much. I'll want to see him every now and again to adjust the band. Alright?"

Harvey might have blushed. His big face seemed to go through a shift in colors, though I couldn't be sure, his skin being black as midnight. I'd been talking to the kid, asking him if the needle hurt. He said, "No, suh, not a-tall."

So Doctor Joe took the boy back into a torture room while we waited another fifteen minutes. I asked Harvey if he'd had a fight lately and he clearly beamed.

"Oh, you bet I did. Big ole knockout, second round. Man, that kid, he went down easy."

"Maybe you just hit too hard," I said lightly.

"No-suh. I wadn' trying to knock him out, just close his eye up a little bit so I could work the inside easier. I was lookin to go ten rounds. He just went down like a stone in water."

"So, what kind of record you got now?"

"Fifteen wins, three loses, seven knockout. Should be moh loses but some these kids, I tell ya, they jest too young and wild, too easy. But I's hoping to go to Birmin'ham first of the year for the big fight. Lots ah money to the winner."

"Good luck with that, and keep working out."

He got out of the seat again and took a few steps then sat back down. He looked more nervous the longer it took. I said, "Don't worry, Harvey. You've got a medical emergency here."

"It's not just that. I—I sho do wish I could ax you over to hit on my bag, Sonny boy, but it jest ain't no good you being there. You una'stand, don' you?"

I nodded. "Yeah, I know. They have bags at the Y. I can go there. But you sure taught me a lot, Harvey. I'm gonna miss your instructions."

"I's jest real sorry."

"Don't worry about it, I understand."

The boy sprang into the room and went straight to the chair next to his father and jumped in it, a little less timid now. Doctor Joe followed behind him. He talked to Harvey standing there. "I want him back in a week, next Thursday. At five o'clock. That work? I should have his brace put together by then. Got that?"

"Yes-suh, we'll be cheer. Thank you, suh."

"Now—" Doctor Joe looked at the boy "—you can get on out of here. I'll see you in a week."

After they left, he turned to me. "Sonny, come on back to the office. I want to talk to you."

He sounded tired, or maybe pissed. I sat on the couch and he get behind his desk, officious like.

"You realize the risk we took today, helping that youngster?"

"Uh huh, I just hated seeing that boy hurting like that. There wasn't anybody else. I knew *you'd* take care of him."

"That's about what I thought," he said with a sigh. "Okay. I'm not angry. Tell you the truth, Sonny, I think more of you for wanting to help him; it shows me who you are. It's just you can't be naïve to the reality of what we have to deal with here. For example, it's against the rules with management for me to service blacks in this building. Truthfully, I don't give a damn about their rules … But just be a little more conscious of our position. Rumors spread quickly in this town. Don't forget that, especially on the subject of race."

He leaned closer my way. "This country, right now, is going into a new phase in its development. It's a revolution and it's going to change society as we know it. And, Sonny, we're sitting in the heart of the opposition to that change. It's a very dangerous and exciting time."

"Yeah, I know. It's this Civil Rights Movement and the guy leading it, Martin Luther King, right? He's the one everybody hates around here, right?"

"He's a big part of it, yes—and great that you know something about what I'm talking about. Anyway, just remember what I've said and try to be more judicious. Alright?"

I really didn't know what to say. He was right. I didn't care if people thought I had nothing against Negroes or even that I was proud to have Harvey Nixon for a friend. But I'd better start caring and take Doctor Joe's advice and just keep my big mouth shut. Or I was headed for trouble.

Chapter 10

I met Doctor Joe's fiancée Jeanne on a Saturday afternoon. She'd driven over from Auburn in a yellow sports car. I could see why she was his fiancée. She was gorgeous. I tried to overlook all the makeup she wore but that was why she looked like a girl on the cover of *Seventeen*. She had long and wavy ash blonde hair that she played with a lot and the greatest legs. The legs weren't made up even though they were impossibly tan for summer being long gone. She wore yellow short shorts and the way she kept the knees locked and slanted, whether she was sitting or standing, I swear they were Jane Russell's legs.

Jeanne seemed nice enough; she hugged me and smiled when he introduced us, telling her vaguely I was a nephew he didn't see often and then boasting what a tennis star in the making I was, which embarrassed me a little cause we'd only played a few times and I was not that good, not yet. She seemed to buy all that without asking me a single question.

She had cold hands, but it was late afternoon and chilly and every inch of her long legs was exposed along with her bare tan shoulders. I'd probably be shivering dressed as skimpy as she was. Still, there was something about her that made my eyes narrow. I couldn't put my finger on it exactly, maybe that she was pretentious. Then I thought, what college girl is *not* pretentious, especially sorority girls? So I just went with how sexy she was and cheered Doctor Joe for scoring such a doll.

Jeanne talked about the long weekend they were taking in New Orleans next weekend. "I know it's not Mardi Gras, but I simply can't wait that long. You're anxious too, aren't you, Joe, sweetie?"

It was nearly five but close enough to "cocktail hour," he said, to have mint juleps. Did I want one? Hell, yeah, I said, and he had just brought out a batch to the backyard patio when Jeanne asked him the question.

He nodded. "Of course, I'm raring to go."

We were sitting where the last bit of sunlight filtered through the backyard woods. Doctor Joe didn't sit. He said, "I want you to hear the new Thelonious Monk album I picked up today. I haven't even heard it yet. It should be sensational."

He went into the house to put it on his hi-fi.

Apparently Jeanne didn't care for jazz cause she didn't say a word. Me neither, really, but it was okay by me to listen to it. Maybe I'd learn to like something else besides rock 'n' roll. Jeanne crossed her arms and did a little shiver, like she was finally feeling the chill.

Except for the meticulous garden Doctor Joe called his "token shrine to enlightenment"—I kid you not—his backyard was pretty much a forest. You couldn't see or hear any neighbors and only part of the sky overhead, no horizon in any direction. The trees stood way taller than the two-story house. It was even cozier with this gurgling rock fountain that rose out of the middle of a deep pond where big koi goldfish breezed in and out of sight under lily pads. He'd put in some kind of small Oriental pagoda at the edge of the pond with a fat, half-smiling Buddha sitting in the middle of it. The structure had finials that looked like pointy little temples, and they were made of gold, or were gold-colored, anyway. And so was the tiled oval roof on it. I might have thought a gold temple was ostentatious except that Doctor Joe explained in India and Tibet and in all aspects of the Buddhist religion and culture, the golden lotus—whatever that was besides being gold—was a spiritual symbol. So, the colors of the peacock were everywhere in the East. I enjoyed looking through his books on Eastern art and architecture, which included China and Thailand and Japan, at the bright colors mostly.

Tiles of a duller earthy color surrounded the pond for about ten feet out in any direction. Geraniums and tulips in round red iron pots ran along two rows of rhododendron shrubs, which lead to the back steps. He said he did everything himself, except build the temple. He went to Atlanta to get the Buddha.

"Yeah, I put the garden in partly as homage to the struggles of the Dalai Lama," he said, whose country was being run over by the Chinese, sort of like the South was getting invaded by the federal government—but vice versa on which one was righteous. "There's a spiritual goodness in Buddhism we could sorely use over here," he said. "Especially now."

The garden could work on you, it was so relaxing, and time just didn't seem to matter, especially when the music he played happened to be really good, like this Monk album.

Jeanne didn't appear relaxed. She was antsy and kept looking at her watch. It was a lovely sparkling silver piece of jewelry that slid up and down her delicate arm when she lifted it. She also had on silver bracelets. I had never owned a wristwatch but if I ever did, it would be one that glowed in the dark. When Doctor Joe returned she sat right up against him to help keep her bare legs warm since the sun had disappeared. She nudged him with her knee. "'Hootenanny' comes on radio in five minutes. You know how much I like the show. Can you turn it on, please, Joe? Baby?"

"Sure," he said, "just let this piece finish. Anyone for another julep?"

He glanced at me.

"Yeah. Yeah, sure," I said happily.

In a bit we listened to some Pete Seeger and Kingston Trio and Carl Perkins on the Hootenanny show. Jeanne talked about the New Orleans trip. She said they would be staying at the Monteleon and that she was really hoping they could get Bananas Fosters at Brennan's and would "most absolutely drink Hurricanes at Pat O'Brien's" and sing "Kansas City" all night long. "Isn't that right, Joe?"

Doctor Joe nodded but didn't seem interested in talking about it. I actually thought her going on about the trip irritated him. He said, "I suppose," and, after the thirty-minute radio show had finished, he wanted to hear a new Ella Fitzgerald album he'd also bought today.

"Would y'all mind a lot?" and he went into the house and turned up the volume so we could hear "Ella's low dips."

"Listen how easily she jumps octaves, in lyrics or scats. What an instrument that girl has, huh?" Ella Fitzgerald excited him more than the folk stuff Jeanne preferred and the rock 'n' roll I liked.

Jeanne talked about a chemistry project she'd been working on and sipped her julep and then went back to talking about New Orleans. "Of course we'll listen to plenty of Dixieland jazz. I do love my Dixieland."

I thought great, have a swell time. I could have cared less where they were staying or where they ate or what they did. I had my own stuff to do, like get down to the YMCA and practice my boxing so I could start getting ready for the next time I was with Herman at the roller rink or a party, knowing damn well he would mix it up. I had to get prepared for Gerald Henry and the Bozos, too, for when they got around to ambushing me for real. And maybe I would have to fight the ex-con that I'd heard was Vicki's new boyfriend and, I'd also heard, was going to beat my ass just because I had known Vicki in the past. I wouldn't know where or when he'd find me, but I had a sick feeling all the time about it. An ex-con! And always in the back of my mind was the threat of the Klan in Sugarman Cole's haunting words, "We'll find you."

Chapter 11

I stopped by Doctor Joe's house after slinging papers in the morning on Thanksgiving Day—on T-Day and Christmas the paper went out just like Sundays, early in the morning. I was hoping he might want to play some tennis and I didn't have to get home until three for our big feast. We were supposed to eat at three o'clock but it always ended up around six, but I still had to be there at three. To help.

It was a sunny day with a crisp fall chill and hardly any wind, a good day for tennis. A good day for a front yard football game, too, if he'd rather do that. I was pretty sure Jeanne would be there and I hoped she would want to play with us. I had been around a couple more times by then when Jeanne was there, and she was still sexy as ever, if not sometimes irritating with her constant sorority girl talk. She was "so excited" for Kappa Delta's upcoming winter rush which promised "some really great girls and I just can't wait!" I heard all about how well-dressed her sisters had to keep themselves at the same time she told us, almost gravely, how many little black mouths the sorority's "Helping Hands" committee had fed last month, and in practically the same breath mentioned the homecoming dance the chapter was planning at the Hilton Hotel Ballroom in Birmingham. They had parties almost every other weekend at their house or over the lane at the Sigma Chi fraternity house.

It was a little disgusting having to listen to that crap. But I still liked being around her cause the things she did and talked about were exciting. I wanted to hear about all she did at Auburn. Her family must have been rich to afford to keep up her expensive tastes and lifestyle. If I went to college, I'd have to work. And I wouldn't even be able to afford the clothes you'd have to wear to be in a fraternity, never mind what it'd cost for dues and stuff. Who would want to be in a stinking fraternity, anyway? That was just for the hotshot rich boys, like the Dudley Willard's and maybe Ledbelly.

When Jeanne wasn't being conceited, she acted really nice to me; she could look straight into my eyes and smile and that smile was sexy. I didn't care if that wasn't the way she meant it; it was the way I took it. I had started to daydream about here, things I knew I shouldn't have been thinking. She was only twenty years old, just four years older than me. When I turned forty she'd be forty-four, big stinking deal. We'd be practically the same age at 60—if anybody could imagine being that old. I was ashamed of myself for the thoughts I had about her, Doctor Joe's fiancée. Doctor Joe was a great friend and I wasn't about to do anything to jeopardize that. But I kept my secret locked out of any conversation we had. Remembering some church sermon, I knew I was a sinner because when the preacher screamed about the perils of temptation with your neighbor's wife, he would harp that if you *think* it, you're as guilty as if you *do* it. He made sure we got the point in that sermon by pointing a finger at practically every man in the congregation and repeating, "*You* and *you* are sinners." He pointed a finger at me, too, and I had never coveted my neighbor's wife, not ever. But if I daydreamed about screwing Jeanne or even just touching her where I wanted, according to the preacher I was just as guilty in God's eyes as if I actually did fondle her lovely breasts. You couldn't even beat off in total privacy thinking about her or that guy's wife without drawing down the goddamn fires of damnation. I was going to hell, sure as sin, so I figured I might as well daydream all I wanted about Miss Jeanne Cochran showing off her tits in tight cashmeres, the girl with the Jane Russell legs.

"Stick around for a little while," Jeanne said to me from inside the house, suddenly appearing on the patio with a bowl of cut-up fruit smothered in whipping cream. It must have been their brunch cause it was only ten in the morning. "You know Joe," she added conspiratorially, "he hates to eat alone."

"Yeah, I know," I said just to say something, cause I didn't know that. "Me too ... You're leaving?"

It wasn't all that warm today but Jeanne wore her infamous short shorts anyway. I guess she always wore short shorts and that was how she kept those legs that tan. She had on an unbuttoned polo blouse and when she bent over I couldn't help but sneak a peek, hoping the cloth would give just enough to see a nipple, cause I was sure she wasn't wearing a brassiere; I would've seen a strap at least. I'd heard college girls didn't wear bras, that they liked to defy society's Puritans. That was something you couldn't help but like about college girls. Her being bra-less in that loose, open blouse was no daydream. It was real, so I was committing no sin by looking, even when out of modesty I tried not to stare.

But, I could have sworn there was something seductive in her eyes when she looked at me just then, like she was saying it was fine and dandy for me to eat her up with my eyes, that that's the reason she took off the bra in the first place. She wanted me to look.

"I'm having breakfast right now," she said. "Anyway, I'm in a rush. Shopping, you know. See you boys later."

I listened to her little MG whine on the upshift for about two blocks. She liked to step on it. That was something else I liked about Jeanne, that she was a speed demon.

Doctor Joe said he was throwing a football party on the weekend, Saturday, to celebrate the winning season for Alabama's new coach, this tough bear tamer who wore a herringbone hat. The Tide made it to a bowl for the first time in ten seasons. The game was Saturday against Penn State in the Liberty Bowl. So he didn't have time for tennis today.

"Heck, I'm not doing anything. I can help you get ready for it. Tell me what to do." And I spent the next two hours climbing up dreaded pine trees in the front and back yards to hang decorations for the party. Out front he had me string a banner he'd painted in big bold letters that read "Go Tide! Whoop those cowardly Lions." It showed up great on the street in crimson-red color. He gave me garden gloves and a long-sleeved shirt so I wouldn't get sap on my skin. The stuff managed to get on me anyway, on my neck and even on my stomach somehow, but that was okay. It wasn't much and he had some miracle stuff that took it off pretty easily.

After that we moved to the back yard to string some lights in the trees around the patio. Doctor Joe didn't climb anymore so it was all up to me. Pearl lead the way around the garage, constantly turning around to see how far behind we were, wanting us to hurry up.

Sure enough the sap got me there too, but I strung colored lights around the whole first flank of backyard trees. It was going to look like a Christmas pageant come nighttime.

While I was in the trees, he talked excitedly about his alma mater and the new coach. He said Alabama had gone through a pitiful losing streak under Ears Whitworth, fourteen loses in one stretch, and after a nine-year dry spell they fired his butt and hired this young coach from Arkansas called Bear Bryant. There were two legends how he got the nickname Bear, he said. One of them wasn't true. Either Bryant was offered a dollar a minute to stay in the ring with a bear or, the one I liked, he had fought a black bear barehanded in the woods of Tennessee and somehow he survived and the bear didn't. I didn't much see how that could've been, and I didn't think Doctor Joe did either by the way he told me the story, a little laughing and head-shaking.

It would've been nice to see the look on Stuart's face when I told him that this friend of mine he'd called a queer ran seven touchdowns as a tight end his very first year for the University of Alabama Crimson Tide, toughest team in America, and that year, 1945, they ended up in first place in the country, winning the Rose Bowl. But if I knew how closed-minded Stuart and just about everybody else was in this stinking town, he wouldn't believe it and wouldn't care anyway. He would only wonder why a dentist was friends with me. You just couldn't get through to some people, no matter what. I wasn't even going to try.

Football was one thing Doctor Joe would talk about. I hadn't learned anything about him when he was a kid. What was he like when he was sixteen, I wondered. How many girlfriends did he have? How many did he have when he was a football star cause I knew he could have had tons. I just figured he stayed too busy studying cause he'd already planned to go to medical school. What he did tell me was he played football because he was too young to fight in the war.

By the time I finished and got the sap off, I had to get home. Mother would be all over me for not being there when my cousins showed up, coming all the way from Birmingham. Doctor Joe thanked me and slipped a five-dollar bill in the pocket of my jeans.

I didn't go to his football party. He didn't invite me. I had to admit I was a little unhappy, after monkeying through half a dozens sap-seeping pines. But I minded only because I wasn't invited. I didn't really want to be around all those snobbish adults.

Chapter 12

I went to the house on Broadmore whenever I had a chance. Doctor Joe didn't seem to mind, my showing up after throwing papers, and I really enjoyed being there. The house was peaceful and quiet except for when he played his jazz on the hi-fi. I hadn't cared much for that kind of music until he got me to understand some of the complicated beats and chord structures. Then I understood what he meant by "jazz is pure art, pure genius."

On Broadmore I didn't have to put up with the nagging I got at home, Stuart hounding me or the foot stomping from the upstairs apartment when they got into their arguments. There was nobody at Doctor Joe's house to fight with over which TV program to watch cause he hardly ever turned it on, and that was fine with me. I didn't laugh much at home but I did at the big house on Broadmore.

You had to climb twelve brick steps to reach the landing at the front door, so it stood high over the wooded lawn and street. Inside was open and airy, nothing like the dungeon of our terrace apartment with small windows and next to a furnace room. Here there were floor-length double windows with light-colored drapes and sheer curtains, which he only closed when it was cold and rainy, and even then it was still light inside. There was nothing ostentatious or pretentious with how he had his house furnished, either. The only thing fancy was that big shiny piano taking up a big chunk of the living room. He said the grand had a much richer, fuller sound than an upright or console. I liked listening to him play on it; the songs he played made the place even more cheerful.

Doctor Joe wasn't picky. I might put my shoes on the couch and he'd look at me but say nothing and I'd remember and take them down. Nothing else was ever said; I didn't get screamed at like I would at home. I could spread out on the carpet, still a little dusty after some chore outside, and play with Pearl. Once I even went to sleep lying there listening to some classical chamber music by Mendelssohn, and Doctor Joe didn't wake me up till it was time for me to leave.

We didn't talk about the other side of life in Woodstock, the side I was from and so familiar with, about the gang rumbles and getting into fights and having to avoid the hoodlums and hallway bullies at school. We talked about music and sports and things I might be interested in trying out, like playing a musical instrument, the piano or guitar maybe. We talked about places to travel, foreign places like Mexico and even California, which seemed foreign to me because it *was* foreign to me, places that I had daydreamed about, those places I'd seen on the desk blotter at his office. He never suggested any field of future work for me but when I got an idea for what I might want to do, he'd go, "Yeah, I can see you as a restaurateur, and you certainly have the presence and personality to work with the public. There's no limit to how far you can go in that career." Always up and positive.

Once when we were cruising in the convertible, he said, "I would bet you're smart enough to make a stock investment," and he talked about me buying a stock "on option."

His longer hair blew all over the place and mine stuck up because it was too stiff to be moved by mere wind.

"It's a cheap and easy way to start off when you don't have a lot of money or expertise," he said over the wind and the pop station I had on the radio. "If the company you buy does good you can make a profit; if not, you haven't lost much. You weigh the risk against the odds and it comes out in your favor with an option—depending of course on the company you go with. So, what do you think, Sonny, you up for it?"

And I said, "Hell yeah."

I went to the bank and handed over $50 of my Harley savings without ever thinking about losing it. He made some suggestions and I chose a brand new offshore oil-drilling company out of New Orleans called McDermott that had just been listed as what Doctor Joe called an "IPO," and I purchased a six-month option-to-buy. Pretty fancy talk for a kid who knew as much about investing in the stock market as horse racing in Florida, which was zilch. We met at the Stock Market Exchange on the bottom floor of the Twelfth Street Building downtown on Mason, the tallest building in town, and he made the contract cause I was a minor. I stood among all these men in dark suits and wool fedoras who watched without any excitement at the ticker symbols track across the overhead wall. To me it was hypnotizing.

Now all we had to do was watch and wait. I could double my investment if the company did what everybody thought it would do, he said. I had no idea what I was doing but twice a week after that, on Tuesday and Friday, I would go to the Stock Exchange and stand by the door and watch the amazing ticker scroll across the wall until McDermott's symbol, "MD," rolled by and see what the price was. Doctor Joe said my choice was a good one since the auto industry was a solid market and what did cars run on but gas and gas came from oil.

"Keep in mind, this isn't Superior Oil and all startups are risky," he warned, "but I've done all right by them." He said when Ford Motor Company went public in '55, he bought a bunch of stock in it and so far had "hit a little gold because of the T-Bird and Fairlane lines."

Yeah, I could see that. I didn't know until then how much of a risk taker Doctor Joe was. But he was also smart and decisive, and I figured I couldn't go wrong paying attention to him.

But it wasn't always stuff about my future or jazz we discussed, usually while listening to Charlie Parker's horn or some Bud Powell bebop piano. He talked to me about this civil rights movement and kind of what to expect. "There'll be a lot of resistance through the Bible Belt and especially here in Alabama. Jim Crow's been the gospel for so long now, it's going to be like moving a mountain to get us to lay down and roll over because the federal government says to."

But Doctor Joe even had a positive view on that. "There will be a lot less bloodshed in this movement if Dr. King's nonviolent principles can prevail," he told me. "I think they will, he's a strong charismatic leader and there seems to be enough faith in his leadership to see this thing through."

There was one more thing I like about the house on Broadmore, before I leave it, and that was when his housekeeper, Deliah, would be there, cause it reminded me of times with Gussy. Sometimes she stayed late, often on Saturdays, to cook his supper. He had guests over a lot on weekends. She was wild in the kitchen and the smells coming out of there were enough to make me linger as long as I could before getting kicked out. She came from the Delta and did a lot of Cajun dishes that had a wide range of exotic flavors, all delicious smelling. Her chickens were always baked golden across the breasts and she'd have some potent French Cajun sauce that smelled so good I couldn't stand it. Deliah had brought whole fish with her, a bass maybe. She would cook it up that way and serve it up that way, she said, the eyes still in the head. She grinned and winked one of her big eyes as if she were joking. It cracked me up that Deliah wouldn't cook potatoes. She was real stubborn about it. I heard her argue with Doctor Joe, "They ain't nothin in a po-tato got any nutrition and I ain't messin with 'em. So don' ax me no mo."

Doctor Joe told me he would sometimes drive her home to Ash Town so it wouldn't take here all night on the bus, which didn't run but hourly on weekends and she had to get a transfer. I could see them driving through the dark streets of Ash, her sitting tall in the seat so neighbors could see her in that white Thunderbird.

One Saturday before it turned dark and I had to take off, and Doctor Joe had drunk more screwdrivers that he normally would in the afternoon, he said, right out of the blue, "Sonny Poe, ..." He showed a playful grin but stared hard until I giggled and said, "Yeah? Well, what?"

I'd had three screwdrivers myself, one more than I remember ever having in the day time over there.

He walked outside with me and we both sat on the front steps. He rubbed his face all over for about half a minute.

I got antsy. "Alright, what is it, Joe?"

He stared out across the long lawn, at the magnolia trees in the street median. Then at me. With a little chuckle, he said, "Impetuous kid. I suppose most middle-teen boys are like that, maybe I might've been too ...

"Now listen to me, Sonny. Let me see if I can say this so it'll be real clear. There aren't a lot of people in my circle who would understand me spending as much time with you as I do. It could become a problem. Rumors might start circulating. So, I'm going to make it official, you are my nephew, the only child of my dead brother, adopted out when he and his wife died and you were a wee baby. This should also satisfy Jeanne, who's getting a little possessive about who I spend my time with. There shouldn't be much flack; you can't very well question the dead. And I don't think there's much chance people are going to call up your mother about it."

He snorted sarcastically.

"Anyway, you can take what I've said and mull it over and then talk to me about going on, if that's what you want."

I beamed. "There's nothing to mull over. Count me in, Uncle!"

Chapter 13

It didn't hit me until later that night, when I was trying to go to sleep and couldn't for Stuart's damn snoring, that Doctor Joe had not given me any reason why he wanted to go on hanging out with me, be my friend. I still didn't know. I was just happy I didn't have to stop going over to his house and everything else because there was so much to learn from him and I had a terrific time doing things with him, and now that I was his official nephew, nobody was going to question all that.

That wouldn't apply to my family, of course. But they were way out of Doctor Joe's circle anyway. They'd never find out I was Doctor Joe's nephew. The best thing I could do concerning them was keep my mouth zipped about anything about Doctor Joe.

For one reason or another I didn't get over there for a couple of weeks. I went on with my schoolwork and throwing papers. It took longer on my route having now to make exact throws around all the Christmas decorations in customers' yards, the silly snowmen and glistening stuff they put inches from their porches. But I didn't break anything, no ripped screens or broken glass. I didn't even knock out lights on those fake Santas and reindeers in the yards or on porches, or maybe pop the string lights on the rain gutters.

I kept thinking about Susie and wondering how she was getting along. Something about the season, I guess, made me want to see her; I was thinking that if she would talk to me I might get her the silver necklace from Sears now. But it had been so long ago since I'd talked to her, I couldn't remember too well what her attitude was. I would go with my hunch that she was still pissed at me.

I wasn't about to try Vicki, not with this new ex-con boyfriend of hers. Vicki was out. Period, no question.

"Hi ya, Susie Q," I said in a singsong chirp that put the Everly Brothers to shame. It turned her off. But instead of cussing me out and hanging up like Vicki would do, she was kind enough to say, "Who's this?"

"Guess," I said and immediately knew I was still turning her off. I quickly added, "It's me, you know, Sonny. The guy that liked you so much last summer." I put syrup in my voice.

"You're a jerk, Sonny. I *did* like you. But—"

"Aw, Susie. I'm sorry. I don't know what happened to me back then. Maybe it was, I was getting to like you too much and I got scared. So I went wandering. You know."

There was silence and I took that as a hopeful sign.

She said, "You know Vicki and I aren't friends anymore, don't you?"

"No, I didn't know that. You two have been friends since kindergarten, I thought. That's awful. I'm sorry."

"Well, it doesn't really matter now. But I have to know if you are still seeing her. I mean—"

"Oh yeah, I know what you mean. No. I am *not* seeing Vicki. I haven't seen her since before I saw you last ... How is junior high, anyway?"

She and Vicki were both still in ninth grade. The thought of that suddenly made her seem so young, like I was robbing the cradle, and it made me pull the phone away from my ear and look sorrowfully at it. I almost hung up.

But, I heard her sigh and that kept me going. She said, "It's hard to avoid her since she's in two of my classes and lives right up the street. Boy, I wish things were different. I wish last summer had never happened."

"Look. I'll call her as soon as we hang up," I said, seeing a chance and begging. "I will tell her I'm only going to see you and that it's over for good with us. I'll tell her you are her friend and have always been her friend and don't let me get between you two. I'll say—"

"Okay, Sonny, don't get crazy. If you promise never to see her again, we can talk about it—us."

"Really? Okay. Great. Promise."

What was I thinking? I didn't call Vicki right away. The more I paced around the living room, the more desperate things got. I didn't want to give Vicki up, not for sure good. Maybe the ex-con would get to be a con again; they usually do, don't they? I kicked at Jody, who was doing nothing but laying there sleeping and jerking his paws, not bothering anybody. I told the dog I was sorry and kept pacing.

But in the end I did the right thing and called Vicki. The phone call really didn't matter and turned out just to be a formality since she reminded me I was the fartface shitbreath that she dumped last summer, didn't I remember who dumped who?

"God, Sonny, are you *dense*," she said, putting the super drama in her voice.

I tried to be true to my word and added, "You and Susie used to be friends. Can't—"

"Ha!" she barked. "Until *you* came along and screwed everything up. Listen, Sonny, I have a new boyfriend who's rich!—"

"Who?" I didn't believe her. I thought he was an ex-con; whoever heard of a rich ex-con.

"Joey Nash. You wouldn't know him, he belongs to the country club. He has a *car*."

Where did the ex-con boyfriend rumor come from? I couldn't remember, but I sure was relieved.

"Nash? Ha, I know him. He's a dog."

The phone went dead in my ear. I thought I heard someone giggle on the party line before I put the receiver down.

I felt better even though it hadn't been much of a conversation. The fact she didn't have an ex-con boyfriend who was looking for a piece of me—what a great feeling. Now I could stop looking down every street corner, around every edge of every building I passed. But I also guess this meant it was really the end of me and Vicki. I could learn to live without that iron bra but it would be hard never again touching the ruinous tits tucked inside the thing.

It was getting late and I hadn't picked up my papers yet. Dusk and night came fast at this time of year. I was hustling to get out of the house when an explosion rocked the whole place.

"Oh, shit!" I knew exactly what it was.

I was glad that Mother wasn't there, or Chance. He would have run to the church in a panic to tell her; he could not tell a lie, which meant he couldn't keep his mouth shut. But Bag-a-bones was at basketball and Mother wouldn't come in till about six o'clock. She was supposed to go shopping today after work.

I would have to depend on Stuart getting home before Mother cause I didn't have time to mess with it. He would be bagging groceries or mopping floors or unloading some refrigerator truck until after dark. But maybe he'd get home in time to clean up the furnace room.

The furnace room was next to our terrace apartment, closed off by a metal door at the end of our hallway. The other tenants couldn't access it, only us and maintenance, and the guy hardly ever went there. I rushed through the shiny door and stepped into a pool of fermenting beer and scattered pieces of brown glass. It smelled like an army barracks latrine. Glass was all over the cellar floor. I saw that the icebox door was blown back against the furnace. The batch must have gotten over-carbonated from fermenting too long which we purposely let happen so it would be stronger. I thought, *There goes my Harley.*

I left a note on the door for Stuart to get his butt to work cleaning up the mess. He was used to that kind of work anyway, cleaning up after clumsy idiots who knocked pickle jars off shelves and broke milk bottles.

I met Susie that Friday night at the roller rink in Midland, a farm town about five miles south. On Friday lots of people came to whirl around the big floor to music that was always good. We met incognito and there were two reasons for that. Susie's mother for one, and the other was Susie didn't want anybody seeing me with her after Vicki got her new boyfriend, Dogface. She said it wouldn't look right. I didn't understand that but I did understand about her mother. Her mother hated my guts. She said when she started high school next year that maybe then we could be seen together—if things went that way.

She was creamy-faced and pretty in tight denims and a fur-collared wool sweater that really defined her plump, high breasts. I skated close to her, putting my hands on her hips, reaching tight around her as we circled the rink. "Devoted to You" was playing, a song made just for making out. I stopped her at the turn and tried to steal a kiss. It didn't work; she was playing hard to get. She wanted to get even. And that was fair, so I just played along.

I finally talked her into taking a ride on the Red Baron.

We stepped outside and right away I noticed some hoods gathered in a dark corner of the parking lot, looking agitated, like they wanted to beat somebody up. Gangs weren't allowed inside the rink so they'd have to ditch their gang jackets and go in one at a time, and that just pissed them off. We had to walk toward them to get to the Baron. Susie didn't seem to notice them loitering around. I took her arm in mine and stepped up the pace before the punks decided to take some interest in us.

They had probably heard some rumor that there might be yankee agitators coming to the all-white rink to start something. Last spring a mixed group of white and black guys, college students, had come down from Chicago or somewhere and tried to buy beer at the army base but were run away without much of a fuss. It got written up in the paper but nobody was lynched or thrown in jail or even beat up. Maybe they were just testing the waters for something bigger later on. Stuff like that had been happening ever since Mrs. Rosa Parks took a seat up front on a Montgomery bus five years ago. She took that seat cause she was too tired after work to walk to the back of the bus and nobody was sitting up front, they said. They should've just let her sit in peace. What the hell's the matter with these people?

Now firebombings in Birmingham and demonstrations in North Carolina and next door in Georgia had the gangs of Woodstock antsy and feeling left out of the action. These Northern agitators infuriated them nearly as much as they did Woodstock's Klansmen. That's what I'd heard, anyway. You could bet the Legget brothers were getting their sorry groups of Klansmen all worked up over the trouble these protesters were causing around the South and plotting something evil if they ever tried to march here.

It didn't have a whole lot to do with me personally, other than the image I could not shake of the sound of that black man getting beaten to death.

I nudged Susie to move a little faster when I saw the four hoods were wearing the ugly blood-dripping crossbones of a westside gang, the Outlanders. I didn't know any of them but I'd heard to join the Outlanders, for one thing, you had to spit-cook and eat a rat that you yourself had to catch. What the frig? Why would anybody in their right mind want to hang out with a bunch of freaks like that? Sickos were all over the place in Woodstock. But mostly from the west side of town.

We huffed it to the scooter before the rat eaters could decided about us. I think they probably noticed this boy and girl strolling out of the roller rink, sweethearts with nothing to offer them short of assault and rape, which they apparently weren't interested in tonight. They were looking for something bigger, so they could take bragging rights back to the west end ghetto and then get drunk at their gang headquarters. Their hangout was probably under a street in a sewer culvert.

The Baron was ailing and I had to push-pedal to get it going, especially with the extra weight of another person. Susie took up the seat so I stood on the pedals and sat when I could with just my tailbone on the lip of the seat. I'd put the bike through the ringer during the last four months and it had started to fall apart soon as the 90-day guarantee was up. The chain kept popping off, the front brake cable wire had finally all unraveled and snapped, the clutch cable was holding on by only about one strand, and I was just waiting for it to go boing, too. But the muffler was wired up pretty good and the headlamp still worked and so did most everything else and we were on our way to the woods. Susie's mother was going to come back for her at ten-thirty "sharp." It wasn't even eight-thirty yet.

The moon was bright that night and we could see each other pretty well despite it being dark in the woods. I left the Baron propped between two sycamores and grabbed the beer. I had stashed three bottles from our first batch of Poe's Suds that Stuart didn't know about and earlier tonight tied them in rags to the underside of the gas tank so it looked like a sloppy repair job to hold the gas tank in place. I knew none of the punks that might be hanging around the roller rink would be interested in stealing a jerry-rigged Moped, and I was right, nobody did.

I said, "Susie, come on over here, I wanna show you this place." I'd never been there before that I could remember, but I made it sound like it was one of my secret hideouts.

We held hands plodding over ground growth and around trees till the forest started to get thicker. Then I took her by the arm and she stayed practically glued to me. Which was what I wanted.

"So where are we going, Sonny?" She sounded a little nervous.

"Just yonder." I didn't have a flashlight and we were losing moonlight the denser the forest grew, so I said, "Here's good, let's have a beer." I spread the towel on the spongy forest floor.

Susie sat on the towel beside me but she was reluctant to drink the beer. "How can you drink it this hot."

"It's beer. You just think I want to get you drunk so I can try something," I said. I was trying to look hurt but you really couldn't tell in the dark, so I had to make it sound like I was hurt.

"No I don't," she said.

"I brought some gum for later, when your mom picks you up, okay?"

She started giggling halfway through the first bottle. Susie wasn't much of a drinker, either that or she was faking it. She let me chase her around a tree until she was breathing hard and had worked up a nice luster of sweat on her neck. She seemed to like me wrestling with her and didn't complain when I put her in a bear hug from behind. I realized then how much difference there was between her and Vicki. Vicki had this great hourglass body that looked so good in a bikini, but she was hard and stout and I just then figured out that was the reason I couldn't do anything with her. Her flesh wasn't soft and didn't give when you held her and caressed her; it was more like caressing a warm manikin. Susie was spongy; I melted right into her. We were wallowing on the damp leaves and brush when she turned to me and I kissed her ripe lips and I didn't feel shy at all with my hardness and in a few minutes I was pushing on her as slow and gentle as I could and not softening but getting even stiffer the slower I went. Susie breathed hard, as if she'd been swimming a race, and she unfolded her legs for me like they were the petals of a blossoming flower. She heard an owl call. I didn't. I didn't hear anything except my thumping heart and hers and her murmuring breath in my ear.

Susie was a virgin but she didn't cry or even whimper. She didn't seem to mind at all when all of a sudden I felt myself pop through, and then she squeezed my back up under my shirt and grunted. I was probably pushing harder than I thought because I just went on in, like a door giving way and barging headfirst right through it. We breathed and listened to the forest's hushed, sweet hymnal. I held her tight in our bed of moss while she cried.

When I got home Stuart was already in bed, on his side. He wasn't asleep. He surprised me, saying, "I got the basement cleaned up. Mother'll never know." And that was all he said. He didn't seem mad that I left him the job or that all our work went for naught or that the Dukes weren't going to have any beer for their New Year's bash. I started to ask if he was going to Georgia now for the beer to get Sugarman Cole off his back, but I really didn't want to make myself feel gloomy, not tonight.

I said, "Good ... Good night."

Chapter 14

Doctor Joe threw another party at New Year's and this time invited me to come. He almost made it sound formal. "Sonny, would you like to come to a New Year's Eve party at my house?"

I jumped. "Hell yeah, I'll be there."

"If you want to invite someone, please do—Susie, maybe? I haven't met her yet."

"Nah, she's way too young." I nixed that idea without even considering it. Susie would probably pass out after her second glass of champagne and I'd be stuck. "I'll just come by myself."

"That's fine."

"You want me to help you get ready?"

He knuckled the top of my head. "No, Sonny, you don't always have to do anything. Just bring your dancing shoes and have a good time."

I wanted to go to his party, I wanted to see who his friends were and how he acted around grownups. But I was real nervous about it, too, and when I walked up the steps of his house that night at nine o'clock, hearing cheerful chatter inside, my legs got weak, cause what I really felt was a pathetic absence to explain why I was there. I wondered what

Doctor Joe would say about me to all the well to do's who'd be there.

I stepped inside and there they were, a dozen of them staring at me, wanting an explanation. Who's the kid in plaid?

But Doctor Joe was there shaking my hand and telling me the punch bowl's in the dining room, help yourself, Nephew.

"This is my nephew Sonny Poe, folks, an up-and-coming entrepreneur and already a tennis prodigy."

He was so cool. I felt a weight lift and a smile rise instantly on my face. "How y'all doin?" I said and headed for some punch. I heard him say it several times to different guests—"Sonny's my discovery. He'll beat me soon enough. You'll hear his name some day at Wimbledon." That was a big fat lie but it sure quenched the fewer and fewer odd looks I got. To keep me busy he put me in charge of the music.

He had said Jeanne may be bringing a girlfriend from college. I spotted the girl right away. There were actually two of them, Bobbsey twins, who had to be from Jeanne's sorority cause they looked just like Jeanne. Both were dressed up in short black, elegant dresses cut nearly to the belly button and down the length of the back with very tight belts on their small waists. They wore glittering high heels that shot them both up as tall as me. Their hair looked nearly identical to each other's, too, blond bouffant that no guy better try to touch. The girls' poses shifted into lots of different curves when they talked to men, and they held their wine at exactly the same distance from their painted lips. At first I didn't have the heart to even say hi.

For myself, I was all spiffed up in a crimson tie and a plaid sports coat of browns and greens and blues. I wore the black penny loafers that Mother got me strictly for Sunday wear. I had waxed my flattop in front of the bathroom mirror at home, then left, telling Mother I wouldn't be home till late. I'd had a birthday not long ago; I was sixteen now, practically grown, and I could tell her I'd be out late and that was all there was to it. She still wouldn't let me use the car, though.

My eyes watered up from the cold wind riding over on the Baron, so I had to drive slow. I pushed the bike in the driveway bushes out of sight of the lights. Despite being spit-shined and in the right attitude, and even though I figured on meeting some educated people, liberals and maybe some black folks, I'd had a sinking feeling about the party, and it wasn't just me who should have seen the trouble coming. Doctor Joe should have too.

The only black person there was Deliah, who worked the crowd with trays of deviled eggs and Ritz crackers topped with liverworts or caviar. There were four people who played in the Salvation Army band who were going to play "Auld Lang Sine" at the bewitching hour. Some local doctors came, Drs. Witt, Kemp and Collinsworth. Dr. Collinsworth used to be our doctor but not anymore. I thought it was over some money owed his office. I sure was glad our present family doctor, Dr. Johnston, wasn't there.

All the wives were fit to kill in evening gowns and lots of flashy jewelry. I wondered if my mother had ever dressed up like these ladies when she was the rich wife of a restaurant owner. I couldn't imagine it. Dr. Kemp was my friend Donnie's father, who was also the rabbi at Temple Beth El. Donnie said he never saw his father, that he might as well be dead like mine. Maybe that was why Donnie was always badmouthing his dad and doing things unacceptable in his religion. I thought I might get up the courage to have a talk with Dr./Rabbi Frank Kemp about why the only son he had hated his guts. I would really have liked to know, but I probably wouldn't try. Definitely wouldn't.

It was too cold to stand around in the Buddha garden so the dining room and den became the gathering spots. In the dining room was where the bowls of purple passion had been set up along with open bottles of champagne, and the connecting den was where Doctor Joe kept his big Fisher speakers next to the French doors and where I kept busy selecting LPs. I ended up stacking the first batch of records in this order: Sinatra, Josh White, Chuck Berry, a Jackie Gleason string romance for slow dancing followed by Elvis' "Heartbreak Hotel." They probably wouldn't want to hear Josh White, especially the doctors' wives, but I put it in the lineup anyway, just because I wanted people to hear some social protest music from a black folk singer. I later threw in a Bing Crosby Christmas album in the spirit of the season. Gleason followed Berry so everybody dancing could catch their breath.

I followed my instinct of normal human psychology to figure out the musical arrangement, only it didn't take long to see it wasn't working out. Not only did most of the guests not dance to Chuck Berry, they didn't dance at all. So they had no reason to catch their breaths. It didn't take long before someone began to interfere with my arrangement by cutting short both Chuck Berry and Elvis after only one song and instead put on *Dave Brubeck Plays London* and another smooth jazz album I didn't know. Someone pulled the plug on Josh White, too, before "Jelly, Jelly" had gone through the first verse, although that didn't surprise me. But I still got irked that my choices weren't appreciated, and I didn't select any more music the rest of the night.

I drank a purple passion and watched Jeanne and Doctor Joe cut a rug to one of Brubeck's pieces. She was great; she could really dance and Doctor Joe had more grace in his movements than you'd expect of a football player. When I finally said something to them, Jeanne's two girlfriends let me get them a drink, but that was it. They weren't interested in any of my questions about Auburn and college life. Their interest was strictly in the bachelor doctors there, including Doctor Joe, showing me how cutthroat girlfriends could be. The other girl told me her name but I forgot it right away..

Doctor Joe's office assistant, Gloria, had come and I got to dance with her once. But she was just patronizing me. I liked Gloria a lot; she was sweet and seemed to like me at the office. But I could tell here, at a party full of rich adults, she didn't really want to dance with a freckled-face high schooler in a stupid-looking plaid jacket. It'd be like dancing with Howdy Doody.

I ended up just wandering around and listening in on conversations. A short guy in a double-breasted suit with pinstripes and a starched white shirt who was presently talking to Doctor Joe got my interest. He wore an ugly iridescent green tie that could have blinded you. He stood ramrod straight and was still two feet shorter than Doctor Joe. He reminded me of Edward G. Robinson playing a big-shot gangster whose sour look said he'd just as soon push a grapefruit in your face as to look at you. I wanted to laugh at him, so buttoned down and rigid. The man's jowls kept tightening from so much intensity.

I eased closer. "…and I'm convinced it'll happen as soon as this spring. It's not the NAACP this time, it's a group called CORE, you might have heard of it, Congress of Racial Equality. Anyway, this group's come out of the woodwork to join in the fun and they're going for some big carnival. We're not sure what it is they're up to, but I'll tell you this, Joseph, all hell's going to break loose. The diehard Confederates are going to scurry out of the woodwork. People could die. The consensus at the AG's is the organizers won't be coming to Montgomery again; they don't need to after that damn boycott and Supreme Court decision."

He nudged closer to Doctor Joe, who seemed to be looking down his nose at the short guy, in amusement more than in earnest. "Joseph, this CORE group might have their party in your town. Matter of fact, I'm convinced of it because there's such a—uh, no offense to Woodstock—but such a strong Klan brotherhood here."

That thing about the local Klan seemed to get Doctor Joe's attention. He nodded and shook his head 'you-don't-say'—like and looked into the short man's eyes. "Sounds interesting, Guy," he said. "Woodstock is your quintessential Southern community, and even without the local klavern being so active, on the whole, we aren't inclined to look positively on anyone supporting civil rights. I suspect you're right, though, our ole boys will welcome the activists with open arms—"

He was being facetious as hell. It was written all over him, but the short guy didn't seem to get that.

"They'll also be waiting with clubs and torches," Doctor Joe added. "Maybe even some rope ... Got any notion what this plan could be? Some kind of street demonstration or rally, maybe?"

Edward G. shrugged. "We haven't yet determined. I don't think it's going to be anything as trivial as trying to enroll some nigra kid in the white school or buy some hamburger meat at the Piggly Wiggly. I think their plan is to make some headlines, just like that damn bus boycott did in Montgomery."

"This your new job, Guy, following on these organizations?"

The stiff man sighed but didn't relax. "The attorney general's still smarting from that calamitous ruling. It allows all of these outside nigra groups to come here and basically do whatever they want. The chief's got three assistants keeping an eye open for any infraction that'll give us reason to kick them out of the state when they come again. It won't happen, but don't tell Sparks that. He and the governor, as you know, are bonded like Siamese on this thing. So, yes, I'm doing some leg work in that respect."

"Waste of taxpayers' money," Doctor Joe said evenly. "This movement's a hurricane that won't be stopped by our antiquated state laws. Better for Governor Kimbrough and your boss to lock down the statehouse hatches and ride it out, just keep out of sight. But I'm preaching at the wrong person, eh, Guy? Still, in all fairness I know you're caught between a rock and a hard place with a governor that's making a mockery of constitutional law and you on the other hand, representing the law itself, being forced to defend these Jim Crow policies—which Kimbrough promotes, of course. I would venture that he's so caught up in his defiance that he can't see that's why Alabama's standing front and center, a veritable bull's eye in the revolution's crosshairs. It's got to be tough on you people down there at the statehouse."

The wires that kept the short man erect tightened a half notch. The only change in his expression was a blink of the eyes. "I'm glad you appreciate my position, Joseph. You're smart to understand," he said. "But if you think I'm about to buck the governor—well, let me put it like this. The attorney general wipes the governor's ass, but he's my boss. So what do I do? … Our office energizes his policies of separate but equal where it applies to state law and we prosecute in accordance. Vigorously."

"Like I said, it's got to be tough on you … Why don't you excuse me, Guy, I need—"

The short man touched Doctor Joe's arm to keep him from leaving. "Joseph, my friend, you got me sidetracked. I haven't got to what I've been wanting to talk to you about, something I know you'll be interested in. You would like to get involved in a worthy cause, wouldn't you, good citizen that you are?"

Doctor Joe turned back fully to the man. He looked interested. "Worthy cause. Hmm, let me guess, it's brother Bill. He's put some crazy ideas in your head. Right?"

"Can't deny I don't see your brother time to time. We talk and sometimes it's about you, your community interests. But, it's not just your brother horsing around. I know you're civic-minded. Weren't you instrumental in convincing a resistant planning commission over here to okay a low-cost health clinic a couple years back? I hear you're in there arguing with the city commissioners sometimes over subjects that can be controversial. Or you might just say my little crystal ball tells me you'd be interested in this thing."

"Only if they're controversial, Guy. Otherwise, all that political-government stuff is boring … I'll bite anyway. What is it?"

"Ha, you'll bite. That's funny, coming from the dentist."

I almost barked too. Not at Doctor Joe's little pun, if it was a joke, which I didn't think it was, but at the man's retarded response. He was a lawyer; maybe lawyers were like that, socially and maybe even a little mentally retarded.

I moved around a little so they wouldn't think I was listening, but I didn't get far out of hearing range.

He leaned toward Doctor Joe again because the noise from people talking was getting louder. So did I. He still stood with a rod down his spine. He said, "A civilian position is being opened here in Woodstock by the federal Civil Service Commission for someone to look into the affairs of government workers. The position would look good on a resume if you ever decided you want to enter public service. What do you think, Joseph, care to bite?"

Doctor Joe rubbed his chin thoughtfully. "'Affairs of government workers.' Sounds a little vague, Guy. What do you suppose that means?"

"Complaints on working conditions, pay discrepancies, charges of discrimination. There are a lot of people employed by the U.S. government in and around Woodstock with all the military contracts, etcetera, and you'll be making recommendations back to Washington. I know you're the person for the position. And you'll get to rub elbows with some ranking brass and bigwigs. I know the judge who's structuring and, I hope you'll forgive me, Joseph, but I've already taken the liberty to recommend you to him."

Doctor Joe grinned. "The pay good?"

He was kidding again, but uptight Edward G. said, "Not much, a few bucks. That's not the reward."

Doctor Joe politely smiled and sipped on a drink. He didn't say yes or no but the short man didn't seem to let that bother him. He went right on into another subject, something that just about floored me.

"Joseph, do you recall a lynching out by the army depot here, oh, well over a year ago now?"

Doctor Joe nodded. He'd looked like he was done talking to the man but it got his attention once again. "What about it?"

"Just curious what the word was locally."

"I'm not the person to ask but so far as I know, it's unsolved. Whitewashed, forgotten."

"Well, we were just wondering if maybe it hadn't been done to draw a little attention over here. They're saying the Klan wasn't involved. Some folks at the capitol are cynical. They think maybe one of these fringe agitator organizations might've initiated it, or at least did nothing to stop it when they knew it was about to happen—that's just the rumor. But like you say, it went for naught. But if it was one of these nigra groups, it showed them that lynchings don't mean a whole lot around here. And that's the reason they might just bring their troublemaking to Woodstock."

I couldn't believe what he was saying. I *knew* the Klan did that lynching, I saw them and I could identify them. It was a boldface lie.

"If I'm understanding you, Guy, you're telling me the AG thinks that lynching might have been the work of CORE or some other civil rights groups? Damn, you people are hardcore, eh."

Guy's chest puffed up a little. He shook his head, which didn't seem to be a response; he'd been shaking his head the whole time he talked, like he didn't believe his own words or he had resigned himself to defeat no matter what he said.

"Anyway, Joseph, I couldn't tell you if we did get involved. But I can tell you it happened on federal land and might've warranted an FBI look, if anyone had cared to call them on it."

Doctor Joe frowned. "And the AG didn't?"

"Sparks detests everything federal, particularly federal courts and in particularly the FBI. Lynchings are a local matter. Doesn't matter that they swung him from a tree on federal property. The national forests is federal jurisdiction, but you go and lynch somebody out there it stays local. Feds don't want to get involved."

"Well, Guy, in the end it was just another Ash Town lynching." Doctor Joe sounded as sorrowful as he did sarcastic.

"There's still that possibility it was a seed. I'm just saying … Stay tuned."

The man had been holding an empty tumbler all this time and now sat it on the glossy dining room table, off the tablecloth. It would stain the wood so I slipped a coaster underneath so quick nobody ever saw me do it. They didn't seem to notice I was there anyway; just a punk kid. But I didn't care cause I'd learned something. It sounded to me like Doctor Joe knew about the man that got lynched.

The short man took a step back. He said, "Damn, I need a drink."

He sounded almost human just then.

Deliah was right there to give him a glass of champagne, him and everyone else around her.

I guess it was Doctor Joe's tradition on New Year's to make a toast before the new year arrived because that's what he did. He made his way next to Deliah, in the middle of the mass, and gave her a big tight hug. Then he tapped on a narrow-stemmed crystal glass with his fingernail. He thanked Deliah for her service tonight and wished her a fine new year.

Then he said, "All y'all listen up a moment. I want to toast the new year, 1960, which I suspect is destined to open a decade of enormous change and enlightenment." He waved his glass around. "Let me toast to the lot of us surviving it. And on that note, here's to the survival of Woodstock itself, seeing in my crystal ball a bitter storm on its horizon.

"And please indulge me with just one last thing; to my new appointment on the federal Civil Service Board. It should be interesting. I'll try to raise some eyebrows."

There was a kind of hesitant laughter from his guests. But then someone said, "Hear, hear," which was followed by others, and then the tall stems started lifting all around. Except for me. I was too young to get included in on a formal toast. Ridiculous. The college girls were probably too young too, but that didn't stop them from gulping it down.

While people made more cornball toasts, I went into the kitchen and teased Pearl for a while. I asked Deliah what her family was having for their New Year's dinner. "Oh, yes-suh, Mr. Sonny, we always have the same, black-eyed peas and good ole greens, you know." I even talked to the Salvation Army musicians, who weren't as full of religion as I thought they would be. Really they were kind of fun, in a dry-humored way. They tuned up their instruments and teased each other that he'd better clean that horn or get one that's in tune. Their big moment was minutes away now.

Doctor Joe was back at it with the short stiff man he called "Guy," when I asked if he wanted me to tend the record player anymore. I was sulking by then.

He looked at me strangely, as though he could see I was upset and was surprised by it.

"Well, sure, Sonny," he said. "Could you put on Ella?"

He turned to his pigmy friend. "Guy, let me introduce Sonny Poe, future tennis pro."

"Oh yeah?" the man said and gripped my hand like a vise, like you would imagine Edward G. Robinson as the mad little gangster would do. I started to give it back to him but changed my mind because I didn't want to do anything to embarrass Doctor Joe.

"Guy Richards, Sonny," Doctor Joe said. "Guy's on the state Attorney General's staff, big shot lawyer in Montgomery."

"Wow," I said, and it dawned on me that I meant it because I had never met anybody that high up. "Do you work with Doctor Peach's brother down there?"

"Bill's also on the staff, fraud division," the short man said. "Too busy to come see his brother, so he sent me."

Guy Richards barked like I'd heard him do before. It sounded like a kid forcing a laugh, or a rat-a-tat cough, like he really was retarded. I knew the laugh was for Doctor Joe, not me. Guy Richards was shorter than me by half a foot, so it was nice looking down into his eyes, which I did, hard.

"So what's your line?" he asked me.

"Newspapers," I said, real cocky. "I'm in the distribution division and plan to climb. Looking to be managing editor."

I hadn't known till then that writing, or taking pictures, for a big-city newspaper was something I wanted to do. But he wasn't really interested in that bit of self-discovery. He showed his disinterest by stepping away without another word for me.

"Excuse me, Joe."

The dismissal hit me a little hard.

"I'll put the record on," I said. If I'd been Pearl my tail would have been clear through my legs. I had to get out of that room so I no longer had to hear folks congratulating Doctor Joe on his new appointment.

But I kept sneaking back to the punch bowl for purple passions, downing them one after the other. I found myself leaning against the double doors in the foyer watching people come and go. I got jealous of anybody who talked to Jeanne, especially the men who were putting their hands on her, those married professionals. She had put her creamy, ash-colored hair up in a bun, leaving only the soft down to touch her long neck, and changed from her black ballroom gown into a tight-fitting pink cashmere cardigan with a big feathery collar. She looked like she was back in high school. You wouldn't think she was old enough to be a doctor's fiancée, about to be "Dr. and Mrs." The thought suddenly made me feel hollow.

She easily handled the lechers with a cool slap on the hand and both she and the man going on like nothing had happened.

She finally caught me staring at her. She grinned and did a little thing with her eyes to alert me she was headed my way. I must have darkened.

"I've been waiting all night to dance with you," she said, as if speaking to her secret lover.

It was my good fortune that just then, instead of Ella Fitzgerald, Jackie Gleason came on with a thousand violins that swept through every corner of the place. I took Jeanne in my arms. I wasted a minute of quick circles before settling to a slow, toe-to-toe rhythm, knowing she was a good dancer and knowing I was just about drunk and so afraid I might sway that I leaned on her. She smelled so good. Like gardenias with something wild and grassy, the bark of a tree or forest sage. I pulled her close and her breasts went against me. I touched her face with mine. Her skin was warm and moist, as thought the night was summer sultry.

I could say nothing. If I uttered anything, I knew it would be wrong and I would hate myself. I didn't say a word the whole dance. Neither did Jeanne. But neither did she seem bored, nor patronizing.

The music was so melancholy I got misty. I wanted to tell Jeanne I loved her. I wanted real bad to kiss her. I knew you could see it in my face, my eyes. It wasn't all sexual, either. I was so relieved when the song was over that I had to sit down. I held on to the staircase railing and dropped onto the bottom step.

She thanked me. "You're a great dancer, Sonny. Maybe again later?"

I think I said yeah, okay, or maybe I just nodded. But I didn't want to dance again with her. Ever. She left to join some other people.

I don't know what got into me right then but I started crying. It was embarrassing, horrible, but I couldn't help it. I spotted the keys to Doctor Joe's T-Bird on the stand and the next thing I knew, I was speeding away from the big house on Broadmore, running from something new and disturbing, something I didn't even understand.

I got out on the highway going to Midland and opened the T-Bird up. I was going nearly a hundred when the lights and siren lit things up right around the stroke of midnight. This was my misguided, miserable introduction to the new year, the 1960s. There was never a thought in my mind to run for it. I pulled the T-Bird off the road too quickly and slid sideways in some mud from the afternoon rain; they thought I was under the influence.

When Doctor Joe got there he shook Mother's hand and put his arm around her to calm her down. They'd called Mother down about two in the morning, after they'd gotten me cleaned up and done all their interrogating. I was a mess. I had thrown up purple grot on the back floorboard of the patrol car and again in the tank.

Mother was ready to kill me. It surprised me that she could be so mad. It should have been Doctor Joe who wanted to kill me. It was his car I stole and might have wrecked. It wasn't Mother's party that I broke up with such cheap melodrama; she was by herself watching the ball fall on TV. And he was the one who had the explaining to do. It was him who would have been responsible if I'd hurt somebody or killed myself, a juvenile that he got drunk in his house. It was some luck for him at least that I had just gotten my driver's license.

But Doctor Joe walked into the cold, brightly lit room as composed and cordial as if he might be seeing a new patient. He said hello to the bunch of mad-looking detectives and uniforms standing around with their arms crossed, sympathizing with them, *Sorry you all have duty tonight.* He shook hands all around wearing that unmistakable warm and friendly row-of-pearls smile. He paid extra attention to my mother. "You've got a bright son, Mrs. Poe, usually much smarter than he's been tonight."

I should have been wrapped up in a white body sheet in the morgue, smashed to pieces in some roadside culvert. Like James Dean. But he played the incident down as though it was merely something you expected from a teenage boy. He was so cool the detectives didn't bother to question him about me. Nothing like, "What's a punk kid doing getting drunk at a party at your house? Who do you think's responsible for his actions? That's right, you are. How's it he's out in your car all alone doing upwards to a hundred miles an hour on such a dangerous night? You mind explaining all that, sir?"

It didn't go like that at all. Doctor Joe got respect rather than suspicion. Maybe just because he was likable and had run touchdowns for the University of Alabama, which he'd somehow mentioned, and that he was a doctor. If he'd been as surly as Mr. Edward G. Robinson, they probably would have thrown him in jail right then.

I looked around at all the people in that small, smelly interrogation room with their eyes on Doctor Joe, standing there as if expecting him to declare the meeting adjourned. In a flash of clear-headed soberness I saw him as a knight in the lair of the enemy, conquering them all without even a swing of the sword, and it occurred to me that the state attorney general had made a good choice in picking Doctor Joe for that new government position. If he could make it so a kid didn't go to jail for auto theft, DWI and reckless driving, he could surely do some good for workers treated unfairly. He could damn well start a revolution if he wanted, I thought. In that lucid moment I glimpsed Doctor Joe making some kind of miracle happen, something a lot more important than getting a small fry like me off the hook.

Chapter 15

It took a little time for me to get back on Doctor Joe's good side. He didn't send me away or anything. He didn't yell at me and wasn't nasty. He just stayed a little cool toward me for a while. For instance, he didn't offer me a beer for a whole month. But I washed and waxed the T-Bird and cut his grass and trimmed enough shrubbery that he finally decided to play some tennis with me again, even if it was freezing cold. You got warmed up on the court real fast playing against him.

Doctor Joe didn't tell me all the nuts and bolts of his new government job, just that he was going to start by looking into workers' complaints at the armory and the military depot. He said he expected most of the complaints would be from Negro workers.

"I won't be getting much support from the local power players or my so-called friends in Montgomery when those complaints turn out to be legitimate and I set about making some changes."

"Aren't you worried there'll be trouble?" I said. "I mean, soon as some folks around here hear you're trying to help out blacks, ... Well, you know what I mean."

"Yes, Sonny, my friend, I know. Don't worry. You don't have to be a mother hen. I know I'm going to rile some people, notably every man on the city commission, who's otherwise a member of the white citizens' council, to the mayor and police chief. But it's what I'm going to do anyhow. That's the contrarian in me."

"Well, you can count on me, if I can do anything to help out. Cause I feel the way you do."

I didn't know a whole lot about civil rights and Negro abuse, but I was pretty sure that I supported integration and all that other stuff. I knew I didn't like the way black people got treated and I especially hated the KKK and everybody who thought like them. Which I knew, like Doctor Joe knew, was just about every redneck soul in Woodstock.

There were a lot of government workers here, at the army arsenal and the depot where munitions and armaments of all kinds like mustard gas and heavy shells from WWI and WWII and Korea were stored in acres of bunkers. That took a bunch of people to watch over and protect. There were jobs in the federal courts, the Social Security Administration, the post office and its branches, and swarms of federal contract employees at Ft. Clayton, a military training base near town where underage kids like me got our watered-down beer on Friday nights, or used to before I met Doctor Joe. Federal employees could have numbered in the thousands. Turns out there weren't that many blacks employed though, and Doctor Joe said the first thing he would request out of Washington was for a more "equitable percentage" of Negroes hired, which he said would probably only come through an act of Congress. But he would pester them about it. Everything in Clayton County connected to federal jobs was now under Doctor Joe's jurisdiction, like he was the new sheriff, come to town to square things in the name of racial justice.

One chilly and overcast Wednesday, Doctor Joe invited me to play at the country club. They had rubico courts there. What a treat. You could slide into a shot, yet still get a better footing, and make the ball spin so much easier than on the asphalt courts at Wells Park. That would have helped my game a lot if I knew how to hit with topspin. Doctor Joe did, and it was frustrating trying to return the bullets he blasted in my court.

I didn't play very well but he said, "You're a go-getter out there, and a good sport. Here, this'll slow your heart rate." He gave me a cold vodka screwdriver he'd earlier made up in a tennis ball can and kept in a cooler. We sipped our drinks from Dixie cups so people would think it was lemonade or water. We sat near the courts by the shallow end of the drained swimming pool. The patio was deserted so we talked in our regular voices. A couple of good swingers were going at it on Court One and I halfway watched. I guzzled the drink and shook my little cup so he'd see, and he poured me another.

The thing that was on my mind had been on my mind since the New Year's party but I couldn't decide if I wanted to bring the subject up or not. From what he said to Guy Richards—his runt lawyer friend from the Attorney General's Office—I figured Doctor Joe knew who the lynched Negro was. But if I asked him and he told me, it would give the victim a name and that would make the dead man human, sort of like bringing him back to life so he could die again in my mind. I wanted to know about the man and at the same time I didn't cause if I knew who he was I would start wondering things like how hard his loved ones must have taken it. I wondered even if he had a family, a wife and children. Maybe he himself was just a boy, no older than me. Why did they hang him? What had been so offensive that they had to smash his skull with clubs?

And then, I figured, Doctor Joe would ask me, "How come you're so curious about the man? He was just another lynched black man who hadn't warranted so much as a funeral notice." Or something along that line. Then I'd have to decide if I should tell him I saw them do it, I saw the faces of the men who killed him. I knew two of them by name. Would he take me to the police and demand I tell them? What would the Klan do to me and my brothers when they found out? Cause you knew half the police department under Bulldog Bradley were either Klansmen or their brothers or fathers were.

I had to consider my oath to Herman too. I thought he had so far lived up to his end of the bargain and told no one. Shouldn't I?

Three or four nights now I'd woken up while the dew was still high, wondering if I should tell Doctor Joe that I'd seen the killing, if I could take knowing who the murdered man was.

I couldn't decide. So I said nothing.

"Listen, Sonny," Doctor Joe said on the club patio. "What I'm telling you about my intentions on this board is in confidence. You know that, right? You know you can't go saying anything about it, don't you?"

I nodded.

"Because I don't think what I'm going to concentrate on is in the interest of the people who got me the job. I'm not certain why they wanted me in the first place; they know my sympathies aren't with segregation. At least I didn't give anyone that impression and certainly my brother Bill knows it. Normally, we're a conservative bunch, medical professionals, but I sure blow that image all to hell. It's going to create some problems for me, I suppose, and that means I'm going to have to watch what I do. You need to know that."

"Sure. I figured that." It seemed such a naïve ambition, expecting to change people's attitude. They wanted things to stay the way they were, forever. You didn't have to look any further than the state's Confederate flag; to see how stubborn and defiant Alabamians were. The attitude ran deep, back to the good old days before the Civil War. It was all the Negro's fault; any good redneck Southerner would tell you that.

Imagining Doctor Joe trying to find a way for Negroes to get a fair shake in Woodstock fed my mind with images of two mythical characters, Ahab and David, because both those guys were going up against such mighty foes with the odds so stacked against them their tasks seemed impossible. All they had was fearless determination and blind faith, and maybe not even fearlessness. They were probably both scared shitless against that walleyed fish and creepy giant. But they were conquerors and so could be Doctor Joe, the new high sheriff standing tall against an honored culture of bigotry.

I should have been worried sick for him because, if anybody found out what he was up to, he'd get crucified. Who knew what they would do. They might just treat him like they would any troublesome black and lynch him. Or just ambush him in the dark and shoot him dead. Leave a knife in his head with a note warning any other traitors to watch out.

We finished off the screwdrivers watching those two guys hit the ball back and forth. It must have gotten Doctor Joe itching cause he patted me on the shoulder and said, "C'mon, let's get in another game. It's going to be dark soon."

Not without some worry, I thought, *Yeah, it's gonna get dark for him soon.*

They had a big to-do at City Hall when Doctor Joe was officially sworn in, even when you could see in their faces how city officials there resented the hell out of the Civil Service Commission for sticking its nose in their town's business. They were all smiles just the same. I guess that was politics, though, smile for the camera and say you care and the next thing you know there's a knife in your back.

His picture on the next day's front page got mangled and unrecognizable when I folded the papers. By the way, my fold never came apart after it landed, even the ones I had to throw over a hundred feet of lawn or gravel or sidewalk. And not to brag too much, but I was the fastest paper folder at the *Woodstock Star*, proved when I won the Newspaperboys Speed Folding Contest. Handily. I folded a hundred papers in two minutes and fifty-three seconds flat, better by nearly fifteen seconds than the next fastest paperboy. There was no prize other than bragging rights and getting nods from some of the other twenty or so paper throwers.

When the customers unfolded the paper they should be able to see the two-column picture of Doctor Joe with his right hand in the air, like he was getting sworn in as a congressman or something. The U.S. and Alabama flags waved in the background above him, the picture taken from below. He was standing on the outside steps of City Hall with a federal judge, a state attorney general who wasn't Guy Richards but was up here for something else, and the mayor and some city commissioners in the background, all of them looking smug. Next to him was the other appointee, a grammar school teacher named Benson Roy, a name that should have been turned around because you couldn't remember whether to call him Mr. Roy or Mr. Benson. Mr. Benson sounded righter. But I was used to his name since Mr. Roy was our substitute teacher in sixth grade. In the picture, Doctor Joe's long hair was blown out of whack and the harsh mid-day shadows on his face made him look older and harder. But he wore that big smile which forgave everything wrong in the picture.

The federal government paid the city to rent an office for the job. He didn't get the room next to the mayor's third-floor suite or even thrown in with any of the nine city commissioners' smaller doubled-up offices. The city managed to find Doctor Joe and his staff of one, Mr. Roy, a windowless room in the basement of the city services' building located several blocks from City Hall. They stored lawn mowers and sewer suits there among other things that smelled. Doctor Joe said going into the place was like opening an old mayonnaise jar.

He said I shouldn't go there.

"How come?"

"Think about it," he said, as if put out by my asking.

Not that I was interested in smelling stale mayonnaise. But I knew there were going to be mysteries worked out in that dark basement and I wanted to be in on it.

We had been playing tennis practically every Wednesday, just us two since Jeanne was at school during the week and most weekends so far this semester. It had been three weeks since his appointment to Civil Service. Winter was on us, with most of the trees naked as molted birds; everything looking dead, like the scenery in this black-and-white French movie Doctor Joe took me to Birmingham to see, in which a knockout finishing-school teacher masturbated herself lying on a bed. It was an eye-opener for me, just incredible. I'd never even heard of a woman doing it to herself.

The wind picked up and whistled through the bare trees. Both of us had dressed in sweat pants and pullovers to play. I sometimes wore a hat with earflaps because my ears would freeze on the Baron. In the winter we could get in only one set before dark. The lights on the public courts weren't very bright but other people still waited and would sure let you know when your hour was up. An hour was enough for me anyway. Doctor Joe ran me hard from side to side on those great corner shots that I could get to but couldn't get much on, so that I returned a lot of lobs. I was getting good at lobs, especially on my weaker backhand shots. But lobs aggravated him, not because he couldn't return them but because he didn't want me getting into the habit of relying on them.

"Lobs are desperate shots," he said when I sailed a beauty over his head that dropped into a corner, which was so good he didn't even try to return it.

"They let me regroup," I countered, pleased with the shot.

"I could've smashed that one. Next time I will."

He was good on his word when he smashed my next lob, which was also well placed to his backhand, and I sort of got the point he was trying to make. He'd been letting me get away with lobbing the ball because I was still learning the game, not perfecting it. I guess he smashed it also because he thought I was getting better and was ready for tougher returns.

We threw our rackets in the trunk of the T-Bird just before dark. Doctor Joe said, sounding excited, "Got time for a drive? There's something I want to show you."

I had time, sure. I only had a short paper for English left to do, a piece of cake. We drove west across Mason Street in the direction of Ash Town. The hardtop was on the T-Bird for the winter, and it was nice and toasty inside. I punched radio buttons till I got the song I wanted, the Everly Brothers knocking out "Bird Dog." I turned it up. "Where we going? This got something to do with the Commission work?"

He turned down the volume. "Sort of. See this street light?"

We were across the tracks on West 4th Street at Richards St., waiting now for the light to change. I didn't need to answer since the light was right there in front of us.

"You ever come out this way for anything, Sonny?"

I could answer that one cause this was the way Herman and I'd come on Halloween for the moonshine. "Maybe once in a blue moon, why?"

"Can you tell the light's red?"

"Sort of."

"I'm not trying to trick you, I know you're colorblind to red and green. The top light is red, like it's supposed to be. Right? That's why we're not going."

"So?"

The streetlights all over Woodstock were dim and it was hard to tell the colors, especially in the daytime. And doubly hard if you were colorblind.

"Last week I was out this way and—"

"How come *you* were driving out here? You're working on something, aren't you? Tell me what it is."

He grinned. He was too excited not to talk about it. "If I tell you, you'll keep it to yourself, right?"

"Yeah, sure I will."

"Last week, red was the bottom color, opposite of now ... Care to guess why it was changed?"

I didn't have a clue. "No, why."

"Who drives this street, mostly?"

"People live in Ash Town, I guess."

"That's right."

And he told me what he was up to. It was his first real probe. Even if it didn't have anything at all to do with government jobs. He said somebody, some rogue cops probably, were changing the signals. "I got an anonymous call suggesting I take a look at this particular light. Many people don't really know what this civil service things is or does, so they call about all kinds of things. I've had folks with good intentions call me about criminal activities, domestic problems. One poor woman said her husband was having a heart attack. I told her to call the operator, then start pushing on his chest.

"But this caller sounded knowledgeable so I took an interest. He said there'd been a lot of police stops at the intersection, twenty or more, but no tickets issued. He said the victims were coerced into making some deal to avoid getting the ticket."

"No kidding? What kind of deal?"

"But first, want to guess who most of those victims are—not most, exclusively?"

"The folks in Ash Town?"

"Very good. Most likely men. By and large, men are statistically more submissive than women dealing with law enforcement. This caller didn't know what these folks were being coerced into, but it's obviously illegal. I'm going to look into it. First, I'm going to find out who's behind the scam, if it's just one dirty beat cop or if it's broader. And find out what these people are getting suckered into doing."

"I'll bet you Chief Bradley's in on it. He's gotta be crooked. And besides that, he lives on my route and his meanass bulldog's always trying to tear my leg off."

His laughter was contagious. I started laughing too, seeing my comment deserved to be laughed at. He said, "Yeah, well a dog does not a criminal make. But I'll take that under advisement."

He wiped off the grin. "It's prejudicial," he said. He'd said that before but now I understood what he meant; whoever was doing it singled out blacks that wouldn't talk back or complain.

About most things Doctor Joe was easy going. I saw him get mad only at himself, say when he'd hit a tennis ball into the net, committing his own error, or when he struck a wrong key on the piano and especially when his rhythm would drift from a lapse of concentration. I didn't think he was a perfectionist. But he wanted things done right. This Civil Service Commission appointment didn't give him policing powers. It was supposed to be only adding up numbers and reporting discrepancies in the workplace, and federal authorities would decide what to do about it.

I told him I had come this way with Herman on Halloween to get some white lightning and that I'd been to my friend Harvey Nixon's house, but I didn't remember the traffic light. I wondered if I'd ever gone through the red light and they let me go because they could see I was white.

"What do you want me to do?" I asked. I was eager to do something. This was a lot more exciting than schoolwork or worrying if Susie was right about thinking she might be pregnant.

Chapter 16

The next day I was over at Herman's house putting away a sack of burgers and French fries we got at Bobby's Bar-b-Que. Bobby's happened to have the best French fries in town and it was two blocks from Herman's. The secret was soaking them in water overnight to draw out the starch. Herman's little sister Brandy, an eight grader now, was growing up fast and that was a lot of the reason I went over to his house lately, rather than him coming to mine. She was good at dancing, too. Could've been that the reason I decided to become blood brothers with Herman was so I could cozy up to Brandy, be nicer than her real brother who treated her like dirt.

The three of us were in the living room playing some of Brandy's 45s, all Elvis. She swooned over Elvis. So did I, I guess.

I watched Brandy dance to "A Big Hunk o' Love." When it finished I said to Herman, "I'm going to spy on somebody over by Ash Town and you're going to drive me over there and be my witness." I just blurted it out without much thought. But it sounded right.

Herman looked at me from the sunken couch like I had said I needed to pee, back in a minute, like I'd said nothing of interest. The phone box was next to his knee with the line stretched tight from the kitchen;

he was talking to a girlfriend while he ate a burger.

"You gotta drive," I said. "Borrow your old man's car tomorrow around five. Will he be home by then?"

"Can I go? Ple-ease?" Brandy said with a French fry hanging off her lip. She pirouetted and popped a hip on Elvis's punctuated vocal. "Teddy Bear" was on at the moment—"I just wanna be your Teh-eh-dee bear." She said lower, "Pretty please, can I?"

Herman lowered the phone, covering the mouthpiece. "Ninth grade you little turd, when you get in ninth grade you can do all kinds of shit, okay?" He was a little too cold, I thought.

"I wish we could take you," I said, "but we could run into a gang. The west side's too dangerous. Okay?"

Brandy's short black hair whipped her face in her dancing gyrations, her slim body contorting almost as good as Elvis with hips moving hula-like except when she would do a quick thrust. The really sexy part was when her hands slid down the arches of her sides and back up to almost touch her sprouting breasts. I had fleeting sacrilegious thoughts of robbing the cradle in my blood brother's home. The room was so cluttered there wasn't room for me to dance with her unless we did it stuck together. I'd always thought Herman was lucky having a little sister, even though she'd been a nuisance most of her life.

He could answer his little sis but not me.

"Or we can go tonight," I said. "Herman, get off the phone a minute. Can you get the wheels tonight?"

I could drive myself but Mother wouldn't let me have the car weeknights. She wouldn't let me have the car practically any night since that college boy messed up the inside of Herman's car, saying it could've been her interior he bled all over. I should have never told her about the incident. But Herman's old man didn't get pissed at us. He said the boy deserved it and shrugged it off. I didn't want to take the Baron to the west side and sit on it by the intersection. That would have just been asking for trouble.

When his old man got home from work he let Herman have the Olds without any conditions—don't be late, don't burn up all my gas, don't squeal the tires—none of the things Mother would have first made me promise.

Brandy did her geography homework, pouting like the pest she used to be, and taking it hard that her brother was such a prick. I would have let her ride in the middle, snuggled up between us.

We drove over there when it was turning dark. People were on their way home from work at 5:30. We parked by a large old brick building with just about all the wire-meshed windows broken out, even on the second floor. You could still read parts of the faded "McMillan Mining Co." sign above the windows. The company had closed down in the late 1940s when its contracts with the War Department dried up. The old building was on the other end of the long block from the BF Goodrich building. That was where the Klan had mobilized that night to set the great blaze in 1929 that gave Ash Town its name.

We had a good view of the intersection and could see some distance down all three intersecting streets. There was only one business that looked like it still functioned and it was catty-cornered to us, a garage with a sign overhead saying "Jackson's Auto and Tire." If the cops were around they could only be on the other side of that garage. At the time the street light colors worked in the right order. I could make out the colors when the light changed despite my color blindness because for a short moment all three lights came on and I could see the difference in them.

"See that metal box over yonder past that car shop, the one on the telephone pole?" I said. "I'll bet that's the switch box and one of 'em throws it from there and another cop makes the stop."

"Who does? Who does what?" he said. He was smoking a cigarette and thumping the ashes through the little window slot. I hadn't told him why we were here. I'd been debating whether to or not, remembering telling Doctor Joe I'd keep my trap shut. But I knew he wasn't going to just sit there without wondering something. I wanted him with me in case I got busted or somebody tried to jump me. Herman wasn't the greatest fighter, but had no fear; he'd fight anybody. I could whip him, no doubt, but I wasn't crazy enough to try it; I'd have to kill him to make him stop.

"I'm trying to see if the cops are catching people running the light,"

I told him.

He gave me a quizzical look. "Why? So what?"

"Do what?" I chirped, like I did with Stuart since Herman and I were now blood brothers and sort of like kin. He didn't understand but I didn't care.

"Huh? What makes you think they're doing that?"

"Don't be an idiot. They're crooked. They're soaking these poor colored people."

"They don't actually get the money, fool. You have to pay for your ticket at City Hall. That's where Daddy paid his … What's with you, you turning into a niggerlover?" he added. It caught me off guard.

"Fuck you."

I really didn't like that answer so I added, "We're going to Ash Town after this to see a friend of mine. I told you about him, he's a boxer. Matter of fact, you ought to take some lessons from him. He taught me and that's why I can beat your sorry ass any day of the week."

Herman reacted like I figured he would. His face got red. I thought he was going to try to sock me in the car. But he kept both his fisted hands on the wheel and just said, "Shut up, Sonny, shut your face."

A dark green Chevy passed us; it had passed us earlier going west, with most of the other traffic. I only noticed because we used to have a '54 Bel Air that looked like it. That was before Mother traded it in on a new '56 One-fifty because the automatic transmission in the Bel Air kept giving her trouble. The trans on that model gave lots of owners trouble; they even dubbed it the "slip-and-slide power-glide." She only bought Chevys and you couldn't talk her into anything else. I liked Ford and tried to get her to buy a used one when she went car shopping. It would have been cheaper, but I couldn't talk her into it. She had to have a Chevy and the One-fifty model was cheap enough that she could afford the payments.

The '54 Bel Air stopped two blocks away and parked facing us. There were some houses there and I figured they lived at one of the houses. I didn't think it was worth mentioning to Herman. It wouldn't have mattered anyway, the same thing would've happened.

Most of the traffic would have been coming from the army depot and the chemical plant where I'd heard folks from Ash worked.

I was starting to get bored.

"The perpetrators aren't out tonight. Let's go," I said. Maybe they'd rigged another light somewhere else. Maybe they'd quit while they were ahead.

"Perpetrators? Shit, man. You know what you're talking about?"

"Hell yeah I know what I'm talking about... They're not here, let's go," I said.

For once Herman didn't argue. He thumbed his cigarette butt out the little window and started the big 88 engine. He whirled the suicide knob several revolutions making his hasty bootleg-turn back east toward our part of town. "Turn around, I told you we're going to Ash Town."

"Don't tell me you want more of that raunchy crap got us into so much trouble before."

"Got you in trouble. I saved your stupid ass, remember?"

He let out a theatrical sigh but made the U.

There was an odor the further you got into Ash Town toward Leonard's Creek that wasn't exactly like a sewage smell, but that's what I figured it was. I had vaguely noticed when Herman and I came here for the shine.

It was suppertime at the Nixons' house. The sweet-potato bread hit me stepping onto the porch. You could smell it even with the windows closed; a lot sweeter odor than you got from the street. Harvey came to the door and barely opened the screen. He was frowning.

"Hey, Sonny boy, what y'all doin' clear out cheer? Did'n I done toll you ain't no good. Git on in here now."

"Thanks, I just got a question I gotta ask you is all." I felt terrible cause I'd told him I wouldn't come to his house again.

Harvey Nixon was all swells of smooth muscle from his neck on down to the belt. A thin coat of sweat turned his skin into shiny black leather, even in the cold winter, it seemed. His eyes and teeth were bright white and stood out under an inspired expression that he always wore like a badge of honor. Maybe all fighters had that look. There was a piece of collard or something at the corner of his mouth that I wondered why he didn't pull in with his tongue.

"Ax me what?" he said as he led us through the living room and past his kinfolk sitting at the dining room table. The table was way too big for the room and we had to walk around it to get to the back of the house. All five people stared as we passed by. A bare light bulb hung over the table. I looked but didn't see any plate with meat, just two big bowls of mashed-up white potatoes and a plate of iron skillet sweet-potato bread, one piece left, and some glasses that had had milk in them. I said hello and smiled like I always did to show Negroes that I was a friendly white, that they had nothing to worry about with me. I always felt uncomfortable when I smiled like that, like I was guilty of something, but I still did it. I didn't notice if Herman was smiling too. He was behind me and didn't say anything.

"How y'all? Sorry I caught you having your supper, Mrs. Nixon," I said to a heavyset woman who looked like she would be Harvey's mother. I hadn't really thought about interrupting somebody's dinner.

The sweet-looking thin woman with shiny hair was probably Harvey's wife. There were three youngsters maybe five to thirteen. The two girls looked at me without any expression at all. But the boy smiled. He knew me from the dentist's office; he knew I was one of the good ones. He anxiously showed me the braces that Doctor Joe had made; they had been in place around three months now and you could tell the difference already. The bumpkin-looking buckteeth were folded in almost enough that it looked like he could whistle without using his fingers. He seemed real proud to show his teeth, even when the silver bracing mostly covered them up. I winked at him but didn't say anything, afraid I might say the wrong thing.

"Now don you worry none 'bout it, Mister Sonny," the heavyset woman said. "Yeah, I knows who you is. It's okay." Her expression was warm enough that I could have sat down and had some collard greens and felt like I was at my grandma's table. "Would y'all like somethin', maybe some this here pie?"

I waved both hands and shook my head. Herman bumped into me cause I'd stopped.

Harvey said, "Okay, Momma, these boys got bid'nes. Let me git hold my jacket and we'll go on out back."

I looked again at the boy cause he kept smiling at me. In his lap was a pair of skates. I got curious why he'd be holding his skates at the table and asked, "Hey, those're nice looking skates. They new?"

He nodded. All of a sudden his whole face lit up. "Got 'em for my birthday. Today! Just listen them ball bearings," he said and spun the back wheels. I walked a little closer.

"Real nice. You're not gonna go too fast on 'em, are you? Till you get the right feel?"

"I already lernt. I'm real good."

"I bet you are. Happy birthday. And I can tell you are wearing those braces like you're suppose to cause your smile looks great. Good job."

He grinned big and went back to playing with the wheels of his new skates, and we followed Harvey to the back porch. The night was dark but I made out the silhouette of a small animal hanging by its legs from the edge of the tin roof. "What's that possum hanging there for?" I asked.

"Sunday supper," Harvey said. "Now, what was it y'all wanted?"

On the side of the yard stood the frame with his boxing bag, at the moment sagging lifelessly, wanting to get punched. The house light put a shine on its upper and lower sections where it hadn't seen much use. It felt good when your bare fists sank into it, the vibration stimulating your arm muscles up through the shoulders and spreading through your whole back.

"You dyin to hit on that thing, ain't you boy?" he said.

"Nah, that's all right. Herman's the one needs to pound on one, cause he's always getting into fights and losing."

Herman punched my arm. It wasn't a friendly punch.

"How come, boy?" Harvey said to Herman, looking him over. He was taller than Herman by a mile and had to look down his nose at him.

"People are assholes, I don't know," Herman said, squirming, trying to slough off the subject.

"Cause he's got all these girlfriends, is how come," I said. "He needs to learn how to fight so he can hang on to one of 'em for more than a week."

"Be mighty glad to pass on to you my secrets if'n it could evah be. But it can't and it ain't no good y'all comin out cheer to Ash. You know that, Sonny boy."

"Sorry, Harvey but I couldn't help it. This is real important.

"Tell me now, what it is you boys want," he said, trying not to show his impatience or fear of our being here.

I hadn't taken him seriously enough before. I couldn't look him in the eye cause I could see how right he was; I just hadn't appreciated it enough before now.

"I'm doing some investigating and I was wondering if you ever got stopped for running that light at 4th Street at Richards, maybe got a fine."

It was subtle but I noticed the flinch. Something had happened. He frowned. "Why? Who you investigatin fo, anyhow?"

"Cause we think they set up a trap to catch people, and it's illegal."

"'We'?"

Dogs barked all around the neighborhood but there wasn't one in Harvey's yard and I wondered why, with all those kids.

"I'm working secretly for the federal government on it and can't tell you anymore than that, Harvey. Did you? Get stopped at that 4th Street light?"

He stared hard at me, into my eyes. "You pullin my leg, boy? Cause this don sound too smart a thing you be doin."

"I swear I'm trying to help you out. It's something in your favor and you can help a lot if you tell me about it. What are you afraid of?"

"I ain't scared. I's mad." He stood there letting his eyes move around. I guess he was trying to figure out if I could be trusted.

Some bushes were in the yard but no trees. You didn't see trees in Ash, none that were tall anyway. They'd all been burned down in the '29 massacre and never had anymore planted.

He finally said, "Yeah, they's nasty cops done it."

My eyes grew a little bigger. "Okay. Now, think hard, Harvey, cause you gotta be sure about this. Did you run the light?"

"I just can't say for sure if I did or if I didn. I drive for a living and I's always watching the lights and everything else. Lose my job I get two tickets in a year, that's in the papers I signed. I didn't think I ran that light."

"You're right, you didn't. They rigged it, swapped the colors to trick you so they could give you a ticket or force you into doing something instead. It was in the afternoon, right? After work?"

"Yeah, bout foe-thirty. Boss let me go early some days. They is somethin' else they don 'stead of the ticket."

"What? What was it they did?"

He hesitated; he didn't want to talk about it, probably cause he was still so angry. And he could also get in some big trouble confiding in me, even when we had known each other for more than two years. But that didn't mean anything. It was a big chance he was taking.

I said, "Listen, Harvey. It would help if you could find some other folks out here this has happened to, too. They won't have any choice but to believe you if a bunch of you got screwed at that red light, and swear to it." I was getting carried away and should not have said any of that stuff, especially since I didn't know what I was talking about.

"You see som'in different when you come up to the house?" he said lifting an eyebrow.

"I noticed the house number is about all."

"Them awnings on two my windows, they's new. Them boys pretty much don give me no choice but to buy 'em. Them other people done talk me into buying for all the windows. Well, they ain't too many windows, thank the Lord, seven total out. But theys also want me to git one on the front door. So we is gitin a awning under the front porch. Hot damn!"

"Holy cow, man." Herman had stood by making sympathetic faces but this was the first time he said anything.

"Yeah. I be paying 'em on time, five dollars come first of ever month. Said they gibe me a special deal cause I got a good job wid the drug stoe. But, Sonny boy, they ain't nutin special 'bout paying foe hundert dollars for somethin we don't even need."

"They give you a copy of the contract, something on paper?"

"No way. They weren't give me nutin like that. They keepin it, foe safe keepin, they says."

"You can remember who stopped you? Can you describe him?"

"Oh, yeah. They was two of 'em. But the one talked was a redhead, red freckles, big arms. I would've liked to box him with them big arms his, see what he got. I knows I got the reach on him."

"So, do you know anybody else got stopped there?"

"I ain't saying. Maybe."

"That's okay, I gotcha. But can you talk to them, ask if they'd like to get out of having to pay all that money? Maybe we can talk again later?"

"Yeah, maybe. How you gonna do that, Sonny boy, get me out of payin them boys?"

"The gov'ment can do it." But I wasn't at all sure of that and it pained me getting his hopes up.

I wanted to tell him who was going to clean up this stinking town starting with the rogue cops who'd put him and his neighbors in this bind. But I didn't dare mention Doctor Joe's name. That lie about working for the government was bad enough, especially with Herman there to hear me say it. Frankly, I sweated Herman talking more than anything else. Regardless that we were blood brothers who shared a terrible secret, I just didn't trust Herman when it came to black folks. What was to keep him from mouthing off something at school? Something like, *You know that Sonny Poe's a goddamn niggerlover, don't you?* True.

Chapter 17

At least Herman hadn't burned rubber leaving Harvey Nixon's house like he had after we got the shine at Jesse's. Maybe he felt as sorry for them as I did, that he could see the kind of crap they had to put up with being black, getting kicked around, having to live and living in Ash Town.

But Herman wasn't sympathetic when it came to me. "What the hell're you up to with this government crap? Just what's going on?" He gave me the eye, like he was the one who'd been scammed.

"Your old man goes to work this way, doesn't he?" I said, ignoring the question. "Maybe they got him, too. Then it won't be just these black folks, will it? Let's ask him."

"No, he ain't been. I'd know. Don't change the subject, Sonny. Give me an answer."

"Okay. I do have connections with the government, only it's in a roundabout way to the investigation going on. That's why I can't tell you anything about it."

"We're fucking blood brothers! You can tell me everything."

"You can tell me why Vicki Smiley dumped you."

"I dumped her, asshole."

Herman laughed gutturally. "Alright, never mind that, tell me about this business."

"You won't start blabbing to impress some hotpants?"

"Hell no, man." He raked a hand across his chest like it was meant to swear on his sacred Boy Scout's honor or something. The jerk. He wasn't ever a Boy Scout.

"My friend works for the government. He's got to clean up Woodstock so it can be ready for integration when it comes."

I regretted saying *integration* soon as it came out of my big mouth. I was so pissed at myself that I didn't much see the surprise on his face. I just heard his usual negative response.

"You are full of shit for sure. Nobody can do that!"

"You'll see. But you better keep your damn mouth shut, Herman. The cops get on to my friend, it could be real dangerous. For you too."

"Who's this friend? I'm your friend."

"We'll call him DJ. That's all I need to tell you, so don't ask me any more about it. Got it?"

He was looking mostly at me as he whipped through the short blocks of Ash Town. When the community had been rebuilt, it was on a grid that was not hard to get into or out of, it just took some time stopping at a stop sign at every corner. The odor off Leonard's Creek lashed out its stink but then died out.

On the books they still called the community Overton District. How it got its popular name, Ash Town, was a true horror story that started with a lynching that lead to the burning of everything standing. In 1927, the story went, a black youngster from Overton snatched a package of Spearmint gum from a white girl on the east side, where he should not have been. Maybe he didn't do it but him being on the east side was reason enough for the white citizens' council, in a secret meeting, to condemn the boy for rape and mayhem, and the Klan took him late one night to a nearby woods where they hanged the teenager and left a knife pinning a note in the corpse's head. That boy was only the first. Men and boys from the settlement began disappearing in the night. Their bodies were discovered suspended in trees in the same woods where the first boy had been lynched. It turned into a frenzy that over the next two years claimed twelve people from the ramshackle company-owned community. Then, on an August night in 1929, the Woodstock klavern of the Klan quit playing around with lynchings and gathered in the nearby BF Goodrich tire warehouse where they were handed torches and went about setting fire to everything in the district, including stores, garages, trees, cars, even the giant 200-year-old oak on the banks of Leonard's Creek. That tree provided shade for summer baptisms. The whole place was turned into an ash heap. All the workhorses and pigs that didn't die in the fire were rounded up and taken by Klansmen for their personal use.

A lot of the Negroes who survived moved away but most stayed and threw up lean-tos because they had no where else to go and they didn't want to give up their jobs at the nearby factory. Jobs were scarce in the Depression. Some of the mulatto kids from the rapes back then still lived in Ash Town today with families of their own, holding jobs where most of the other residents held jobs, over at Vulcon Industries and the Fort Clayton Army Depot. That meant a lot of Ash Town's current residents were employees of the federal government, some the very people that Doctor Joe said he would focus on.

Herman and I had just passed under the light at Fourth Street and Richards when a car pulled up beside us on Herman's side. It was so close at one point the side mirrors bumped.

"Pull it over," the man not driving said. He didn't speak too loudly because he didn't have to. Herman had his window down with his elbow sticking outside. His arm could have been hit or crushed, that's how close the car came to us. I guess Herman wanted to show them he wasn't chicken. The idiot.

It was the same dark green '54 Bel Air I'd seen earlier. It pulled on in front of us and cut us off, like out of a gangster movie, the setting a dim, glassy-wet city street. The street here wasn't glassy but it did have a matted oil trail running down the middle of both lanes.

Herman stopped the Olds.

The driver of the green Chevy got out and hefted up his trousers by the belt loops. His flannel shirt was rolled to the elbows, exposing pale muscular arms. It was about fifty degrees outside but he looked too tough to ever get cold. He walked with a swagger up to Herman's side and leaned into the window, not worried in the least about getting his face blown off from the double barrel 12-gauge I might've held in my lap. Herman's old man's '49 fastback after all was a reputed hoodlum favorite, especially with its wheel skirts and sitting low to the ground. I kept my left arm where it rested on the back of the bench seat, not wanting to move a muscle; it felt awkward, like I was scared. And I had plenty reason to be scared of him, Herman too, since I recognized the man.

"Where you boys been tonight?" His grin was full of threat, as if he already knew where we'd been and didn't like it one bit.

"How come?" Herman said in his disinterested tone. He wasn't surly.

A carpet of red hair covered the man's arms, a redhead. Harvey described the cop who pulled him over as a redhead with big arms. He was the cop, only out of uniform. I would have known he was a cop anyway, the way he immediately started bossing us around.

"We're just out ridin 'round, no reason," I said quickly, before Herman came out with something sarcastic, egging them on. "On our way home for supper."

"You boys been over to Ash? Up to no good in there?"

"Yeah," I said, "but we didn't score nothin. They was all sole out. Know where we can git some?" Talking hick meant I was too dumb to lie.

"Weren't you boys stopped out here earlier, right over on that corner there? And don't make no question out of it. I'll do the questioning."

"Yeah," I said, thinking real fast, "we was arguing over who bought it last 'fore we went in to buy it this time. It's his time, *I bought it last!*" I practically whined. Herman played along with a shrug.

Then I said, "Are you the po-lice?"

That ticked him off. "Get out of the car, both of you."

"How come?" Herman said, this time sounding damn surly. "We didn't do nothing. Who are you, anyways?"

The man reached in and grabbed a wad of Herman's shirt and pulled him up against the doorframe. "The man you don't want to ask that to … Who're you with, shit-for-brains? You ain't no gang member I ever saw."

"Hey, we ain't associated with no gang. Go to Woodstock High," I shouted.

"Then you must be Boy Scouts working on your merit badge. Now get the fuck out of the car!"

Herman suddenly slapped open the door, catching the man with the upper frame against his forehead. It hit him hard and by surprise and he fell out of view, a thump told us he was on the asphalt. Herman opened the car door and stepped out. He looked around for something. He was focused. I supposed he was looking for a rock to hit the man with.

I was out and around the car in a second. "Herman, look at me! Come on, let's get out of here." I grabbed his arm and pulled him back.

By now the other man was almost on us. He wasn't wearing a police uniform either and I didn't see a gun or a sap in his hand. He was a lot bigger than the man on the asphalt, moving slow like a wrestler. He ignored us and crouched beside the redhead, never even looking at us, it seemed to me.

Herman flew back in behind the wheel and waited till I got in, then he burned rubber backing up and around the other car. I was glad he didn't try to run over the two men. We blew by them. I watched in the outside mirror the man on his knees holding and wiggling the redhead's head. It looked like the redhead was dead.

"Holy fuck, man. We're in one shitload of trouble now, thanks to you," I shouted. The shouting helped me cool off. "You think they got the tag number?"

"They didn't get it. But they'll remember the car, guaranteed. All they gotta do is ride around in the right area till they spot it parked. And they got me."

"Why in hell did you hit him, anyway? Shit. You could've just backed out and outrun him."

"He was an asshole."

"Yeah, you're not wrong there."

And that was it. That was the way Herman functioned, picking the most simplistic way of satisfying his needs or handling a situation. But back there he might have been right, and I had to admit I did get a rush seeing the asshole go down like that. Who's to say what might have happened if we had complied and got out of the car. What were they going to do, how far were they willing to go, not even knowing what we were up to? I would've liked to play that out, just to see. But not Herman. He just responded by instinct, which was primal and virile as a baboon.

Still, part of me was glad he did it.

"You know who he was?" I asked in a voice barely audible over the engine roar.

"Fuck yeah, the crooked redheaded cop that stuck your nigger friend with the awnings. That's who."

"That's true, but that's not all. Think about it. You ever see him before tonight?"

Herman glanced at me. His dull eyes suddenly came alive. "Wait a minute. Oh, man."

"Yeah, but he doesn't know. They never got a look at us that night, remember?"

"Oh, fuck."

He drove a couple of blocks east then turned south and drove halfway to Midland before doubling back, taking different streets. All that time I watched the expressions change on his face, going from very pissed to very frightened to somewhere in between and even level-looking, which was an expression I didn't see much from Herman.

"Where the hell are you going now?" I said when he headed back in the direction of Ash Town.

"Fooling 'em," he said, grinning wildly.

Moments later he pulled over behind the store where we'd been parked about an hour earlier. The Chevy was gone, nobody around. The intersection was quiet as midnight. The traffic light flashed its colors in correct order, red to amber to green, top to bottom. I looked hard but didn't see any blood where Herman had dropped the redhead.

"I guess you fooled 'em." But I wasn't so much of a hick to think that for a second.

Chapter 18

I would've bet most of the policemen in town didn't know anything about the new Civil Service position, that its appointed commissioner—Doctor Joseph Peach—was going to nail at least a couple of them for crimes against the people. They were about to have a rude encounter with real justice, I thought in my fantasy. If it did happen, I just hoped it came before those two caught up to Herman and me, and I was praying the redhead would be too embarrassed by a couple of kids getting the best of him to tell his Klan buddies.

But I decided to wait until Harvey Nixon talked to the other traffic-light victims and got back to me before I told Doctor Joe my good news. That way he might go softer on me for breaking my promise not to tell anyone what he was up to. How beautiful it would be if I could give him a list of people who'd been scammed by those cops.

It took the whole weekend before it sank into my head that that wasn't going to happen. There was no way the Ash Town residents would stand up to the crooked police; the law was not on Harvey Nixon's side. I also realized that keeping Doctor Joe in the dark was just plain wrong. It was putting him more in danger.

I waited until Sunday night and then I called to tell him what I'd found out. I got as far as saying, "I went to my friend Harvey's house last night and, man, you won't believe—"

His big voice butted in. "We'll talk later." And the phone line went dead.

It was as abrupt as he had ever been with me. But he knew our phone was on a party line, and I thought back to the times we'd talked recently by phone. It was me who'd called him and he'd made the conversations quick and pointed and officious. Was I retarded or what?

I was anxious all during school on Monday, and it was one of those days where you learned nothing, which made the day even longer. Two of my classes were babysat by sub "teachers" who didn't know diddly about history or biology. To show you what they knew, in biology we watched half of *Blackboard Jungle*, which the teach said was "social commentary on the state of modern juvenile delinquency." That had absolutely nothing to do with biology. Then, we had study hall in history where it would have been appropriate, in my view, if the subs had coordinated in advance so we students could see all of the damn movie.

The boredom left me thinking about the evil phantom I'd thought about again last night. Lying in bed, I'd see a man's shadow on the wall. The figure hovering, pointing a gun at me. I imagined him as the cop and his plan was to ambush me in an alley on my paper route. I could see him string up a wire across the drive, real tight, so when I rode by it would take off my head. Or he would jump me with an ax from the roof of a garage. I knew the very alley where the dreams took place, too, the alley close to Bulldog Bradley's house where some apartments stood on top of the garages, blinding your view of beyond. The cop lying in wait was the worst dream and when I rode the Baron, I was constantly looking over my shoulder, imaging him swinging the ax at the back of my head.

I had to shake the ghost or I was gonna go crazy.

I made it through the school day without the real cops busting in the classroom and cuffing me. After the 2:50 bell I ran out to the Baron and headed to the newspaper plant.

It was an ugly, gray, cold day where my breath stayed smoky the whole time I was outside. The magnolias along Broadmore were the only trees on my route with leaves. The big, magnificent trees still spouted white blossoms when everything else looked dead, even the evergreen pines dripping brown needles by the millions. Before I finished throwing papers, I cruised by Doctor Joe's house. I didn't figure he'd be there and he wasn't. The smokeless chimney and drawn curtains made the whole house look like it was shut down for the season. It was nearly four o'clock and if I picked things up I could get to the medical building by four-fifteen, before he left. I didn't want to go through another night with those phantoms chasing me. Maybe Doctor Joe would know what to do about the redhead cop.

I finished a little after four and headed toward his office. The T-Bird sat in the "Doctors Only" covered area of the parking lot. One other car stood under the tin, a shiny new Buick. I guess these doctors kept bankers' hours. It was quiet in the hallway, as if it were a Wednesday. I tapped on his private door. I heard a rustle and in a second he opened up with a phone at his ear on a long, stretched line and let me in, making a keep-quiet gesture with a finger pressed against his lips. He pointed for me to go into another room and I went into the lab. But I didn't take my ears away from his office and I could hear his voice. He asked into the phone, "How did you find out?"

His tone was flat and dead serious and he asked the question in a half voice, which was so low I barely could make it out. There was a delay and dead silence that felt like a cold wind blowing down the hallway into the lab, like the door to Alaska got left open. He said a couple of uh-huhs, like he was listening to a patient complain, and then, still flat and serious, said, "Well, officer, I certainly do thank you for telling me, for confiding in me. Thanks again. So long."

I dashed back into the lab and pretended to be interested in some skeletal molds of people's teeth lying on the work counter. I thought, *That's that damn redhead cop he's talking to.*

"Hey, Sonny," he suddenly said behind me. I almost dropped the lower jaw of somebody's mouth. "I'm glad you're here. Now is as good a time as—"

"I know, I know. That's why I'm here." I was ready to square with him.

"Well, come on in and let's take a look."

He pointed to a torture room.

"Huh?" I said.

"That troublesome bicuspid of yours, come on. I'm done for the day and it won't take a minute."

I went ahead in front of him and took a seat in the big chair. I was relieved that he didn't seem upset with me, but that was still there, waiting.

I hated the dentist chair; it was like the electric chair. It always seemed to be a cold, dark day when I had to see the dentist. Before Doctor Joe came along, I would walk in the deep concrete ditches all the way to the Tenth Story building downtown where Dr. McMahon worked on me with his broken drill; always on a Friday and always raining or stormy clouds looming. Half my teeth had silver fillings already. Well, nearly

I sat down and right away Doctor Joe touched something with the air gun that made me holler. It was a cavity all right and it was working into a nerve, he said. That's why it hurt eating chocolate and knocking back Cokes. He said we'd better repair it now, before it got any bigger, and had me mix up the amalgam. I'd helped out in the torture room once when his nurse was out sick. Nervously, I had followed his instructions with the air, water, suction and cotton pads. He said because I was left-handed I would make a good chair assistant.

He wanted to do the job without deadening my jaw since the cavity was still pretty small, just take a tiny bit of drilling. It took thirty minutes and hurt like hell, especially when he hit me with the water and air, which it seemed like he used about every three seconds, one or the other.

I kept watching his eyes as he worked, looking for a clue to what that phone call had been about. But I saw nothing that helped me. His big clear eyes were focused only on the work at hand, which was making me squirm and flinch and sweat with pain. It occurred to me he was punishing me for misbehaving.

I helped him clean up the room and put the instruments in the silver canister to sterilize overnight. After that he got around to it, "You have time to stick around for a bit? Want to talk."

"Okay, I guess so." He turned off the torture room lights and we went into his private office where it was quiet, almost dead silent.

While he made a drink, I blurted, "I gotta tell you something. It's about me going to Ash Town. It was a bad scene and I couldn't help it—"

"Alright, slow down …"

His shoulders were slumped. He looked upset. He poured himself a drink from a bottle of Chivas Regal and dropped in two ice cubes from a half-size ice tray, shut the small refrigerator door and leaned back on the couch and sucked down the drink. "Sorry, I'd better not offer you a drink tonight."

He made himself another, but only sipped this one. I slouched in the chair on the outside of his desk and swayed side-to-side with my legs stretched out and crossed at the ankles.

"Be still," he said, "I can't get a bead on you."

"You're not going to shoot me, are you?" I grinned but it didn't help. I sat up straight. "Joe, I'm sorry. I should've never taken that damn Herman along."

He flinched on the mention of Herman then fingered his hair and gave me a bemused rather than dirty look. "Okay, Sonny, tell me what you did and what happened. All of it."

I told him I went to check out the streetlight that he showed me at 4th Street, where the cops had set up their trap. I said I asked Herman along because I needed him to drive me there.

It gave me a little satisfaction saying, "Harvey Nixon did get stopped at the light, he told me so. But instead of paying a fine they forced him to buy awnings for his windows."

Then I got to the two cops who pulled us over wanting to know what we were up to. I told him one of them was the same cop that stopped Harvey Nixon at the light. "At least we know one of the crooks," I said. "He's a redhead."

When I told him Herman slammed the car door on the cop and knocked him out, Doctor Joe grimaced and hissed through his teeth. He sure didn't like hearing that.

The thing was, I didn't tell him everything. I didn't say I told Herman I was working undercover for the government. It was as good as lying to keep that from him, but I just couldn't come out with it.

He got up and paced two steps at a time in the narrow room. He said, "It wasn't the smartest thing to do, going out there like that. But it's done. Now we have to keep you from anything connected to me, to Civil Service ... Got any suggestions?" He looked at me hard-eyed.

"You bet. I already told the redhead cop we were out there to get some shine for Saturday night. When he wanted to know why we were parked at the corner earlier, I said that me and Herman were sitting in the car arguing whose turn it was to buy it."

Doctor Joe narrowed his eyes. "That may not have convinced him; he'd be suspicious. Anyway, whatever they do, it won't be official. They won't try to arrest you; they don't want anything connected to their scam on record. Let's just hope they bought your story. The cop will want to square things for getting knocked down by a couple of kids, and that's very troubling."

Then he asked me what I was afraid he would ask me. "How much does Herman know? What did you tell him?"

The last thing I wanted to do was keep lying to him, but that's what I did. A boldface lie. "Nothing more than what I'd talked to Harvey about."

Doctor Joe seemed to accept that. He trusted me. I felt awful.

He said, "You know who that was on the phone when you came in?"

"Uh-uh," I said weakly and braced myself.

He stood and poured more Scotch into his glass then went for another cube of ice.

I sat on the swivel chair and asked sheepishly, "Was it—was it the redhead cop?" My question sounded more like an admission of guilt.

Doctor Joe looked tired, like all he wanted to do was just shut his eyes and sleep. "No, it wasn't him. It was a police officer, though. The same person who alerted me to the streetlight shakedown."

"A cop did that? Wow." I could suddenly breathe again. "Who is he? I swear I won't tell Herman, or anybody else."

"I don't know his name. He won't identify himself, and it's better that way. I do know why he wants to help me out, though. It's a personal matter with him and he's concerned. He should be."

"How come? Why would a cop be telling you things like that? He's not in on it?"

"He may be the only one on the force who isn't on the take. He confided in me because he wants to see some justice brought to the people of Ash Town; it's why he's giving me this information. To make a long story short, he's in love with a woman from Ash Town."

"A black woman? Holy shit." I was so flabbergasted I didn't even realize how much of an idiot I sounded like.

"Yes, that's right, Sonny, she's a Negro and he's not. It may sound crazy to you, but stranger things happen. It gets even crazier; he says they want to marry."

"They're both crazy. Don't they know anything?"

I knew the sigh; it was impatience, something he didn't express often. "Look. I know you haven't seen much of the world, but believe me life and love aren't so narrowly focused everywhere."

He suddenly arched his head and grinned approvingly at me, like I'd just passed him with a swift backhand. "On second thought, you are perfectly right to say this guy is crazy, that both of them are. Because they don't live somewhere else, they live here."

"I guess," I said, but I was changing my mind and thinking those two people were just gutsy and brave enough not to be afraid and go after what they want.

Doctor Joe stretched over and patted my knee, like he was patronizing me, and said, "But love is a strange animal, kid. And so is its flip side, hate. Either one can overpower the rational mind and that can end up destroying people. My brother Carlton could attest to that."

I hated it when he called me "kid" but I forgot it cause he hadn't ever said anything about his other brother. Or his family for that matter. Except that I was supposed to be that brother's son and that brother was dead, along with his wife. Which might all just be made up.

The few things he had said about himself were so vague I couldn't even draw a picture. About all I knew was that Doctor Joe grew up on some kind of plantation over in Mississippi, and that was about it. I couldn't tell you what religion he was or what his father's occupation was. But they were rich. I was pretty sure of that much. Doctor Joe may have played football on scholarship but he went to four years of medical school and all that stuff afterwards that cost a lot and his little brother had gone to law school. I didn't even know if his parents were still alive.

He didn't make me ask, *What thing?* He said, "It wasn't Carlton's affair that disappointed me but the cowardly way he handled it."

"Carlton's your big brother, my 'uncle?'"

His nod was so easy I couldn't be sure it was a nod or a shake. "The difference between him and my friend on the police force," he said, "the officer isn't as impetuous as Carlton. Maybe that was age alone. Carlton was still a teenager. And his lover was younger than him. Illiterate, third generation out of bondage but still a field slave under my father's dominion. We called my father the Baron, or the Monster when his tyrannical behavior turned intolerable."

"Baron like the Red Baron? A baron's not bad, is he?"

"Like the czar, the oligarch, the barbaric khan."

"Oh."

"Anyway. His girlfriend's name was Sarah. Sarah was an April butterfly, just as lovely and just as innocent. She was milk chocolate. I though she was mulatto though nobody seemed to know. I spied on her in my childish curiosity when I learned about them and it was easy to see why Carlton fell for her, so vibrant despite all those forbidden drawbacks. But they had no possible hope for a future together, not when you were part of the Baron's kingdom in 1940's Mississippi. There was only one escape for them."

"How old was she?"

"Younger than you. Two ill-fated youthful lovers. As the firstborn and heir apparent to the Baron's 'throne'—and that's the way the bastard thought—Carlton couldn't afford to get caught screwing around with the help. Trysts with blacks were permissible and commonplace in private but don't broadcast it. But Carlton didn't give a hoot who knew. I think that was the rebelliousness in him, against his father. He flaunted the affair. He played a dangerous game and he lost. He escaped the only way open to him."

"What happened?" I said, so excited my voice squeaked an octave higher.

He sat his tumbler on the desktop, empty but for the remnants of an ice cube. His face grew longer. I knew whatever happened with his brother was not good cause he talked about him in the past tense. He looked me in the eye and I began to squirm. I wanted one of those Scotch drinks.

"You remind me of Carlton, same curiosity, same impetuousness," he said, quick grin changing into a drawn face. "You remind me of—"

He cut himself off too fast not for me to notice, especially because he put a hand over his eyes and I saw the corners of his mouth turn down. It was odd.

"What is it, something wrong?"

I saw his eyes were watery. "No, nothing. I just had a thought, not important."

I was moving around, my leg jumping. "What happened to him, your brother?" I said. I should have just sat there listening. Doctor Joe was a patient man, though. It was one of the things I liked most about him. I thought I was even learning how to be a little more patient myself because of him.

He gave me another pleasant look, tolerating me, and then, as calmly as if he might be talking about filling a tooth, he said, "Hanged himself in the stable. Nineteen-year-old kid gone before he knew anything about life. Sarah wasn't seen anywhere around the plantation again. I moved away a few years later."

"Oh. I'm sorry," I said, but I was shocked. I had expected him to tell me something bad but not that, not suicide.

He exhaled a big breath and stood up but didn't go anywhere. "Anyway, I'm reminded of that event some twenty years ago because of the predicament this man is in. I just hope he and his girlfriend aren't in for a similar fate."

"Yeah. Me too."

"By the way, Sonny," he said, "have you ever seen the Negro schools in this town?" It seemed to be a question out of the blue.

I looked away. I didn't know if he wanted me to answer. I'd never thought about black kids' schools. I never even thought to ask Harvey Nixon how his children were doing in school. Did they even go to school? What were Negroes taught about the Civil War? Did they have to learn algebra? Did their high school have a football team and who did they play and where did they sleep at their away games? The questions flooding my mind made me realize even more just how little I knew about the unfairness of being black.

"I—I don't," I said feebly, embarrassed.

"Well, I can tell you the two schools serving their communities are shameful. But, here's some good news. The federal government has legislated funds to upgrade or build new schools in distressed districts in some of the Southern states. They were earmarked for public white or black schools, both. Now the funds are finally being put to use. Woodstock is included in this first phase and it's going to a Negro elementary school that's very much needed."

"Well, that's great."

"My officer friend said there's a groundbreaking ceremony in a couple of weeks."

"Righteous," I said.

"The only problem," he added, "our town leaders aren't too happy it's not a white school getting built. It's just hard to believe they'd not want to see the town's children have better schools. Period."

"That'll show 'em, huh?"

"My friend could lose a lot more than his job with the force for making that call to me. And I'm getting a little worried about my own position, too. It seems I'm getting something of a reputation around town that I didn't realize or want. That could explain why I haven't heard anything official on this groundbreaking yet. They want to keep me in the dark."

I felt a sudden guilt spear me, wondering if snooping around Ash Town, the trouble I had with those cops, didn't have something to do with it.

He ran a hand through the length of his disheveled hair and gave me this pathetic look. "I wish I hadn't gotten you into this mess."

"You didn't do anything. Besides, I'm not scared."

That didn't mean anything to him. He just sighed. He added, "I didn't finish telling you what else the man said. He's heard there's going to be a disruption at the ceremony. He didn't call them out but he meant the Klan has plans to show up. He advised me to be careful if I'm thinking about going. Which of course I am."

"Oh, man."

He suddenly frowned. Something just occurred to him and he stared hard at me. "Don't you even think about showing up at this thing, Sonny. Do you hear me?"

I nodded vaguely and sat there a little while until he shut his eyes, and then I got up and said thanks for doing the filling, and left.

It was dark and I hoped the headlamp on the Moped would surprise me and stay on this time till I made it home.

Chapter 19

I stood on the porch of the Browns' squat clapboard home for a moment before knocking, looking out beyond the narrow, freshly cut front yard to the quiet street. Mr. Brown had parked the '49 Olds on the street instead of using the driveway when nothing was in the driveway. They didn't have a trailer or fishing boat or another car to take up its space. I wondered why Herman hadn't talked him into pulling it in, getting it out of view. So it wouldn't be easily spotted by the crooked cops.

With no moon at all, it was one of those nights as dark as deep space. On the way here I kept looking over my shoulder in that darkness for the hatchet that would have glinted under a street light before it plunged into the back of my head. Right before my skull split open and my brains ran out, I'd get to see the shadowy cop's bigass grin. And the terrible laugh that would be the last sound I ever heard.

I tapped on the screen door. I came to find out why that shithead Herman hadn't called me all weekend.

Brandy opened up. She looked delicious and knew it, wearing flaming red short shorts and a mini pajama top so loose and thin I could see her sprouting breasts, already well formed, mounds with perky little tips.

"Hey, Sonny, whatcha up to?" Brandy had perfect, snow-white teeth. I was into teeth these days, noticing just about everybody's.

It was business with me and I didn't want to get distracted by Brandy's sweet scent. "Is he home?"

"Well, yea-ah. He ain't going to be out, not looking like that."

"Like what?"

"Like a smashed pumpkin head. You haven't seen him? You didn't know?"

"Haven't talked to him, no. Know what?" I squeezed by her since she wasn't moving out of the way to let me in. I put a hand on her bare arm and wanted to accidentally on purpose brush against her but I held off. I could get up close dancing with her later, if I stayed that long.

"He's out in the back, sulking I guess. Don't tell him I called him a pumpkin head. Pretty please?"

"Sure. You doing your homework? Wanna dance in a little bit, maybe?" Her mother was the only one of her parents I had to worry about, but Mrs. Brown was at the laundromat down by Scarborough Drug Store and wouldn't be home for awhile.

"Maybe. Daddy's watching TV, though."

I could hear the TV going and smell the cigarette smoke. Sounded like Johnny Yuma was on, one of my favorite shows. I stepped around so as not to get in his view and said, "Hey, Mr. Brown, how's it going?"

"Goin fine, boy. How you?"

"Good. Been better, but good. Say, where's Herman?"

"Out yonder." He pointed back toward the kitchen then stubbed out a Lucky Strike in a half-full ashtray on the arm of the couch.

"Is that *The Rebel* you got on?"

"Yep."

"I love Nick Adams."

"Yep."

"You been fishing lately?"

"Nope. Wish."

"Deer hunting?"

"Same."

"Yeah, me too. See you, Mr. Brown."

"Yep."

I found Herman lying on the bed in the back bedroom. The room used to be a porch. Herman had helped his old man enclose the screened windows with corrugated tin and smaller aluminum windows last year when Brandy started having hissy fits to have her own bedroom. There wasn't much insulation on the porch so it got cold in winter and hot in summer. They called the room "out back" or "out yonder" or "the porch," depending on who was talking. Not "Hermie's bedroom." But it became Herman's bedroom soon as it was finished and Brandy got the real bedroom.

Herman faced the wall. "Let me see," I said sternly.

He turned and I had to look away. "What the fuck happened?"

The face was worse than a smashed pumpkin, all swollen in black and blue and red bulbs, like onions of different sizes. Black ants ran along his lower lip below his chin in two places. He sure wasn't any Tony Curtis now. Even his hair had lost its sheen.

He clasped his hands behind his head on the pillow and said, "Man, the guy comes out of nowhere. Like Wile E. Coyote, you know? BAM—ouch! That hurt—Anyways, he starts punching me 'fore I knew what happened. Then, beep-beep, he's gone."

His "beep-beep" sounded like "weep-weep" with his lips so swollen.

"I didn't even get a look at him. Wouldn't know him in a line up. He was that fast."

He did a lot of lisping and slobbering but I understood most of what he'd said, and I was skeptical.

"Who? Where?"

I thought he was frowning but it was hard to tell. "Hurts to talk, shitbreath. Roller rink Saturday night. I was messing around with this chick. Man, did she have some knockers."

"Save the bullshit, just give me the facts," I said. My Sergeant Friday imitation. "Her boyfriend did it, right?"

He nodded. But he wasn't looking at me and I wasn't buying it.

"Bullshit, it was that goddamn redhead cop, wasn't it? Don't lie to me, Herman. I'm not like your little chickees who believe anything you feed them."

I tried to sound real mad, though I wasn't. I felt sorry for him mostly. He had to be in a lot of pain. I thought getting my tooth drilled without Novocain was a deal till I saw him and thought about the doctors grinning over him while they sewed up his split lip. He wasn't numb now, it had worn off nearly two days ago.

He sat all the way up, then he stood. I thought he was going to topple over. He swerved like a street drunk, but he finally got his footing. "I ain't lying, goddamnit. I don't lie to my blood brother."

I guess that ended that. "Well, what about the cops on Friday? Did they find you before you got beat up? They would've found you before me. You had the car."

"Ain't heard nothing. Kinda surprised."

"You didn't call all weekend. I been seeing cops everywhere and they've all got red hair."

"Now you're bullshitting."

"But I'm scared. Where the hell are they? Why haven't they found us out yet? Something's not right."

"Well, I only know they'd be more interested in this government guy than us, if he's on to them. Which you say he is, right?"

"Why would you say that, man?" I was perplexed. "How would they even know about that? I mean, we only made them think we were out for some shine. Those cops had no way of connecting the government and what we were doing out there." But I was remembering Doctor Joe just an hour ago telling me the cops might be watching him. Maybe the two cops did know somebody was on to them.

"Yeah, that's right. That's all," he said in a garble. "They know they're crooks so they're lying low, hoping we'll do the same. Figures. Don't it?"

I got up and walked out of the room. I was tired of trying to make excuses for him because I was hoping he hadn't blabbed when the redhead cop beat his ass, if that's what happened. I had to think about it. I just wished I hadn't told him anything in the first place.

The TV was off and Mr. Brown was nowhere around. He'd gone to bed already. He was working the early shift these days. Brandy was lying on the couch on her stomach with her feet swinging behind her and a pencil in her mouth, making it look like she was sucking on it.

She batted her eyes at me. Got me going right off.

"We'll have to keep it low," she whispered, grinning up at me. "You want 'Hound Dog' or 'Teddy Bear?'"

Brandy Brown was really tempting and what I was about to say took all my powers of resistance. I found myself grimacing like Doctor Joe would, in agony. "I gotta go, my old lady's gonna skin me. Next time, though."

Her little pout said there wouldn't ever be a next time. But I knew better. Brandy could change her tune in the blink of an eye; she was only an eighth grader after all.

Chapter 20

I made it over to Susie's on a cold, blustery afternoon before her folks would get home from work. They showed up about the same time, about five-fifteen. Her little prick of a brother spotted me parking the Baron outside their chain link fence and ran out screaming something about Phil taking off my head, I'd better get lost.

"He'll slaughter you, skinny." That would be Susie's big lug of a new boyfriend, I figured.

Sir Stevie was a nasty little guy but I had no choice but to deal with him if I wanted to see Susie.

"Go screw yourself, punk," I said softly and with a smile. "Tell your sister I'm here."

"My mother has strictly forbidden you to enter the house when she's not here."

Damn, where'd an eleven-year-old learn to talk like that?

I pushed him aside and knocked on the back door. Susie was right there. I hadn't seen her behind the screen.

"Hey, Sonny. What're you doing here? Mom'll be here in thirty minutes."

"Well, if you must know, I came to see that sweet little brother of yours, that's about to get a knuckle-burn on his noggin if he does anything to my bike. What's up? How you doing?"

When I asked her that she just totally lost it. I had to get the screen door opened and grab her before she collapsed and busted her head on the kitchen floor. I managed to get her into the living room where she did fall like a brick, but on the couch. I sat next to her on the floor. I kept looking toward the kitchen to see if Stevie was snooping. He was but he didn't come in the room.

I leaned close to her ear. "It's not because of—? Is it? Have you said anything to your mother or anybody else?"

"Oh, *God*," she said in a soap opera voice that carried all the way through her small house and into the street, no doubt.

"Come on, Susie. Talk to me."

"What's there to talk about, Sonny, you jerk? You know what's the matter. I think—it's been how long now?"

"Only two months. It's too soon to know, isn't it?" I asked, not knowing about those things but thinking it wasn't right. I didn't want to know, either. I didn't even want to say the word, because, who knows, she just might be panicking and I didn't want to re-enforce her fears.

Her face was puffy and reddish, full of healthy color, her lips plump and inviting. I got on the couch and slid up real close to her and touched her face with the back of my hand like I was reading her temperature, like my mother would do me. I just wanted to touch her.

"Mom'll be coming home anytime."

I stood. "Look, Susie. No matter what happens, I'm not going to skip town. Promise. I am not going to abandon you just because you might—"

She wiped her eyes and looked up at me from the couch. She pulled in her legs and put her hand under the side of her face, like she was about to go to sleep. "You mean it?"

"How much more time before you know for sure?"

"Not long, Sonny. I think it's already been enough time to know for sure."

She started bawling again but softly.

"Sorry," I said. "Say, have you gotten back to being friends again with Vicki?"

"We've seen each other a little," she said, sniffling now.

"Good ... I better take off. Remember what I said, okay?"

"I will remember. You remember, too."

Chapter 21

On Wednesday after throwing papers I stopped by the medical building to do some studying. That wasn't against the law so I wasn't worried. I had some algebra and a paper to write in history on anybody I wanted to write about so long as it was a politician from Alabama. Any time in the state's history. Could even be today. The course wasn't "Alabama History," so I don't know why Mr. Peters limited the paper subject to this state, because if you think about it, the world outside is much more interesting. I mean, look at ancient Greece with all its philosopher politicians, a goldmine for this kind of paper, or even our neighboring state Florida, which was totally corrupt. Pah! … Anyway, Doctor Joe was educated in Alabama and knew bigwigs in Montgomery. He was sure to have some good ideas about picking somebody.

He wasn't thrilled to see me. He didn't want me at the office, grimacing as he emphasized it wasn't safe. But he gave in when I asked him to help me with my paper.

His little office was quiet and studious, like the public library's second floor cubicles. They kept all the stuff that wasn't fiction on the second floor, like Freud's works. But here I could drink Coke or stretch out on the couch to read. You weren't allowed to bring your Krystal burgers and Cherry Coke into the library. But that was good cause I sure didn't want to be distracted smelling somebody's hamburger while I was reading about some girl so fixated on her daddy's penis she dreamed of killing her mother. A jealous girl can be very dangerous.

He poked his head out to look up and down the hallway. "Where'd you park the bike?"

"Behind the dumpster. Nobody saw me come in, I'm sure."

He seemed satisfied with that.

I sat at the desk and Doctor Joe headed back into the lab to finish a new retainer for Harvey Nixon's boy. The boy was progressing right along, he said, and following instructions. I told him about the history paper and asked if he'd give me some ideas. He was glad to, I could tell.

"Let's see, you could do it on Hugo Black, who became a supreme court associate and was a liberal Democrat. Kind of a tedious body of rulings that are probably too boring to interest anyone in the tenth grade, probably even the teacher. There's always Big Jim Folsom, ex-governor, if you want to do something pat. He was actually a big supporter of the Negro, but also a flagrant thief. Pretty fascinating stuff. You can draw information easily on him," he said. He didn't seem too enthusiastic, though. "Or, you might like someone more obscure. Ex-congressman Teddy 'Big Daddy' O'Brien, for instance, a truly colorful character who was as crooked as he was charming, a notch or two less than Huey Long, so he didn't draw much national attention."

"Who's that, Huey Long?"

"Another colorful politician who ran Louisiana for an era after the Depression. Milked it, actually. You'll get to him soon enough in school."

"Well, what makes this guy O'Brien fun?"

He laughed. "Yes, fun, good way to put it. He could wheel and deal. For one, he got decidedly rich heading the Prisons Reform Committee in the '20s by selling prison labor to local businesses. Time served was forgotten for those poor bastards. A colossal scam that was wide open on the books. The racket is still going on even though it's been outlawed. Nobody seems interested in fixing it."

"I'd bet you could, huh?"

His eyebrows lifted on a grin and he seemed to consider the question, then said, "Matter of fact, I might look into it."

"I'll bet the prisoners were all Negroes, weren't they?"

"Smart kid. Better than ninety percent, because Negroes made up that percentage ... I'll give you some references on Big Daddy," he said, "but don't use only this aspect of his tenure, right? The man might have been rotten to the core but he got some good things passed, too, like pushing through liquor licenses in some mid-state counties—so today I don't have to drive so far to get that vodka you like so much. For your purposes, he was just a lively, personable politician who ought to be fun to write about."

"Okay, I won't."

I asked, "Have you learned anymore about the ceremony for that new colored school? Maybe what the Klan's planning?"

He shook his head. "We'll have to see, but I did alert the *Star* so they could have a photographer on hand. I think they'd planned just to use the standard Washington press release on it. This is a big deal and I want to see it gets some real news coverage."

"Do you have a gun? Cause you're gonna need it if they show up."

He frowned at me. "I hope you're not serious, Sonny. Arming myself won't solve anything. You can't deal with extremists that way. It's just playing into their game. Let me give you a little social studies lesson. Cultural revolutions don't depend on the use of arms. Look how the great leaders handled revolution, Gandhi, Tolstoy, the Dalai Lamas through centuries of repression and invasions. Our own Cherokee Indians, disastrous as their peaceful resistance was against moving their nation and the subsequent deadly 'Trail of Tears' march relocating their tribes, would have lost many more of their people if they had picked up weapons and resisted. What they did was smart. They appealed to the U.S. Congress and it got them independence, even if it did mean settling in new lands. The point is they escaped genocide—"

"I'd still take a double barrel with me if I were you. It'll give them something to think about if they start burning things down."

"Well, kid, for one thing nothing's been built yet to burn down ...

Let's do a hypothetical; what would you do, if you were in my position?"

He had me. I already knew I wouldn't shoot anybody; I discovered that about myself the night they had me up the oak tree, sweating for my life after that lynching.

I gave easily. "You're right. I take it back. Pretty dumb idea."

"Glad you recognize that. You want to start your project now?"

I guess he noticed I didn't. He said, "Well, I've got a proposition for you. Do you want to get involved, do something for me?"

"Yeah, you know I do. What?"

"A little investigative work. You seem to have an interest in sneaking around, doing that sort of thing." He grinned saying it but he might as well have shaken his finger at me. "You can work independent of me. So it shouldn't cause a problem."

"I'll do it, whatever it is. What is it?"

"Careful what you volunteer for. At least find out what the assignment is first."

"Okay. What is it? Then I'll volunteer." I wanted to try to make up for my blunder in Ash Town and was ready to do anything.

"Go to the county records section at City Hall and make a list of building permits taken out by Decker Building and Designs, but just those for jobs in the Overton District, Ash Town as we know it."

"Okay, sure," I said.

"Remember, Decker Building and Designs. I want you to get addresses for permits pulled for awnings and any other jobs they might have done there. Sound like something you can handle?"

"Hell yeah, I can handle it. Ah, which section is that stuff in?"

"You'll find what you need in 'Planning' or 'Building.' You can figure it out, that's part of the job. Tell any nosey clerk as little as possible, that you're there on a school project, a paper you're doing on historic architecture, something like that. Be vague, don't ask for help. Right?"

"No help, right. Think there are a lot of them, these permits?"

"I've been out there, seen more than twenty houses with shiny awnings. Those people need curtains on their windows, new paint, better cars. Certainly not awnings. I'm just guessing Decker did all the work."

"I'll get started Friday. Won't have time tomorrow, big papers and

I have to stuff them first. Is Friday okay?"

This looked like my best opportunity to ask Doctor Joe for a favor. Wouldn't it be something if I could take Susie to the drive-in in a Thunderbird! *Some Like It Hot* was playing and she was dying to see what Tony Curtis looked like dressed up as a girl. So was I. I couldn't imagine; I could only think of Herman dressed to look like a girl, which was a real laugh and impossible to imagine. Since I was doing this snooping favor for him, I thought, *Go ahead, what's to lose.*

"Are you gonna be around, say, Saturday?" I started off, "cause I was wondering—See. ..."

"Most likely. Jeanne may come over. May. Never know with her."

"Uh, what would it be like if I washed the T-Bird in the afternoon, if it's not too cold? For nothing! Cause being white it needs it more often. Prob'ly pretty dirty right now."

He looked at me and grinned. "Well, genius, as a matter of fact, white will cover up dirt better than a dark color, despite what would seem to be the contrary. That's one reason I chose white as the color. What do you say to that?"

"White is great! God, what if it was blue, baby blue? Or black. I couldn't see your car being black."

He leaned back, content looking. His eyes were a little narrower but he still wore the grin. A grin on Doctor Joe looked like a big smile on anybody else. "So what's up, Sonny? You've got a date and need some money. No, you said for free—No, wait again. You want to borrow the T-Bird for a big date on Saturday night. All washed up and looking sharp. Am I warm?"

"Can you read minds? Susie wants to go to the drive-in and see *Some Like It Hot* with Jack Lemmon and—"

"Marilyn Monroe. Great movie, very funny."

"Don't forget Tony Curtis is in it too ..."

"One condition."

"For what?"

"For borrowing the car."

"Yeah? Great! Anything, what is it?"

"No speeding this time."

Chapter 22

It wasn't raining on Friday afternoon so I finished my route quickly, just after three-thirty, and scooted downtown to City Hall. I'd been inside the huge building with the clock tower only once that I could recall. That was with Mother; I was pretty sure we'd gone there for something that had to do with my being alive. I'd noticed ever since then the clock in the tower always read ten minutes after noon, or midnight if you were down there late at night. An inset plaque outside the front door said the stone palace was built in 1887 in tribute to the "founding fathers of the City of Woodstock, Seat of Clayton County."

It was big and quiet inside, like a mausoleum; I mean, the ceiling was way up there and the floor was marble which made echoes as you walked. I didn't find a listing in the directory for anything under "Planning," but there was "Building Services Division" and I climbed the wide stairway to the next floor and went down a big, dim hallway till I came to the door that had those words printed on the frosted glass.

The big room had a smell of musk, old paper and freshly sharpened pencils. The smell and stacks of tall cabinets reminded me of the cluttered living room of Mr. Waring's upstairs apartment where I took Saturday violin lessons until the end of fourth grade, up till when Pops passed and we went broke. I liked Mr. Waring's bowties; I didn't remember him ever getting mad at my disinterested bow squeaking and laziness to learn sheet music. The clutter made me feel claustrophobic, though. You couldn't breathe easy in his room. It was like that here.

I strolled through a forest of file cabinets tall as me till finding the counter where I asked a droopy woman looking ready for bed to point out where permits for building things were kept.

"Right over yonder, young man." She gave me a curious look, just what Doctor Joe warned me about. *Don't talk to the clerks.*

"Now, what on earth would you want with boring old permits?"

I was ready. "It's my grandma, ma'am. She sent me to gather up all I could on a house she's wanting to buy to let us live in, me and my three older sisters. We're orphans, you see, Mommy and Daddy got kilt in a automobile crash out past Midland after New Year's. But thanks for asking. Goodla told me I'd better find out what she wants without any help or she wouldn't buy the house. She means business, too."

"Oh. Well, good for your grandma, sonny. Sorry bout your folks, that's a real shame."

Doctor Joe was right, it wasn't hard to find the permits drawn by Decker Building in the Overton District because there were none. At least not for awnings. I looked all through the files that listed "Overton District" for work by "Decker Building and Designs" and found only one in the Overton area. That was for a room addition, taken out twelve years before now, in 1948. The only other permits were for water heater installations and various plumbing jobs which I suspected were legitimate, though they weren't drawn by Decker Building and Designs. Different plumbing companies like "AAA Ace Emergency Plumbing" filed those permits. Hardly any permits had been pulled for work in Ash Town and I knew why. Those folks couldn't afford to pay plumbing companies to do the work; anybody could figure that. They'd do it themselves off the books since it was a lot cheaper than paying a company. The few I saw would've been widows or elderly folk who didn't have a choice cause they didn't know shit from Shinola about U-traps and union fittings, never mind trying to crawl under a sink and work upside down. Stuart had taught me some stuff about plumbing in an old house we used to live in before we moved to the apartments, where they had a maintenance man.

At first I thought it was odd, that I was on a wild goose chase and I wondered if Doctor Joe had put me up to this as some kind of test or because he just wanted me to feel useful. But then again maybe it wasn't odd at all. What if Decker Building never drew permits because they didn't want any record of selling those people awnings? That they didn't want the money showing on their books? Doctor Joe would not have known that. It couldn't have been that permits were expensive cause they weren't, $3.75 to $9.00 each on the ones I saw, all for various things like outside light installations and running electricity to a garage.

I found something else, too. It wasn't all that odd, but it was still interesting. On every record I looked at for Overton properties, it said Kimbrough & Sons Builders built the houses, and all in 1930, the year after the fire wiped everything out. I only noticed this because the governor of the state was named Kimbrough, Edward "Moose" Kimbrough Jr., and he was from Woodstock. So I figured it would have been his father's company, and he would've been one of the "Sons." Some kids my age didn't even know who the governor was. Our social studies teacher, Miss Thackeray, had asked one day and only about a third of the class raised their hands. Me included. That amounted to six kids total, five girls and me. I was the only boy in class who knew who the damn governor of Alabama was. To be fair, I probably wouldn't have raised my hand if I'd never met Doctor Joe, cause it was him who got me interested in that sort of thing, politics and government and civil rights.

Anyway, I suppose there was nothing unusual with all the houses being built by Kimbrough & Sons, a company in the business of putting up whole subdivisions of prefabricated structures, like the houses in Ash. It just caught my attention.

I went through as many listings in Ash Town as I could—probably thirty—in the hour I spent there. Then the droopy clerk made her announcement so everybody checking records knew they had to complete their business by four-thirty. She announced it over a loudspeaker: "The door will be closed and locked at four-forty p.m. Please conclude your business …" I only saw about five people in there when I left at four twenty-five.

When I stopped at the big brick house on Broadmore the next day, Saturday, Jeanne's little yellow MG was in the driveway. The canvas top was up and a see-through sticker of letters across the plastic window read, "W A R   E A G L E S." There was an "Auburn" bumper sticker too.

I sat on the Baron at the curb for a moment considering whether I should go on up and ring the bell. I smelled my armpits first then looked down to see if I was fit to even let her see me. The jeans had holes in both knees and my tennis shoes were ragged, strings loose. I could smell gasoline on me somewhere from my bike breaking down last night after I left City Hall; it ran rough and smoked. I had to push and pedal it home and worked on it till after midnight, finally figuring out the carburetor had a bent floater pin. This morning I helped Mother with chores until Sears opened at nine. Mother felt like being nice to me and drove me there without even a fuss. She wanted to get herself and us boys some new underwear and socks. I was very lucky they had the part I needed in the warehouse cause I didn't have to wait for it to be ordered, which would have left me stranded for a week or more. It took me almost till delivery time to fix the Baron but I got her running proper.

I started to just go on. I could see Doctor Joe later, after I got cleaned up, but I didn't. He would want to know what I found out; he wasn't going to call me on our party-line phone to find out. And there was no way I had forgotten he was going to let me wash his car today. I had my big date with Susie tonight and had permission to use the T-Bird for it.

Jeanne answered the bell. "Hey, Sonny, what's cookin'?"

It was the middle of winter but she wore those tight yellow short shorts that left hardly anything to your imagination. Her hair was in a bun, a chignon. That style was a method of tightening the hair into a hard ball if a girl felt insecure or defiant, both of which meant she was feeling unsexy. I'd learned that from Freud's case studies. So why was she in those super-sexy yellow shorts? It confused me but I felt strangely relieved knowing her mood was the "look but don't touch." Now I wouldn't have to try to impress her. I could just get down to the business at hand.

"Doin' swell, Joe in?"

She held onto the edge of the door, like she wasn't going to let me in, like I was some door-to-door salesman and she didn't want what I was selling. It occurred to me then that I hadn't ever seen an engagement ring on her finger. She had some rings on, but no band or anything with diamonds, and I thought that was what you wore when you were somebody's fiancée. Especially a showy girl like Jeanne Cochran, Kappa Delta, Miss Phi Beta Kappa in the making, and Mrs. Joseph Peach to-be.

Probably I was just jealous.

"Yes, he is. Wipe your shoes on the mat, we don't want mud on the rugs."

Damn. She sounded like a wife already.

"How's school? You studying hard?" I asked. I wiped my tennis shoes but there was no mud on them. It hadn't rained in two or three days.

"Yeah. Real hard," she said, almost sarcastically, as though she wanted me to know she *wasn't* studying hard. She was trying to confuse me, I guess, but I didn't let it bother me.

"Where is he?"

"Oh, out back raking leaves, I think. Or tinkering around with that damn car."

"You don't like the T-Bird?"

"Sure, it's just he spends too much time with it. You know, like it's his little baby or something."

She was jealous of his car. I understood that. "Well, that little MG is pretty hot, too. You don't like it?" I said. Maybe I meant to provoke her.

But she didn't bite so I walked on through the house to the backyard.

He *was* tinkering with the T-Bird, bent under the hood shining up the chrome air filter.

"Hand me that quarter-inch socket," he said. "I'll be done here in a second and you can get busy washing, maybe throw in a wax job, huh?"

I frowned.

"Just teasing you, lad."

Pearl jumped in the air waiting for me to greet her. I scratched her between the ears and she immediately did here thing—dropped her head to the ground but leaving her butt in the air for a pat. I had never seen a dog do that, but Pearl did it every time she saw me. It was the weirdest thing and always gave me a charge. I patted her rump and then pulled on her tail. She showed her teeth.

Doctor Joe said, "She's touchy with the tail. One of those dog things."

He closed the hood and wiped the tools and his hands equally long with different rags. "Let's talk out here. No need for Jeanne to be in on this conversation. Right?"

"Yeah, I guess. What's with her, anyway? She seems different."

"Don't mind Jeanne. She can be moody."

He squinted. "About the information, did you get it?"

That wasn't much of an answer about Jeanne, but that was okay. I didn't really care anyway, but I would still slow dance with her in a second, if she wanted.

I couldn't help it, I had to ask, "When's the wedding?"

His eyes darkened, like a cloud came over them. It was amazing.

"Did I say something wrong?" I asked.

We sat in the cold wrought iron chairs at the patio table.

"No, no. You've probably been wondering for some time. Truth is we haven't set a date."

"Why not? I mean, she's been your fiancée for a long time, ever since I've known you, anyway."

He did that thing with his long fine hair, ran both his hands through it all the way to his back. "It's complicated, Sonny. I told you before that relationships can sometimes be guided by irrational or immature emotions that stand at times to bring out the underside of a person's nature. I'm not saying that's necessarily the case with Jeanne and I, but there are—well, like I say, complications. Let's leave it at that for now, all right? … Now, how about this thing with the permits?"

It was chilly in the shade of the trees. Pearl came over and laid her head on Doctor Joe's shoe. He was wearing leather boat shoes.

"Did you get to City Hall?" he asked, sounding bored.

"Hell yeah I did."

"Well? Do I have to keep asking questions? Such as, what did you learn?"

I felt stingy and said, "What do you think I learned?"

He switched tunes and played along. "Nothing. You ran into a nosey clerk who sent you packing."

"Well, you're right. Except the lady didn't interfere. I found the records and just like you said, nothing there. No permits drawn by that company, Decker Building and Designs, for any awning work in Ash Town. Ever. Period. They must have done it without getting permits, is all I can figure."

"Doesn't surprise me."

"That I didn't find permits? Then why'd you send me?"

"It just doesn't surprise me. I wasn't sure. Now I know. Now we have at least one thing to nail them on. This is strong evidence." He looked at me. "Good job, Sonny. You are my go-to man."

"Yeah, but don't you have to get a complaint from the folks that got taken in, to go after them?"

"Wouldn't that be something? But those folks are scared to death as it is. They are not about to point fingers at a white police officer …"

I knew that all along. "Well, what's next? I mean, how are you going to bust the crooked cops?"

He looked around as if wondering where Jeanne was. He said, "I'm getting thirsty. You?"

"Yeah, but I gotta go in a minute and deliver my papers. So maybe some ice tea?"

I liked my ice tea unsweetened, but I always had to ask for it that way cause everybody and their help loaded it with sugar otherwise.

We went inside long enough for him to mix a drink for himself, something with a "Rose's Lime Juice" and some real lime, and my tea, then went back outside. I gulped my ice tea and watched the giant goldfish breeze through the water under the lily pads.

He said, "It shouldn't be hard to nail them if I can talk some of the victims into corroborating. At least I hope to get them to show me the contracts they signed. I get that, I have something to bring the county prosecutor."

These deep furrows dug into his forehead. I knew what he was about to say, that that guy, the prosecutor, was a crook too. So I said it first.

"You think he'd favor the cops don't you?"

He nodded. "Most likely. I don't really trust anyone in office. What a damn shame that is."

Pearl tried to resettle on his foot but he pushed her off.

"There's not many people in power we can count on. In fact, I don't know anyone, except the officer who called me with the tips. And I depend on him."

"I hate to tell you," I said, adding to the troubles, "but those folks out at Ash? They aren't going to show you any contract they signed, because they didn't get anything on paper. At least Harvey Nixon didn't, and I bet none of them did. Harvey said they were holding them for 'safe keeping.'"

He only nodded. "Well, I'll see Harvey Nixon when he brings his son in next week. See what he has to say."

"Let me go talk to him," I said brightly. "Harvey trusts me."

"Don't think so, Sonny. If anything comes out of this thing, though, you can feel good for what you've done. I'd better go it alone from here."

"I'm not scared, if that's what you think. I want to help."

He stared at me inquisitively. "Well, let me ask. That redheaded cop got a good look at you, right? And we're pretty sure he's running the streetlight game, right? There's a reason why he hasn't paid you or your friend Herman a visit. And that's the thing that worries me to death, Sonny. What are they up to. They could have pulled you aside already."

Before I could catch myself, I blurted, "Maybe *he* beat up Herman. Maybe Herman really was lying to me—"

"Hold it. What are you telling me?" he said, a hard edge in his voice.

I grinned like the kid with his hand in the candy jar. I'd learned from my fifth grade teacher Mrs. Rose that nobody is smart enough to get away with lying, you'd get caught sooner or later. Abraham Lincoln said it, she said. I had lied to Doctor Joe. I'd kept from him what I told Harvey Nixon and Herman, that I was working undercover for the government. I still couldn't bring myself to tell him. But I had to say something about Herman.

"Herman got beat up pretty bad last weekend. His face is still a mess," I said. "He was going after some girl at the roller rink and her boyfriend punched him out. Which sounded just like Herman—except I'm not so sure."

Pearl got up and walked away. She didn't want to hear me try to weasel my way out of my own mess.

"How badly was he hurt?"

"Black and blue. Will have to eat soft food for a while, and he probably can't even brush his teeth yet. I don't think they broke any bones in his face."

He looked glum. "They handed him a hard lesson in meddling where he's not supposed to. I'd say there's a good chance Herman told them what he knew. And he knew about the rigged light at 4th, right?"

"Yeah."

"Then there's little doubt he told them who you are and what you were doing there. Not good, Sonny. It'll also jeopardize whatever case I can make since they'll now be scrambling to cover up the awning racket."

"This stuff's not going to mess up my chances to wash the T-Bird this afternoon, is it?"

He shook his head, sighed. "Holding back like that will always comes back to you. I hope you've learned something here. But I never renege on a promise."

Jeanne appeared suddenly. Like a genie had just materialized her, poof. I guess seeing her all of a sudden hit me as a little odd after what Doctor Joe had said about her—or about relationships that I took to mean him and Jeanne.

She walked past me and sat on Doctor Joe's knee, kind of worked herself into his lap and put her arm around his neck, running her finger along the rim of his ear. Real sexy. Her hair was still in the tight bun. My theory wasn't holding up. I just gave it up, confused and feeling even more ambivalent about Jeanne.

She said, "There's a patient of yours on the phone. Says it's got puss and hurts so bad she can't even swallow. Yuk."

Chapter 23

I really hadn't appreciated what a nice day it was sitting in the shade of the pine trees in Doctor Joe's backyard garden. But occasionally between these intermittent winter days of rain and cold wind that would absolutely convince me I wanted to quit throwing papers, there would come days like this when the sun burst through chocolate skies and warmed up the air and gave your skin color. You could shed your jacket and roll up your sleeves. It was central Alabama weather at its best. But this kind of day was also dry and that caused my hands to crack and bleed. Then again I didn't have to wear that silly-looking toboggan scooting around on the Baron. The ointment Mother gave me helped some with the chapped skin.

The air didn't feel wintry, it felt romantic. I was dreaming of Susie, at the drive-in, snuggled inside the two-seater T-Bird.

I had one block of papers left to throw, and decided after that I'd head on over to Calhoun Street and meet Susie's mother before I came over to pick her up tonight. I had to get that over with once and for all anyway if I expected to take Susie out. I just had to make a good impression, so when I got to her house, I'd have to remember to button up my shirt and tuck it in and shape my flattop with a little spit.

But all that didn't matter cause I never made it to Susie's; I didn't even make it through my route.

The first time they drove by the car slowed down and they just stared. I was hunched down on the curb working on the Moped. The master link had popped loose and the chain dropped on the street, laying back there like some greased-up dead snake. I used a piece of the wire that was still on the bike from the beer-toting jigamadig that night I met Susie at the roller rink and jury-rigged the chain together till I could get a new master link, which wouldn't be till Monday. I didn't know how much longer the Baron was going to last. It seemed to always break down on weekends, leaving me high and dry for some way to deliver my heavy Sunday morning papers—without having to beg Mother to drive me around or, God forbid, let me use the car.

The shiny new Impala must have swung around the block and this time when it came by it stopped in the street at the corner. Four boys got out and looked me over. They leaned against the Impala like the cocky hoodlums in *The Blackboard Jungle*. They left the car engine running for some reason. It was a gorgeous car, a hardtop, meaning it had no center post to interfere with your arms, just open space. It looked brand new too. Two-tone sky blue and white with straight shiny chrome lines and swan fins that fanned out with those hypnotic triple taillights. You couldn't help but admire it, even idolize it.

I recognized two of the boys. They were from my high school. Twelfth graders, rich kids. One, the driver, was Dudley Willard, Jr., or the second, "II." I didn't remember which or much care. His old man owned Dudley Willard Chevrolet. His slogan was "Dudley'll Do You." Real lame. Should've been Dudley'll do you *right*, but the slogan was at least honest because he did you all right, did you in. He did Mother in on her '53 Chevy by about three hundred dollars, she said. But that was nothing to the way they screwed blacks over. He didn't have one black person working on his lot, not even to wash up the used cars. But Willard Chevrolet would sure sell cars to the Negroes and I imagined with terms that cost them a lot more than what white customers got. I mean, there just wasn't much question about that.

It wasn't Dudley, II, who got to me first and kicked over the Baron.

That was Josh Winningham. Winningham played on Woodstock High's varsity football team. Offense, I think, maybe a lineman. I didn't go to many of the games since the Rams were such losers. I liked college football anyway, the Crimson Tide, the Auburn Tigers and Georgia's Dawgs. Winningham was a bully. You wanted to avoid him in the halls. I couldn't avoid him right now.

"What the hell you do that for?" I screamed and moved to pick up the bike. What did he have against me, I wondered. It surprised me and so I didn't have time to get scared or fighting mad.

"You're a fuckwad, fuckwad." His tone was nastier than his lame vocabulary. The other three were behind him now. My bike was losing gas and it looked like oil was leaking out, too. I picked it up and stood it back on the stand and Winningham kicked it over again. I jumped over the Baron and tried to grab his throat to strangle him to death.

It didn't work. My hands never got a grip on his neck. They were all on me in an instant pulling me apart at the limbs, like some medieval torture device. Then I got scared. Someone punched my face with what felt like a rock or brass knuckles. I thought I felt my cheekbone shatter but it could have been my nose instead.

I squirmed to get out of their grip. They weren't saying anything so I didn't know why they were attacking me. I screamed, "What'd you want? What'd I do?"

I thought my arms were coming apart at the shoulder joints. It was hurting like hell and I was getting more scared that I might get really hurt. But I could move nothing but the midsection of my body, my hips. I tried to swing them back and forth. Then I heard a whooshing sound and it felt like someone had plunged his hand into my stomach and pulled it out, the stomach and all my guts behind it. It took my breath and I may have passed out because I didn't know if I could move my hips after that.

I couldn't say anything cause I couldn't talk. It was all I could do to suck air into my lungs. It felt like they had exploded.

All of a sudden I landed on the ground, except it wasn't the dried-grass lawn I hit, it was the sidewalk concrete. But I didn't care. I could barely make out figures of people through my watery and swollen eyes.

The left eye was surely permanently shut. A fifth figure vaguely appeared in my vision now and he was bigger than the football players and he was black.

Harvey Nixon.

Harvey moved behind two of the figures and I saw his big hands grab the necks of those two boys between him and me. He pushed them together. I heard their heads crack and their voices groan. The silhouetted figures remained in my vision after they collapsed. Then I saw the other two figures disappear too, except they didn't fall. They ran like hell, screaming something like, "Oh, shit. Damn nigger killed 'em."

I saw the little white, beautiful pickup truck with the words "Scarborough Drug Store" scribbled in cursive on the driver's door. The driver's door stood open.

That Harvey was there to save me was nothing short of a miracle. They were going to kill me and I could do nothing to stop them. It was such a helpless feeling that I swore to myself, when they were pulling my limbs apart, that I would never let myself get caught in any such predicament ever again and to get myself strong enough that I could get out of something like this if it did ever happen again. And I was feeling pretty sure it would happen again. I was even more sure that Harvey Nixon was going to find himself up shit creek for saving the life of a white boy from white boys.

He wouldn't let me sit up. "You jest stay right there, Sonny boy. Don't move a muscle till I can find out how bad you is hurt."

He ran his hands over my midsection, squeezed and poked and asked, "How's that feel?"

"Like shit. Is my stomach still there?"

"We gonna have to git you to the hospital. I'm gonna pick you up real easy, okay?"

"Okay."

He did and he sat me in the passenger's side of the white truck and made me hold a rag to my face. The rag vaguely smelled of gasoline. Then he went back and picked up my paper bag and bike and put them in the bed, leaned up so more oil wouldn't spill. I rested my head against the back window and looked out the door window through my only good eye. There was a small colorless pool of something left on the sidewalk, maybe gas from the Baron. I hoped it wasn't oil, or my blood. I noticed how still those two boys lay there and then I shut the eye. I knew I was hurt and wanted to get there fast. I knew I was in bad shape because I had never wanted to go to the hospital again after getting my tonsils out when I was six. Then, I woke up sick as a dog from the gas they knocked me out with, nor could I talk for a full week or eat anything besides awful scrambled eggs. Except they said a little ice cream was okay, and Pops brought me different flavors every night from his shop, Pop's Ice Cream, during that week. I could see the rest of my family from my makeshift bed in the living room, smelling good food, and remembered my older brother laughing at me.

"Don't talk," he said, "jest shake yo head, okay?"

I nodded.

"I seen them boys befoe. They up to no damn good, ridin round after school looking fo trouble. Idle hands is the devil's tools … You know 'em?"

I nodded. "They—"

"Shh. What you think they wanna come and beat up on you like that fo? No, never you mind answering that. We'll git to that later. You think maybe they is connected to them dirty cops what made us git them awnin's?"

"Hadn't thought of—"

"What I tell you, boy? Jest nod, nothing moe. I bet that it. Well, I s'pect they got a good look at my face, them other two what ran. Oh, I didn't hurt them two lying back there, not too bad. They's just knocked loony. They be awright after ja-while."

"How you know?" I got it in before he could stop me.

"You get hit nuff, you know. Here we is." Harvey knew what he was talking about since he was a professional boxer himself and I let the thought of those boys' chances of croaking, or surviving, fade in my mind.

He didn't pull all the way up to the emergency entrance. He looked around nervously, I suppose looking for anyone who might see a black man with a bloody-faced white boy that they would surely report to the law immediately. It was broad daylight.

"I'll walk up there," I said. "I can make it. I'm feeling better now ... Harvey, I would've been minced meat if you—"

"Don't you go worrying 'bout it now. Just go in there and don't scoot around the side. You heah me? You could be hurt bad. I see that your motorbike git home, okay?"

"Okay."

"Can you make it okay yo'sef?"

I nodded and stumbled forward.

But I did slip around the side. The pain in my stomach wasn't as bad now and I figured it was just the pain from getting hit unexpectedly in the tender parts. As for my eye, it was closed tight. I knew I was suppose to put something cold on it, like a piece of steak out of the icebox. It was the bleeding from the cut on my cheek that sent me to the hospital the next day, only because it needed stitching to stop the flow.

I was a mess all through the night, but Mother was worse off than me. At least I knew she really did care about me. She cried. She prayed for me, too. Praying wasn't going to cut mustard but it made her feel better and for that I was glad she said those nice prayers. I tried to hold cold bacon against my face and sleep; have you ever tried that? I had to change bandages on the cheek a few times and Mother gave me some aspirin and forced me to take some cod liver oil, which only put me in the bathroom before daybreak. Why the hell she gave me that I didn't know; I guess she was just in a panic for her son's life. I had to get a sub for the route and that was always a hassle cause I would get the calls at home from customers who were looking for their paper, always steaming mad cause they didn't get their Sunday paper. I didn't go to school on Monday or even the day after; it wasn't until Thursday that the swelling in my cheekbone went down enough that my words could be understood by human beings, and on Friday I finally went back to school.

What I couldn't get out of my spleen was why those twelfth graders jumped me. If they were just up to no good or if somebody had sent them, as Harvey said. I thought that somebody might be the redhead cop. He'd found me out and this was his revenge and his warning to stop snooping around in their crooked business. Did that mean Herman confessed to them before they beat his face in? I didn't want to think so, but I sure was leaning that way. I set myself to see him soon as I was on my feet.

But what bothered me just as much as being set up by those cops, and a terrible worry about what's to come for Harvey Nixon, was what those people might be planning against Doctor Joe, if it was his investigations that made them come after me. That would mean they knew I was working for him as a kind of private investigator …

Yeah, my new slate, Sonny Poe, P.I.

Chapter 24

He denied it.
He said there was no way he would rat on me. "How could you think that? You're my fucking *blood brother*." Herman was in total disbelief.

Or doing a pretty good acting job. I wished I'd know which.

"What's the guy's name who beat you up at the roller rink? Or the girl you were messing around with? You always know who the girl is."

He couldn't tell me. Said he never got that far with her, and also that he'd never seen either one of them before. "She coulda been from Midland. She coulda been from fucking Arkansas."

He was too defensive. Herman was fearless and never defensive. He got mad because I didn't believe him. Not hurt or disappointed, which would be the reaction from most friends. Not Herman, that wasn't how he worked.

There was one reason I thought he might be telling me the truth—he wasn't asking me anything now about my investigation for the government or the man I referred to as "DJ." If it had been the cops who attacked him, they would've demanded that he find out all he could about me and this DJ guy and probably granted him a little time to find out before paying him another visit.

I dropped it for the time being; I had my life to get back to.

There was a lot of homework after a four-day absence. Algebra worried me, considering my promise to Doctor Joe to always keep up. But how are you supposed to concentrate when your face is still throbbing and your eye still mostly closed and unfocused? And speaking of my face, they said my nose was dislocated and fractured. It would be permanently crooked. That was all right with me, cause I figured a crooked nose makes you look experienced and gives you character. I only worried whether I would be able to breathe through the left nostril cause it was still swollen shut on that side. I couldn't do sit-ups, my stomach was so sore, and once the stitches were out, they said I'd have a permanent scar on my cheek just about where my nose was bent. More experienced.

Susie wasn't happy at all for getting stood up Saturday night and I couldn't blame her. She didn't get to see *Some Like It Hot*, she said, trying not to pout about it. But when I called her the next Monday, which was as soon as I could work my jaw enough to make words understandable, she started bawling, even though this time it was over me. That was nice of her.

The next week, my kid brother came home after school with a white bag of milk chocolate from Woolworth's that must have cost a dollar and a half. Since I still couldn't chew anything more than grits and tomato soup, I thought he was being a smartass, looking to get a good laugh for himself and for Stuart, too. But that wasn't it.

"Naw, Sonny, you can eat it later, soon as your mouth works again," he said, "just hide it somewhere I won't find it."

Funny kid, that Bag-a-bones. He was just being nice and doing what he would've wanted if he was in bed all busted up. Chance was all right and I didn't hold it against him that he went totally by what the Bible taught. I guess that was why he was still in Scouts—and I wasn't—and why he was captain of his YMCA basketball team, the Wolves, which made it all the way to divisional finals, where they lost.

… At school on Friday, my first day back, Miss West read us a short story called "Dry September" that she said we should think about over the weekend. On Monday we would talk about what we thought the story was really about. Miss West had become my favorite teacher because she didn't seem afraid to talk about anything. She was the one who taught me not to turn and stare when you heard someone come in the auditorium late. It's rude, she'd said. I was all ears listening to the story because it told about some rednecks going after this Negro to lynch him for maybe doing something to a white woman, or maybe not. I had firsthand knowledge of a lynching. I had a hard time staying with the story. I thought it was really bold of her to read that story out loud. It took pretty much the whole class time, and all that time students kept looking at me as if I was a leper or a worthless bum, with pity or disgust. They couldn't have known about the lynching I saw. It had to be my beat-up face they were gawking at, deciding if the rumors they'd probably heard about how it happened were true. I had no clue what those rumors were.

After class I cornered Ledbelly and asked him what the hell. He shied away and didn't want to talk. But I kept at him as we walked outside and stopped under the portico to get out of the rain. It was a cold hard rain that covered our voices.

"I didn't get beat up on the west side, if that's what you're thinking," I said.

"Shit, then what did happen?"

"Is that what everybody thinks, then?"

"I don't know what anybody thinks. I thought it might've happened at the roller rink. You like to go down to that place, don't you?"

"Yeah, sometimes. But that's not where I was. Do you know anybody on the football team?"

"Yeah, sure. Who?"

"That punk Josh Winningham. Dudley Willard, too."

"They did it? What the hell are you messing around with seniors for? Winningham's just evil."

"I never talked to him before in my life. Till him and three of his buddies attacked me on my route. For no damn reason at all."

He looked at me disbelievingly. "You think I'm lying? … All right, then. You tell me why they jumped me. Huh?"

He kicked at something invisible and started to move on. I grabbed his jacket.

"C'mon now, Belly, be a sport. Tell me why I got my face beat in. Why did they do it, smartass?"

"Well, they probably did it, I'd guess."

"You'd guess."

"Yeah. But—Look, Sonny, I've known you a long time, right? We had some fun times. Right? But those guys, they'll beat up *anybody* they think's a niggerlover—Right?"

"What! Is that it?" I was stunned and that was all I could get out of my mouth.

I let Ledbelly go and headed on myself to my next class. I was getting looks by kids who knew me and some who didn't and, by their expressions, knew something about me they didn't like—and it wasn't my ugly-looking face.

Those seniors didn't beat me up for being a niggerlover. They didn't even know Harvey Nixon was my friend. How would they? For all they knew he was just a good Samaritan who happened by. But a black man coming to my rescue would've been why they spread that rumor around school while I had been out recuperating. It still wasn't why those boys tried to kill me.

Which reminded me to go to the grocery store after my route today, if it stopped raining. I wanted to take Harvey and his family a turkey for saving my life. I was going to buy the biggest one I could find.

I looked for Herman between classes but never saw him; he played hooky more than anybody I knew. I was wondering why he didn't say something to defend me while I was laid up so these rumors wouldn't spread. He probably thought the same thing about me, the more I thought about it. Then it occurred to me that maybe the seniors were the ones who punched on him too, not the jealous boyfriend or the redhead cop. It could've been the cop who had the football players take care of both of us. That was only a guess. And the question about Herman came down to whether he was a friend, my blood brother, or a traitor, Judas Iscariot.

Nobody the whole rest of the day asked me what happened to my nose or how did I feel. Thanks, everybody, for nothing.

Chapter 25

If the Moped hadn't broken down on me, I might have gotten away from the those guys. I could've darted into alleys, slipped in between houses without fences or clotheslines. I knew the area real well. If I'd had a Harley, I wouldn't have to go across lawns. I could just speed straight up streets. There was no way they would keep up with me on foot even if they'd been all-American running backs. And I could've easily outmaneuvered a high-powered Impala. You can lean a Harley at high speeds and I knew lots of narrow passageways and dark pockets where I could hide.

There was over $350 in my savings account; I only had Susie to spend money on now and since her mother had told her never to go on a date with me, she probably wasn't going to cost me anything anymore. Three hundred and fifty wasn't enough for a new Harley 165 but that much should get me a pretty good used one.

Stuart wasn't about to sell me his. But his was a Hummer, anyway, only a 125cc. Too little.

I rode the Baron down to the Harley shop to check out what they had and see if they would take mine in trade.

"You're shittin me," a mechanic in a jump suit said. He'd come out of the back shop to see what a guy riding a Moped wanted in a Harley store. It was a dumpy showroom which you could barely make out from outside, looking through those oily windows, and it smelled of gasoline and stale cigar smoke. It had some raunchy-looking bikes and some gorgeous ones on display. The mechanic said he ran the shop and made all the deals. The boss.

He laughed looking at the pathetic Baron, how it was all jury-rigged and looking like it wouldn't hold up for one more mile. I didn't let it bother me cause he was right, and he wasn't going to let a worn-out pedal-bike be seen in his Harley Davidson showroom, such as it was.

"How much for that one right there?" I pointed to a fire engine red 165 with fantastic chrome buckhorn handlebars. The buckhorns were sort of shaped like a couple of swans' necks back to back. Coolest bike I'd ever seen.

"That one? She's been sold already."

"You're shitting me." I wasn't going to take any of his crap. Why would it be on the floor if it'd been sold already.

The mechanic grinned off the side of his greasy fat face. "Tell you what, hotshot, that guy don't want her, I'd let this one go for three-twenty-five, not a damn penny less. How's that grab you, kid?"

I walked over to the bike, slowly, thumbs locked in belt loops with my fingers tapping against my jeans. I sat on it. There was a sticker on the gas tank that said "SPECIAL! $299." The son of a bitch. I checked it out, all shiny and looking brand new except for some burn on the chrome exhaust pipe and maybe a little wear on the handlebar grips. The chrome tailpipe wasn't factory, it'd been added. I'd bet it was a glass pack, too. It had a little over 2,000 miles registered on the odometer. Not bad.

"Mind if I crank her up? Take a listen?"

"Tole you. She's been sold already. Better git off."

"Let me crank her up and maybe I'll give you the three-twenty-five. Right now, cash up."

I didn't need Mother to co-sign; I was sixteen. I even had a driver's license. This was the bike I wanted and I didn't care if he was cheating me out of the twenty-five bucks that I could have used to buy a sissy bar for Susie, or any girl. Stuart would go crazy with jealousy when he saw it.

The mechanic chewed the cud and he squeezed pimples on the hairless part of his cheek. Then he wiped his nose with a rag that had dark grease on it. He was disgusting, even to look at. I wondered how Harley Davidson headquarters ever got some dope like him to run a business in a town big as Woodstock. Maybe he was a good mechanic, and I hoped so in case I ever needed him in the future, but he sure didn't belong behind a cash-register counter.

"I like you, kid," he finally said, to my surprise and pleasure. "I'll do it. Lemme get that sales tag off and you can roll her outside and crank her on up."

He gave me the red Harley for three-twenty-five but threw in the tax and also put a thirty-day guarantee on it that said the bike ran and wouldn't break down on me or he'd fix it. Insurance? Ha. Nobody ever got insurance on a motorcycle they paid cash money for.

I was glad that the chrome tailpipe didn't have a glass pack, which would've made it so loud I'd wake up the neighborhood on Sunday mornings. It was a regular muffler inside the chrome but still had that deep Harley grumble. Susie would have to ride snug with me and hold on.

I was so happy riding my new Harley that it wasn't until I found myself out State 131 halfway to Bessemer that I remembered the Baron, still leaning against the wall at the side of the shop. I didn't care; nobody would steal a rusty old Moped with its muffler tied to the frame and its puny little bicycle seat in shreds. The air hit my face like sand in a storm. The bike took the dips like it was supposed to, merely passing through clouds, and with those fat tires I could lean on the curves till the foot rests scraped. My mind filled with all kinds of plans, how I'd drag anybody who didn't have a V-twin, what girls from school I'd take on joy rides, or just riding up and down Mason Street showing off my new Harley.

The next day before throwing papers, I gave Bag-a-bones a lift to the shop so he could wheel the Baron home. I decided I'd let him have it for nothing.

Chapter 26

Doctor Joe took the news of my beating pretty hard. He blamed himself. I figured he'd get over it sooner or later and so I just kept it out of our conversation when we met to play tennis the next Saturday. Jeanne was with him again, so it wasn't hard to keep our talk on other things. I wasn't sure if he'd clued Jeanne in on the investigations, but the fickle way I felt about her anymore I didn't much care one way or the other.

Since my nose was still a little swollen and there were splotches of blue and black under the eyes, Doctor Joe didn't want to take us to the country club where I'd get the contemptuous stares, so we waited at Clayton Park for a court to open.

Spring weather brought people out of the woodwork and there were plenty of them in the park. I idled Red slowly around the parking lot and up close to the number one court where people mulled around, halfway watching some hard pounding match that was going on. I gunned it before shutting down the bike. Just showing off. I'd already named my bike *Big Red*, after the army unit Nookie Grimes's old man served in during the war, The Big Red One. Cause it was red and it was as tough and gnarly-sounding as his old man.

The three of us would play a rotation game rather than inviting a single to join us. Doctor Joe popped open a fresh can of Wilson balls as Jeanne and I took the frames off our rackets. We all did some stretches, Doctor Joe jumping around on his toes like he was back on the football practice field. Jeanne was looking Jeanne-gorgeous in her white tennis outfit, that short skirt rising when she bent over to pick up a ball. It was pretty hard to see her as just a tennis player. I tried anyway. She bragged she played a lot with her sorority sisters but I doubted that. She could hardly keep the ball in the court. But she also admitted she wasn't very good. Making an admission wasn't like her, but it was something in her favor, the way I saw it.

"Harvey Nixon punched out the punks that attacked me. He saved my life," I said.

"Huh?" said Jeanne.

Doctor Joe did one of his famous facial grimaces, making it look like he was in excruciating pain. It may've been the best I'd seen. "That's good he was there for you, but it wasn't a very smart thing for him to do."

"Yeah, I know. He knows ... I took a turkey and a ham over to his house this morning and left it with his mother."

"Well, that was kind of you, Sonny," said Jeanne. "Who's Harvey Nixon?"

Doctor Joe said, "What did he do, exactly?"

"Four of them jumped me and Harvey happened to be making a delivery. He spotted me getting trampolined. He just popped a couple of their heads together and the other two ran. They're rich kids, live in the Woodlands. At least a couple of them, Dudley Willard and this punk with the Rams, Josh Winningham. I have a hunch why they jumped me."

"Trampolined? What *are* y'all talking about?"

I could see Doctor Joe hadn't kept her up and that I shouldn't say anymore. She didn't like being left out. She'd started to pout. He was going to pamper her.

He placed a hand on her shoulder, the size of it making her look small. "Honey, it's nothing to fret over. Did you notice Sonny's face?"

I couldn't believe it. He was being facetious. I noticed then that she still didn't have on an engagement ring.

"Of course I did," she said, sounding a little putout. "I was just wondering why nobody has said anything to me about it. Do I have to come right out and ask?"

I said, "I got into a fight, that's all. Happens all the time. It happens to me because I don't belong to a gang. I'm what you call an independent. Gangs like to pick on independents."

Doctor Joe shook his head with a wry grin. "That's not exactly correct. He was probably attacked because these rich-kid delinquents got wind he has a black friend. That would be Harvey. So they jumped him when they caught him alone. Cowards, basically. I know that doesn't bother your sensibilities, Jeanne—that Sonny can call a colored man a friend. Does it?"

"What bothers me, Joseph, is that you keep this stuff from me. Don't you know I'm taking poly-sci and I've got this liberal prof who's for the nigras' civil rights all the way?"

"Educated people usually are. But are you?" Doctor Joe sounded argumentative, like he was trying to get her riled up, again surprising me. I did know that he got riled hearing anyone call Negroes "nigras" because it was a patronizing, halfass effort to acknowledge Negroes as human beings. Maybe he thought she had no interest in civil rights, that she was too enamored with her own social life at Auburn University—where there was not one black student on campus—and maybe that bothered Doctor Joe's own sensibilities. It did mine when I found it out.

When Jeanne headed back to her pout, I stepped in. "We're both a couple of the biggest niggerlovers you ever saw. Right, Joe?"

He frowned. He also rolled his eyes. I knew I sounded like a yokel but I didn't care. I wanted her to hear it so she'd know that I was in with Doctor Joe on something that might not include her, which was something like an admission I was jealous and envious and maybe even halfway in love with Jeanne Cochran.

"Let's play some tennis," said Doctor Joe, somehow looking content. "Jeanne, you ready to take on the boys?"

Chapter 27

I thought I knew what Miss West's story was about. I raised my hand soon as she asked, "Well, class, did you give Mr. Faulkner's story some thought over the weekend? I hope you all had a wonderful weekend, by the way. Yes, Sonny Poe. I see you're eager to give your interpretation. We'll start with you then."

"Well—Oh, thanks about having a good weekend. Mine was great." I didn't tell them why cause it would have just sounded like I was bragging that I'd gotten a Harley Davidson motorcycle and they hadn't, but I wanted to.

"Why, thank you, Sonny. Go right ahead."

"I was thinking that those guys didn't really know what happened to the old spinster woman, what'shername, or even if anything actually did happen to her. But they didn't have any trouble blaming that colored boy for perpetrating a crime—"

Some giggling stopped me. I guess it came from me using the word "perpetrating." Herman had had the same silly response. I'd learned that word in my investigations for Doctor Joe—in this real-life case meaning the awning company and some dirty cops, the perpetrators. He'd used it sometime, I guess.

"No, I mean, there was the barber, the only good guy in the story, you know, who had enough sense to be reasonable around a bunch of hotheads. I think the whole thing is about what happens when you make a rumor that might not be true, how instead of solving anything it only causes problems. In this story it caused a murder. They didn't have to lynch that guy. They didn't even have a reason, other than—"

And then I heard the word itself whispered from behind me, loud enough for the whole class to hear: *"Niggerlover!"*

I turned, despite what Miss West had taught us about looking back. I wasn't the only one looking at Chucky Barnes. He glared back at me with a self-satisfied grin and then around the room. He might as well have stood up and taken a bow the way other kids reacted, doing everything but applauding. Nobody looked offended but me, I guess. Maybe Miss West. I looked at the faces around Chucky; a couple of boys were even nodding, to show him he had their vote.

"Whoever said that stand up right now," Miss West roared. "I will not tolerate any such language in my classroom ... Who was it?"

She was looking straight at Chucky but she couldn't prove it was him anymore than I could. But the class was not going to get down on him, or, as in my imagination, get a rope and string up the tub of lard. Not because they didn't know he said it; they did. But because his saying it brought into light just what they wanted to hear. They wanted the niggerlover's head.

It was a meaningful moment for me personally. I could see into my near future some more black-and-blues coming. But at least it confirmed the rumor about me. Now I knew what I was up against at school. One more worry I had for my health.

The road ahead was vague; I couldn't see myself, for instance, going through two more years at Woodstock High School.

But what I saw for my friend Harvey Nixon was a lot scarier and made me a lot more nervous than I was for myself. It wasn't just rumored that he beat up some white boys. It was a known fact. I would've bet my new Harley that the Klan was already plotting their deadly revenge. What I didn't want to see in my imagination but saw anyhow was a pair of dangling legs in the dead of the forest night.

But Harvey Nixon was not like the Negro in "Dry September." He wasn't about to go down without a fight.

Chapter 28

It might have been convenient for Doctor Joe that the school groundbreaking ceremony was on Wednesday, his afternoon off, but it wasn't for me. I had to skip school after lunch to get there before it began and I was going to miss algebra.

The plan called for building a new elementary school right on the corner where me and Herman staked out the altered traffic light, Fourth and Richards. They were supposed to tear down the old McMillan Mining building and erect a three-story schoolhouse. With a playground in the place of the dilapidated building next door. It would serve the children in Ash Town and outlying areas as well.

The last thing Doctor Joe said to me about this event was, "Don't go, understand?" So I hid Big Red three blocks away in the alley parking lot of the Hello Cafe, where the smell of barbeque filled the air. White folks didn't go to the Hello but I had been there a couple of times and I could say those folks didn't know what they were missing. Flaky barbequed beef ribs with white loaf bread served on a heavy paper plate with a tall glass of cold milk. Harvey Nixon sent me.

The auto shop across the street from the activity was out of the way but close enough I could see the makeshift stage and gathering, so I settled in there to watch. Nobody seemed to be around at the garage or inside the tiny office. Mechanics aren't doctors who take off Wednesday afternoons, especially when they were Negroes who didn't make squat for a living. They were either gone because of this event or sleeping underneath a couple of jacked-up cars in the garage. There was a rocking chair out front that I stood behind, under an overhang that put me in the shadow. The lumberjack shirt I wore blended right in with the red brick. I stayed quiet and still. That infamous 4th St. traffic light hung in a direct line between me and the event.

There were cars parked on all four streets of the intersection, except where people were. Mostly Chevys and Fords but also a few fancy Oldsmobiles and there were two black Cadillacs on the Richards Street side.

I was a little disappointed not to see a high school band or any festivities for that matter. It was supposed to be a celebration, after all. The crowd wasn't as large as the congregation gathered for the courthouse preacher on a Saturday morning. Doctor Joe said he called all nine Board of Education members to attend and had Benson Roy, his Civil Service assistant, try to round up as many teachers as he could. He said it was to "make a show of force to recognize the positive impact on education in our black community." I remember his words cause he sounded like he was practicing a stump speech and I asked him jokingly if maybe he was planning to run for public office. I couldn't tell if he thought I was being serious but he answered, looking pleased, as if I were serious, "You never know what I'm likely to do, my man. But I'll do whatever I can," and blah blah blah.

I thought, yeah, he's going to make a run at it some day. Maybe, when I went to college, I could be one of his aides or pages or whatever you called congressmen's gofers.

None of those invited people showed up except a couple school board members and Mr. Roy. There were no blacks on the district school board, of course. The others probably just didn't see any reason to come or couldn't get off work.

A kid on a bicycle and one on roller skates heading down the street stopped like the suddenly panicked Road Runner when they spotted the line of uniformed policemen, at which they skedaddled back the way they came, toward Ash Town.

People milled restlessly on the sidewalk in front of the boarded-up factory, like they were anxious for someone to start the thing. I counted a total of six white people, all men. Chief of Police Vernon "Bulldog" Bradley wore a black uniform that made all the gold ornaments and stripes on his coat jump at you like fireworks. I recognized Mayor Tompkin in his standard three-piece suit that was always too loose and then Doctor Joe and Mr. Roy. Doctor Joe had on a muted yellow blazer over an open-collared shirt and beige slacks, looking loose and snazzy. The other two white men wore fancy pinstripe suits, which made me think they were the yankees from Washington. Doctor Joe stood there patiently with hands clasped in front and managing an expression that meant to show he was pleased with all things. Except for the six cops that I didn't count as anybody, others in attendance were black folks, several women among them, wearing bright dresses and big droopy hats, quick-stepping around with smiles on their broad faces. There was no traffic at all and the air felt heavy from the silence of it.

I knew they were here somewhere, I just couldn't spot them. Their invisibility spooked me more than if I'd seen them somewhere lined up in their white pointy hoods. At least when you can see your enemy you know what you're up against. I wondered if Doctor Joe felt the same. He didn't look around or act like he was concerned at all with the Klan. I knew he hadn't forgotten that cop on the phone telling him they were going to disrupt the groundbreaking; he was just being cool, being himself.

One of the fancy suits finally clapped his hands and then stretched his arms wide as if there were thousands of people in front of him. It reminded me of Reverend Carmichael inviting the flock down to the podium to be saved by Jesus. I had done it twice, once just to help Herman down to the rail after the Spirit grabbed him so fast and hard it took away his legs. Jesus didn't stick with me either time; Herman, I wasn't sure about.

"Okay, we'll have all four distinguished men next to me cut this ribbon to commence the groundbreaking for your new Archibald Grimké

Elementary School. Ah, in just one moment," the man said in a yankee accent that tried to sound Southern but failed miserably. "But first let me welcome your distinguished mayor and chief of police. Mayor Tompkin, Chief Bradley. Gentlemen, take a bow, please."

Neither the mayor nor the chief bowed but they did produce strained grins that made them look like embarrassed schoolboys. I might have laughed if it had been funny.

The speaker mispronounced a couple of the people's names and then made a big show of taking a pair of hedge clippers the other man in a shiny suit held out like the winner's trophy. That man had pulled the clippers out of a duffle bag on the sidewalk. All four put their hands on the handles of the hedge clippers.

A short Negro woman snapped pictures with a box camera held under her chin. There was no way she was a photographer with the *Star*. The only black people working for the paper I'd seen were janitors, which made the newspaper more progressive than most businesses in Woodstock. She must have been a yankee. She zipped around, weaving in and out of people to take her shots. I found myself wanting to break from my cover and run out there to talk to her about her work cause I liked the idea of being right out in the middle of an activity no matter what it was, snapping pictures that would capture just what was going on. I thought about the night of the lynching and what might have come of it if I'd gotten shots of the Klan clubbing and hanging that man. It would have made the front pages of newspapers all over the country, all over the world, and then that poor Negro would have been somebody. A picture of them roping and hoisting the blood-stained body, that would have made all those yankees and congressmen stand up and take notice of just what in hell's wrong down here, of what the Civil Rights Movement was for. That nameless victim who didn't even get an obituary in the *Star* would've become famous, I'd have bet.

The woman photographer suddenly turned her camera away from the crowd and I looked to see why. The two kids on the bike and skates were back. Behind the boys was a group of black men and women walking in a line wide as the street. They'd come out of Ash Town.

The yankee at the podium saw them and lowered the hedge clippers and fell silent. Seeing him stare, everyone else turned and those smiling faces suddenly dropped cold. If there had been a band, the drum would have gone silent and the clarinets squeak out a final rough note. The photographer snapped and wound until her camera ran out of film and she had to reload.

Doctor Joe stood in what had been the back of the crowd but now was in front facing the line of Negroes, who stopped about twenty feet off. Harvey Nixon was among them. A woman I recognized stood next to him, his wife, I thought. I looked for Jesse, the bootlegger, but didn't see his face. The group looked like they'd all just got off work and hurried right on over here. I couldn't imagine they were armed, though I suppose they could've had weapons hidden in their coats. But they didn't look angry.

The two kids hung behind. I didn't recognize until then that the boy on the skates was Harvey Nixon's boy, those skates had been his birthday present. He didn't smile so I couldn't see the braces Doctor Joe made for him.

Surprising everyone there and especially Chief Bradley, Doctor Joe spoke and spoke loud. "Come on up here and be part of this event. It's your new school that will open here. This is a celebration, folks."

And they moved closer. Doctor Joe held out a hand like he wanted to shake every person's as they came closer. I wish I'd thought to bring my Brownie.

I watched the six police officers draw weapons then and hold them by their legs and stand with their feet separated. I thought, *Watch out, people*. Still standing on the wooden porch of the auto shop, I looked everywhere for a white robe. Where the hell were they? Could his informant have been wrong?

Most of the people in the original crowd seemed paralyzed at first, then they started to shift around again except now they looked a lot more nervous and awkward, like a chain gang that scrambles without going anywhere. I think they all sensed something was about to happen and that they were at the heart of it. It seemed to me like Mayor Tompkin wanted to get his famous smile working but wasn't having any luck. He kept looking to Chief Bradley to take control. I thought he was fed up with the whole situation and wanted the chief to lock up the entire mob. But nobody was rowdy, nobody was shouting. The group of about 30 Negroes, who'd strangely appeared there like ghosts out of the old Overton District, just stood there without moving. They didn't seem to want to join in. I was hoping they had stepped out to demand justice for the illegal awnings forced on them, which some of these officials knew about. Maybe they didn't know what to do next. They needed someone to lead them and he was standing right there with his hand held out to them. Doctor Joe.

All kinds of feelings took painful swipes at my heart, fear, shame, feeling cowardly because I hid in the shadows and did nothing. Harvey Nixon knew me; I believe he trusted me and maybe I could help persuade them to join with Doctor Joe. Maybe they would even start a protest, right here, right now. But something far more poignant and sorrowful occurred just then, and it hit me hard and deep, something that would bury itself into my core and stay there for as long as I lived.

The blast of the gunshot quelled every movement in my vision, and people looked where I looked. His new skates remained laced and lay lonely on the street, as if they'd been dropped on the back porch after using. The boy on the bicycle fell over and seemed to hug the asphalt, and the boy who'd been in the roller skates lay a few feet away, still and facing the sky. A sea of red stained the pair of overalls on his lifeless small body.

I didn't even know Harvey Nixon's son's name when it was my fault he was now dead.

Chapter 29

It was the hardest thing I'd ever done in my life, going to that boy's funeral. His name was Harvey Nixon, Junior and they called him "Junior." He was only eight years old. There was so much crying going on that no one had the will or the energy to be mad. It was just so sad.

They had the Zion Baptist Church children's group sing the Battle Hymn of the Republic and it tore out my heart. I couldn't find a voice to sing with them and not many others could, either. Even the black children of the choir had a rough time at it, having to read the words and be as brave as they could to labor through the task.

Doctor Joe stood by me. He was dark, and not just because of what he wore. It was like a black cloud had engulfed him. I'd never seen his face so grim or his eyes so dark. His eyes got moist but he held up strong against his emotions. I knew he wanted to let go and bawl like the rest of us. He was human and a freedom fighter and he felt the pain of that boy's death as much as I did. But he stood tall and held my shoulder to keep me from sinking into the quicksand under my feet.

There were some other white people there too, my mother and little brother Chance and a few I hardly knew and now wanted to know. The sorryass mayor and police chief didn't show up but a platoon of cops did, looking like Nazis storm troopers in their high boots and shiny-brimmed hats. They stood in a strake line in the back of the church and later way back in the cemetery yard. Most of the other whites were strangers, yankees and news people from Birmingham and Montgomery and Atlanta and who knows where else. That little black woman who had taken pictures at the event was also there. I didn't even think about talking to her today. Doctor Joe showed me a copy of the *Atlanta Constitution* which ran pictures on the cover that he said were hers. In one of the pictures the dead boy lay on the grass where the blast had knocked him down and another shot of his skates in the street and a picture of Jackson's Auto, from where they determined the shot had come. You could make my image out in the picture but only as a shadow. I hoped they wouldn't start asking questions about the shadowy figure. I'd probably end up getting accused of being a lookout or maybe even the shooter.

Nobody there saw the person who fired the shot. The coward did it from inside the garage. The loudness from the gunshot still rang in my left ear. I thought I'd gotten a glimpse of the man, of several figures scrambling out the back. They weren't wearing robes. I couldn't tell if they were white or black. That might be useful to know because if they were Klan then that meant they would have earlier run the shop employees out on some threat and hidden inside and waited it out, like jackals in the dark. And the real mechanics could identify the men. If they only would.

There was only the one shot and it had a clear purpose—the Klan getting its revenge on Harvey Nixon for attacking the white boys who beat me up. *Me.* That's what it came down to. If it hadn't been for me befriending Harvey in the first place, this would never have happened. But as I thought about it, Harvey would probably have helped anybody out of a jam like the one I was in. He was good to the bone, and any fair-minded person would know his action was the heroic act of a foolish man.

Chapter 30

It's funny the things you might do to take out your anger over something.

The day after young Harvey Jr.'s funeral, I put on a pair of hard-toed boots before delivering papers. They were Stuart's army surplus boots, but he didn't wear them. I never saw them on his feet even when he sometimes meticulously polished the boots at night. I asked him once recently, "What the hell you use those clodhoppers for, anyway? You don't wear them."

"Kick butt," was all he said. Gang activity, I figured. But I guess that was a fair answer, and that was what I intended to use them for too, to kick butt, or rather hopefully a bulldog's choppers.

It was a weekday and on weekdays Chief Bradley was at work, probably right now collecting his share of illegal payoffs that patrol officers collected from speed traps they had set up around and outside town. Doctor Joe said the police, like the county sheriff's boys, worked on a fee basis, which meant they got a cut of the fines once they were paid to the court. I would've bet it was illegal as hell to do that, somewhere in the United States Constitution or the state code. But law agencies in states and cities and counties and even unincorporated areas around the Deep South used the fee-basis system on a regular basis to cheat people out of money.

Chief Bradley's wife went out to do her shopping in the afternoons when I was tossing papers and she would put the dog in the yard behind a short chain-linked fence where the ground had long been dug up around the corner posts. I guess neither one of the Bradleys cared whether the dog got out, or they would've filled in those holes. But then, he was the chief of police, who was going to complain. But that dog was a menace not just to me but the whole neighborhood where little tots rode merrily up and down the sidewalks on tricycles and kids jumped rope and young girls played hopscotch. They called their stubby bulldog Rex, and Rex especially didn't like anybody on wheels; he was just as ferocious going after little trikers as me.

Well, now I was on the back of Big Red rumbling through the neighborhood, and I could go a lot faster than the wheezing predator could on those stubby legs. Old Rex had been chasing me for years and never drawn blood, although he'd gotten hold of my pants many times and a few times tore them. Back when I rode the Flyer and even the Baron, I had to sneak up on the chief's house, toss his paper then pedal like hell to get out of there before Mad Rex heard the paper hit and made it under the fence. He especially hated me and my whistling jeers when I'd get by him without him seeing me. He probably wanted revenge on me as much I did on him.

The house where Rex resided was downhill from the block before, so I could idle silently by and then throw the paper; that didn't wake him. By now he seethed up a lather appreciating that I could give him the slip.

I didn't have to worry about him catching me on Big Red, but today I purposely took it slow, gassing it a little in advance to give him time to tear under the fence and get all worked up in a snarl of foam and drool, going into his phlegmatic breathing like he might croak before he reached me. You might call me a mean and nasty dog hater after hearing what I did next, but I liked dogs as well as anybody. It was just that Rex had it coming; he'd intimidated every kid up and down the block way too long and it was time he learned some dog manners.

The chief's block was early in my route and I skipped it and came back when I'd finished slinging papers so I wouldn't be weighted down for a quick getaway. The sun was still high enough that it wouldn't get in my eyes as I honed in on the snarling beast.

The only thing I could feel when I made contact with Mad Rex's jaw was a jolt up my leg. The contact was solid. I braked and turned in time to see him still in his back flip tumble. I almost felt sorry for the little devil, but I got over that quickly. Rex picked himself off the street and wobbled off in the wrong direction from home. He was dazed. I thought I heard him moan. I never heard a bulldog moan. He plopped on the grass between the street and sidewalk and lay his drooping chops between his paws and then I did feel bad.

I got off the bike and walked over to him, slowly cause I didn't trust Rex at all. Then, lying on the street where I got to him was the thing I wanted to see. A tooth. A fang. I forgot about checking out Rex and picked up the tooth, wiped the blood off on the grass, and examined it. It was whole. A perfect hit on the very first pass. How lucky was that?

I tore off the longest loose string from my *Woodstock Star* paper bag and tied it tight around the grossly yellowed tooth where it was indented at the gum line so that it was like the pendant on a necklace—later I could get Doctor Joe to drill a hole through the root and I'd use a fishing line. I hung it off Red's speedometer so that the tooth flashed in the sun, hanging like the booty of a conquering cavalryman. I wasn't at all ashamed that the conquered menace was a dog in the place of a ruthless Klansman. You had to start somewhere.

Chapter 31

"Get on up! Both you boys, out of bed, *now.*"
Mother's voice could be harsh, especially on Saturday morning when she had no toleration for anything, us sleeping past seven, say.

I pried open my eyes to see her looming in the doorway, hands on her hips like a mule driver. "I mean it. Let's go, Stuart, Sonny. Up! Chance has been up for half an hour already ... Today's your father's anniversary, in case you two didn't remember."

Meaning not the anniversary of his death or their wedding but his birthday. She wouldn't say "birthday" though, she always said "anniversary" for some strange reason. It meant we had to put on our Sunday school suits and go to the cemetery and lay some flowers down and listen to her prayer for him. And then get a lecture about being no-accounts.

Stuart didn't argue with her. He crawled out of his side of the bed and grunted like a bear sniffing through the woods. I knew it wouldn't work throwing the pillow over my head and forgetting my surroundings, kind of like the ostrich burying its head in the ground. I could see the humor in that comparison and went ahead and got up.

After some chores and breakfast—Mother cooked up grits, biscuits and scrambled eggs, one of her wonderful specialties—we put on the charcoal suits she'd bought on discount for taking three of them. And that was the after-Christmas sale Christmas before last. None of the suits fit us now but we had to wear them cause it was "tradition" to dress up for Pops's "anniversary." We piled in the Chevy, Mother driving slow as a grandmother, and went across town to the westside where the graveyard was, Oakwood Gardens, and drove the quiet little lane that curved through some ancient eastern hemlocks and Jack oaks around to where Pops lay at rest under a modest headstone in the shadow of one of those hemlocks.

The day was bird-chirping, a clear, warm, chigger-free winter day, and the cemetery was as countrified and serene a place as you would ever see. It might have brought joy to visitors just because they were alive and able to enjoy the wide-open beauty whereas their loved ones at their feet could not. But it wasn't joyous. It wasn't joyous to anybody who came there just because of the reason you went to a cemetery, to reflect on life being over. Death. It wasn't because my father was buried here that I didn't feel any joy, not today, but because I kept thinking about an eight-year-old boy who would never grow up, who couldn't hear a bird chirp or feel the warm sun, not a damn thing ever again.

Mother made us take hands after she placed two roses in the cup on the left side of his headstone, which had only Pops's vital statistics printed on it, no Mark Twain poem or cheerful quotation to reflect the lively personality older men had told me he had. I noticed Stuart and Chance both pulling on the butts of their tight pants. I guess I'd been doing it too.

"Lord have mercy on our souls," Mother said, looking not at Pops's plot but straight out into the trees and blue sky. "We hope and pray that Buddy has not left your kingdom, that he's been good enough to stay another year. Amen."

"Amen," all us boys went and swiftly let go hands and stood away from each other. Now we were suppose to privately reflect on Pops with good thoughts. I tried to just remember what he looked like since there weren't many memories I had of him. He was so tall I could barely make out his face up there and that made it hard to draw a mental image of him now. I knew he had a face like a skeleton. It was narrow and bony with inset dark eyes and black eyebrows. Nothing like my face, I thought, although one man who knew him commented on how much I looked like ole Buddy.

But Pops had a smile you could remember. Big and wide and lots of white pickets showing in the middle of his shadowy face. He had a way of teasing me with his eyes and hands that I could never guess where they would come from before they attacked. Usually get me somewhere in the ribs but lots of times on the feet when I was in pajamas, or behind my knees. I would almost faint from riding so high up on his back or shoulders.

Mother said Pops was not ordinarily a religious man, but when his drinking got so bad that it affected his work and began to make him sick, he finally saw the light and took to God.

I remember getting snippets out of Mother about his death. She wouldn't say much about it, just that his accident was divine providence or luck of the Irish or his fate. "Wasn't his destiny," she said adamantly, "cause his destiny was success." She added, "But I guess it was too late to reach God when your father finally came calling."

And I had said, "But I thought God forgave everybody. He's suppose to forgive you of your sins for nothing in return. All you have to do is just asked Him, right? Isn't that right?"

"Evidently, that wasn't the case with your father. The drinking killed him even when he tried to ask forgiveness. He was just too far gone, Sonny."

I wanted to know what she meant by "even when he asked forgiveness." Nobody in the family would tell me much after he died. Uncle Tommy who was my favorite uncle told me that Pops tried his damnedest to put the bottle down and went to the preacher for help and that was when he had his accident.

I didn't give up seeking answers, and after a long time I was able to finally piece it together. Pops had been out drinking after he'd made his pledge to stop and felt so guilty for breaking the promise that he made his way through the woods to the preacher's home late at night looking for something, forgiveness, God's mercy maybe. Drunk as a coot, he probably thought he was doing the right thing. He got close enough to see the light in the window of Reverend Carmichael's but he couldn't see the ground in front of him. That was the light that might have brought him everlasting salvation, but then he tripped in a rock bed and stumbled head first into the stream that was running high. The fall knocked him out and broke his neck. That light in the reverend's house went out just about the same time as he must have drowned.

Out early the next morning to pick blackberries, Mrs. Carmichael found him. That was on the Fourth of July.

God must have decided Pops shouldn't reach the preacher and He let him go. He could have uncloaked the moon so Pops could see where he was stepping. He sure didn't forgive Pops, which was all my father was after. Just simple forgiveness. Was his drinking such a bad sin that there could be no redemption? Pops never hurt me or my brothers. God wouldn't acknowledge my father's humility and answer his call, and that's why I couldn't trust Him. And goddamn Him for it.

I didn't want to think God let him go because Pops hired blacks in the kitchens of his restaurants, even when it was breaking the law under Jim Crow. But I vaguely remember there was a big uproar in the church when he put a Negro over the griddle. Surely that wasn't an unforgivable sin, especially since the customers didn't stop coming. They came cause the food those black cooks cooked was delicious. Pops had a fried pork chop on his lunch and dinner menu at Buddy's Café with potatoes and gravy customers raved about, that kept them coming back. I guess good food let you slide with Jim Crow.

I knew something bad was coming when Mother took me aside to have "a little talk;" we walked behind the hemlock, blocking out my brothers who stood around looking bored. I thought it was probably about making her go with me to Harvey Junior's funeral. She'd never been to a Negro church in her life and I knew that alone had made her awfully uncomfortable. I was glad she went, though.

"Sonny, about Doctor Peach. I—I've been hearing things, Sonny," she said very somberly, almost apologetically.

Not much could throw me for a loop after what I'd already been through, but that did. I should've known bad rumors were bound to start circulating sooner or later. Still, it made me feel guilty. "It's just awful things I'm hearing, son. I want you to tell me it's not true. That he's a good man, that he's just generous and kind and that's all."

"Not true. Whatever you heard is not true, Mother. They're rumors because he's on the Civil Service Commission and he's trying to get some people jobs and better pay. Frankly they are colored people, Mother, and people don't like it around here when anybody wants to help out Negroes."

"Who-what people are you talking about?"

She didn't know anything and I didn't have the energy to try and explain it; Mother was a simple white Southern Christian woman, just a mother who worked hard at making a living for three infantile sons. "I hardly ever see Doctor Joe. But I know he's just trying to do what's right. He doesn't tell me what's going on. Okay?"

She mulled that over and then said, totally off the wall, "Your Uncle Tommy wants to take you hunting. I want you to go."

"Okay, sure. Deer hunting?"

"I believe. Can you get that Carlile Oldham boy to substitute for you? I think you can depend on him."

"Better him than asking Stuart, right?"

She glared. She knew as well as I did you couldn't depend on Stuart to sub even though he had time and could get to work at the store after. Stuart thought throwing papers was beneath him. In my opinion somebody needed to bring him down a notch or two. But it wasn't going to be Mother.

She wasn't through with me. I could see in her focused eyes she wanted to make sure I didn't escape without some lesson. "I don't like it that you bought that motorcycle, Sonny. It goes too fast, it's dangerous."

"I guess."

"You didn't use good common sense spending all your savings on one thing, anyway."

"Yeah, but I don't nearly get run over anymore."

Chapter 32

I was shining the chrome on my "dangerous" Harley when Nookie Grimes drove up in a boxy old '46 Chevy Fleetmaster. Big car painted a puky baby blue that looked like the paint had been slapped on with a dried-up brush. It had uneven streaks down the side and paint on the chrome, on the hood ornament and grill, and on the silver rings holding in the bug-eyed headlamps. I started to ask him if he'd painted it but something else entirely came out of my mouth. "Stuart's still at work."

I am pretty sure I mentioned that Nookie used to be my friend and Stuart stole him. Or looking at it another way, that he sold me out for Stuart and the Dukes cause Nookie wanted to belong to a gang and he only used me to get there. I guess he was considered too much of a two-timer to get into a real gang, like the Outlanders, the raunchiest gang in town, probably cause he didn't have the guts to eat a greasy rat.

A couple of other boys were in the car too. He got out but they stayed put.

"That's all right, Sonny. Don't really care, cause I was hoping to see you."

"Oh, yeah? ... That your latest car? Nice color."

He looked at the bulky Chevy. Other than its puky color, it looked more like a gangster's car than Herman's old man's '49 Rocket 88 cause it was so big. You could probably stuff seven or eight guys in there, each of them with tommy guns swinging out the windows.

"The old man painted it," he said sorrowfully. "Said he used to paint at Ford over in Marietta. That would've been before he got fucked up, even before I was a gleam in his sorryass eye."

"I always liked your old man." It occurred to me to tell him I named Big Red after his old man, or his army unit, but I didn't think he deserved to know it.

"Anyways, what're you up to tonight?"

I didn't answer. I didn't have any plans but I didn't want him knowing that. It was Saturday. I wasn't going to a basketball game or to a movie or a dance or a party. I didn't have a date. I had nothing to do but stay home and watch Lawrence Welk with Mother. Jesus.

"Prob'ly got a date. Waiting around to find out for sure. Why, what's up?"

"Man, you don't want a date," he said excitedly. "We're going to Georgia to get drunk. I thought of you cause you said you'd been once and knew where the cheapest beer was."

That was true. I had told him that, but I was lying through my teeth. I just wanted him not to run off with Stuart.

When I didn't respond he said, "You won't have to pay for any of the gas. Whadda you say, man? We're gonna get *drunk*."

"Okay, sure. Hell yeah."

"All right. We'll be by to get you around seven. Be ready."

I'd never gotten to go to Georgia and it was something I really wanted to do. I heard you could get a gallon-pitcher of beer for seventy-five cents at the bars in Kantville and a couple places on the Chihegee County road, which were the closest after the state line, and they didn't even ask you for an ID.

Seven o'clock rolled around and so did the puky baby blue Fleetmaster. Mother'd made her famous spaghetti and Herman didn't show up to eat after he'd been invited. That was peculiar. Herman never missed Mother's spaghetti. I figured he had a date that was just too hot and it was her or spaghetti. There was always a first time. So I had an extra helping.

"C'mon, man, let's hit it," Nookie hollered from the driver's window, his bare arm hanging limp outside the door. It was dark and chilly but the other boy in the front seat had his window down too, I guess for the cigarette smoke to escape.

I crawled into the backseat with the other kid, a heavyset hood type with greasy hair hanging down like it had been plastered on his forehead. "Hey, man, Sonny. Nice to meet you."

"Rick, you too." I shook his hand.

"You play football?" I asked, from his grip.

"Wrestle's all. How bout you?"

"Shit. Tell me you're kidding. I play tennis."

"Fucking girl's game, tennis."

"Yeah, you can pick 'em up pretty easy if you know how to play," I said, pissed but trying to salvage something.

The other boy wasn't but fifteen years old. He was going at that young age to Georgia to get drunk in a car driven by a wild man. That thought made me remember that I'd wanted to go to Georgia when I was thirteen, so I couldn't talk, I guess. His name was Butch something.

Nookie really was a wild driver. You had to go through a national forest to get to Georgia, meaning a windy, mountainous two-lane road where there were no lights, just reflectors at the sharp bends. There were about five dangerous sharp curves in several places and the homemade crosses and little Catholic shrines to the dead shined in our headlights as we screeched around those curves. There was some good lovers music on the radio, being Saturday night, like "Teen Angel" and "'The Great Pretender," but it just made Nookie sad and foot-heavy on the accelerator. My fingers dug into the door grip most of the way through the forest and I started thinking the trip would only be half done when we got there; we had to come back. It made me a little queasy wondering how that would turn out. I already regretted coming with these idiots.

The first place we got to after crossing the state line was only a liquor store, not a bar, so Nookie started questioning me cause I was the one supposed to know where it was and I told him I forgot, I was drunk, remember. I ran in the store and asked where a bar was and the guy said about a mile and a half from there. He was right. A joint called "Boondoggle's" was lit up with Christmas lights all around its exterior and beyond into the trees. The sign further said it offered pool, dancing and beer. It was our place.

It was crowded inside with all ages and kinds of people. Some of them didn't look a lot older than us but most were grown and dressed like they'd come out of the deep woods, wearing overalls and plaid shirts and baseball hats with stuff like "John Deere" and "Shakespeare Fishing Tackle" stamped on them. The scant number of women sat at tables in one area on one side; you couldn't tell much about them. Nobody was dancing. These people weren't college kids from Atlanta, that was for sure, but I still thought, Shit, Georgia. What a great state.

We grabbed a table soon as this couple left and ordered two pitchers of whatever they had on tap, which was Pabst or Falstaff or Jax. We got Jax. It cost more than seventy-five cents, though. But there were four of us to split it at fifty cents each.

Country music screamed from a jukebox. At the moment Loretta Lynn was ripping out a lively one about a honky tonk gal. Pool balls cracked on four tables. I was anxious to play. I put my dime inside the lip of the closest table. I played in the Y's pool tournament and thought I was damn good since in the last tournament I made it all the way to the semi-finals. I could bank and cross-bank and shoot long straight balls right into the pocket. And never took a lesson cause nobody taught pool; you just learned to play by playing.

The guys I was with all smoked and I had to bum one. Butch, the kid, gave me a Camel and a light and offered a kick in the butt to get my lungs going. We sat with our elbows on the table and Nookie said we should play a drinking game that was based on your ability to hold back a grin or a laugh when staring down another guy. The one who broke first didn't get to drink. I couldn't do it. It cracked me up just looking at the wrestler's chunky, pockmarked, stern face and then the pimples on the kid's oily, adolescent nose. I didn't find anything funny about Nookie's face. It was pale, sour, covered in alligator skin. So he caved in first and I polished off a tall one.

It didn't take long before everything was funny. I wasn't by myself begging to stop the stupid game.

Luckily, it was my time at the pool table. This lanky guy broke them for eight ball, the game of the house. I'd rather have played rotation, but who was I to challenge house rules?

He said, "You wanna play for a beer?"

"Nah, I got some already with my buddies over there."

"You wanna play for a dollar?"

"Nah, not yet. Gotta get warmed up first. You hold this table long?"

He didn't answer and that meant he was a hustler. So I beat him. It was bad luck that he scratched on the break. His break was so good that it scattered everything around the table and left the low balls in the best position and I ran the table on him. He never got another shot.

The next guy was an old timer with a gray beard and a potbelly. His cap read "Jesus Lives in Kantville." He looked like a tow-truck driver. He asked me the same thing. "You wanna play for a beer?"

He'd probably seen me run the table on the lanky guy and decided he'd show the kid a lesson. I figured right away that he was really good so I passed.

"You wanna play for a dollar?" he asked, just like the other fella. I thought it was déjà vu.

About then Floyd Cramer came on and I had to park my stick and listen to the start of his beautiful slip-noted piano in "Last Date." I didn't know how to say what it was about Floyd Cramer that I liked so much until Doctor Joe demonstrated his style on his piano. It made me appreciate him all the more.

"Well, do ya?" the tow-truck driver asked.

"Hell yeah, sure," I said.

I broke and separated them good but nothing went in. He pulled out a gorgeous stick from a carrying case and I thought, *Uh oh*. While he took his time screwing the parts together and chalking it up, I went over and finished off my glass of Jax and said, "I might have to borrow some money before the night's over."

None of them looked too happy with that. They probably didn't have as much money as I did and were going to hit me up for the next pitcher. Maybe that was the real reason Nookie wanted me to come. I knew he didn't have money, not with an old man that stayed too drunk to even work and a mother who was just as bad off, spending their welfare checks on booze and sometimes getting Nookie some Krystal burgers.

Nobody answered or even looked up at me. Both pitchers were just about empty. I quickly filled my glass, which emptied that pitcher, and then they all looked up, scowling like dogs showing their teeth. "Jesus, I'm only taking my share ... I got a game going. Be back in a minute."

The man didn't take a dollar out like I did, so I slipped mine into my front pocket instead of putting it on the rail. He had a couple of easy sinks then took a long bank shot that I would never have tried; he had easier shots. The cue had to fit between two of my balls in front of the pocket and there was hardly any light between them. And that was from the bank. I watched carefully to see if his ball would touch mine. If it did, he'd lose his shot. It didn't. He made it. It was a miracle shot. I'd been suckered by a real pro.

It wasn't until he shot his last ball before the eight that he got anxious and messed up. The cue scraped the eight ball before it touched his, knocking the angle off and his ball didn't fall. I chalked up the cue tip and powdered my hand and went to work. I guess I'd hit my peak beer level cause I didn't miss another shot and left myself with a straight in on the eight. It fell and I said, "Good game."

"Double or nothing," he said. I couldn't tell if he was mad or just the quiet type. His face didn't show me anything.

"Okay, but isn't somebody else up?"

"Chester. He don't mind. I'll rack 'em."

"Okay," I said, but I was not pleased.

I guess they all knew each other over here in this neck of the woods. Maybe they were all kin. Chester must have been the guy leaning against the wall behind us. He didn't say anything and didn't seem in any hurry or bothered by having to wait longer, so I added, "All right, double or nothin'." I felt cocky enough to say, *Your funeral*, but figured it'd be better if I kept my mouth shut in a place where I was the stranger.

I couldn't believe how my stick was working. He had one chance, but I had left the cue trapped behind a cluster of my balls and all he could do was bank blindly and hope he hit something. They didn't play like we had to play at the Y. Here, you didn't have to call your shots so there was some chance of luck. But not for the truck driver with the potbelly and the fancy stick. This was a quicker game than the one before.

"Double or nothing," he said, same toneless voice as before. He was so stoic I couldn't figure him out. But then everybody here seemed to be like that. I looked around the smoky place. There may have been a dance floor over on the other side of the bar but nobody was dancing even though some great dance music—like Floyd Cramer—blasted from the jukebox. They all looked like, I don't know, like zombies, like a roomful of wigged-out John Carradines as Count Dracula. Except for the girls, but they just stayed seated, didn't smile or look at anybody. So I guess they qualified as zombies, too.

"Nah, that's enough," I said. "I need to drink. You can have the table, though."

I hung up the stick and waited for him to cough up the two bucks. He didn't seem begrudged to do it. "Thanks, play you again later, maybe," I said.

Looking for the bathroom, I couldn't help but notice two guys sitting cozy-like at a small table away from the action, like they were just observers. They didn't look like zombies; I thought they were beatniks. So I said, "Hey, cats, what's hanging?"

One of them wore a neatly trimmed beard. Both had long hair tied in the back and strong, nice-looking faces. One wore a sweatshirt with sleeves cut short at the elbows and baggy high-wasted slacks with a corduroy belt drawn real tight against his thin waist. He wore a gold necklace. The other guy had on a sea captain's hat and wore an unbuttoned flannel shirt over a T-shirt. They were drinking some foreign-looking beer out of the bottle. I needed to describe what they wore in detail because it was just what I thought beatniks would wear, and to show that they weren't just two more zombies. What were these two guys doing here, I wondered.

"Hey, daddy-o," one said brightly. "Not too much. How 'bout yourself?"

"It's a blast here, ain't it, man? Zombie land?" I said. "Where y'all from? Or going? Cause I know it's not anywhere around here."

"Ha. How true that is, friend. Well, let me put it to you like the poet might have it: We're riding the high, flying through space, time, money, just blasting through the mad universe. San Fran's where we're due." The guy talking looked at his gold wristwatch and he added, "And, cat man, we are very, very late."

"No shit? That's great, man. Boy, would I like to go there sometime. You driving?"

"Sweet Hudson coupe, right outside that door. So many miles, so many roads, hard to fathom. And—"

"That is why we write it down, cat," the other one said. "Say, you're a classy-looking kid, you from around here?"

"Hell, no. I'm from Bama."

"Eh, too bad ... Then, whadda you say, want to bug out to the coast? Free the bind, take to the road? Be a real mind-bender."

The thoughts and visions that suddenly poured into my mind were in themselves mind bending. I saw tall beautiful people who always smiled and walked about in the bright sunshine with a sense of fulfillment and wonder and without a pinch of hate in them. I saw the sign over our shop on Market Street: "Peach & Poe's Bistro and Troubadours," just like Doctor Joe and I had fantasized opening if we ever went to a big city together, like Atlanta. But San Francisco, man, that would be even greater, unbelievable.

"Big thought, huh kid? Well, someday. You be smart. It's cloying here, better you move on."

Dazed, like I was one of these zombies, I went back to my table and sat down where Rick was arm wrestling with Nookie and winning. The kid, Butch, looked drunk already. His head lolled.

"The next one's on me," I said brightly.

I ordered from the bar then went over to the jukebox and found one of my favorite singers and punched it to show those two cool cats I had some class even if I was from Alabama. But when I looked up and back at the lone table in the rear, I saw they were gone, already split for California, for San Fran. I visualized a sputtering coupe merrily speeding into a western sunset. Kind of like John Wayne on a horse but not quite.

We finished off the pitcher in about ten minutes, I'd say, and I decided to be the hero and get another one, choosing the Pabst Blue Ribbon draft this time. My song came on then and I started waltzing my way back to the table with the full pitcher in hand.

It was as if a dam broke and flood water swept through the place by the breathless reactions of the zombies, everyone of them looking drowned and dumbfounded, if the undead can look dumbfounded. I had to suppress a smirk of satisfaction.

The bartender came from around the bar, wiping his hands on a soggy rag for some weird reason. He cast a stern look around the room and said, "Who put that nigger shit on?"

He stared at me. I guess because I'd been dancing in slow hillbilly. I figured true Southern zombies like these would freak out when they heard Nat King Cole. I was right. I picked "The Very Thought of You," a magnificent song sung in the sweetest voice I ever heard. Doctor Joe had the album and we played it over and over.

"We don't allow that coon shit in here, boy," the skinny barhop said, staring me down.

"Well, how come it's on the jukebox then?"

I shouldn't have said that, but how could I resist. It was just so stupid to freak out over a damn song, especially a beautiful song.

The man's face swelled up like a cantaloupe and I thought it was going to explode. I wanted to laugh at him, his bloated hatred.

About then Nookie grabbed my arm. He said to the bartender, "We're going, sorry about that."

Rick jerked the kid up and we were out the door and in the Fleetmaster in about ten seconds flat. I guessed somebody would enjoy the pitcher of Pabst I left on the wet table.

Nookie made the tires spit gravel sliding onto the highway and we fishtailed away. We were heading the opposite way from Woodstock. He turned and said, "You're trouble, man. I can see why your own brother wouldn't let you in the Dukes ... We're gonna go on over to Atlanta and we're going to drop you at the next gas station I find."

"Atlanta? What the hell for?"

"Business. And none of yours."

"How'm I supposed to get home, huh?"

"We don't much give a shit, do we Rick? Call that guy with the T-Bird, see if he'll come get you."

I guess I was drunker than I thought cause that made perfect sense to me. "Assholes," I said lamely and hunkered down till they pulled off the road by a phone booth glowing like a huge bare light bulb.

It wasn't that late, about ten o'clock. I had enough money that I could have taken the Trailways home, but there probably wasn't one running this way till morning. I didn't think they traveled the county roads, anyway.

"Let's go, out," Nookie said. "You got a nickel for the phone? Want me to call for you?"

What a friend, I thought, don't do me any favors. But I said, "Yeah, you call."

"What's the number?"

The booth was only about three feet off the damn highway. The wind behind a big semi might've blown it right over, me inside. But there wasn't much traffic.

I dialed the number and gave him the phone. Nookie said I was this guy he met in a bar at the Georgia line and that I was drunk and getting into trouble. He told Doctor Joe I was at the second gas station he'd come to across the state line out SR-8. Nookie must have been halfway sober cause that was pretty good directions. "Better get here fast. No telling what he'll do ... No, I can't stay, just passing by ... Yeah, he gave me your number to call."

They left me standing by the phone booth. My jaw locked tight as I watched the boxy car disappear into the darkness of night, heading back toward home. The dirty bastard.

I went inside and had some potato chips and tried not to think anymore about how I got suckered again by that two-timing Nookie Grimes. I watched cars drift in and honk for the guy to come out and pump their gas. The Quaker State station was bright enough to sober you up, a billion watts of light blistering my eyeballs. There was only the one guy to pump gas and check the oil and he didn't move too fast.

"Closing up, you gotta go outside," he finally told me.

At least it wasn't raining. I sat down and leaned against one of the pumps. I didn't have to wait but an hour.

It wasn't the T-Bird that pulled in; it was our car and Mother was driving it.

"Get your butt in here, Sonny Poe. Right this minute," she said before she'd even come to a full stop. Doctor Joe was sitting by the window next to her. He didn't grin. He just looked serious.

I crawled in the backseat and shut the door and stared at the two gas pumps as still as tombstones.

"You smell like a brewery. Have you been smoking too?"

"Pretty much broke even," I said smugly and said hi to Doctor Joe. "How come you brought Mother?"

"Never mind how come he brought me. I'm here. You're drunk. You ought to be ashamed of yourself. Tomorrow you're going to church in the morning and there's no ifs ands or buts about it, do you hear me, mister?"

Doctor Joe wasn't talking. I couldn't see his hands; they were probably clasped together in his lap, the man of patience. He stared at the road while Mother drove. It was pitch dark in the national forest with nothing but woods on either side of us. When we passed into Alabama Doctor Joe watched both sides of the road. I was glad to be in the car, safe and sound, with people who cared about me.

Suddenly, Doctor Joe said, "There they are, Olivia, just as I thought. Maintain your speed."

I didn't see anything but an unlit billboard that showed the name of a stupid gas station, grabbing my eye with a buxom gal bending over just to show us some great tits and a scrumptious butt as she pumped gas into a car. Or maybe she was washing a car, I didn't see which and didn't much care.

Mother was driving at fifty-five mile an hour without altering the speed, regardless of the hills and curves. It made my stomach rise taking those "Slow Curve Ahead" turns at that speed. But I was still glad not to be coming back with Nookie behind the wheel.

I finally blurted from the back seat, "They couldn't stand the song

I put on." I still couldn't believe how those zombies reacted. "That's why they kicked us out, cause I played Nat King Cole. Bunch of Neanderthals."

Doctor Joe turned and grinned pathetically at me, like he might next pat the moron's head, like I was the Neanderthal. "I can see that," he said. "They almost killed him in a Birmingham performance four years ago. Boys from Woodstock … Who was the guy that called me? It wasn't one of your friends?"

"Yeah, used to be. Nookie Grimes. He's a traitor."

"You watch your manners, son," said Mother. "You know he's Stuart's friend. Besides, he comes from a tough place. It's hard on him." She didn't move her head an inch, just stared at me in the rearview. I shifted out of her view.

"Sonny, why do you think they dumped you?"

I didn't know, but it was getting clearer why. "I—I don't know."

"I can tell you it wasn't because you were responsible for your group having to leave," Doctor Joe said. "It was arranged before you left. They were laying a trap, Sonny."

"Yeah, I got it." I didn't want to talk about this in front of Mother, and I was wondering why he did after the rumors about him. Didn't he know she had heard about them? My head started to spin and hurt on the thought; I couldn't recall what I'd said about it. Knowing me, I probably hadn't said anything.

The thing coming clear to me was how dirty these people were. They set up this trip to catch Doctor Joe with me, drunk, on a lonely road at night. It was as scary a thought as my nemesis phantom cop lying in wait with his hatchet, and it was real.

I looked at Mother's red face looming in the glow of dashboard light. She had fallen into a driving trance and didn't sway from her steely-eyed focus, gripping the big wheel hard enough that her pointy knuckles looked like little pearl onions. I hadn't ever seen her so tense. I wondered what Doctor Joe had told her on the way to get me. He must have told her something about his investigations, about me.

I leaned my head against the window, and that's all I remember of that night.

Chapter 33

I probably wouldn't have taken the class if the Y hadn't offered it for free. But they did, so I started my "Body Building for the Atomic Age" on Saturday morning. I could barely walk or even move a chair on that first Sunday. It got better as I lifted and I worked out every other day in the Y's gym. I could already feel my muscles getting harder and bigger after just two weeks. It was great to feel strong. The instructor said building your body would give you tremendous confidence and you wouldn't be afraid anymore.

It was true. Already I no longer feared the phantom cop's presence. I didn't think about his swift blade raised in the air when I stepped in that dark closet and when I sped down that narrow alley. The phantom stopped chasing me and I slept fairly peacefully with the crabapple shadow on the wall, even as the wind blew the shadows just as hard in the springtime as it did in the winter.

I wondered what I would do if Gerald Henry decided to pop me on the nose now. Would I pulverize him then and there in front of his gang of Bozos? It would probably take only one swift poke to knock him flat, an uppercut would do it. But I wasn't going to do that. The instructor also preached at us not to be aggressive. "Don't go out there looking for trouble just because you'll be strong and feeling fearless," he said. He was serious. And he looked like Mr. America, so whatever he said went. He said his bodybuilding was an Eastern martial arts, and in that school you never started a fight even though the training was strictly physical, without the mental discipline you got in the true martial arts training. But I guess it was a little or he wouldn't be teaching us to stay out of fights.

The air was crisp like it was in the early fall but now the dogwoods bloomed cotton-candy white. It was going to be Easter in a few days, which meant I had to go with Mother to sunrise services. I didn't really mind except for the praying and all the stuff about Jesus rising from the dead. You had to skip over a heap of reality to believe anybody could rise from the dead, though I guess Jesus wasn't just anybody and that's why so many people could believe it—because of who He was, the Son of God. But the mornings on those Sundays were always beautiful and inspiring, if that's the right term, at least it was something that made you feel really good, sitting on the dew-damp hillside when the sun came up and bathed you in golden warmth. Plus we always had bacon and biscuits with our breakfast at my grandma Goodla's afterwards. Yeah, so I kind of liked Easter Sunday mornings.

Since I'd been lifting, my brain seemed to be working better and I started getting homework done faster. I didn't labor on algebra. I even wrote an English paper in an hour. An hour! Finished before supper.

I found myself with time to go to City Hall and look up what I could find on Ash Town. I hadn't forgotten that it was the governor's father, Edward Kimbrough, Senior, who bought the property after the big fire and built the place up again.

I stepped inside the musky Building Services Division room where they kept the planning and permit records, where the droopy old lady kept her eye on everybody and gave me a friendly nod of recognition when I passed her counter. I was hoping to find something that would tell me what interest back then the governor's daddy had in building there. You didn't have to be top of the class to know there probably wasn't any money to be made off it.

What I found was pretty amazing.

First off, the structures the people lived in prior to the burning of Overton weren't real houses, so no records existed to show that any kind of structures had originally been built on the thirty-two acres. There hadn't been running water, sewage or electricity. According to official records, it was undeveloped land. The records went back to 1893 when the Overton District was first established as a "future planned community with a business district" that didn't seem to ever realize that future. As everybody knew, the KKK burned the shacks down in 1929 and ran all the colored folk out. Then, right away the parcel was purchased by Kimbrough & Sons Builders for $792.35, which included fees and pre-paid taxes. I didn't know if that was cheap or not. But it seemed Overton was just a useless ash heap. I couldn't figure why the Kimbroughs wanted to build a community there. Because that's what they did, they built the community that had been planned but never completed nearly forty years before. The records showed that the plan was submitted and approved with permits authorizing the construction of one hundred and ninety houses and a two-acre site for commercial use. The wording was exactly the same as it had been written in 1893: the property would house a "planned community with a business district."

While I was mulling this over, I saw on the fold-out map in the record book that two of the adjoining properties on the east side of Overton had long belonged to the U.S. Department of War, but the north end of the Ash Town property line was land also owned by the Kimbrough family. One Jeremiah T. Kimbrough, Esq. purchased it in 1912. I looked up and glanced around like I'd discovered buried treasure.

I found the page on that property and discovered that Jeremiah Kimbrough had completed the construction of Vulcon Industries there just as World War One commenced. Vulcon was a chemical plant with two big smokestacks that still spewed out black smoke today. It was common knowledge Vulcon made mustard gas used against the Germans in that war. They still produced poisonous materials, commercial stuff like bug and plant sprays.

It made me wonder if maybe the Kimbroughs didn't have something to do with the burning of Overton, if maybe they started the rumor that the boy assaulted the white girl and that the KKK was just following the

Kimbroughs' orders to lynch those people and to finally burn the whole place so the family could then buy up the property. But the question was why did they want it?

I didn't know what I had, if I had anything at all. Doctor Joe would figure it out. I couldn't wait to get to him with the information. I could hear him saying something great like, "Damn good job, topnotch investigating," and smiling and calling me his go-to man.

I wrote down all the figures and names of people buying and selling the properties and folded the paper into my back pocket, the one on the right side cause my billfold went in the left back pocket, and then I got out of there just as the lady clerk yelled to wrap it up. You could tell in her voice she was dead serious about locking the door "in exactly five minutes." Sounded like Mother.

I stepped into the bathroom across from the hall and stood in front of one of the wall urinals. Every sound echoed from the marble floors. The booths behind me had swinging doors and I heard one swing open and then swing back and forth as a man left the room without washing up.

I didn't hear the person walk up behind me but a hard voice spoke in my ear. "You're a sneaky little bastard, I'll say that for you." I knew the voice.

I stopped pissing immediately and got some dribble on my trousers. I turned. It was the redhead from the 4th Street stoplight, the Kluxer who was part of the lynch mob that summer night in 1958 that, for me, started it all. He was in a policeman's black uniform and armed to the teeth. I tried moving toward the washbasin so he couldn't bash my head against the hard marble wall. He didn't try and that loosened me up a little.

I noticed in the mirror that I was almost as tall as him, my image blocking out most of his face. I turned around with my hands still wet.

"What'd I do?" Act dumb. It couldn't hurt, I figured.

He sneered. "Don't play games, Poe. What I want to know is what you were up to that night your friend got lucky with his car door. You remember, he knocked me for a loop."

Maybe Herman had been on the up and up and hadn't told him anything. Or maybe the man was just playing me for a fool.

"We just wanted some shine. Like I said."

His eyes glistened and his hand lifted off an unsnapped holstered gun, a big gun. The hand made a meaty fist that he brought up to my chin. I remembered what Harvey Nixon had said about the size and length of his muscular arms, and that he would like to try the man out. Harvey had the reach on him. I wished he was here now to find out. Before he used the fist, the cop stopped as if some other impulse overpowered him. He eased back. Maybe he was just trying to scare me. If that was the case, he did a good job.

"There's some men want to talk to you outside," he said stiffly. "Follow me."

The sun was almost down and the shadows off dull government cars stretched long across the mostly deserted parking lot next to City Hall. My Harley was near the steps I walked down, leaning on its kickstand, heavy looking, itself casting a long shadow. I followed the redhead and walked on by Big Red, wishing I could just hop on and ride away. I felt a wind move the hair on top of my forehead. It needed some wax.

I'd noticed the redhead's nametag on the flap of his right shirt pocket. It said "Roach, D." *Roach* sounded about right for a dirty cop. I tried to guess what the "D" stood for. "Dipshit" seemed right.

He stopped and leaned in the window of a fine-looking Pontiac Bonneville, just like he'd leaned into Herman's old man's '49 Olds at 4th and Richards. Then he turned and nodded toward me standing 20 feet back. He waved me over. I gave Red a last desperate look and then stepped over there. There were two men inside the car. Not a soul was anywhere in the giant parking lot. They both wore white shirts rolled up to the elbows and had on dull ties pulled away from unbuttoned collars. Not that I had much experience with police detectives, except for that New Year's blunder, but those two looked the spitting images of TV detectives, like you'd see in *Peter Gunn* and *Dragnet*. Unhappy thick faces and crew-cut hair, a cigarette hanging from the mouth of one of them and between the stained fingers of the other.

Roach said, "Here you go, get in."

It was a two-door and the driver was going to have to step out to let me in. The driver said to Roach, "Frisk him."

He made me lean against the car. The hood was too hot to put my hands on so I just held them over it like I was warming over a campfire and pushed my knees into the fender for leverage. He felt under my arms and around my chest and down to my crotch. He patted my pants and I thought he was going to reach into the pockets and find my notes on the governor's crooked family. At least I thought the family was crooked; wasn't everyone that high up? I had the motorcycle key in my front pocket along with a nickel's worth of Double Bubble and some change, and in my other pocket a jacks ball I found somewhere, plus the billfold in my back pocket. But Roach didn't make me empty the pockets.

"He's okay."

"Get in," said the driver, who was thin enough that he lifted forward the seat without getting out. He didn't smile but he wasn't unfriendly.

They didn't tell me their names but asked who I was, my full name and birth date and where I was born. I told them. The back seat was a lot lower than the front and it let them almost hover over me, which wasn't very comfortable, two big men hanging their arms over the seat and pushing themselves at you. They could have been regular officers out of uniform but I didn't think so.

The first guy spoke. "You wanna guess why you're here talking to us, son?"

I shrugged. Of course I knew why: they wanted to know how I knew they were running a traffic-light scam to cheat black folks out of money they didn't have. But I kept my mouth shut.

"I hope you're going to cooperate," he said. There wasn't any malice in his voice. "I'll just cut it down to this. You know the dentist, Dr. Peach, don't you?"

I nodded. "Yes, I do."

"Good. That's a good start," said the detective on the passenger side.

He went on, "Just how well do you know him, Sonny? Can I call you Sonny?"

"Sure. He lives just off my paper route and I've seen him outside washing his car. He has a T-Bird, 1956. The best year."

"Isn't it true you play a lot of tennis with the dentist?"

"I wouldn't say a lot."

"But you have played with him before, right?"

"Yeah."

The guy pushed a little closer to me. It seemed his head grew a little, too. His eyes narrowed to slits and I started to get nervous. "He ever try anything with you? You know, put his hands on you, suck your dick maybe?"

"Hey, Curt, take her easy," the driver said.

"All right, kid. Sonny ... Well, did he?—Do anything like that?"

"Hell no. He's got a fiancée," I said and tried to make my voice as hard as I could. But I was scared shitless.

How big was this rumor, I wondered, how far had it spread? I hadn't thought that much about Stuart blurting out his nasty comment at the table that once; Stuart never thought when he said something, stuff would just come out with whatever was in his half-dead brain. I knew on that day you could add homophobe to his many other prejudices and mental limitations. That was going to hold him back forever. Maybe my brother started the rumor.

The guy named Curt tried to grin but you could tell he was hot underneath. I guess he must have really thought Doctor Joe was a homo, which I guess makes some people get so worked up they go berserk. This man was one of those people, I thought. I might've said: *What damn business is it of yours, shit-for-brains?* But saying something like that to this hothead would be like asking a Klansman to hug a big buck Negro.

The driver seemed more reasonable, even-tempered. He said, "Look, son. We're not saying that he's a homosexual or that he's after you because you're a freewheeling kid. We don't care. May not think so but even Curt here don't care. It's just, this dentist's been messing around in police business, upsetting people downtown and getting the niggers all stirred up with his talk about better jobs and pay. We got enough problems with Northern agitators, we don't need your dentist friend making the problem worse. You see? We just don't want that happening here ... Let me ask you, do you even know what I'm talking about?"

I wanted to say, *Hell yeah I know what you're talking about and it's crooks like you that me and Doctor Joe are going after.* I wanted to say it with all my heart, but I didn't have the guts. Also, it would've been pretty dumb.

I looked down at my knees and shook my head like I was lost.

"Well, he's a troublemaker and has got to stop his meddling in other people's affairs. It's the right thing to do. Now, how can you help us do that, son? You got any suggestions?"

I didn't look at him when I said, "There ain't nothing *I* can do. Sorry."

"Well, la-de-da!" Curt said, squirming. He was getting restless. He grabbed my chin, his thumb pressing hard into the bone, and lifted my head to make me look at him. I thought better of knocking his hand away.

"Innocent as a lamb, huh? Never did nothing illegal, that right? Not even stole a car out of Willard Chevrolet late one night about a year and a half back. Around Halloween, wasn't it? Never siphoned gasoline out of cars from the alley off Broadmore Terrace?—What was that for, your mother's car?—Never stole cheese crackers from the drug store countertop either, I suppose."

I pushed his hand aside so I could talk. "How'd you know about the car, I brought it right back? Nobody saw me."

"Used cars, they don't keep much gas in the tank," he said almost friendly-like. "You found that out when you got off the lot, brought it back it was empty. Out of the goodness of his heart, Mr. Willard didn't press charges against you boys for that stunt. Think you're a slicker but you ain't nothing of the sort. You're just a punk kid."

I knew right then that it was Roach and these men who'd gotten Dudley Willard Jr. and his football buddies to beat me up. It was probably them who had Harvey Nixon's little boy killed, too. Him acting as a Klansman, not a cop.

You could say I didn't have much leadership growing up since my old man wasn't there and I tended to get into mischief frequently. But that was before I had any reason to think about a future, before I believed in myself. Now, I was cured. Way I figured it, I'd been saved by Doctor Joe, kind of like getting saved by the Almighty. All past sins supposedly forgiven.

I'd practically forgotten about taking that car off the lot, largely because I'd been drunk at the time. But I remembered that I had only wanted to see if Ledbelly had any guts. I tried to get him to drive it but he only lowered on the chain so I could get the car off the lot. About ten blocks away Belly hollers, "It's going to run out of gas! Look at the fucking gauge." I turned around and we put it back on the lot just like we found it. We didn't get stopped, and nobody was the wiser. Now, I guess I'd have to change my mind a little about Dudley Willard, Senior, even if he was a crook and a bigot and his vicious son tried to kill me. There was some good in his corrupted heart.

"What we're trying to say, Sonny," the detective behind the wheel said, "is it looks pretty obvious. Grown single man playing games with a boy, letting him come to his private office on his days off, the New Year's shenanigans you pulled in his car. They should've stuck him in the can for that one. Look, I could go on but you get my drift. Even if it ain't so, anybody could make that assumption and lots of people are making it. You understand the seriousness of this thing?"

"I guess."

"So then, let me show you this piece of paper. See if you wouldn't have any objections to signing it. Here, read it."

He handed me a single page that looked real official. It had the letterhead that said "District Attorney of Clayton County" with about three sentences below, which stated, as me talking, that Doctor Joe had "fondled or molested me on more than one occasion."

The driver went on, "Before you say anything, consider this. There's money in it for you ... Look, son, we know you don't have a father and your mother works her butt off to make a puny living for you three boys."

"It ain't that hard a thing to do, kid. It doesn't even say he ever copulated on you when we all know damn well he did." That was Curt, whose voice rose as he talked, getting hot again.

I thought it was as low as they could sink bringing my mother into it and that right there was enough reason that I wouldn't sign their goddamn paper. But I wouldn't have signed it anyway, if they'd offered me a thousand dollars. Maybe if they offered to shoot me where I sat in the back seat of the Pontiac, then I might have thought twice.

I guess they could tell I was getting red cause the driver added, "Three thousand dollars, Sonny. You know what that will do to ease your mother's stress and help you and your brothers? And nobody will ever know you did it. Promise. We only want the dentist to stop his interfering. Okay? Here's a pen. Go ahead, son, sign it and take this bundle."

He actually had a roll of money in his hand. I couldn't tell how much. It could have been $3,000, but it didn't matter. My decision was set in stone. There was no way in hell they could get me to sign that paper saying those things against Doctor Joe, and it made me wonder what my choice meant. Did it mean I would follow Doctor Joe to hell? Cause that's where he was headed.

But refusing them gave me a sense of power, too, even if I didn't quite understand it. But it felt gratifying and oddly calming.

They let me out unharmed. The driver said, "Be careful where you go, who you see. We're there."

Chapter 34

They tried to bribe me on Tuesday. Now it was Thursday and I couldn't put off talking to him any longer. Waiting two days was as nerve-racking as when I'd piddled around afraid to tell him about Herman and me in that first encounter with the redhead cop, Roach. Things had gotten a lot more serious since then. Doctor Joe's reputation was going to be ruined, if it already hadn't been. But I wasn't scared now; that was the only good thing.

I didn't call Doctor Joe from home. I called his office from the phone booth in Woolworth's before heading out to deliver papers. Disguising my voice by making it deeper, I said it was Dr. Perry from the second floor needing to speak, if he could break away for a minute. Dr. Perry was an oncologist or something and maybe they wouldn't know him all that well in a dental office.

"Sure, Dr. Perry," said Gloria, who sometimes acted as receptionist. She could've recognized my voice and played along cause Doctor Joe had prepared her for oddities like this and told her to carry on normally.

"Thank you," I said and stammered to keep from calling her name.

A moment later he said, "This is Dr. Peach."

"It's me, Sonny."

I didn't tell him anything except we needed to meet somewhere besides his house or office and he suggested the Hitchin Post on the west side. I didn't remember ever saying the Hitchin Post was my father's first restaurant, but he knew I didn't like going to the west side. But meeting out there was smarter. That wasn't a place they'd be watching.

The Hitchin Post Drive-In had gone to the dogs. It needed painting. They could at least have washed the windows. The place had turned into a hangout for hoodlums so it really didn't matter that the owners didn't keep any of Pops's black cooks. I mean, because hoodlums didn't have any taste, and they weren't here for food anyway. You used a speaker at each slot for ordering, same as when Pops owned it, everything still under a space-age roof. The roof looked new but the speakers were the same, only rusty.

There weren't many cars at four in the afternoon and only one motorcycle, mine. By now I viewed pretty much everything around me with a suspicious eye. I noted the occupants of each of the cars. Only youngsters, which didn't raise any flags. Smelling rain in the air, I had parked Red under the awning up against the backside of the main building.

I slid into the T-Bird. The motor was running, defogging the window. It felt extra warm inside, like you would want it if you were under the weather. Doctor Joe sat in a slump, his long legs competing for space with the steering wheel. He held open a book called *Bhagavad Gita* … He seemed to be concentrating hard. I thought he hadn't even noticed me for a second, but then he closed the book and looked my way. His eyes were puffy and bloodshot. I figured he was coming down with a cold.

I didn't like seeing him that way, cause he looked vulnerable. "You okay?"

He tried a smile but it collapsed. "This is the book that influenced Mahatma Gandhi," he said simply and then glanced at the girl carhop taking an order down the way. I watched her too. She held the tray awkwardly at shoulder level. She wasn't on skates. She walked quickly, maybe because of the darkening sky that had snuck up pretty quickly, and just then a windblown thundershower let loose and the girl's short skirt blew around, giving us a real nice, quick view. Like that movie with Marilyn. She had to hold it down in front and back and only one hand to do it. She jumped at a thunderclap but lost not one French fry on her tray. She was good.

Doctor Joe suddenly laughed and shook his head. "When it rains it pours," he said, crazily.

"What's the matter, are you sick?"

He tried the smile again and it had some comfort to it, but not enough to count. Mostly he was just sad looking. "I wish. It would be a relief to have something I could look forward to getting over. If only it were that simple."

His voice wanted to break but he didn't let it. He breathed large, then said, "They've taken my license."

"What? No! How can they do that? They *can't* do that."

He glanced at me, blinked, then turned back to the windshield. "Somebody in power doesn't like you, he speaks to a member of the board or someone connected ... Officially, they've suspended my license while my *case* is under review. I can't treat another patient."

"Holy shit, man. This is serious. Wha—what will you do, Joe?"

He looked at me with cow eyes. "These things don't get reversed— that doesn't look good for the board's image. Board of Dental Examiners, a bastion of equity and dispassionate objectiveness. I'm basically dead in the water, Sonny. No matter where I go."

"Who? Do you know who did it? What's this case about?"

He kept staring into the downpour. "Does it matter? Really? But, no, I don't know who did it or what their reason was, so there's nothing I can defend, not at this point at least. They don't have to reveal who brings complaints. The board's not a democracy."

I didn't know what to say. What could you say? It was terrible.

"But no doubt someone here in Woodstock doesn't like what I'm up to. And it's not any of my patients, that I know of."

It occurred to me that Doctor Joe all this time had been so sure of himself he never believed they would go after him, try to stop him. I couldn't bring myself to tell him they tried to bribe me. Ruinous stuff about him. Or mention the rumors; maybe he already knew.

"Don't you have to accidentally kill a patient or maim them for life or something real bad for them to lose your license? It's not right they don't give you a reason. How can you defend yourself?"

He sighed but that was all. He tapped his horn at the girl in the plaid skirt who was running past us again, her tray now empty. The overhead partition shielded her and the drivers' windows from the rain. She gave the T-Bird the once-over and then snuggled up against his door. Flirty. Pretty, too. She probably went to school in Midland. Or maybe she didn't go to school at all; maybe she was a teenager with a baby and had to work for a living cause her parents kicked her out for getting pregnant. Poor girl. She could have been Susie.

"What can I get for you, sugar?" I decided she had the baby and got kicked out and took this job cause she didn't know how to type.

"Tall orange juice and an extra cup of ice. Is that possible?" Doctor Joe said.

"Sure. Back in a jiff."

I said, "You're probably not in any mood to hear what I learned at City Hall about Ash Town, huh? Do you even care anymore?"

He brightened a little. Then he looked curiously at me, his eyes glimmering as if some of the rainfall had splashed into them.

"Would you tell me something interesting?"

"Would I not?" I said. "Did you know the property was bought by the governor's old man after the Klan burned it down? Thirty-two acres of ashes that he didn't wait around to build on. To the tune of a hundred and ninety houses. You know why?"

"Why do you think?"

The girl was quick with the orange juice. He gave her a dollar tip.

"Thanks, y'all. Holler, you want something else."

He poured half into the extra cup. I held it up while he poured. "Drink?" he said then, and grinned at me. It was nice to see a better face. "Can you drive okay afterwards?"

He'd never asked me before when I always had to get somewhere after we'd been drinking. "Hell yeah I can drive. Even better."

His grin broadened. He put a hand on my knee and squeezed like he was squeezing juice from an orange. "Ouch, okay," I said and he let go.

"Sorry. Didn't mean to hurt you. I'd never hurt you, Sonny, you know that, don't you?"

"Yeah, I know that … This thing's really got you down, huh?"

I held the extra cup as he poured from a flask. He kept looking at me like there was something he wanted to say but maybe didn't want to say, too.

"Here's what I think," I said. "I think the governor's daddy wanted that land first off cause he could build a company town real cheap using convict labor from Clayton Prison or some other jail. He wanted a company town because Vulcon Industries—the chemical company next door?—because he owned it too and could get cheap labor from his colored tenants. I'll bet you could find out if the employees at Vulcon back then lived in Ash Town. I'll bet you'll find out they were treated like slaves, tied to the company town. I'd even bet that what you discover could get the governor thrown out of office today—maybe even thrown in jail … Or, if you blackmailed them, it could get you your license back! … Then you could move to San Francisco and be a dentist."

He listened, amused, then shook his head. "No kidding?"

I said, "I wouldn't shit you."

"Well, that is some exploring, some theory, my man. Super sleuth Sonny Poe—Say that three times after your vodka screwdrivers … You might have something here. I especially like that Vulcon Industries also belongs to the Kimbroughs. Or did. But even if they no longer own the company, there's something to your marvelous investigating. It's worth a closer look. Here's to you."

We touched cups and drank. He stared at me for a moment, as if making a study out of me, then said, "You are one amazing fellow, Sonny Poe."

He *was* making a study of me

Chapter 35

I left him sitting in the T-Bird, myself feeling real good, pumped even, despite all the troubles. I pulled my cap down tight over my eyes to keep the hard pellets from blinding me on the ride. I wasn't about to put a windshield on Big Red, because, how would you feel the wind in your face?

That night I couldn't sleep. I lay in bed for a while listening to Stuart's gurgling and snoring. I wanted to write something in my diary. Things were developing fast and I had to get it down. But what I ended up writing surprised me.

I slipped into the bathroom, which had become my journal-writing office, the toilet lid my desktop. I put down something about these events and how fast they were coming—and heading—the wrong way. *Terminal* or *final* were words I thought of but didn't use. Everything seemed to have no good end and nothing seemed redeemable. A rumor was like the deadliest cancer where I lived; it could spread quickly and it destroyed just as quickly. I'd bet if I lived in a big city outside the South this rumor would be laughed out of town and the dental board would never have used such nonsense innuendo crap to get rid of a dentist as good as Doctor Joe. It was like I was trapped in the Dark Ages and had been all my life. But all of a sudden outside events, like the consequences from meeting an open-minded man who'd made me see things from his viewpoint, had brought some light to my limited, miserable vision of things. That sorry brother of mine could sure learn some things from him; he could have used Doctor Joe's light a lot more than me. And I could go down a list of other people but I would then be missing the point of who I was and where I was going.

I wrote, *It's not fair he lost his license when he's probably the caringest dentist in this town. It's the petty corrupt people of Woodstock who are such religious phonies, uptight prejudiced prudes and rednecks that have put him in such a lousy place. And I'm glad he's not giving up. I'm not either. The hell with everybody, all my friends who aren't my friends anymore. The truth is even if Doctor Joe were homosexual, I wouldn't give a damn, not one iota, and I would love him just as much.*

I had to stop writing and reread *I would love him just as much* … Did I write that?

When I started back I scribbled, *DJ would fit better in another time, like he said his idol Adlai Stevenson would.* (I just then decided it wasn't safe to use Doctor Joe's name in the diary; so I went back and inked out every time I wrote it and put in instead, "DJ." It was to protect him since the journal might some day be discovered if I had an accident and say went into a coma and died. I didn't know why; it just seemed right.)

He talked a lot about the presidential candidate Adlai Stevenson, how his liberal ideas were so far ahead of his time they couldn't be appreciated by all the elected lamebrains who actually did run the country, or advocated policy according to constituency wishes—Doctor Joe would have said it like that, not me. I was only mimicking him.

I thought Doctor Joe belonged somewhere else. I was thinking of those two cats I met at Boondoggle's zombie house on that Georgia roadside dump and the places they'd traveled and the place they were headed to next, San Francisco. It sounded like Doctor Joe's kind of city. Mine too maybe. I decided to study up on San Francisco and maybe New York City to what kinds of attitudes people had over these things keeping the South bogged down in its own turmoil. And then try to talk Doctor Joe into packing up and moving where he might be happy.

But I knew what he'd say. Something like, "Who else is going to help these people? You want me to throw in the towel when I'm just getting started? No can do."

Why, why, why was he so stubborn, so driven? Something made him like that. I wondered if all his impossible ambition started with his brother's suicide; I just couldn't believe that his brother's affair with a black girl could be the reason. There had to be more to it. Maybe it was in the Eastern teachings he followed, some connection to the "goodness" he'd once told me that was the core of the spiritualism that guided his beliefs. Whatever it was, I knew he wouldn't go anywhere until he saw this Civil Service thing through, until he did something for the people of Ash Town. So damn stubborn.

I still had to put up with school, and the next day, after nearly forgetting all about Sugarman Cole, I had a run-in with him. Getting my history book out of the hallway locker, I backed right into him. He was stalking the corridor. His aftershave made me sneeze, which I aimed at my locker door. I didn't get close enough to him that night in the woods to know if he smelled that strong all the time.

"Sorry," I said, "didn't see you."

He wasn't carrying any books, so nothing flew out of his hands. He said nothing and just stared at me like he was trying to figure out who I was.

I helped him. "Stuart Poe's brother. I told Stuart it was all right with me if he gave you some of our beer—Did he?"

He was about to say something, I thought, when a curly-haired blond in a plaid skirt and bobby socks walked by, gave him a look, and he took off behind her, strutting in a way nobody less than Brando could pull off but him, The Sugarman. He mystified me and I was beginning to wonder if he was a real person or some fabrication of my imagination.

I got through the day without having to fight any punks who hated me because of my views on the Faulkner story.

After school I sped over to Sears for the bracelet I'd ordered from the catalogue nearly a month ago, a sparkling silver half-heart charm for Susie that cost me $12 plus two dollars for shipping or something.

It was foolish spending that much money on a stupid charm. But I felt bad that I hadn't seen her much after losing our virginity together, to each other. But she hadn't been much fun to be around, crying all the time from worrying she was pregnant. I sure couldn't blame her; that's why I got the charm.

I drove over to her house on Calhoun Street right after throwing papers to give it to her. I had about fifteen minutes before her mother got home. Her father wouldn't be home today for another hour. Her little brother was there, as usual, but I just pushed him aside after he warned me again that "Big Phil" would take care of me when I least expected it. "How many Hula Hoops can you do in a row, Stevie, three, four at most?"

He gave me a nasty look and grabbed the Wham-O on the back porch. Then, without a word, he went into the yard and started twisting and twirling. He didn't have enough shape to hold the hoop up for more than one-and-a-half turns, which lasted that long just on centrifugal force. But it kept him busy and I went into the house calling Susie's name.

She caught me in the kitchen and I felt my face lift seeing her so buoyant. She looked fresh and lively. Her face glowed as if under a luminous halo. She was going to give me some good news.

"Oh, Sonny …"

She couldn't get another word out and she didn't have to. She looked as good as that moonlit night in the woods. I slid my hands under her arms and pulled her off her feet in a hug that put us close, giving me pause to consider sneaking her into the bedroom, if there was time before the wicked witch barreled in and caught us butt naked in bed. The thought died quickly recalling the night I spent with the twins, Donald and Ronald, sleeping in a tent out back when their mother peeked in and caught all three of us in a sweaty race to see who could finish beating off first. This would be a lot worse than that embarrassing episode.

I forced myself to break from her creamy lips only when the door slammed behind us.

"I did it, douche bag. Five. Now pay up." The little twerp was pulling on my shirt.

I wondered what he meant by pay up. Did I make him a bet?

There was no way of figuring that I would suddenly burst out laughing. But that's what I did, and it wasn't at the eleven-year-old goofball standing there with a hand out, serious as he could be, or even that Susie wasn't pregnant anymore. I think it was just a sense of levity overwhelming me, an instant of lightness in a world that for me had gotten weighted down with too much nastiness and sadness and fear. I think it started in school today when I realized Sugarman Cole couldn't touch me.

"I want to meet your mother," I told Susie.

Chapter 36

Herman wasn't home but his little sister was and she was all by herself, wanting me to dance with her to Elvis's new one, "Stuck On You," which she'd just bought with her allowance. Her mother hated Elvis the Pelvis but drove Brandy to the record shop so she could dish out half her weekly dollar allowance on the 45. The flipside was "Fame and Fortune," which you could fast dance to, too. At least Brandy could; Brandy fast danced to everything, even "One Night" and "Love Me Tender," if you could believe that. I'd have to grab her forcefully and hold her real tight to keep her from breaking off in her Elvis jitter, which she was great at.

"Sure," I said nonchalantly, as if I was almost but not quite interested. "Where's Herman? When's he getting home?"

"Don't know, don't care," Brandy said, pouty-faced. She turned from the door and I followed her into the womb of the cluttered living room. I watched her sashay, her tight little hips moving like she was swimming.

"When's Mr. Brown getting home?"

"When he usually gets home and that won't be for a whole hour. Mother'll be late, naturally."

She batted her eyes and I wasn't dumb enough not to know what she was driving at. "Put it on," I said.

She did and we danced till I was sweating on my forehead and neck after only playing the record twice.

"I can get you a Nehi."

"I could take you for a chocolate shake at the drug store instead." I didn't want to stop but I was thinking of Susie, feeling like I ought to be true to her, at least for a while. Besides, Brandy was my blood brother's little sis. If I did anything, even just felt her up, it would be like incest or something.

I put her behind me on Big Red and made her hold on tight with her legs hugging mine like she was trying to fit into my clothes. It wasn't necessary cause she had her own foot rests, but, you know.

After we sat down at Scarborough's soda counter, I took a package of peanut butter crackers off the rack and laid it in front of me to make sure the jerk making our malts knew I only had one packet. I never liked the kid; he was probably the one ratted me out to the cops. Since Brandy said she liked malts better than a shake, I got one too. And it was better. She took a Wonder Woman off the rack cause they didn't have any teen mags and climbed back on the stool like a little girl climbs in a chair and started looking at it from the last page.

"How come Herman hardly goes to school anymore, you know?"

"He goes every day ... Why? He *doesn't*?"

"Yeah, sure. I guess I just don't ever see him, our classes being so different." That wasn't true. There was something else going on with Herman.

"Where is he right now?"

She didn't answer. She was in some kind of malt and comic book trance. She reminded me of her brother. You could holler "Boo!" right in Herman's ear when he was reading a book but he was so tied up in it, it wouldn't even faze him. You could pinch him and he still wouldn't notice. The guy could concentrate. Brandy was like that too. "Does he ever come home after school in the afternoon?"

She didn't even hear me.

"Boo!" I said in her ear.

"What?"

"You don't have to put up with him treating you like shit, you know."

"How come?"

"How come? Jesus." At least I had her attention.

She slurped the last of her malt through the straw then tipped the glass above her mouth and tapped the bottom to help the last clump down. I did the same.

"Who's he been hanging out with lately, you know?"

She suddenly beamed at me. "Take me for a long ride, Sonny. Please? I love going fast."

"Yeah, me too, Brandy ... Tell you what—"

"What?"

"You sneak around and find out what your brother's doing and a week from now I'll take you down to Midland. Maybe go skating."

She beamed again. "Like a *date*, Sonny?"

"Hell no. Just going riding, all right? Forget the skating."

I could have guessed she'd go into her pout, but she was so quick to do it and so exaggerated with it, I was still surprised. I paid. We left. She stayed clammed up on the short ride to her house. Even when I reneged and said okay, we'll skate, she wouldn't make the deal to spy on Herman.

He was outside, sweeping the porch. I revved the engine before shutting it down to make it backfire through the pipe. Brandy ran past him into the house. I walked up, cool-like, trying to swagger. If I'd had longer hair, I would have flipped out my comb and gone to work with it, Kookie-like.

His face just about looked normal now, a trace of purple under one eye.

"So how's it going, man? What's with the broom?"

"Promised Mom."

"Uh huh. Always do what you promise, do you?"

"What's that supposed to mean?"

"I don't know. It just makes me dizzy seeing you with a broom. Tough guy like you."

He leaned on the broom handle. "What's eating you, Sonny? ... Say, you been working out?"

"Where you been? I can't ever find you. Even your little sister doesn't know what you're up to. She thinks you go to school every day."

"You think I gotta clear everything I do with that little fag?"

"Jesus, she's a sweet kid. Why do you treat her that way?"

His face began to change color. I knew what to expect since I'd known him most of my life, and he was about to swing the broom or a fist.

"Don't get yourself too worked up," I said, "but you gotta tell me the truth. And don't give me any crap about being blood brothers—how could I dare think this or that about you. I want the fucking truth. Wasn't it Roach that got to you, beat you up? You do know his name, right? Didn't you tell him we knew about the traffic light scam? That that's why we were there that night? I gotta know if you squealed or not, Herman, cause they're after me now and this thing's gotten serious."

He didn't get mad and he didn't get superior, either. These Brown kids were surprising me all over the place today. He got sheepish and I was sure he would say, "Yeah, that's the way it was. Sorry." But he didn't do that.

He said, "So, brother, when you gonna let me drive your Harley?"

I closed on him. Let him take a swing, I'd like it.

"If my muscle teacher hadn't told us not to use force—If he hadn't meant it, I'd punch your ass out right here, Herman, you cocksucker."

Chapter 37

Despite it being spring, it was colder than a witch's titty up here in north Georgia. Uncle Tommy wanted to sleep by the creek so we would already be close to the deer early, and we had thrown a tent and crammed in a sleeping bag. Sometime in the night the tent fell over on us and we pushed it off to breathe. It didn't take long before my face turned numb. I thought my lips might fall off cause I couldn't feel them when I brought a finger out to test. I was glad Uncle Tommy said it first.

"Shit, hossfly, it's colder 'an witch's titty. Let's get in the car."

The best hunting was in north Georgia, he said, and we were up around Whitefield or Hatfield, I didn't really know. Or much care. It was somewhere in deep woods with narrow roads, and I was with my Uncle Tommy who knew his way around up here and I didn't worry about a thing. All I cared about at the moment was getting unfrozen. His car had a great heater and in no time we were laughing about nearly turning into icicles. He broke out a bottle of shine, the dark kind which I didn't care for but he said was the best you could get. He took a snort and passed the pint to me. It was okay, better than I thought it would be. There was no sediment that I could see.

"Think we'll get us a place tomorrow. Do this trip up right, what do you say?"

I said if that's what you want, like a tough mountain man. Uncle Tommy saw through that and laughed. He laughed himself into a smoker's hack. His hacking would start first thing in the morning till he got a cigarette going. That seemed to settle down his lungs.

He lit a cigarette now and took another sip of the charcoaled moonshine. It must have been only about midnight. "It'll be colder when we get started at four, but all we gotta remember is there's a whitetail with our names on it out there," he said. His face glowed. He had blue eyes, like Mother. "They've seen some ten-pointers and better in these parts this year."

"That big, how are we going to get it back to the car?" I said, visualizing us hauling a two hundred or even three hundred pound deer out of a ravine and up the mountainside.

"Gut and haul. We get us a big one, we could move a mountain. You won't even notice. We better get some sleep. You want the front or back?"

"Back."

"I'll just step out and finish this smoke. Cover up cause the engine's going off in five."

"Okay, Uncle Tommy. Night."

The covers came up to my nose. They couldn't touch me here, in the heart of the forest. I guess that's why I had the dream I had. It was clear and seamless, no jumbled-up chaos like most of my dreams of late. We were in a boat on the Coosa trolling for surface bass. The sun glittered across the water. I was teaching Chance how to cast. The reel didn't backlash once and he quickly picked up how to use it. A shadow passed over. It was a yellowhammer circling with something caught on its leg that kept it from flying away. Uncle Tommy cranked up the motor and we laid a wake to the river's edge where the fishing line attached to the bird was hooked in the overhanging thicket of arrowwood. I said I'd get it loose. For some reason I wasn't afraid of the yellow jackets and bumblebees swarming the blooms covering the bushes. I spread apart the vines and there was an orange-colored door that I easily opened and stepped through into a playground where Harvey Nixon Junior swung on the bars with me as a youngster. We were both about five years old and giggling, playing tag. No one there made us separate to different parts of the playground. There was only laughing and screeching from children on the swings and seesaws and jungle gym and in sandboxes. I remembered the yellowhammer flying around up there in circles. It might as well have been inside a birdcage and you can't keep yellowhammers caged. They will keep flying into the bars until they kill themselves. I left the play yard and closed the little door and unsnagged the filament line. Back in the boat I pulled the bird in by the line and when I had it against me, I saw that the line was not attached at all to its legs, that the line just ended at one of the bird's claws. I put the yellowhammer on my shoulder and told it to fly away, we were busy fishing. It wouldn't go. We had live bait in case we wanted to go after brim. I gave the yellowhammer a fat nightcrawler and it guzzled it then chirped and flew above us. The bird dove into the water like a waterfowl. I knew what it was doing. It was showing us where the surface bass were running. I told Chance to cast his line over there and he did and he brought in a two-pound bigmouth bass. The bird then flew off into the tall pines and, I guess, started knocking on wood cause that's what I heard that woke me up.

He rapped on the window again. "Want some flapjacks, hossfly?"

Four o'clock had come and gone. The light of day nearly burned my eyelids. I sat up and looked around. Uncle Tommy grinned and shook his head to tell me it was too late to hunt. I crawled out of the car but by then he had disappeared. We were parked off the road far enough in you couldn't see the car from the road.

"Hey, Uncle Tommy, where'd you go?"

He popped out from behind a tree working on his fly, having some trouble with it. "There's this little diner that has real syrup for your flapjacks."

"Yeah?" I muttered. Then I said, "Hell, let's shake a tail," cause I started thinking what hot pancakes with real maple syrup would taste like.

Uncle Tommy was a salesman of some kind, something industrial.

He had a territory that covered Alabama north of Birmingham and east of Decatur and also northern Georgia to Chattanooga in Tennessee. He had regular customers up here so he knew where all the good places were to sleep and eat. And he knew the backcountry. He said they had the best moonshine. I believed him cause the dark stuff we had last night went down smooth as a milkshake, sort of. At least when you compare it to the rock gut you got from Ash Town.

They gave Uncle Tommy a new car every two years and he always got a Pontiac, a great car. This one was only a year old. It was big inside, big enough to stretch out to sleep, or oversleep.

Uncle Tommy lived in Birmingham. We didn't drive up there too much to visit. Sometimes at Christmas or Thanksgiving or to see our divorced grandfather. Uncle Tommy's two boys got bored when they had to come to the sticks of Woodstock, so we didn't see much of our cousins. Which was fine with me since they were more Bag-a-bones's age.

At breakfast he said, "So tell me what you've been up to, hossfly. High schooler now. You been making the grades?"

I had a mouthful of bacon and pancakes and couldn't answer just then. I shook a fork to hold him off a minute. "So far getting As and Bs, A in Algebra. That's the toughest one."

"No kidding. That's better than anyone else in the family ever did. I know Olive wasn't much for studying. The smartest of us, too. She was a good hand on the farm, though, that one. Someone helping you study, maybe?"

"I didn't know that about Mother. Always thought she had it easy till Pops kicked the bucket."

"No, that's not right, son. And he didn't kick the bucket. Your father had an accident and died."

"Same thing. Damn, this is good," I said to get him off my back. "You know how to pick 'em, Uncle Tommy."

After a moment he said, "You want to shoot some grouse this afternoon, hossfly? That white tail will wait till the morning."

I said I sure did and after that big breakfast he drove to a place that had log cabins for rent and we got a room with both a fireplace and a gas heater. We dumped our gear except for the guns and headed right back out to find a field.

"There's this old boy lives up aways we can ask where to go. Won't take long, 'sides, he's got the good shine. Okay with you?"

"I'm with you."

Way back in the hills was this tin-roofed house on stilts that looked like pictures you saw of places people in the Depression lived. It sank in the middle of the porch and you could see right through the middle of the house to the back woods, like they'd built a tunnel so cars could drive through it.

A skinny old man sat on a rocker on the porch. He wore the very overalls you'd expect to see on a mountain hillbilly. He seemed to be the only person around. The man got off his rocker and limped about a hundred yards to greet us. He put his head inside the driver's window and said, toothlessly it sounded like, "Well, how-do there, Thomas. Y'all come on up to the house, set a spell."

"Can't, Hubvert. Not today. Taking my nephew here bird shooting in the afternoon. You know where's best for grouse this time a year?"

He gave us some crazy directions and Uncle Tommy nodded like he understood perfectly, not repeating any of the turns or landmarks or questioning them. "Take you bout a hour to git there from here. Want some shine while you are here?"

"Now that you mention it, Hub. Thank ye kindly. The boy's big enough he can take a snort. Ain't you, hossfly?"

"You bet."

We had our snort and then another on that leaning porch even though Uncle Tommy said he didn't have time to sit today. I propped against a porch column and Uncle Tommy sat on the edge with his feet dangling like a kid's. The emaciated old hillbilly worked his squeaky rocker. He had a heavy porcelain jug by him and that's what we drank from. It was better than the stuff we had last night. Uncle Tommy took two pints with him. He gave Hubvert some cash and said thanks, he'd get by in the next month or so.

It took a few minutes short of one hour to get to the big field, some of it off-the-road driving. Uncle Tommy didn't care if he wore out the shocks or shook screws loose over washboard paths since he'd get a new car in another year. He laughed telling me that, his voice vibrating from the bumps.

He'd brought a bunch of guns. We took the 12-gauge double-barrels for grouse. He gave me a brief safety rundown, which I already knew about, barrel always facing forward, never get in front of another shooter, or fall behind either. Don't cock the hammer till you raise the gun, but that was hard to do when suddenly a bird would spring in a flutter ten feet in front of you and you'd be groping to cock it while the bird darted away in an unpredictable pattern, but always away from you.

We got plenty of chances to shoot and I brought down three grouse, all of them from about forty feet off. Uncle Tommy took one out of the sky and missed a bunch. So did I. My shoulder was going to be sore tomorrow.

"That's about all we need for chow tonight," he said. "Damn good shootin, hossfly. You've done this before, ain't you?"

"Couple times, yeah."

"Yeah? Who with? Who taught you to shoot like that?"

"Guys, punk friends. I guess I'm just naturally a good shot." I wasn't going to tell him Doctor Joe had taken me quail hunting in the fall, that he showed me how to lead the bird and anticipate and be quick to fire. I got some then too.

It didn't get by me some of the things Uncle Tommy was asking. "Who with?" and "Did someone help you study?" Mother put him up to taking me on the trip so he could talk some sense into me about my wayward ways. She'd suggested it on Pops's Day. "Your Uncle Tommy wants to take you hunting." She'd said it out of earshot of my brothers. I knew she just wanted him to give me a lecture on the company I was keeping, mainly Doctor Joe, although Uncle Tommy hadn't yet mentioned his name. If I gave him the chance, he would.

But I was having fun being with my uncle and didn't want that stuff to interfere. Especially with the deer hunting tomorrow. So I was avoiding his prying. When he wanted to start his lecture, then I'd probably just deny it all and say Mother didn't know what the hell she was talking about. You know how women are, how they can think the worst, especially when it comes to their children. Don't you, Uncle Tommy?

He cooked some dark beans in a pot in the fireplace, big blackened pot that mortar fell into when the fire blasted around it. He called them, "mortar beans." It took about two hours to clean four birds, which didn't produce as much meat as either one of us thought. The cabin didn't have much in the way of spices and cooking utensils to do them up right, but the way Uncle Tommy halved them and fried them in a skillet in their own skin fat with just pepper and some sprinkles of moonshine, those grouse were delicious.

We drank from shot glasses and played cribbage for nickels that he lent me. Uncle Tommy drank more than me and pretty soon I was taking the nickels that we'd placed on the corners for whoever got there first. Cribbage was a cinch. Counting combinations came so easy that I never hesitated discarding and I think it made Uncle Tommy try to go faster too. But he needed more time cause he was throwing away pairs to my crib, even a 7 with an 8. He was the first in mother's family to graduate college—University of Georgia—so he had to be smarter than the way he played cards. If he was just letting me win cause that's what he did with his kids, then let him. That was okay by me.

"If we get a deer tomorrow, what are we going to do with it? I mean, are we going to take it to Woodstock? Or your house? Freeze it? Cause we don't even have a freezer."

"I'll take care of it up here. There's some folks will butcher it for us. We'll put her on ice and divide it up at home. What cuts do y'all like?"

"Don't have a clue," I said. "Whatever you don't want will do, I guess. I don't even know if Mother likes it. Probably, though."

"Oh, yeah, she grew up eating venison. You could figure her favorite cut is the haunch roast. Prime stuff, or the fillet. We'll see she gets it, huh? … You know what, hossfly, four o'clock is gonna come in a hurry. You ready to hit the hay?"

I guess he decided to give up with the questions. I figured he didn't want to get into it any more than I did. Let's just have us some fun hunting, whadda ya say there, hossfly?

My breath blew out like horse steam in snow, except there was no snow anywhere. Just cold, maybe 15° or 20° down in the north ravine where we moved like mice against a slight wind as far down as we could get to the stream, which was mostly frozen. The .30-06 felt light after the meatier twelve gauge and I was eager to fire it. I hadn't ever fired a gun with bullets this big. Both times I went deer hunting before I used a shotgun with a pellet load and I never even came close to popping me a buck. I didn't have to be as close this time, just make a good shot, cause one was all I'd get. You didn't want to wound the deer, say by shooting it in the rump and letting it run so another hunter could pop it when it was slower and easier to bring down. I wasn't going to shoot unless I could see its chest or side. I wasn't going to shoot it in the head. No way. I wouldn't shoot it on the run, either. I had sure put the limits on myself, but those were my rules. Rules of moral conduct, you might say. We'd talked about killing the animal on the way down to this area and Uncle Tommy agreed with every one of my rules. So I had his word he wouldn't shoot either unless he had a clear kill shot.

I had chambered a round as we entered the woods and headed downhill. Ready, even if it was still dark.

We were by the creek now, the air to our face, waiting silently. Light had just started seeping in from the top of the woods. I looked at Uncle Tommy behind the tree next to me. His turquoise eyes were wide open and clear as creek water. He had a look of anticipation and excitement on his face mixed with a calmness that told me he was not the kind to panic in a hunt. In that moment a vision of the lynching two years ago lay before me and Uncle Tommy was Herman, whose dark eyes collected tears and whose fear of watching a man being murdered turned to panic. If Uncle Tommy had been him, would he have tried to save that man? Would he have put a shot in the air, if we'd had any bullets left, stepped out and confronted the angry mob? And would I have stepped out with him?

The doe came upon us quiet as a snowflake. I didn't hear her or smell her, yet there she was, bending to sip from the stream, not fifty feet from us. I glanced again at Uncle Tommy. He was telling me silently, pointing to his eye, *Where there's a doe there's a buck.* I got it and firmed up the rifle in her direction. We waited, barely breathing.

To kill a deer was a rite of passage. That didn't mean it suddenly made me a man or raised my esteem to some kind of warrior. But as my bullet passed through his lung and his heart and the legs collapsed under his lifeless weight, the lightness of some sweeping change lifted me and I felt like a conqueror, like I had surely passed into a new dimension—which would strengthen me for the dangers I knew lie ahead.

Chapter 38

Heading into that alley on my route where the nightmares of my own beheading once forced me to tread cautiously, I spotted him. He had parked between two garages where a small T-Bird couldn't be seen until you were right on it. Had it been the evil cop of my nightmare, it would've been curtains. I could not have stopped before the wire got me. But it wasn't that phantom. Doctor Joe stood by the T-Bird, in dark clothes, looking gloomy, defeated.

"Didn't mean to startle you," he said.

"Didn't." I wasn't going to tell him what I had against the alley. "Your whitewalls are getting dirty, want me to wash them?"

He glanced at a tire and smiled tiredly. "Can we talk?"

It was the quietest place on my route, if you didn't count a snaggle-tooth bulldog on the occasional prowl. Not a soul drove or walked through this alley until the residents came home from work. That would be nearly two more hours.

I got off Red, left my paper bag on the ground and got into the passenger's side of the car. With the hardtop on and windows up, the car had a new-leather smell you didn't notice riding in the open air. That book he was reading before lay on the seat, the *Bhagavad Gita* or *The*

Lord's Lay Commentary ... followed by a bunch of other words. I picked it up and mindlessly thumbed through it. I'd been thinking about him and worrying like hell since they'd taken his license. But I wasn't going to risk calling and neither had I heard from him till right now.

"Please tell me there's something good to report," I said, "that that's why you've found me."

"I wished I could, Sonny. I'm farming out my patients and shutting down the practice. Not a fun thing to have to do."

"Where's Gloria going?" His assistant/Girl Friday.

He shook his head. "She has a daughter to raise. Did you know that?"

"Bastards," I said, spitting the word. "Well, what are *you* going to do? Will you move away? To Atlanta?—And what about Jeanne? How's she taking it?"

In a gloomy way, he seemed strangely at peace, like he was resigned to accept his fate rather than the Doctor Joe I knew who would go all out to defend himself. That man would run over his problem, like he would run through football players getting to the goal.

"Let me read you a passage from this book," he said, flipping pages close to the end. "This is a spiritual philosophy that's free of dogma and the kind of religious trappings fanatical evangelicals like my father used to punish and control his children. This book is rubbish in that man's view. And thus for the likes of me. These verses hold me together.

"Listen ... *'There are two types of beings in this world: divine and demonic. Those of demonic nature know not what to do or refrain from; purity is not found in them, nor is good conduct, nor is truth ... Holding this view, these ruined souls, small-minded and of cruel deeds, arise as the enemies of the world, bent on its destruction ...'*

"This type sound familiar?" He looked me in the eye. "I'm not going to see you again. It may already be too late for me; but hopefully not for you. I want you to accept that."

He tried a grin but the look turned into the same sick-dog look he had the last time we were together, when he told me he'd lost his license. I knew he was right, but it already was too late for me. That bribe by the cops showed me that, the rumors at school. Still, I didn't want to give up knowing him. He was my teacher, my friend.

"Why don't you just quit this great quest you're on, huh?" I said, suddenly mad. "It's just going to get you hurt. Or killed!"

He seemed lost in thought now, and I felt like my chest was going to explode. I felt horrible that I'd held things from him, the bribe and telling Herman about investigating for the government.

"We could run away to New Orleans. Anywhere. I can't stay here anymore either."

He gave me that tired smile. "Yeah, let's run away to New Orleans. If that were only possible. Listen, Sonny. You know I like you and over this time you've become more important to me than just a youngster needing some guidance. I think you know that … It's given me a lot of joy being around you, expanding your parameters, hopefully, just doing the things we've done—believe it or not I've enjoyed teaching you tennis, and I do not like chasing balls. You're a quick learner, open to most anything new. And that's rare … Now they've warped our friendship into something perverse and terribly wrong. But as for the way most people judge human relationships, and given the demonic nature of these folks you call rednecks, you can see how the rumors would spread.

"I know, I know, before you blow your stack, that it's nobody else's business. Unfortunately, kid, that's not the way things work in this society, especially not among obsessively righteous minds like we're dealing with—"

"Yeah," I interrupted, "I know." I was on the verge of spitting it out—*They want me to sign a paper against you!*—when he suddenly broke down. His shoulders shuddered like the ground under him shook. He heaved. He couldn't get air. It was terrible to see him like that. As far as I was concerned, though, it didn't cost him anything, not with me. All I saw was another dimension of him, a sweet, human vulnerability.

I put both hands on his shoulder and let my arms sway with him in sympathy. Then I gave him a hard shake.

"It's all right, Joe," I said. My voice sounded weak. "Come on now, I know what you're saying and I know you are right. It—It's just going to be hard. There's still so much to do. We're supposed to go to Mexico, remember? I haven't beaten you at tennis. I wanted to learn golf … What will I do without you? Please, Joe."

He barely lifted his head. He sniffled. "There's—there is more to it than that, Sonny. It goes so much deeper—"

They didn't come in a black and white cause I would have noticed. And I would've bet Chief Bradley didn't send them either. I glanced out the window to see Roach, the redhead cop—my demonic nightmare in the flesh. He stood right in front of the T-Bird with his arm raised with an object in his hand.

"Look out!" I cried and grabbed Doctor Joe's neck to bring his head out of the way. It must have looked obscene to Roach and to the two other rotten bastards appearing attack-ready next to him. I ducked just as Roach let go the missile, a rock I thought, that when it hit turned the glass into a gauzy blindfold and left me wondering what would fly through the windshield next. If it would be bullets.

Doctor Joe acted first, and fast. He threw open the car door and got out. "Sit. Don't move," he commanded.

I obeyed for only seconds, and then I heard the shouting start up and I jumped out. They had Doctor Joe surrounded. I recognized the other two as the detectives in the Pontiac who tried to make me sign the statement for three thousand dollars that Doctor Joe performed lewd acts with me. Roach wasn't wearing his black cop's uniform.

Doctor Joe stood there as cool as he might stand in a huddle on a football field, arms hanging loose, taller by inches than all them. They looked more nervous than he did. But they weren't talking like they were nervous.

"Whadda we got going on in that cozy little car?" said the bulky hotheaded detective Curt, his words slurred by venom. He was the largest of the three men and just about as tall and big as Doctor Joe, though his bulk fell to his belt.

Doctor Joe stood his ground. "That stunt you just pulled is assault with serious intent … You have some identification?"

Curt sighed as his arms went around Doctor Joe in a kind of body-twisting bear hug. It pinned his arms to his side. Doctor Joe didn't do anything; he just allowed them to have their way. That threw me. Roach took the first swing, a blow that glanced off his flinching jaw.

"Let him go!" I screamed and ran toward them. Doctor Joe didn't react other than trying to dodge the blows coming his way when I was sure he could have broken loose. The redhead stuck his fist out so lightning fast I didn't see it coming and it knocked me off my feet but not out.

Doctor Joe looked down at me and started to say something, but a fist thrown by the third man caught him square on the back of his jawbone and he reeled, almost taking Curt down too. I thought I saw his eyes roll in their sockets but he didn't go to the ground.

I got to my knees and balled my left hand into a fist, then sucker punched Roach in the groin. It hit the mark cause he dropped like a concrete gargoyle would tumble from a building. It surprised me how fast he collapsed. I got to my feet and kicked at Curt's shin to make him release Doctor Joe. I was wearing my brother's boots again today, thinking I might take another shot at the chief's dog. He'd started back to growling at the kids, which made me decide it was time to kick out his other fang. I must have missed the shin cause the big man didn't even flinch.

"Don't, Sonny, it's not the way," Doctor Joe said, still wrapped in those long arms. Robbed of wind, his voice sounded weak.

The third detective surprisingly didn't come after me. I kept my eye on him and he just stood there waiting for Curt to steady Doctor Joe so he could try another shot at knocking him down. I was about to try my steel-toe on him when Curt suddenly gave Doctor Joe a hard push forward and let him go. Then he turned for me. I guess I had connected with his shin after all. I ran behind the T-Bird but he didn't chase after me. I thought he might pull a gun and start shooting. Doctor Joe was on a knee on the gravel alley.

The two detectives then went to Roach, who was sitting up now and breathing in deep gasps. They each took one of his arms and helped him up. He rose slowly, grimacing, groaning once.

Doctor Joe was wobbly but his eyes were open and focused on the three of them. "This windshield has to be taken care of," he said in a low, even voice.

Blew me away. I was mad as hell. I wondered how he could just let them bust his car and his jaw and just tell them he wanted a bill for the windshield.

I knew the redhead had a temper. I'd seen it on 4th Street in Herman's car and again when he'd snuck up on me that time in the bathroom at City Hall, wanting to slug me; it was the intent on his face that made it so obvious. He now stood on his own and I thought he might come after me.

Looking sharply between us, he said in a voice so pitched it wheezed, "Only thing I hate more than a useless nigger is a goddamn fag … Vengeance is mine saith the Lord. Faggots will suffer a living hell on earth, burn for all eternity. You hear me, *Doctor?*"

His hand was shaky when he pulled a gun out of the back of his pants and aimed it square at Doctor Joe's chest.

I thought, *Oh, lord, this is it, this is the end.*

Chapter 39

He would tell me later it cost nearly $500 to get the T-Bird fixed. New windshield, new leather upholstery on the driver's seat, fixing the damage the bullets did to the inner body and trunk lid when one of the slugs ricocheted and dented it to where you could see the lump on the outside. The other slug went as far as page 300 in his spirituality book and lodged there. He could afford the repairs, "no sweat," he said.

Then, why couldn't he go off on a South American cruise and let this whole thing blow over, I wondered.

What frustrated me the most was him not doing anything to protect himself, just letting those thugs knock him around. He said fighting back didn't accomplish anything. "Don't you have to try and defend yourself if you're getting beat up, though?" I argued. "That's what I tried to do."

But he stood his ground. He went by "Gandhi's model," which was don't fight back with violence. You are the "good one," so you seek goodness through nonviolent ways. He believed that. I know, I had just seen him put it to the test in real life. The same approach Dr. Martin Luther King, Jr. took in his teachings of nonviolent disobedience guiding his Civil Rights Movement.

They might beat him but he was not going to let the thugs and the crooks intimidated him. Just because they were this close to shooting him dead—and me too—and had already ruined his dental practice and probably his career and now were destroying his reputation, all that was no reason for him, in his thinking I guess, to either fight them or to run from them. I would have rather he take his stock market wealth and open that coffee house in San Francisco. And after I finished high school, he could bring me in to serve espresso. *Peach and Poe Bistro*, something like that. I just didn't think he was seeing the best picture of what his life could be.

Or he was crazy. Those men, and especially the redhead whose hatred I thought spilled into insanity, they meant business. They were out to get Doctor Joe. Who knew what they would do next, how far they would go.

I got the message on a piece of paper inside a sealed blank envelope and delivered to my house by my girlfriend Susie Pendergrass. I say "my girlfriend" because I hadn't been with another girl since Vicki last summer, so I guess Susie was it, my official girlfriend. Her mother thought so after I'd finally met her, and Doctor Joe must have too since he sought her out to deliver the message.

If he wanted to see me again, and he did, it must have been something big, something he needed me for.

We met just after dark at the roller rink in Midland. The roller rink may not have been the safest place since you got a lot of hoodlums and gangs hanging around, having nothing better to do than look for trouble. But that made it a better place to meet than, say, the Y or the drive-in again. With so many different kinds of people there, who was going to notice.

It was Saturday night and usually by eight o'clock you couldn't make your way around the rink without bumping into people, kids, chicks. But tonight you could even do turnouts and fling your arms. They didn't have couples-only times on Saturdays; it was open skating all night, free for all. I whizzed around accidentally running into girls in tight sweaters, saying "'scuse me very much" in my Elvis voice as I grabbed them around the waist and helped them regain their balance. I kept my distance from Doctor Joe but still whizzed past him a time or two to hit him with my skate wake, tease him. He'd told me he wasn't allowed to skate growing up but, as athletic as he was, he held his own. They played Buddy Holly's last album, *That'll Be The Day*, I guess as a salute to his memory. You didn't want to be reminded that he was gone, it being so recent, but it was great skating music, so you just skated and sang along with the songs and put out of mind that our idol would never sing another song.

I had parked Red near a floodlight seeing the leathered-up hoods hanging around in the shadows. They smoked and drank shine and kept an active eye on everything, like they were guilty as hell, expecting the law to rush them any minute. I didn't like running into gang members cause it usually got me a black eye or a bloody nose; it was because I stared back at them and that was a no-no, unless you wanted to fight. Just stupid. But with Doctor Joe with me, I didn't worry at all. Even when he was sworn to nonviolence, Doctor Joe had no fear of mere punks. You could bet he had knocked down tougher guys on football fields. That was a big reason I liked to go around with him; I felt safe, invincible even. Even when those cops attacked us and he just took it.

After a while, when it was safe, we had a Coke in the wing close to the entrance/exit. His face was still puffy and discolored where they hit him, so he was being extra cautious. My face was still sore from Roach's punch but the bruise was gone. It still hurt when I laughed.

"Are your teeth all right? Anything loose or chipped in there?" he asked. It was his first comment to me after a week of wrenching silence and wild speculation over his well-being. I didn't even know if he was alive or dead. He hadn't been at home when I drove by, which was every day.

I shook my head. "Are yours? You got hit a lot harder than me, I heard the crack."

"I'm good. Just madder than a hornet. Look, I know what I said. That I wasn't going to be seeing you again. But when I tell you why, you'll be glad."

"Heck, I'm just glad to see you again, to know you aren't a body in the morgue. What is it?"

"In a minute."

He finished his Coke and, just like Brandy with her malt, he turned it up and tapped the bottom to get the stuck ice down.

"Don't you remember what the dentist told you about ice cubes and jawbreakers?" I said in a stern voice.

"You are right, Dr. Poe." He spit the ice back into the cup as if taking me seriously. He was like that sometimes, driven to make sure he did the right thing, whether it was laying off the ice or putting down his fork cause he was eating too fast, or trying to change the behavior of unchangeable rednecks.

He stayed with the serious note. "They're not following me all the time. That means the whole organization—if it's that at all—is not involved in these attacks on us. It may just be those three; they may be renegades or were sent by the Klan."

We were standing by the wall so nobody could get behind us and listen in. "It's not them that got your license pulled, is it." I tried not to sound sarcastic and he didn't take it that way.

He shook his head. "I see your point."

"They're just goons for someone higher, I reckon … Joe, there's something I have to tell you."

"Yes?"

I looked down. We still had on our skates and the tips of them faced each other, not quite touching. "The two guys with Roach that attacked us, I'm pretty sure they're detectives. One is named Curt, the one who put you in the bear hug. Well, those two tried to get me to sign a statement and offered me money to do it. A lot of money. It was about you." And I told him what was on the statement and how much money they'd offered to give me if I signed.

His face reddened. "I'm sorry that you had to go through that. It must have been frightening."

I wasn't expecting him to apologize. That was my place this time. "Well, I can tell you they aren't getting anything out of me in the future, you got my word … There's something else." I looked at him and a sharp bark slipped over my lips. "It's about Herman." And I gave him everything, that I'd told people I was working for a government agent. I looked at him for a reaction. He wouldn't give me one.

"I tried to get Harvey Nixon to round up others in Ash who got scammed at that light, so they would all sign up as a group and help you bust open this thing—"

"As a group, yes, that's it," he said. He liked that idea.

"What do you mean, that's what?"

"Working together as a group, it's the only way to get anywhere."

"I guess," I said, confused why he hadn't gotten mad at me. "But they're not going to do that; they're too scared … I—I'm sorry for not telling you this before, Joe. It would've helped you understand what you're up against, not plowing ahead in the dark."

He looked out at the skaters. In a moment a smile crept onto his face, soft and welcome as a banana split.

"You were trying to spare me. It wouldn't have mattered if you'd told me this stuff. I wouldn't have stopped. I may have gone about it a little differently, that's all. I wouldn't have strung you alone this long for one thing."

He was grinning now. "No, listen. I've been researching a little into the history of Ash Town," he said, looking squarely at me now and not the crowd. He sounded excited and that was great to see. "Because *you*, young man, my go-to man, made some very interesting observations."

Without even working my skates I could feel my heart speeding up. "Tell me," I said, sharing his excitement.

"Hotshot newspaper boy coming up with all this suspicious stuff on chemical plants and ownership rights and squatter abuse. Amazing, and you pegged it, too … The Overton District had been a concrete storage yard through the first world war, then went out of business. Sharecroppers came in, set up camp. It's not very clear what the Klan's motivation was for destroying the campground. People lived in lean-tos and shelters of scrap tin. You have to think what a miserable place in winter. There was nothing of value there."

I said, "The Klan doesn't need a reason to destroy things."

Doctor Joe glanced at the skaters. "Getting a little loud, and hot," he said. "Come on, let's move outside."

"Make like we're a couple of toughs? Hey, I got it. We'll be Dukes, a little spit on your hair to slick it back."

He didn't know what I was talking about. I laughed. "Never mind. Yeah, let's move outside."

The place had started to fill up, getting to the way it was supposed to be on Saturday night; that's why it got stuffy. I was glad to get out in the crisp air. The only people around were kids walking into the roller rink. The hoods weren't over there in the shadows, not that I could see. I couldn't see the T-Bird either cause it was parked in the dark reaches of the lot. We walked to the bike rack where I'd put Big Red in the light. Doctor Joe leaned against the bike rack and I sat on Red. He looked at the bike like it was the first time he'd seen it.

"You're mother doesn't think you should have the motorcycle. Thinks it's too dangerous." He grinned, shaking his head. "But what do mothers know, huh? About danger, I mean."

"Yeah. But she might've been right to say I wasn't being practical, spending all my money on it."

"You didn't borrow to buy it, did you?"

"Hell no. Paid the sucker cash."

"And you have a regular income, don't you?"

"Yeah. That's right. As a matter of fact I've already started building my savings back up."

"How'd you do wrong, then?" he said, and that was the last word on spending and my lack of common sense.

"You recall what your theory was?" he asked but didn't wait for me to answer. "That the governor's father used prison labor to build the subdivision?"

I nodded.

"Well, as it happens, convict leasing was legal in some places, until the Thirteenth Amendment ended it. They outlawed it here in Alabama in 1928. That was a year before Kimbrough Senior bought the property. So he knew he was breaking the law using prison labor for the construction. That's one thing. You could say that by itself wasn't going to get him in any serious legal trouble since, as I told you some time ago, using prison labor was legal and widespread for a century. He could criticize it as just another federal law butting into states' rights, and so on—just like they don't recognize the new federal integration laws now.

"But what piqued my interest is that Kimbrough & Sons leased the entire site to the U.S. Army as a munitions dump. But that's not what it became. Apparently the army never took notice that Kimbrough had already built 190 houses there with young Kimbrough Junior, our current governor, in charge, so the army set aside only a small section of the property for bomb-disposal use.

"That's not all, either," he went on, talking a little faster. "Vulcon Industries? What did you say about it being next door?"

"Uh, that it hired the Negroes who lived in Ash? Probably dirt cheap."

"Exactly. Not only that, Vulcon required its workforce to purchase those properties, else they didn't get a job. I read a few of the archived real estate contracts those people signed and, just as I guessed, Vulcon held their mortgages. The chemical company had a captive workforce and got most of the salaries back that they paid out through the mortgage payments which they'd overpriced to begin with. The Negroes were literally slaves. It was basically a company town.

"The people didn't see it like that, though; those folks had a real opportunity to work and own their own property. They signed on, eagerly. The Depression had just started and they got a roof over their heads, not lean-tos, and a company store that offered credit. It's still that way today.

"The bad news is very bad, deadly," he said, shifting his weight, "Vulcon manufactures toxic chemicals. It produced biochemical weapons in both wars. The arrangement with the army's armory next door was to bury waste on the armory grounds. That was the neighboring property, remember, Ash Town. I could find no record where the unused canisters got buried.

"After World War Two, Vulcon made chemicals for widespread commercial uses, DDT and PCBs. It's legal and they still manufacture it.

"The contract with the army was only to dispose of war-effort materials like the mustard gas and ordinance canisters but not the company's commercial product waste. That waste material goes somewhere. Can you guess where, Sonny?"

"What does that mean? What's wrong with DDT and that other one? What are they, anyway?"

He stood and wiped off the back of his pants. He wore tan slacks and a pinstriped button-down Arrow shirt that with his jacket off made him look dorky circling the rink with a bunch of ponytailed bobbysockers.

"Your mother grew up on a farm, didn't she?"

"Uh huh."

"Well, no doubt they used dusting powder on their crops and it was probably DDT, an insecticide. It kills indiscriminately, not just boll weevils and potato worms but good insects, ladybugs, mosquito eaters. Small animals, birds. If a human ingests DDT, you could get seriously ill. That happens to farmers.

"And then there's the waste that comes in the manufacturing of it, both ground waste and sulfur dioxide from the smokestacks. Vulcon has two smokestacks, you've probably noticed. I'm guessing they dump their waste in the stream running through Ash Town. I've seen Leonard's Creek; it can run fast in the spring; it runs year round all the way to the Coosa."

"Is that what I smell that's bad out there, the creek?"

"Yep. I'm guessing the surrounding ground is saturated with toxic waste as well. Medically, we don't know the lasting effect or how much exposure is unsafe, but it's likely to have some carcinogenic effect. It can cause liver cancer, affect the immune system, create respiratory complications. Suffice it to say, living in Ash Town is very unhealthy."

"Ho ly shit," I said. I knew that most of those people had been there a long time; their parents raised them there.

I said, "So you mean the corruption goes all the way up to the governor himself?"

"That's right, all that way," he said. "Not that you haven't done enough, but now I need you to do one more thing. Get word to Harvey Nixon about this, tell him to spread around what I've told you. The people living there all need to be informed. They have to keep the kids out of the creek, and no fishing. The sooner they move out of there the better off they'll be. It's a poisoned wasteland."

"Okay, yeah. I will," I said, ready to go over there right then.

Maybe he read my mind cause he grabbed my arm as if I was about to take off. "Look, Sonny. This is something very dangerous I'm putting on you, telling you this stuff. Believe me when I tell you that I feel terrible for doing it. But you need to know. Just in case something goes wrong—you understand? People have to know."

I didn't say anything. Nothing was going to happen to him. How could it? He was way too big, way too important.

"I don't like asking you to do it, but I've got to get to Montgomery now to get something done about it. Hopefully they aren't the people responsible for my license revocation … You remember Guy—"

"Sure do, from the New Year's party. Weasel that stuck you with this Civil Service thing."

He didn't like hearing that but I didn't care. Guy Richards had way too much snake oil on him. I guess you had to be like that, though, to get that high up in politics.

"Well, regardless, he's the person I know in the Attorney General's Office who can get me an audience with the man. Listen to me, Sonny—"

"Doesn't your brother work there? Couldn't you tell him instead?"

"Not positioned right." That was all he said about his brother. Maybe they didn't get along, like Stuart and me.

He continued, "For the people in Ash Town, this is bigger than their civil rights. It's their health, maybe even their lives. I need to see the AG himself, I have to convince him to investigate Vulcon. If it comes to it, I'll threaten to go to Washington. But first I want to give these SOBs in the statehouse an opportunity to do the right thing—and I've got a little ace up my sleeve."

I couldn't help it. I just blurted out before thinking, "Are you crazy? You think that crook's going to help? He *works* for the governor. He won't help you, Joe."

He planted his feet and I could tell a lecture was coming.

Chapter 40

Doctor Joe said he should be back in town by Wednesday but would see me only long enough to relate his news, if any. He said the Hitchin Post would work. I said it could be risky there but he wouldn't change his mind. I said good luck and told him goodbye.

I watched him walk in a long, sure stride toward the dark end of the parking lot. I was hit by the thought of how all alone he was in this impossible battle. Don Quixote facing the great windmill or that crazy man Ahab shouting down the great whale—as if little human words would get him anywhere. I watched him disappear in a sheet of darkness, like the vaporous flame off a match, and I wondered if this would be the last time I saw him. The thought gave me such a hollow feeling I nearly bolted after him.

I knew that showed weakness. Well, maybe I was weak.

I felt alone, too. But at least he had given me something to do. It wasn't much, just relate some information. I wanted to see Harvey Nixon anyway but I hadn't yet worked up the nerve to face all the sadness in that home.

I straddled my motorcycle and wiped a blur from my eyes.

It took three cranks to get Red going, but once she sparked I felt better; I had control, power under my hands. I got adjusted, coat zipped, shoelaces double-tied, no hat or goggles. I goosed the throttle, feeling the vibration running through me. His white Bird pulled out of the lot and I was about to split behind it when I glimpsed some kind of ruckus at the entrance to the rink.

A handful of guys in black leather suddenly stumbled outside onto the pavement. I couldn't tell if they'd been pushed out or were backing out as a come-on to someone still inside, an invitation to rumble on the asphalt. I hadn't seen those jackets go in when Doctor Joe and I were talking. They would have come up from the other side of the lot. I looked closer and saw the gang was none other than Gerald Henry's West Side Bozos.

A couple of the punks shot them a bird back inside and I knew then the management had booted them out. You couldn't miss the rink's policy on gangs. It was posted on the wall as you stepped inside—"No gangs allowed. No exceptions."

I killed the engine, deciding to stick around and watch the action. I should've known the Bozos would move on in a whimper, which is just what they did. But then two cars came roaring into the lot, their brights on, one running very close behind the other toward the entrance to the rink. I thought they might crash into the place, but the cars stopped right about the spot the Bozos landed out front. One car pulled next to the other. The engines continued to run and the headlights lit up the roller rink.

The lurking cars intrigued me, just sitting there like metallic cats stalking the place. Why didn't anyone get out? Something strange was going on and I could sense people inside gawking out the door into those bright lights. The tension felt electric.

When the car doors finally opened and the occupants stepped out, I felt sure everybody else was as surprised as me. I knew who the people were even though I'd never seen them before.

After depositing the passengers, the two cars backed up and moved away toward the far end of the lot, out in the dark where Doctor Joe had put his car.

The group didn't move cautiously as I thought they should have.

They walked headstrong toward the entrance and right through some people out front, as if the group didn't see them or were seeing them as just fixtures, like street signs or trees.

They were young but older than me, college age and probably college students. And absolutely from up north. You didn't see anybody with hair like that down here, puffed up like mushrooms and high-waisted trousers with big belts. All four of the black males were too puny to intimidate anyone. Skates hung off their shoulders as though they'd actually come to skate. The others in the group were white, including two girls, one with dirty-looking long straight brown hair parted down the middle. The other girl had the same ironed hair and was dressed in boy's long roughed-up jeans. Two of the three white guys were husky but studious-looking, wearing flat round glasses and buttoned-down plaid shirts. They had no sideburns or ducktails; they weren't mean and they weren't fighters and they would've been a lot more at home at a pep rally instead of this tough, die-for-Dixie roller rink.

It would have been one of those civil rights organizations that sent them and I would've bet that they had scouted out roller rinks across Alabama beforehand and determined the one in Midland, with its racists policies proudly displayed—"We reserved the right to refuse Negroes entrance"—would get some press after their people were beaten and sent to the hospital. Or sent to jail.

The group held hands, stayed tight. They were keenly aware of where they were. I saw two of them trembling, like they'd been standing too long on an icy Chicago street. The group stopped for a second, maybe to reconsider, but then moved slowly inside. I wanted to think they were out of their minds, crazy from brainwashing. Like kamikazes. But that wasn't it. They were aware and afraid of the danger, and it reminded me of those black children walking unsteadily and scared to death into that white school in Arkansas, in Little Rock. Even with the army escorting them, those students were scared to death, you could see it even on the TV. Like those nine, I thought this group was about as brave as you could get. I mean, it took real nerves for them to walk into this place when they thought they knew how vicious Alabama's rednecks were.

But they only knew what they'd been taught in a classroom, not how bad it really was.

Why I got off the Harley and ran up there and fell in behind the group I couldn't really say. It was impulse, and crazy. My heart raced. But it felt right, like I was *supposed* to join them. My brain seemed to go on some kind of primeval instinct, not reason. But it wasn't the healthy instinct of survival because I was afraid. It was the instinct to find definition ... Maybe. No one else thought like I did since not a single other person joined in.

It felt like standing in front of a firing squad without time for a last smoke; I drew hard looks. My legs tried to buckle. None of the people in the group seemed to notice I was standing with them. I guess they were all too nervous to notice.

One of the black guys showed some ghost-white teeth to the girl in the ticket booth while pulling out his wallet, as if he thought he could then slip into his skates and begin gliding around the rink, maybe pick up a white girl. And maybe the management would put on Nat King Cole for him, too.

The ticket girl's skin was as ghostly white as the boy's teeth. She was too dumbfounded to say anything or even make a face; her jaw had stopped in mid-chew. It was then that two men suddenly stormed out of the nearby glassed-in office quick as jacks out of the weeds. You could see they weren't going to exchange cordialities with the kid wanting a ticket.

"You see that goddamn sign, jigaboo?" the burly one said. "Huh, see it?" He pushed close enough that his very long, very red beard brushed the kid's lost chin. He was about fifty years old and wore a hunting shirt with the sleeves rolled up to the elbows, a blanket of red hair on his thick freckled arms. He didn't need to get worked up cause he looked like he'd been worked up the last forty of his fifty years. "I'll tell you one time and that's it. Each and ever one of you yankee agitators got one opportun'ty to turn around and march your asses outta here. And I mean now!"

They'd cut the music and the big floor was morbidly lifeless.

The guy by his side was the brawly guy's opposite, paper thin, bug-eyed, big Adam's apple with a short-barrel pump shotgun cradled like Satan's baby across his arm. I watched his finger move inside the trigger guard when the big man started shouting. He wore no expression and that worried me a lot. Other people gathered behind the gun-toter and behind the visitors, surrounding us, all of them swelling and pulsating, like a pack of wolves, ugly faces growing uglier, spitting on the floor, a few guys anxiously circling. I pushed between a black kid and a girl and grabbed their hands. Hers was clammy and boneless. It trembled in mine. The black kid's hand was sickly hot.

The group stood silent. Outwardly, they didn't flinch. One of the white students spoke up, his voice clear, "You are denying us admission? Is that correct, sir?"

"Charlene, you call the sheriff right now, you hear me?"

Everybody looked at Charlene in the booth. "Yessir, Mr. Prichard, yes sir!" The phone was already in her hand, her unsteady finger working the circular dial from memory.

Prichard turned to the student that back-talked him. "Oh, you gotdamn right I am, boy. You niggerlovin' foreigners think you can come in here, do what you want, pretty as you please. We got ways down here, boy, and they don't 'llow no niggers mixin' with our white girls. This here's private property and yous' is violating my legal rights. Those rights says I can shoot your meddlin' asses if I am so inclined. You get me? …"

I kept a hard eye on the silent skinny one holding the shotgun, which he'd now pointed at the Negro with the wallet still out. While manager Prichard shouted, I whispered to the white guy who'd spoken, "He ain't messing around, you know that, don't you?"

He nodded quickly without looking at me.

"You better get the hell out of here. Fast!" I said. "Don't wait for the cops, they ain't your friend."

He turned to look at who was talking to him. His blue eyes were dull and determined. I saw his lips tighten against his teeth and I saw his surprise of realizing what was about to happen. He understood these people were serious. But, still, he didn't back off. That he would *still* stand up to the man like that, I had to admit, was the only thing that gave me the courage to stand there too.

There was no way these college kids were getting inside. They knew it and they weren't leaving here scot-free. They knew that, too, knew it before they even arrived in Alabama. The mob around us now was seething, mumbling things—"Take 'em out?" "String 'em." A venomous voice whispered, "Sew their balls where they eat." Any movement or gesture from one of the activists and that shotgun was going off. A wrong facial expression could have done it. These headstrong yankees were cooked and I was too.

Someone behind me pinned down the heels of both my shoes. He didn't say anything, just breathed on my neck. The odor was vomitous, like romano cheese on pizza. I felt the air suddenly shift behind me and I succumbed to that dreamy fear of a two-by-four slicing air toward my head. Then I flinched for real when something fell softly on my shoulder. I looked and saw it was the head of a baseball bat, tapping the shoulder, telling me something. I wasn't sure what.

Voices became mumbles as Charlene cradled the phone and said in a loud cry, "They on the way, Mr. Prichard. Be here in a shake."

My theory was that if it hadn't been for all the young girls, out on Saturday night with girlfriends or dates, there would already be blood on the floor, the management worrying later about cleaning up the mess. Us southerners were of a singular mind when it came to being chivalrous with our young white girls. We also protected to the bitter end if necessary the name of Jesus Christ Almighty, the Confederacy and of course the good name of all our mothers. We even let sentiment guide us in those beliefs.

I worked up the courage to turn around to see who it was with the club. I had to blink against the blur that seemed to keep me from focusing cause I wasn't sure I was seeing right. He looked at me as if he didn't know me, then nodded toward the entrance behind him, telling me to leave. He motioned with his head again. Sugarman Cole hadn't said a word when he released that foul air and tapped my shoulder with the club. He just tweaked his head, again now, as if to say, *I'm giving you this one. Get on out of here.*

I did. I stepped out into the breezy, clean night air hating myself. I held my breath and just about prayed to God not to hear gunshots or the awful sound of clubs pounding flesh and bone. Instead, headlights raked across me, followed by sirens abruptly screaming. Two patrol cars came to a stop at the front of the roller rink. They were Woodstock police cars, black-and-whites, not the dirty brown cruisers of the Sheriff's Office. I was sure Charlene had said, "Sheriff! For godsake, hurry …"

An officer from each car hustled inside with sidearms drawn, disappearing as fast as it took me to wonder again why Sugarman let me go. I tried to listen from where I stood but there was too much running-around noise.

The sudden pull on the back of my jacket just about caused me to lose all the control Mr. America, my bodybuilding instructor, told me never ever lose. I almost swung an elbow first and looked second.

It would have been a mistake.

"Sonny, let's go," Doctor Joe said in a hurried-up voice. "Now."

"Jesus fucking Christ. What are you doing here?"

"Tell you later—Come on now."

"What about them? They ain't gonna make it." I was practically screaming at him.

He tried to calm me with a smile, and it worked. Why would he be smiling at a time like this, I wondered. He must have had good reason. But, still …

He said, "I called my friend on the force."

"What? How'd you know?"

"I saw the cars arriving as I was leaving. I saw blacks inside the car and headed for a phone. That's him in there now. Don't worry, I'm sure he'll get them out safely. Let's go. I can't afford to get caught up in this. He doesn't want me seeing him, and that goes for you too. It's for his safety."

I stared at him in amazement, wanting to say thank you, thank you, thank you. He saved those young people. But I guess he knew that already.

"I'm on my bike, remember."

"Okay, but this time I'll wait to make sure you leave. I know you, you'll butt right back in there. That's something we've got to work on, Sonny. Get on your bike and leave, got it?"

"I guess. Right."

"I was thinking you might want to catch Harvey Nixon at the drug store. I think it would be better if you didn't go to his home. Alright?"

"Well, I'll see what I can do … Good luck in Montgomery and thanks again. You saved those poor bastards."

He nodded. "I mean it. You've got to go about your business, go to school, deliver your papers. See Susie. Now go home. Please."

This was another goodbye. He dropped his head and walked again into the darkness.

It occurred to me the dark was now Doctor Joe's friend, his protector. He could hide there. Like a thief on the run. It was as bad as being black. He wore an albatross that in this country, in Alabama, the South, was worse than being a criminal. Now he had to move about as night creatures move. Who would vouch for him, for his good deeds? Well, I thought, for what it's worth he's got me.

Before I left the parking lot, I wheeled into the shadows and found the two cars that had dropped off the civil rights workers. They were parked next to each other with their car engines and lights off. Both had Alabama tags—the words "Heart of Dixie" stamped on a yellow background. I threw down my kickstand but let Red idle and walked over to the driver's side of one of them, a fairly new Packard, '56, big four-door that could hold six people easy, eight as skinny as those kids were.

"Listen," I said in a low voice. "The cops are taking your friends. They're going to the Woodstock jail. Call your yankee lawyers first. They're gonna need some help tonight."

"Okay. Thanks, friend." The driver was a white college-aged kid too who looked scared shitless, like he thought I might pull out a pistol at any moment and start blasting.

"Are y'all with CORE?"

He looked suspiciously at me but then nodded.

"Well, if you're planning to march through here sometime, I could help you out, give you information that might help you. I can give you my number."

"You serious?"

"I can be your fucking spy. You want it, my number?"

He quickly handed me a notebook like the one I used in my algebra class for problems. I wondered why they would have a school notebook in the car but wasn't about to ask a question stupid as that.

I put my full name and phone number on that sucker and handed it back.

"Thanks, man. Really. Be cool."

"You are welcome, man. You be cool too."

I hustled off into the night, free as a bird on the outside but trapped in my heart at the fate of those brave college kids.

Chapter 41

"You's a good boy, comin out cheer wid dem kind words, Sonny boy."

I also brought along an appointment date I'd made for his family, all seven of them, at the colored health clinic to get their blood checked out. I handed him the card without saying anything. He gave it the once-over. His scrunched-up face showed about a hundred questions.

"I'll tell you why in a minute. Can I come in?"

I didn't want to go against Doctor Joe and I didn't mean any disrespect against him or against Harvey Nixon for coming to his home. But I couldn't count on running into Harvey at the drug store and it seemed more urgent than Doctor Joe made it sound. Even though he was the medical expert, not me.

There was still some daylight left at five in the afternoon and if the enemy lay in wait out here it didn't make much sense to park two blocks away, but I did it anyway. Nothing suspicious caught my eye as I walked along the narrow street Harvey lived on.

Losing their young boy was hard enough for the Nixons to get through, they didn't need more grief from the likes of me. But they were about to get some anyway.

He let me in. He said his wife was at the café waiting tables and his stepfather was out fishing Leonard's Creek. I cringed hearing that. He probably fished that creek all the time, the catch a treat at family suppers. His two daughters were out back and his wife's mother and his mother were in the kitchen fixing supper. I wondered if they were waiting to cook the older man's catch.

"Harvey, can I ask you—Did your folks live in Ash when it got burned down? And your wife's?"

He nodded and said, "Not Cissy, she from Blueboro. But Mama, yeah. She come through fine. Pops, no. He one them die not long after. Why you wanna know fo'?"

"You called your daddy 'Pops'? Me too. My Pops, he's dead, too … How is your mama feeling? She in pretty good health still?"

He frowned. "She okay, mostly I guess."

"You think I could talk to your mama about it, that time back then, I mean?"

He frowned again. "What you up to show do sound like some mischief, Sonny boy. Why you so inna'rested in the burnin? That be one dark time nobody wanna talk about round cheer, huh?"

"Yeah, I guess. But I gotta talk about it. There's some things you have to know, Harvey. And they ain't good, especially since you've been here so long and probably don't owe anymore on your home."

"Shee-it I don'. I's owe a bundle and now moh cause of dem dang awnins."

"Yeah. Well, we're gonna try and set that straight. Don't pay a penny more. It's all illegal. Hear me?"

I waited till he nodded. He took a seat in an old cloth recliner by the living room window. It spit out puffs of dust high as his face. He didn't even notice. I stole a stiff-back chair from the dining room and straddled it close to him.

I could hear some pans or something clanging in the kitchen but nobody was talking in there.

"First off, that doctor's appointment is to see if any of you have lead poisoning or anything bad in your system ought not to be there. It's because of the chemical company, Vulcon. They are dumping poisons in the crick you fish in."

He leaned forward not two feet from my face. He wasn't mad-looking, not yet, still just puzzled. But he was interested and that was good.

"Yeah?" he said.

All of a sudden I burst out crying. I couldn't explain it, it just happened. When I found my voice I started talking fast as a grammar-school girl between lots of gasps, "Oh—I'm sorry—Your son is ... he's dead cause of me ... and I just can't help feeling so bad about it—For your family. Please, please—Can all y'all forgive me, ever? I can't stop thinking ... thinking if only you hadn't been there that day when those boys beat me and pulled them off me, it wouldn't have happened, Harvey. Your boy would be here. If I had never ridden in the truck with you. Oh God, I am sorry, Harvey. I'm so sorry ..."

I just trailed off into a black hole where there was no light and no forgiveness, just a blank nothing. He couldn't forgive me. I couldn't forgive myself and I couldn't forget it. But then he said something that seemed like a candle light down at the bottom of that empty black hole.

He laid his heavy hands on both my shoulders, squeezed them and patted me affectionately, his hands big like Doctor Joe's. "It the way it is, Sonny boy. Ain't no blame on you. You kant hep that you is white, huh?"

I stared at him while wiping my eyes on my shirtsleeves and sucking air, trying hard to dry up and not start again. I wasn't sure just what he meant. I thought he meant that *he* couldn't help it that he was black and that was why trouble fell on him, not me. But either way, it's just the way things are. It hurt my face to have to smile but I did it just the same and said, "I hate it that there's so much hate for you, Harvey. For all y'all. I—It's going to change, though. Just you wait."

"It don' rightly seem so, been this way so long."

I sucked up the snot cause there wasn't a tissue in sight and got to what I'd come to say. "They've been sending that poison down the crick for as long as they've been in business, and that's a long time. The stuff's in the ground under your feet, too. Nobody has ever investigated it until now, until my friend with the government found out. He sent me to tell you about it. He's in Montgomery right now making a big stink about it."

I gave him a moment so he could think about that. Then his eyes lit up and he said, "You know they's impot'unt folk over at Vulcon and in the state gov'ment who ain't gonna take kindly to your man, even if he in the gov'ment too."

"Yeah, I know. He knows."

"You don't una'stand, boy. Most us'ns in Ash, we work over Vulcon and they's good jobs."

"Maybe so, Harvey, but they are cheating you and they are poisoning everybody that lives here. People are gonna get sick if they ain't already. That just ain't right. It's gotta be stopped."

He swelled like he was going to take a stand against me. "Lookie here. Some them pot'unt people up there, I mean they gots some half breed mulatto chil'en all growd up now still livin in Ash, the gov'ner fo' one and they is just happy to—"

"The governor? You say the *governor*?"

"Sho' nuff. They's one lady what's good neighbors live right over yonder." He pointed toward his back yard. "His own flesh'n blood. But she know better than go round talkin 'bout it. You too, young Sonny boy. Don' you go tellin *no*body 'bout that neither."

"Course not, Harvey."

"They maybe seven, eight still here from the burnin', all them half-blood from some pot'unt white mans, show's the cream set on top the milk."

Among all the other graft and abuse, Ash Town was a sex playground for some rich white men before it became a killing ground and a heap of ashes. And the man who was now our governor had been right in the thick of it. Doctor Joe would have fits when he found out; he would want to know right now, too, while he was still at the statehouse. I was thinking it might give him some artillery to get the Attorney General's attention. How could it not? He could argue how bad it might be for Governor Kimbrough's future, in office and in his citizenship, if his loyal Alabama voters learned that all that fun he had with shanty black girls back in his youthful construction days had made him the daddy of some little half-and-half picaninnies. And by the way, Mr. AG, I'd like my dental license back.

I thought real quick and decided I should call Jeanne, maybe she'd know how to reach him.

Harvey leaned back in the dusty chair looking thoughtful. He said, "I tell you another thing, young Sonny. One them by name a William Earl Johnson, he live out cheer all his born day. Everbody know the gov'nor, he also William Earl daddy. Why that man get stole in the night summah fo' last and strung to a tree, I nevah una'stand, cause he don do nothin wrong. Nothin … William Earl, he a good man."

I tried to go back in time. Just one minute was all I asked for. I didn't want to believe I heard it. He was talking about the man I saw beaten and lynched in the forest that night nearly two years ago. And now I knew his name, a name I'd prayed I would never know.

Chapter 42

I wanted to get away, but Harvey held me with his story.

"William Earl coulda been the son a the gov'nor, but them all the sudden findin out ain't why they lynched 'im. No suh."

I stared at the wall that had nothing on it but one framed photograph of some real old black people who posed without smiling. I pictured the man, William Earl Johnson, on his ride to the woods and thought of the horror of that ride. They would've taunted him, spit in his face, degraded him. That was the teasing part of it, their way of working up the bile. I went through it before, in Miss West's class as she read the story, a black man crammed in a car among sweaty, agitated white men on his last ride; William Earl Johnson knew what to expect, too, that it was the end of time.

I stood and walked unsteadily to the front door and looked up and down the street through the curtain-less window. I didn't see a squad car or a green Chevy, but there was a white cat creeping slowly across the street, about to pounce on something camouflaged in the bushes that I didn't even see.

I had not noticed the new awning over the front door when I arrived. Harvey had scoffed at having to purchase it because it wouldn't provide a damn bit of protection from anything, not rain, wind, sunlight, peepers, dirty cops, nothing.

I listened for sounds and heard some girlish squealing. That would be his two daughters playing out back. I heard a thud, like a stick hitting the punching bag, something his son would have been more likely to do than the girls. Maybe I'd just imagined it.

I turned and looked at Harvey again. He seemed more anxious to finish talking and I knew I had to hear what he needed me to hear. "Then wha—why did they do it? What for?"

He hesitated. Not like he was still afraid to confide in me, but rather searching for the words. He said, "Nobody give a hoot he be only half black. Nobody round cheer give one cent he be a fancy one, neither, or that he worn't married to nobody. He didn't never bring no harm to nobody. Oh, William Earl was fussy sometime', even uppity wid some folk. He could talk you two mile a minute. And sing? That boy, he was a jaybird. He sho' put on a show at the club come Fri'dy night. He sho' was a wire round cheer. That William Earl …"

His face was warm and affectionate telling me this, like he was talking about a loved one.

He went on. "He fussin' all a time at dem white boys what put up his new awnin' and they laughin at him all the while. Well, I reckon they go tell the Klu Klan and then … Well, I sho wish I could git my hands on one them god damn Klan men what don it."

Too much was going on in my head and in my heart and I had to sit down and just breathe. I thought how astounding this moment was. Here I sat, me, this white boy, in a Negro's home being told these very intimate things just like I was part of Harvey Nixon's own people. As deep in Dixie as you could get, where blacks *never* got personal with white folk, not even with the white children these old nannies like my Gussie have raised, I felt like I belonged.

I looked at Harvey and my eyes welled. "I saw it, Harvey."

Squirming in the chair, I told him what I'd never told anyone before. "I saw it happen. They beat him and then they lynched him. He … he was out of his misery before they got the rope on him."

Chapter 43

The visit with Harvey Nixon took up the afternoon and now I was having to deliver papers in the dark. Customers stood in their yards with their arms crossed waiting for me. I didn't even think most of them looked at the damn thing, except when something exciting happened like the Ruskies launching Sputnik before us—bully for them—or maybe to clip the grocery coupons and this week's Green Stamp specials.

"Yes ma'am, it won't happen again. Thank you." I said that about five more times before throwing the last paper.

It was my proclivity to snoop that took me by Doctor Joe's house before going home to supper.

I figured I'd just check to see if he left Pearl there while he was gone. This being Monday, I guessed he'd still be in Montgomery and the house would be dark as a graveyard.

But it was not. I kept guessing wrong so often lately that I told myself right then and there, Don't ever make another guess about anything, not even about something simple like when Mother's going on the warpath, or something more complex, like Susie couldn't be pregnant.

The light came from deep in the house, the kitchen, I thought. There was light in the backyard but that would be the floodlight.

He's back, I thought and pulled into the driveway, all the way to the back, right up behind the yellow MG with "W A R E A G L E S" pasted across the rear window. I didn't see the T-Bird. This wasn't a holiday, why wasn't Jeanne at school studying her butt off for that Phi Beta Kappa pin? Then again I thought, Okay, she's here to do something for Doctor Joe, like feed Pearl. Then I reminded myself again not to make guesses, I was wrong every time. It was a proven fact.

Then I thought, He must have phoned her to go to the house for some reason; he left the oven on. Sure. He hardly even used the oven. Deliah did. Then Deliah left it on. Sure again.

I mashed the doorbell so disgusted with myself for still guessing on things that I hadn't given a thought what to expect or what I'd say to her.

It took a while but she got there and opened up, or rather she cracked the door about five inches and stuck her face in the small open space. She looked alarmed and her eyes traveled all around but not on me.

"What's the matter?" I asked seriously.

"Wha—why are you here? Did you want something?"

"Joe's not back, is he? I didn't see the Bird."

The door didn't budge. I felt like sticking my shoe in the crack because I had a sudden feeling she might shut it. I guessed she might.

"What are *you* doing here, Jeanne?"

Her eyes kept darting, now trying to think up something, but she didn't answer.

"Listen, Jeanne, I gotta talk to him. Do you have a number where I can reach him? Is he staying with his brother? I was planning to call you tonight to find out. It's important."

"Well, just how were you going to call me? Did you get my phone number somehow? How?" She sounded incredulous. I wasn't surprised.

"I *don't* have your number. I was going to figure that out, maybe call the administration office at Auburn, get it that way."

"Silly boy! They don't give out information to strangers. You didn't know that?"

Normally that would have stung me into giving up, but I didn't let it. I'd interrupted some fishy business and she was trying to put me off.

That only made me more curious, and suspicious. That was troubling because I wanted to believe Jeanne was true to Doctor Joe even if they did have some pretty good spats. I'd hoped that we could be friends when all this trouble blew over. But deep down I didn't believe it would ever be that way. And right now she was up to something.

I heard a noise behind her, a thump. It wasn't Pearl; she would have greeted me with a bark before I rang the bell. It sounded like someone slipped on a step, heavy like that. I pretended I didn't hear it and Jeanne pretended too. Which told me absolutely that someone was with her.

"He's asked me to fetch him something that's very private," she sniffed, in a tone that meant a peon like me was not privy to knowing what.

I sighed, and meaning to be sincere, I asked, "Jeanne, what's the matter? How come you're treating me like the enemy? I'm not."

The door was cracked open enough for me to see her fist ball up and go straight onto her gorgeous hip—Yep, she had on short shorts again. I had to admit just the way she looked was a big part of the reason I was trying to understand and forgive her. It could've been that seeing her in those skin-tight shorts made me think of holding her, dancing with her.

She slumped, giving in a little. "Sonny, Joe and I are going to be married some day. I don't want to say this to you, but I am just trying to discourage you. There won't be a place ... Do you understand?"

Well, that one did sting. But I didn't care. "Yeah, I guess. But where's your engagement ring? Wouldn't you be wearing one? How come you've never said anything about getting married or even being engaged? Huh?"

"Well, if the bastard—" and she cut it quick as a guillotine's slice.

"So, then," I said, "it's him. *He's* the one don't want to get married. Is that it?"

"No thanks to you, you—" She made it too easy.

Then I slipped my foot into the doorway. But she didn't try shutting the door so I pulled it back out. I tried again. "Listen, I have to reach him. Will you help me or not?"

She turned bitter. "I'm afraid not. He hasn't told me where—"

I shook my head and looked her dead in the eye. "My mother used to tell me, 'Don't speak before you think.' Jeanne… who's in there?"

She slammed the door.

I was very discouraged with Miss Jeanne Cochran, Miss Sorority Highbrow. She just managed to show me what a phony she really was.

But I still didn't know what she was up to, so I decided to find out. I rolled Big Red along the side of the house and parked her behind the tall border shrubs, out of sight of her car and the street. Then I eased around to the backyard. A row of high windows lined the garage. I checked inside for the T-Bird and Pearl. Neither. I dashed past the kitchen light behind the lily pond in the patio and into the backyard trees out of the illumination of floodlight. I watched for movement.

In a moment the upstairs lights one by one started going on and then off. Very quickly, the downstairs rooms began to glow too. She was going room to room for something.

I anticipated her and the other person making a dash for the car and then I would jump out and surprise them. Tackle her if I had to, to find out what she'd taken. I waited. The kitchen pantry door had a broken spring in the latch that if you jiggled up and in it would open, and I was getting so antsy I was about to go for it. But I held off. When they made their dash for the MG, I'd see. Be patient; that was something I'd learned the importance of in my muscle-and-mind class, not only from Doctor Joe.

A noise you did not want to hear when you were hiding out behind someone's house came from around front. It was the sound of more than one car pulling close, stopping. The muffler on at least one of them was blown out. That one grew silent. I didn't know how many there were but they weren't leaving.

Chapter 44

I took a breath, swallowed hard and eased back around the corner of the house expecting to see a green Chevy and maybe a cop cruiser. Their spotter saw the lights and they were coming for Doctor Joe.

But when I had them in sight, I could see I'd guessed wrong once again. It wasn't cops. My throat had gotten too dry to swallow. The three cars that had jumped the curb and now sat idling on the front lawn were all 1940-model Fords, two coupes beat to hell and a rusty pickup. Bunch of jalopies. Four heads that I could see were inside the gray coupe, and they seemed to be talking to each other. Some of them could have been cops but all wore the white robes of the KKK.

When they cut the headlights and started opening doors, I moved back out of sight. Double-timing to the back of the house, I broke in through the pantry, noticing first the glow coming from the opened refrigerator. There should've been some Miller High Lifes in there. I'd never seen it without beer. The light was still on in the kitchen. I crept into the dining room and through the hallway to the foyer. The floor creaked under my shoes; I'd never noticed that before now. The skinny dress windows beside the front door had coverings but I would still have seen the glow if they'd set fire to a cross in the yard; I figured the hole was getting dug right now to put the thing in the ground and it would soon flare up. No sounds came from outside but I didn't dare get near the curtain to peek, not with the kitchen light at my back.

I whispered, "Jeanne? Jeanne, where are you? We've got company. Come on now!"

She stepped through the door of Doctor Joe's study, which was beyond a short passageway underneath the stairs. There was light coming from the office. The guy stepping out behind her was Joe College himself, with the argyle sweater draped across his shoulders under a shock of wavy gold hair, the dazzling white pants and brown penny loafers. Looked like Pat Boone if you could imagine him without that creepy smile. Both of them disgusted me.

He stood back as Jeanne came on me in a rush, wearing a guilty smile big enough for the both of them. I was now by the staircase, where I had stood that night with her in my arms, dancing, breathing in her sweet-tangy gardenia fragrance, as I remembered it. She got close enough that I had to breathe through my nose instead of the mouth in case my breath stunk. She laid her arms right on my shoulders and wiggled herself so close every part of her touched me. I could've melted. I could've forgotten all about what she was up to or what she had in mind. I might've sold my soul to the devil just to kiss her.

"Company?" she said without perplexity. She had no reason in the world to get worried just because of me.

Then I remembered, *The fucking KKK is out there.* That broke the spell. "You've got to clear out of here, Jeanne. They're outside, they're going to burn—"

I lost the next moment. We all did, at least Jeanne and me. I couldn't say about the frat fella. Several seconds may have passed or a number of minutes. The blast came so swiftly it was impossible to shield Jeanne from it. We both went off our feet and through the air. I say both of us, but I really couldn't tell what happened to Jeanne. I just assumed she hit the wall when I did because as I came to, she was unconscious next to me, close enough to be in my arm, her legs splayed in the way a doll's legs can get twisted sideways. It scared me to look. I grew wide-eyed. A trickle of blood seeped from her hairline in front of her ear.

I took her hands. They were limp as the paws of a sleeping dog. I put my ear to her heart before I realized I couldn't hear anything, certainly not a heartbeat. I think I started to panic. She might be dead, or dying from bleeding inside her brain. What could I do about that? Then I remembered we have pulses and I placed two of my shaky fingers on her wrist and tried to calm myself long enough to feel for one.

Yes, I felt a pulse. I tried to pull one of her eyelids back by pushing back the eyebrow and it worked but that didn't tell me anything except her rolled eyeball was still in its socket.

I dry-washed around my face and head and looked at my hands. No blood. My head didn't hurt much and I didn't feel lumps. There was no blood on my clothes, either.

Where was the frat guy? "Where are you?" I thought I had shouted the question but I could only feel a vibration inside my head. I couldn't hear my voice.

The blast had shattered the front door and blew half of it onto the staircase about five stairs up, and the panes and cross sections that flanked the door were blown clean. I figured the curtains saved us from the spray of glass. It was a big explosion, not a simple Coke-bottle Molotov. They must have used dynamite.

I wanted to black out again, I could feel it coming and quickly stretched out in a push-up to speed blood flow to my head and took deep breaths. I couldn't let myself go out, not with the flames licking the floor around us and smoke rolling through the room.

I stumbled trying to lift Jeanne onto my shoulder. One of those flames jumped up into her shiny hair and ran through it fast as wind through a wheat field. I smothered her head into my chest, then knuckled up enough strength to get her up before our clothes caught fire. She wasn't that heavy. I was just weak and dizzy but I got her moving and very quickly we were out of the hall and in the kitchen, then out the backdoor and into the airy trees. I didn't even remember taking a breath.

Jeanne coughed and spat phlegm and rapidly blinked her eyes. She would be okay. She stood up, or tried to; her legs, which had been in that awful-looking position, gave on her and I grabbed her arm. She tried again and did it. Her singed hair was a little shorter and smelled something awful.

I felt sticky pine sap pulling the hairs on my arm and mumbled, "Piss!"

"What? ... Wh-where's Greg?"

I realized I could hear her; my hearing was on its way back. I called Greg's name a couple of times and didn't hear him answer. "You hear him?" I asked.

She shook her head. I cringed watching her knead her bloodshot eyes again.

I didn't want to say what seemed obvious, that her friend Greg must have been knocked out in the blast and was still inside. There was nothing to do but head back in, and I did.

"Stay put," I told her.

The heat in the front was too intense and I could get only to the back end of the hallway where I screamed for Greg again. Still no response. The fire was getting bigger by the second. I could see it spread across the ceiling in the foyer and up the stairs like it was running a relay race with itself. I couldn't get to the study. He may have retreated into the room and hopefully broke through a window and escaped. I hoped so cause they would figure out a way to blame Doctor Joe if they found him burnt to a crisp inside his house.

I rejoined Jeanne whose begging eyes dropped when I shook my head and made the mistake of looking sorry. We watched together while the fire ravaged the house. She stayed close to me, even leaning on me, but that was just out of helplessness.

I imagined that guy burning in there, his flesh bubbling, bursting. How horrible it would be to go that way. I'd much rather be shot by a firing squad or gassed in the chair.

"You know they're gonna want to know what you were doing in Joe's house."

She tightened her grip on my arm and put her face against me. She wouldn't look at me. Her long hair on one side was burnt all the way to her head. It wasn't quite so creamy luscious now and it would be a while before it was again.

Doctor Joe's important possessions were going up in flames while we stood around and watched; there was nothing I could do. He had his investment records in his office and some expensive gold and silver pieces, which might survive since they were in a safe. He'd shown me a rare Prussian gold coin. Once he brought out a sack of heavy Spanish silver pieces and we used them as chips in two-handed poker. He had hundreds of record albums, trays of color slides, and lots of framed pictures on walls of him in his football uniforms, photographs of himself with friends in Europe when he was a student. There were pictures of Jeanne, too, but those could be replaced—if he ever chose to.

But I knew the biggest loss would be the autographed sheet music he had been collecting for years because he was putting together a book. They were jazz scores from already famous black artists. He had been going to lounges and taverns, wherever Thelonious Monk or some other big musician would be that he could get to, and worked his magic on them. He told me once, "Monk's a tough negotiator, let me tell you. Bad as Miles Davis. I paid dearly for 'In Walked Bud'—way too much. But it will be priceless someday." He said he was doing the book to celebrate black artists, pure and simple, not for money.

I had teased, "You want to show that all blacks aren't the jungle bunnies this sea of idiots all around us thinks, right?"

"Yeah," he had grinned, "something like that, if you leave off the jungle reference. Music is the one way Negroes have been free to express themselves. It'll be an important historical document some day, this collection. In your lifetime, you watch."

Jeanne started to tremble and I thought she might be going into shock. Maybe she realized how bad it was for the guy who'd come with her. She clutched me tighter.

I sure didn't want her collapsing on me now; we had to get out of here. I tried to keep her thinking. "Jeanne, we've gotta leave. Do you understand me? Jeanne?"

She let go my arm. Her voice quaked. "You thi—think he's in there? Do you?—Oh my God!"

"He's a big boy. He probably got out through a window. Okay? He's probably fine. Now—"

Fire suddenly burst through the upstairs windows, spitting out glass and flaming fabric. We buried ourselves deeper in the pines. The unleashed flames licked at the brick exterior as black smoke began billowing off the slanted roof like steam off molten lava, and then the flames burst through the highest point of the house and shot skyward into the night. We stood mesmerized by the crackling fire even as the heat kept backing us away.

Chapter 45

It started to worry me that she wouldn't leave. She didn't seem to grasp that hanging around the scene of a crime was no good for her, and this was definitely a crime scene. I had to get out of there, too.

"If they catch you here, who do you think they'll blame?" I said. "It ain't gonna be the Klan. Down at City Hall they all hate Joe, that's why they did this. Don't you understand that, Jeanne?"

She finally got some sense in her head and let me help her into her car, dazed and worried and frightened as a little girl in a dark woods. She seemed to shrink down to nothing in the seat of the little MG.

I got away after her, just ahead of the first fire truck. By then, the house was surely totally gone. The time it took them to get there only led me to think the Klan also controlled the fire department and told them in advance to take their time responding to calls on Broadmore, that they should go find a kitten to rescue first. People had gathered under the street-side magnolias and I couldn't be sure they didn't see the MG leave, or me. It helped that yard trees largely blocked the driveway from view and most likely all eyes were on the blaze.

Riding Red out of town on 131, I drifted for a while and let the cold air sting my face. I was trying to sort things out. I loved the wind on my face, but I couldn't sort anything out, so I headed back.

It was nearly eleven when I killed the engine and pushed the bike down Herman's long driveway to the tool shed in back, then stole across the dirt yard. Everything was quiet except for some crickets going at it and the hiss of some cat I must have spooked. The light from his back-porch bedroom guided me. When I tapped Herman quickly appeared in the small window. His eyes blew up like the devil had come for him. Way too nervous. He was still running scared.

The door creaked open and then the screen creaked open.

"What the hell?—" he said quietly.

"I wanna spend the night. No big deal."

"You smell like a campfire, where you been, man?"

I was here because I didn't know where else to go. Certainly not home; that's the first place they would look. Call me paranoid, but I had this gnawing suspicion that Jeanne went straight to the cops. I imagined her saying, sobbing and hysterical, that she'd stopped by Doctor Joe's to water the hanging ferns when she spotted me—you know, that little highschooler always hanging around Dr. Peach's? It had to be him that did it. She would be all worried and wanting to know about Greg, too. Had he been killed? I hope that boy gets the chair for murdering him.

I was guessing they hadn't hesitated to put out the APB on me.

So now it came down to whether Herman could be trusted. He's got his opportunity right now, I thought.

"You got me up, tell me something."

I raked clothes off a chair and sat. It was the only chair in the cluttered room. It went with the yellow formica and chrome kitchen table he used for a desk. He'd dropped one of the leafs and pushed it up against the wall to save space. School books were piled on the table along with comics and more clothes. I saw a shiny new rifle propped over in a corner next to his .22 but didn't say anything. The gun was bigger than the old single-shot. It infuriated me to think he'd gotten it from the dirty cops as a reward for squealing on me, telling them it was my government friend who had figured out the streetlight scam.

"I just need to get a little shuteye, okay? Then I'll tell you everything. Just let me sleep a while."

"Fuck no, man. Tell me now."

I looked up at him, into his stare. "You gonna turn me in again?"

He sighed in disgust and walked out of the room without saying anything. Herman had changed since his beating. It seemed to me he had gotten more contrite and in control of his temper. The metamorphosis of Herman Brown, I thought. My class had just learned that word from a story Miss West assigned us to read. She wasn't reading to the class anymore after that story about the lynching and the row it stirred over me. I couldn't figure why she chose a story of some sheepish little guy turning into a damn cockroach. It was like science fiction; it *was* science fiction. I didn't understand anything about the story except that the word in the title, *"Metamorphosis,"* meant the little man was transformed into a giant bug. Herman might have changed into another creature, a rat, say. But he'd also had a lesson in fear and I could see the change from that. Maybe I had changed too.

I followed him into the kitchen where he stood at the open refrigerator holding a package of baloney and staring blankly as if hypnotized by the interior light. I spotted half a banana cream pie in there with lots of wavy whipping cream and shut my mouth before I drooled.

"How 'bout a mayonnaise sandwich, you mind?" I said.

"Go ahead, but keep it down," he said.

"Thanks." I got the stuff out and went to work. He let me have a slice of baloney too. We tiptoed back into his room.

I was bone tired. I could feel it especially strong after devouring the sandwich. "Let me just shut my eyes for a little bit, huh?"

The next thing I knew jays were trilling in the cherry tree outside the thin aluminum window. I made out the tweets of finches frolicking in the bramble, and there were dogs somewhere, maybe talking to each other across yards, Good morning to you Rufus, You too, Brutus. I felt great, as bright-eyed and bushy-tailed as a Walt Disney creature that thumps. Until I remembered.

Hearing Herman's weird bubbling that was him snoring brought me back, or down, to who I was—a fugitive on the run, chased by a monster you could never escape. I elbowed the snorer.

"Herman. Herman! I gotta go. Wake up."

Only his eyes opened, like Frankenstein coming to life. "Huh?"

"I need some money. Can you lend me some? I can pay you back later. I've got money in my savings account. C'mon, man. Herman, get up."

He sat up rubbing his eyes as if he was unscrewing the lid off a pint of white lightning. Then he scratched his head and farted and half-grinned. I thought he'd woken up happy too, until he said, "Oh, fuck. This ain't Saturday."

He frowned at me. "What'd you say?"

"Look at me. I won't be going to school today. Seven bucks, alright?"

The hands on his Roy Rogers wind-up pointed to 6:04, too early to make a phone call.

"You gotta do me another favor, too. Call Carlile Oldham. You know him. Call him before you go to school and tell him I need him to deliver my papers this afternoon. Okay?"

He lurched to get hold of my shirt. "Sonny, what's up with you? You said you'd tell me. So give."

"Alright ... First off, I didn't do anything wrong," I said and told him enough to get him to back off. "I saw this house get burned down over on Broadmore. I saw who did it, too. The Klan. They don't know I saw them, but I did—Just like with me and you in the woods. They weren't there to burn a damn cross; they threw dynamite in the place."

"Man alive! Did you recognize any of them? Were any of them the same ones?"

I wanted to see how he would respond, and now I knew. "It was dark."

He might have noticed the heat rise in my cheeks, but he acted like he didn't. He wasn't interested whose house it was or how I was actually able to see the KKK do their work. Which, it seemed to me, meant that Roach had taught him how to get answers out of me without drawing suspicion. It was looking more and more like the end of my lifelong friendship and blood brotherhood with Herman Brown.

I didn't have to dress, just wash my face and pee and of course brush my teeth. I used Brandy's little yellow-and-blue Snow White toothbrush, thinking in a moment of high longing that the worst about Herman meant I wouldn't see her again.

Herman gave me the seven dollars but not without wanting something for it. "Where you going, anyways?" he asked, sounding casual.

Seven dollars would get me to Montgomery. "San Francisco," I told him.

"Shit, man. Really, where are you going?"

"That's where I'm going. Come see me when you grow up."

All things considered, I still couldn't be a hundred percent sure about him. "Thanks for the dough, I appreciate it … Herman, I don't know what you think of me anymore, but I ain't doing nothing bad and I'm not out to get you in any trouble. If you got beat up cause of the trouble at Ash Town, I'm sorry. I'm sorry I drug you into it. But, man, I really need to know if they got to you or not. It's okay if you told them what I was up to out there. I understand. I would've too. But listen to me. I'd tell you so you'd know where you stood. Can't you do the same for me—if that's what happened?"

I guess he just couldn't fess up, cause he went into that zombie trance like he did the last time I questioned him. That's the way Herman was put together, or the new person he had metamorphosed into. He probably resisted them at first, but in the end he talked. It was like that night in the woods when he held tough all the while they beat William Earl Johnson to death and then, after it was done, he had to bolt.

All I got from Herman was a perplexing moist-eyed stare, like he was screaming inside to right things with me but was too much of a rat to follow through.

But the house wasn't surrounded by cops and I cranked up and shot out of there without being stopped or chased by a green '54 Chevy or an Electra Glide or any other vehicle with bad guys. So at least he didn't turn me in while I slept or stop me when I snuck into the other room and whispered morning wishes to warm, cuddly Brandy. That was something good I could say about my friend Herman.

Chapter 46

I stopped at Scarborough Drugs cause they had a phone booth around the side of the front door that was mostly out of sight of traffic on busy Tenth Street. I didn't act nervous. I didn't jump when a car backfired coming off the hill or a biker revved his glasspacked V-twins.

I tried to put things together rationally. Jeanne's friend Greg could've escaped out the front while Jeanne and I were knocked out; he had been standing farther back than us when the bomb exploded. So there might not be an urgency at all for them to nab me. Maybe I wasn't even reported to the cops. The spectating neighbors were being good guys, minding their own business cause they liked Doctor Joe and didn't want to say anything against me for his sake; I knew some of the neighbors were friends and even patients of his.

So maybe I could take it a little easier, just be vigilant.

I called Mother at the church. It was a little before 7:30. She usually didn't get there till a few minutes before eight, but she could've gotten to work earlier cause, knowing her, she was too nervous worrying about where her number two son was to sit still. She had to move when she got worried. And where else would she go?

I was right for a change. She answered, "First Baptist Church. This is the Reverend Daniel Carmichael's office, Mrs. Poe speaking. How can I be of service?"

It was a mouthful. She said it every time she answered the church phone and that was plenty through a whole day, five days a week. I reckon she had it down pat after more than five years now.

"Hey, Mother, it's me. I—"

"Oh, Sonny! Where have you been? I've been worried sick wondering wh—"

"Listen, Mother, I'm sorry I didn't call. There was a fire at Doctor Peach's house last night. They burned it down."

"Yes, yes, I know. Preacher Daniel called me in early to take calls. He lives out Broadmore now, you know ... Sonny, listen, son, he called me here just minutes ago. He—"

"Reverend Carmichael? I thought—"

"No. Joe Peach. He—"

"Wait. Is the church phone on a party line?"

"No. Why?"

"What did he say?"

"Sonny, what have you gotten yourself into? Don't tell me you had something to do with that fire. Oh, God, I—"

"Hell, no, Mother. The Klan did it, I saw them. They used dynamite. They wanted to kill him, Mother. Anyway, I think the cops are after me about it cause I might've been spotted leaving, and I think they might arrest me cause I know they are in with the Klan."

"But they haven't called or come to the house ... Well, what were you doing there? Why would they want to arrest you, Sonny? Oh, son, what are you involved in? ..."

She sounded despondent and I needed to ease her mind. "I haven't done anything wrong, Mother, okay? You need to believe me. Neither has Doctor Peach. Does he know about his house, did you tell him?"

"Yes, I told him. He didn't know. He was shocked. He was just real upset about it, I could tell. But he only asked if anyone was hurt."

"Well, wouldn't you be upset—if you owned a home?"

I could practically feel the chill in her silence. She said, "I'll have you know we owned a great big home, young man, in the Woodlands."

"Sorry, Mother. I didn't mean it like it sounded. What else did he say—something he wanted me to know? He called you, didn't he? It's pretty early."

"Well, it *is* what you meant, Sonny Wayne. I can't help it if we don't have money. I'm trying to do the best I can, but it's not easy raising three boys all on your own. You think I asked to be poor. Whiskey did it. I pray every day you boys won't start drinking. I'm not worried about Chance, he's a good Christian boy. But you two, the way you cuss at me and don't tell me *anything*—I can only pray you'll turn out good ... So you just mind your manners, Sonny Poe, and be thankful for what you do have. You hear me, son?"

And Mother was the person that preached to always think before you speak!

I held the phone just far enough from my ear that her voice wasn't a scream. It was when she got like this that I remembered how much I hated my father for dying, for ruining her life because he didn't have the self-control not to. I felt guilty and ashamed and sorrowful and miserably sad when Mother started in like this. I always looked for an escape and since I couldn't get away from her physically, I tranced myself into thinking I was running through the woods as fast as I could go, flying, dodging limbs and stumps and vines and seeing the blue, cottony sky whiz by and listening to the birds as I raced agile as a cat through all those trees.

"I'm going to get rich, Mother, and take care of you then. Take you to Paris, okay? One of these days. You'll see. I'll make something big of myself and then you can rest easy."

I heard her sigh. I sensed the frown unfurling on her forehead and her eyes starting to dry. Maybe she used a tissue to blot them. She sniffed. She didn't say anything and that was a good sign. It meant she wasn't mad anymore.

When she spoke she was clear-voiced as if there'd been nothing fussed over. "He wanted me to tell you he talked with 'some important people,' that's how he said it, whatever that meant. He said you'd know, that he was sorry he didn't have time to tell me about it. But he had time to tell me that much."

"Is he still in Montgomery, did he say?"

"He didn't say where he was."

"Did he leave a number, by chance?"

She didn't answer and I knew that meant no. Mother didn't want to look dumb and I didn't like having to ask her any questions that would make her feel that way.

I told her she was the best mother in the world to put up with a kid as bad as me, that even Stuart wasn't as bad as me. She got a little mushy and told me I wasn't all that bad, just didn't have any common sense and that I was headed in the wrong direction, I should have a good talk with Preacher Daniel to help get me straightened out. I said okay. But I had no intention at all of taking that road. Pops had gone to Preacher Daniel for a straightening out and look what happened to him.

"I might have to miss school, Mother. Can you call and say I got pneumonia or something? I got it, a moccasin bit me out fishing on the weekend, but I'll live, just had to stay in Birmingham with Uncle Tommy and Aunt Tilly to heal. It's almost true—"

"And why is that?"

"I promise I'll tell you everything just as soon as all this gets cleared up. Promise. I've got to go now, Mother. Bye."

I hung up before she could start screaming again, cause I knew she would. I knew Mother through and through. The thing is she was mostly right about everything she accused me of. I didn't want to think about the kids I might have when I got to be a parent, if they treated me like I treated her. I really felt guilty when I turned things around like that and saw me in her position, what the little ingrates could be like. I felt even sorrier for her and more ashamed for not being a better son. I thought, I mean it, I'm gonna make things easy for her some day. I knew that bum Stuart wouldn't and that left it up to me, second in line.

I was on the highway headed for Montgomery before really considering how to find Doctor Joe there. Hadn't he told Mother he had already met with some people? Probably saw that midget attorney general Guy Richards yesterday. That would mean he was most likely done and might already be on his way back to Woodstock.

We were supposed to meet Wednesday but he called for me this morning. That meant he must have some good news he couldn't wait till Wednesday to tell me about. I could hope, anyway.

I pulled off at a diner/gas station with a tall "EATS" sign just off the road and went in for some breakfast and to rethink things. There was a jukebox next to the door and it was going this early in the morning. Hank Snow sang, "I'm Movin' On." I thought, Yeah, that's what I'm doin', and it got me in a mood.

"Mornin' shug, coffee?" She wore a plain, fairly clean apron and had a pencil stuck in her hair that she grabbed quick as a frog nailing a fly and held poised over her pad. I guess she got a better look at me and decided I didn't want coffee. "Orange juice, maybe?"

"Just water, I reckon. That special on the window, it come with grits?"

"Now, what kinda ques—Course it does, shug. That what you hav'n?"

"Biscuits too?"

She nodded this time.

"Yeah, make 'em scrambled, please."

"Comin right up, hon."

I sat there at the cash-register corner of the counter nodding my head and foot to the arousing beat of Johnny Cash, and before you could say cockadoodle doo a couple of times, I'd eaten everything on my plate. It was a fine meal and nobody disturbed me to ask if I wanted more water or just what in hell was a kid like me doing out here on a school day. It was a place that minded its own business.

I went into the bathroom for a minute and then paid the $1.04 bill and left a nice tip of 30 cents because I thought it was cute that she kept pencils in her beehive. I twisted out a toothpick and stuck it in the corner of my mouth, then put on my jacket and walked out. I felt as cool as those cats headed for San Fran.

My mind was on that when it occurred to me I'd made no headway on which direction to take, back to Woodstock or forward to Montgomery.

It didn't matter. The green '54 Chevy parked next to my bike decided for me.

Chapter 47

Roach sat on Big Red, sidesaddle like a girl, looking especially mean in his duty blacks. The shirt alone, official and serious with its yellow sergeant's chevrons and big silver badge, could intimidate you. The gun, cuffs, sapper and other stuff on that thick black belt made him lots scarier. He wore a motorcycle cop's tall black boots, like a Nazi. The big, hot-tempered detective named Curt took his time opening the passenger-side car door and lazily got out. Every time I'd seen him he wore a white shirt with a loose skinny black tie, just like now. There was no sense in running, so I walked on over.

"Just don't look like you can keep yourself away from that queer dentist, do it, son?" Roach said, like he was disappointed. He even shook his head a little. I didn't think it was a question. "I'm guessing by now you're one too ... What brings you way out here on a school day, eh kid?"

I shrugged. I wondered how he found me out here, and that made me start wondering again about Herman.

"What kind of mischief you been up to, say around eight last night?"

"Whaddaya mean?" I asked, dumb as mud.

"'What do I mean,' he says." His words dripped so thick with sarcasm I hardly recognized them as words. He added, "What I mean is you don't ask the fucking questions, punkass. You answer them ... You a niggerlover too, ain't you? Just what kind of boy are you? You must a been born in outer space cause you didn't come from around here."

Curt barked. He thought that was funny, I guess. He moved around behind me. I wasn't too worried cause I'd parked the bike right out front of the diner and they could see us from inside. I thought that would keep them from doing something like attacking me.

I was wrong. Once again.

The stick came out from behind Roach like magic, in one full swoop, and didn't stopped until it caught me in the sternum hard as a thrown baseball. The blow numbed me all over.

It was like I was drowning; I could not make my lungs work. I was sure the detective held me up cause I had no legs and I didn't go down. Everything around me funneled down to a narrow edge of light, a single speck in a sea of black. I tried real hard to breathe but I just could not and the tiny light went out like a candle in wind.

I don't remember what happened then but I hadn't lost consciousness cause I could hear an unintelligible noise piercing my eardrum. I felt like I was floating in space with ice picks repeatedly getting shoved into my ear.

It must have been Curt shouting. It must have also been Curt that I heaved on since he suddenly let go of me and I collapsed like a tuckered-out hound. I puked up grits and bits of sausage and laid there for what seemed like precious hours until I was breathing again. I didn't stir even from the nudge of that stick in my shoulder blade. That is, not until the pokes got hard enough to get me moving.

"I guess that smarts, huh?" Roach said and rapped my knuckles with the stick. Another great blast of pain ran up my arm and spread across my neck and chest.

I rolled up on an elbow and almost retched again from the shock of flexing my stomach muscles. I was one of those people who never threw up, even when the best thing you can do is get rid of the sourness on your stomach. Like when you had too much moonshine and needed the poison out of you before it did you all the way in. But I didn't have a choice this time, it just happened.

"Wh—what? I don't—Just tell me what you want." I was hurting and tried real hard not to sound quarrelsome.

Curt tossed him a towel after he'd finished wiping off his trousers and wingtips and Roach threw it on me. "Clean up some …"

After a second the detective said, "I gotta tell you, kid, you are in some serious trouble. We know you were there last night, that you burned down that house … Sounds pretty bad, don't it? But there's a way you can redeem yourself. You don't really want to go to Thornton House, now do you? Honestly?"

"Ha!" snorted Roach, "It'll only be for a year—then they'll throw him in the Big House where all the real fun begins."

I righted myself and tried to level my eyes on him. "I knew you'd try to blame me—"

I cut it short but it wasn't easy—kind of like stopping your racket mid-swing to let a ball drift out—but I really needed to keep my mouth shut. I must have flinched getting ready for another killing punch cause Roach started to chuckle. The detective joined in. Laughter didn't come easy for either one of these men, you could tell by the way they could only make grunts instead of real laughs. I reckoned they were too cynical and perpetually angry to see much to laugh about. They only became cops so they could beat up folk, or throw them in jail, or lynch them. They were raised full of hate. But that didn't make me feel sorry for them.

"All you gotta do is sign the paper we showed you before and you're free to go," Curt said in a voice of silk. "Whaddaya say, kid? You wanna stay out of Thornton. You know they got reason to call it 'Torture House,' don't you?"

I kept my eyes on the big glass window of the "EATS" diner, hoping somebody would see and come to my rescue. Everybody in the place got there before me; I knew they were through eating. But nobody stepped through the screen door.

"I suppose," Curt went on, "that we gotta figure out where a dumbass kid like yourself could come up with the kind of explosives that would blow up a house. Eh, Dutch?"

The big detective wore a magnificent smirk. It might've been partly from having to smell my vomit on him when he couldn't just go and change pants.

Dutch Roach. "Dutch" probably wasn't what the "D" on his uniform nameplate stood for. He said, "I got a notion. That other kid with him out at Ash that night? Don't his old man work at the armory? And don't they have tons of explosives just sitting around out there?"

"Hmm. Might have to have a talk with Mr. Brown and his boy."

Roach said, "All right, kid, get on up now. You leave us no option. Time to go for a ride."

They put me in the backseat and I didn't resist, though I was frantically trying to figure a way to bolt. They were either going to take me to jail or to the woods. It was a crazy thought, but dying in the woods fell on my sensibility with some small sense of comfort. If that turned out to be where they were taking me, I'd have to count on my disbelief of the afterlife being the opposite of what I thought happened to you after death, which was nothing except that your body rotted or was turned into ash. And that left two choices, as bible school had hammered into me, you either went up to heaven or down to hell. I wondered which one it was for me.

"He's slippery, keep your eye on him," Roach cautioned. Curt got in by me in the back.

Roach walked into the diner; that black uniform looked awfully hot even in fair weather like now. He eased the screen door to a soft close going in and removed his shiny hat, the courteous and pleasant police officer. He leaned casually on the stool where I'd eaten breakfast and started talking to my waitress. She apparently hadn't seen the nice policemen cream me right in front of the huge window or watched me writhing and puking in the dirt. Now she craned her neck looking through the written-over window, nodding with serious attention at something he was telling her. A couple of patrons also turned and glared out the window. I breathed a little easier, thinking there was no way they were taking me to the woods now, not after establishing witnesses on my behalf.

But I had been wrong before when I went to guess what was going to happen. Just about every time.

Roach let the screen door slam behind him. He walked over and straddled Big Red, kicked up the stand, put the gear into neutral and walked the bike under the gas station overhang and into the garage. When he reemerged, he was wringing his hands as if my bike was dirty.

Chapter 48

The cell was so dark you would think sundown had come, but it was only the middle of the afternoon on a sunny spring day. At least out there, outside. I imagined the basement cell was a lot like the little cellar room the city had begrudgingly allowed Doctor Joe to use for his Civil Service Commission office, the one that smelled like stale mayonnaise. It smelled worse here, of urine, putrid sweat and vomit. Maybe some of that was me.

I never appreciated how much I would miss delivering papers.

But ever how bad this garbage dump was, it was better than the cold, damp earth under the pines where I might have been. I kept thinking, if I'd been black, like William Earl Johnson ...

I'd been here about an hour, listening to cars stop and go and the drone of machinery somewhere nearby. The jailhouse itself was quiet; I guess I was the only prisoner awake at the moment, or maybe the only one here, which was fine with me. I'd earlier asked the jailer if the activists they'd arrested at the roller rink Saturday night were here.

"You part of 'em?" he wanted to know. Hell no, I told him, I just happened to be at the rink when they tried to overrun it. "Damn yankee agitators," I added so he'd know whose side I was on.

He bought it, said, "Yeah, they got sprung. Swarm of highfalutin' lawyers say they from the NAACP come in first thing Monday morning with a writ of habeas corpus they got from one a them niggerlovin' federal judges over in Hot-lanta."

"Shit. Hope y'all gave 'em something to remember 'fore they left."

He looked sharply at me. "Just what's that suppose to mean, buddy?"

"Just wondering if they got what they deserved's all."

"Well now, whadda you think, hotshot?"

"I don't think any a y'all would be that dumb."

He laughed as he locked me inside the piss-smelling cell. Before the jailer left he peered at me through the barred slot with a lunatic's grin and said, "Guess you'll just have to go on thinkin."

You didn't want to get locked up in the Woodstock jail anymore than the rotten Tijuana jail, where you had to come up with five hundred dollars, no matter what your offense was. So the song went. I'd been singing it softly since the door slammed behind me.

My gut and breastbone were tender but it didn't feel like something was torn or broken inside. That surprised me, as hard as the stick had hit.

They did their interrogating when I first got here, used the same room where I had been grilled on New Year's for being drunk and speeding like a fool and feeling sorry for myself. But now it was a lot more scary and real than then. Oddly, I could sense the presence of other miserable souls who'd been in the grilling room before me, the combined fear of ghosts trapped inside these drab concrete walls shouting at me to keep my mouth shut, don't tell them anything, ever. There was a stale, sickening odor, too, like buckets of sweat had been splashed all over those painted walls and would never evaporate, and that I would've bet made detectives loathe having to spend time here too. Maybe for that reason they would cut the interrogation short. I could've told them they weren't going to get anything out of me.

I found myself sweating under the shaded light they actually pulled down from the ceiling. It burned the top of my head, my face, my ears.

Curt, the gorilla, liked to let me know where I stood, it seemed. "Here's how you can look at your future, kid. You're going straight over to Thornton House. No bullshit, no hesitation. That is, unless you decided to cooperate with us right here and now. You've got about two seconds to decide. Your last chance."

I nodded, looking at my lap, trying to keep my nerves from showing at the thought of Thornton House. Everybody knew about the asylum where they took youths considered too violent, uncooperative or psycho to go to juvenile hall or even regular jail, those "special" delinquents you would never hear about again. The "Thorn" as kids called it, not "Torture," although that was probably more accurate, was an old beat-up brick place with a high, rolled-wire wall in the sticks not far from Midland Roller Rink. They say the electricity worked half the time and there was only one toilet, in the yard, for all those boys. You could probably even see and hear the rink from there, hear all the kids out there having fun while you were looking out behind those grungy mesh-wired windows.

"You're acknowledging; good going. Let's see how long you can keep it up. Tell me what you were doing at the house of Dr. Joseph Peach last night, Monday." His tone was formal and grave but softer than when he'd tried to bribe me with money to sign the paper blasting Doctor Joe.

Roach had put his nightstick on the table right in front of me. They'd taken off the cuffs and I was free to move my arms, free to grab the stick and try to swing my way out of there. I got the feeling they were hoping I'd try, cause you could see in their leering eyes a craving to hurt me worse than they already had. I believed they liked putting folks in pain. They thought up creative ways to do it. The whole purpose of being police officers, at least for these two, had little to do with keeping the public safe, protecting the innocent. Rather they were out to hurt whoever they wanted—blacks, drunks, punks, yankee agitators, anybody who wasn't of the redneck persuasion, freaks like them. They were here to make the public live in fear of what they could do to you. God help you if you were black and sitting here. Or Doctor Joe, if he were here now. They would probably beat him to death with clubs and brass knuckles and blame it on some toughs in the cells downstairs.

Roach said, "Answer the damn question."

I looked up. "Sorry, I didn't hear one. You're asking me to tell you something I don't know nothin about," I said, whiny-like. I couldn't see that I had any other choice but to deny being at Doctor Joe's house.

"You trying to provoke me, boy?" Curt said evenly, almost amusedly. "You're going to tell us you were *not* at twelve twenty-four Broadmore Terrace last night? Is that what I hear you saying? I'd think twice, I was you, because everybody in this room knows you are lying. In fact, you weren't the only person there, were you? … Look at me when I'm talking to you, boy."

When I looked up at him I flinched like I was about to get hit again. It was impulsive and on purpose, too, cause it might get them to worrying in case I ever went to court that I could scream they beat me. Maybe they thought I could sound convincing and that would be enough to keep them from actually hitting me again now. I didn't know for sure if Jeanne had run to them. Neither was I positive Herman had broken down and talked. I just didn't know. I needed Doctor Joe to advise me.

"Can I please call somebody? My mother?"

Some luck came my way just then. Bulldog Bradley stormed into the room hollering.

"Goddang it, Dutch, ain't y'all finished with the kid yet? …" He looked at me and grunted, or snarled. "Never mind him right now, I need both yous. There's a ruckus—"

He seemed just then to recognize me, the kid who'd knocked on his door every month for the past five years collecting the $2.35 bill for the *Woodstock Star*.

"What the hell? This ain't him, is it?" His voice was pinched, like he couldn't believe I was the "him" he meant. My only source of comfort was the thought of the dog fang that dangled off Red's buckhorn handlebars.

"Yep, that's the one, why?" said Curt, glowering at me. "We ain't getting nothing out of him. Whaddaya wanna do with him, chief?"

Bradley turned back to me, that same look of disbelief in his eyes. "That's the one, huh."

I hated myself for being stupid enough to be in his jail, helpless to get up and walk out. It was a real sense of oppression I felt. That upped my understanding, and my sympathy, of blacks southerners. I glanced at the inviting bopper on the table and I saw myself going for it, swinging it hard as ole John Henry and taking off Bulldog Bradley's head. I was breathing hard and getting dizzy just thinking about picking it up. He must have noticed cause I saw the thick-breasted police chief's eyes flare, his hand drop to his belt as if to unsnap the holster strap on the pistol that he didn't wear anymore.

He suddenly threw a hand in the air, dismissing me like so much spittle. "Put him on ice. I need you both. Now!"

The tall detective made a motion to hold me where I was until the chief and Roach left. Then he got close, showing me this sadistic, crooked grin, and said, "I'll tell you this, boy. When a dame's involved, you gonna have trouble. Just a fact."

"What?" I said, but he just smirked and nodded to the jailer.

"Hands behind you," the jailer said and cuffed me.

I appreciated Curt's piece of advice cause that made it pretty clear Jeanne got to them.

I paced back and forth in the tiny cell, bumped the toe of my shoe on the iron door, turned, took three steps and touched the opposite wall and turned back and did it over and over again. A sliver of light streamed down from a slit in the wall eight feet up that was supposed to be a window. A thin line of daylight filtered into the dusty cell but I couldn't see an inch of sky. This must be solitary, I figured, the one for those special people they want to work on secretly.

I started thinking about Harvey Nixon and all the grief I had caused him and his family. Never taking into account in the beginning the trouble he could get into being seen with a white boy in his truck. I had only been showing off, thinking how hip it was to ride around with a Negro because of some reckless need to show off that I didn't have anything against black people. In his humble way he tried to discourage me—"What you doin' comin out cheer in the daytime fo', Sonny boy?" Too polite to just come right out and run me away like he should have. He knew what would happen when he stepped in to keep the football players from beating me to oblivion. He did it anyway. Harvey sacrificed his little bit of safety in a world that hated him for only one reason. It was heroic; he was my hero.

I could have pounded my head against the concrete wall; I deserved it. That wasn't going to bring back little Harvey. Nothing could do that. It wouldn't do him or anybody any good if I was brain dead, so I vowed then and there to devote all my energy and wit to helping the Civil Rights Movement. And that meant sticking by Doctor Joe, all the way, no matter what the consequences.

The distant machinery droned on.

In a while I heard, "Psst," outside the cell. No one showed their face. The hiss came again and a voice followed it this time.

"Sonny Poe, that you?"

"Hell yeah," I said.

"Keep it down. Have you signed anything?" He spoke in a whisper. I didn't recognize the voice but it wasn't the harsh voices of the men who'd been hovering over me like feral cats.

"Not yet. Who are you?"

"Don't look out here. I can't let you see me. Got it?"

"Okay. I won't look. Can you get me out? I need to go. Please."

I remembered reading about the snake-headed Greek lady, Medusa, who before going into a murderous rampage was a guardian angel. I wanted to look.

"Who are you?" I asked again.

"Just listen. And keep your voice down. They are out to crucify Doctor Peach and they're holding you just to get—"

"I know who you are," I blurted. "You're the officer that called him about the school groundbreaking. Right?"

"Shh. None of that talk. I've told the doctor they're holding you. He—"

"How?— I need to talk to him."

"Just you shut up and listen." A pause then he said, "You ready to listen?"

"Yessir, sorry."

"He should be back by now. I told him to lay low; they put an all-points on him. They got one of their judges to sign off on it. But he's here anyway. A stubborn man, your friend."

"He's that. But what's there a warrant for? What're they saying he did?"

"It's better you don't know anymore about it. But if you want to help him, keep your trap shut when they ask you anything about him. Have you made an admission so far?"

"Hell no. They didn't like it, either."

"Good. That's very good. You're a brave kid, eh? There's a chance they'll send you to Thornton. But I don't think they will; too many people know about you and'll step up ... They didn't hit you, hurt you in any way, did they?"

"Only about tore my guts out, but that wasn't here. Here, they sure wanted to, but, no, they didn't touch me. They're trying to nail me for burning down his house. The chief stormed in and broke things up—lucky for me, I guess. Why do they want to arrest Doctor Joe?"

"Sorry, kid. I'm not going into that. I gotta go. You just hang tight."

"Why's everyone so anxious around here?"

He hesitated, then, "Chief's gone crazy over all the NAACP activity lately. Total overkill. Some Negro reverend is threatening to sit down at the lunch counter over at Woolworth's. He wants a show of force down there to watch the reverend have his lunch."

His tone was dry as funeral music, like the whole thing was ridiculous. So I added, "Yeah, that's stupid alright."

"You ain't wrong, kid. Even the federal law says the man's got the right to sit there but that ain't stopping Bulldog. Wasting the troopers' time. I gotta take off. Just remember, keep your mouth shut and try to stay calm if they get the chance to go at you again."

I said, "Wait a minute, sir. Can I ask you something? ... Uh, did you come from somewhere else, up north maybe?"

Since I couldn't see him, he was just a disembodied voice, like he wasn't real, but the bark-like laugh he gave me was real enough.

"You figured all cops are racists, on the take maybe? Well, I'm glad to show you that ain't true. Me, I'm born and raised in Midland. I see it like this: if you don't like yourself, you just naturally turn that bitterness on someone else. For us ole Southern boys that'd be the black man. Got handed down from Daddy and Grandpa and on back, a contagious disease of the mind that hung on tight after we lost the right to own people—*because* we lost that right. Us good ole boys just kept on hating till it's grown beyond fixin, and now the federals are stuck with stepping in, trying to put some damn sense into our stubborn heads. I'm a cop because I think I can save a little bloodshed, and we are going to see a lot of it in the next few years cause these diehard segregationists just can't give up the ghost. They'd rather die than ever think about that one question that gets them riled beyond reason: 'Would you let your daughter marry one of 'em?' That right there puts it all in a nutshell. That's what it's all about, kid, breaking that barrier. Now, I gotta split so I can get over to the Woolworth's 'fore my white brothers knock that reverend's teeth out—Maybe I can talk some sense into some fool heads, save a little blood from spilling."

I knew he wanted to marry a black girl from Ash Town, so it was nice to hear him explain it just for my benefit. He hadn't answered my question. Or maybe he had. Anyway, what he said made me feel better and made me feel worse, too. It was enough to sickened me thinking about it, cause he was talking about my history and my life, simplifying how disgusting and sad and narrow I and everyone else around here were. Up till now I didn't know any difference.

What if I had been raised in California, say among the wildly diverse commoners in John Steinbeck's country that I'd read about in eighth grade? How would my life be different, cause I knew damn well it would be, a lot different. What would my parents have been like? Even if my family had been migrant Okies still picking the cabbage fields, they would have been better off than here. I guess that wasn't exactly fair to say since my old man was dead and you can't get much worse off than that. Maybe I would already know what I wanted out of life, how I wanted to spend it. But whatever I did, it would sure be brighter than growing up in a cesspool of hate.

"I'm sorry, but please, one more thing. Doesn't your girlfriend live in Ash?"

"Hey, I told you, don't talk that stuff. Not ever; they'll have my head on a stick."

"Yessir, you're right. But you need to know that Ash Town is full of poison from that chemical plant, and if there's people there you care—"

"I know about it, yeah ... Listen, kid. You're a good person, doing what you're doing, the way you think. Take a piece of advice. Get out of this town. Get all the way out of the South. You owe it to your health. I know, I'm in the business."

Chapter 49

Mother bailed me out with a hundred dollars borrowed from Reverend Carmichael's slush fund, which was kept in a metal box in her desk down in the church basement. The preacher told her to take what she needed.

They put this lesser charge on me of truancy and aiding and abetting a fugitive and left out even a hint of charging me with arson or anything malicious, any felony like causing the death of a college boy named Greg. So it turned out a bluff, just like the officer said, no big deal. Still, I was going to have to answer to a judge or truant officer for running around fancy free during school hours. They would come at me thinking the worst, like I'd planned on robbing the "EATS" diner. So I wasn't completely off the hook.

I got Mother to drive me out there to pick up my bike. She didn't want anything to do with me just then, but at the same time she was doing all this stuff for me. She complained and screamed but still did it.

"I'll tell you this, mister, you are going to use that motorcycle to deliver your papers and nothing else, not even to get to school—You still have a bicycle and you can ride that. You understand me?"

I nodded and cracked my window to get some of the hot air out of there.

"Oh, and I heard again from Joe Peach," she said casually, as though commenting on rainy weather. Saying his whole name as though I might not know who she was talking about. Just being nasty.

"When? What'd he have to say?" I tried not to shout.

She took her eyes off the road to give me a hard look. "He *said*, 'I'm sorry, Mrs. Poe, for all the worry that boy's causing you.' It's getting to be a broken record with him … And he's not going to be our family dentist anymore. Stuart won't go to see him anyway."

"That figures. Tell me, how much has he charged you so far?"

She gave me a murderous stare. Any other dentist and we would have had a huge bill that Mother couldn't have paid off in 20 years.

I didn't let her see my eyes roll. "Did I tell you thanks for getting me out of that stinking hole? Well, thank you, *thank* you, thank you. What'd he say?"

"You know him, he wouldn't talk on the phone about his business. And I don't like it one little bit, either … But, when I told him I got you out of jail, he was very gracious. He said he'd see you sooner than later. Oh, and don't look for his car, he said he's not driving it. That's about all. See you where, Sonny? I don't want you seeing him, you hear me? That man is trouble, nothing but trouble."

"Okay, Mother … Thanks again."

I was pissed at Miss Beehive at "EATS," but I didn't go inside to find out why she didn't send anybody out to holler at those dirty cops. I went straight to the garage where I had to pay the man $5 for "storage."

"Helluva lot cheaper than Impound," he said.

Riding my beast was sweet, like being hunched atop a big bird. It raised my spirits and I wanted to soar. The engine roared at two-thirds throttle. I kept having to slow down to stay around the speed limit of 55 mph. I wondered if Roach or a crony would follow me. I didn't know; I didn't think so, but some other greedy Nazi lying in wait behind a bush could still ticket me.

Under a coagulated sky twilight fell fast and all that humidity brought the flying insects out early. Riding fast, they had trouble getting out of my way and zapped me all the harder for it. I didn't care; I just lowered my head and pulled my brow down over my eyes like half-lowered shades and kept my lips tucked tight. Lip hits hurt for days and they didn't look very inviting for the girls to chew on. Headlights were popping on by the time I pulled into the Hitchin Post. I kept my eye peeled for anybody suspicious and didn't gun it for once.

The drive-in wasn't deserted but it sure didn't have the booming business it used to have when Pops ran it, the way I remembered it. Once back then I snuck out here with a boy whose older brother had a car and who I talked into letting us kids tag along. I wanted to see how Pops acted around other people since he was always working and rarely home. He used the big warm memorable smile I remember about him on everybody, even the troublemakers. There were as many stations now as Pops had back then, but it was never enough for all the cars. Guys circled around waiting for one to open up, honking and jockeying when someone left. Pops and one of the white cooks had to come out and break up a fight that broke out over a spot. Trouble from some west side hoodlums. As far back as then I didn't like that he opened a restaurant on the west side.

I spotted Doctor Joe in a car at the farthest station from the restaurant. He stared back at me from the driver's window of an old Ford coupe, gave a little wave. I couldn't tell exactly what year the car was, being so plain. It didn't have any chrome or even wheel skirts and whitewalls. I'd guess a 1950 business coupe, a piece of crap. But he melted in with the other low-rent patrons. He had fallen to this, below the status even of my family. I felt sorry for him; he never had to sneak around in the dark before.

I parked Red near the garbage dumpster behind the restaurant and walked up the catwalk to his car, turning again to look for anyone who might be following.

I said eagerly, "Joe! Man, am I glad to see you. I've got to tell you about Ash Town and the gov—"

First thing, he showed me an abundant smile then hugged me, right out in the open under the rotating blue-and-red neon lights, big bear hug that he eased up on since I couldn't get air. I felt his body shaking. He prolonged the hug as if he was afraid to let go. It was starting to get embarrassing; it reminded me how the preacher will shake the hell out of your hand after church and won't let go when others are waiting their turn to make sure he knows they showed up for his sermon.

When he finally let go, still holding my arms, his eyes were moist.

"I am so sorry, Sonny, so so sorry," he said. "I know it was bad, did they hurt you?"

"That's all right. It's not your fault."

He shook his head. "Everything that's happened to you is my fault ... Are you okay? Don't just say you are."

"Yeah, yeah, I'm good. A little sore in the chest is all." I hadn't convinced him; he still had that hapless puppydog look. "Joe, really, it could've been a lot worse ... You've got it worse than me, come on. It's your house they burned down, and it's you they're all bent out of shape over. They used dynamite; they wanted to kill you!"

"The house was insured. I'm just thankful you escaped the fire."

"Yeah, but I just—I was just driving by; I didn't do anything—"

"I know you didn't. Don't worry. My friend on the force let me know what happened to you, that they had you in jail, interrogated you. Put you through all that. I am just so sorry."

"I talked to him. He came to me when I was there. What a great guy to be a cop. He seems to know everything that's going on, even with the Klan. They've put out a warrant on you. You know that, right?"

"Let them catch me if they can."

He talked like he didn't think they could catch him. I was glad to see he had that kind of confidence cause I sure didn't.

I said, "You'll never guess what I found out."

He frowned. It wasn't the right time for guessing games, so I got right to it.

"Our governor had at least two children with black girls back when he was rebuilding Ash Town. These two are still there—one anyway. The Negro that got lynched summer before last? His name was William Earl Johnson. He was one of the two.

"I saw it happen, Joe. We were out there drinking beer, Herman and me, over by the depot. We both saw it. They weren't wearing hoods. I know who did it."

He stood there, leaning against the car, staring hard at me. "Who?"

"Roach was one of them. I can identify others."

I watched his eyes light up at the mention of Roach. His voice was low and menacing. "Then we can nail him."

He didn't believe in revenge. He was a peace-loving person. But when Doctor Joe added, "We can put the sonofabitch away," the menacing tone in his voice gave me a chill. It sure sounded like revenge.

"Hell yeah we can," I said, my jaw clinched.

He surprised me again, saying, "You are one amazing young man, Sonny Poe."

"I wished I'd told you sooner. It would have helped if you'd known."

He waved me off. He was thinking hard; I imagined seeing his thoughts pop out in little comic book balloons all around his head. "Do you think Herman will come forward, identify any of them? If he will, it might lead to an indictment."

"I don't know about him, but I'll sign in a second."

"Your word alone won't do it, since Roach assaulted you. But if Herman will speak up … It might work."

"I don't think he has the guts but I'll talk to him again."

"Alright … Sonny, I know they're after you—"

"Yeah, but don't go feeling sorry again. We just have to get …"

I let it trail off cause I could see the gloom start to spread over him again. He looked like a little boy about to cry. He was a little boy sometimes. He took things real hard, too hard.

"It was Jeanne," he said. "What I mean is, it was Jeanne who told the police you started the fire. A neighbor saw her MG leave after the house was in flames, then saw her pick up a man down the street. Jeanne went to the police the next morning. My officer friend read her statement."

I was real thankful to hear Greg made it out.

"It was convenient for her to blame you. She's a little jealous. The police know you didn't start it, but they want that defamatory statement signed, so they went after you … It all comes back to me, Sonny. It's on my head, this whole thing."

I said, "Well, here's what happened. Jeanne was up to no damn good." I told him everything that happened then and added, "I wish I didn't have to tell you this, Joe, but I think she was there to steal something cause of the sneaky way she was acting; she lied to me and had a guy with her named Greg. You know him?"

He shook his head. He didn't seem surprised or upset. I guess he had way bigger things to worry about than a cheating fiancée.

"I know what she was after."

"Huh? You do? What?"

"Something in the safe. The safe's supposed to be fireproof, so it should still be there."

"What is it?"

"I probably should've married Jeanne three years ago. Would've put me in a lower tax bracket, much as it's cost me to send her to college."

He snickered, "Might have salvaged my social image, too."

"So what's in the safe?"

"Jeanne's family works for us. In the fields, inside the house. Several generations now. Around the turn of the century, the Peaches finally gave up using only blacks on the plantation. You wouldn't know she comes from sharecroppers, would you? She breaks the mold, so ambitious. And aggressive. I was attracted to that. A few years ago she got into some trouble and we kept her out of jail. Falsified an alibi, basically. Pretty serious stuff. Her case is in the books over in the Jackson courthouse, if you care to look it up. What's in the safe is her signed confession to the crime. I asked her to draw it up as an incentive to keep herself out of trouble. And she has done so, up till now. Now she's ... she's changed."

"It's me, right? She doesn't want me around. I know, she as well as told me point blank."

"There's that. There's her sorority ranking, gone to her head. She's fickle too, I think, knowing she could never go back to her roots. It's a rough time for her. I imagine with our strained relationship of late she thinks I'd turn her in. But she doesn't know me. Jeanne is free to do as she pleases. I thought I'd made that clear to her. She's already proven she's on the right path. Now, I don't know."

I looked at him like he was crazy. "She broke into your house, she lied to the police. That doesn't sound like the right path to me."

"Well, Sonny, she had become attached to me—or the security I provide. Turns out, she's just a gold digger, aggressive in the wrong ways, not the girl I thought I knew and supported all this time. We weren't ever engaged; that was a ruse I used to placate the country club crowd.

"She's doing well in school. She has goals. I destroyed the confession months ago. She doesn't know it."

"Damn … You think the Klan coming when she was there was just a coincidence?" I said.

"Can't see it any other way."

"What'd she do? What was her crime?"

I could tell by his half-shuddered eyelids he wasn't going to tell me. If I wanted to know about Miss Jeanne Cochran I'd have to go to the Jackson, Mississippi courthouse and dig up the case for myself.

Chapter 50

Suppertime had crept up on us and brought cars coming in and taking up slots. A waitress in a fluffy checkered skirt moved quickly to take orders.

Doctor Joe stared into every car that pulled in. So did I, searched inside until I was satisfied they weren't goons. I got the feeling he was waiting for them to come for him, that he expected it now.

"Let's get in the car," he said and moved to the driver's door and I went to the other side. I was glad to get away from the nibbling gnats; I was starting to scratch.

"You hungry?" he asked.

"You bet."

He punched the button on the two-way on the post outside his window and ordered. A hollow voice crackled back what he ordered and he said that was right: two large orange juices and two hamburgers without mayonnaise, no pickles on one, and one fry with extra ketchup.

You knew the fries and ketchup were for me. Doctor Joe wouldn't eat French fries unless he made them at home, or Deliah did, with his own grease, olive oil or something like that.

"What did you find out in Montgomery? It must be something good."

"In the future, I'll have to listen more closely to what you think about people," he said. "I'm speaking of Guy Richards. You were right. His only interested in me is keeping tabs on civil rights activities here. So when I brought up Vulcon Industries and the pollution problems in Ash Town, he'd heard enough. Said it wasn't his jurisdiction—which of course it is; it's exactly his jurisdiction and his business. So I had to explain that the FDA will be interested to know the plant's poisoning our town. That got him interested."

"Yeah, that's the way to stick it to him."

Doctor Joe let out a little grunt. "But Guy's not one to be threatened. Cool as a cucumber, he advised me to forget about the FDA because I have more pressing personal problems with the criminal investigation his office is launching into my activities with the Civil Service Commission."

"No. That's crazy! It's crap … Why?"

"They've already signed a criminal complaint. Mind you, he gave me this warning 'as a friend.' Which is why he didn't have me nabbed on the spot, I suppose. He suggested in so many words I would stay in better health if I leave the state soon as possible. Apparently, I've been taking bribes to secure federal jobs for certain people, white people of course.

"He'd planned to have me arrested anyway. See, if they can sue the federal government—and me, since I represent it—for denying blacks equal employment, the state of Alabama looks to the civil rights people, and the feds, like the black man's hero."

He shook his head and sort of laughed. "Needless to say, I never got around to asking him to put in a good word to the dental board."

"That sonofabitch. I told you," I said angrily, uselessly.

Doctor Joe raised the window a few inches so the girl with our tray of good-smelling burgers and fries could situate it on the edge of the glass. She'd brought us orange juice the last time too, thought that was in the T-Bird, but I guess she remembered us or the orange juice order cause now she peered inquisitively into the car. "You guys don't like Coke or somethin'?"

"You'd think, wouldn't you? OJ's healthier," Doctor Joe said pleasantly and put some bills on the tray that probably included a big tip.

We both went at the greasy, paper-wrapped burgers with gusto. "Don't eat it all in one bite," I had to remind him, sounding like Mother, and just like a scolded kid, his burger, what was left of it, went quickly back to the tray. Cracked me up.

"I didn't leave Montgomery with my pockets completely empty," he said, slyly. "Before we got into it, Guy got a call from the state police, apparently warning him that some group was planning another demonstration somewhere in the state. Guy started screaming into the phone about 'those goddamn foreign agitators trying to take over his state.'

"When he calmed down, he said he'd be ready for them. He had a plan.

"I managed to figure out that it's CORE. They're arranging an integrated bus trip through the South—"

"Yes!" I said, spewing hamburger bun crumbs. "I told those guys to call me. I hope they do, I can help them out."

"I reckon you could at that. Anyway, if I'm right, the AG will call on the Klan rather than the state police to obstruct the bus. That way the state keeps its hands clean … Sounds like they dubbed it 'Freedom Rides.'"

He took a dainty bite out of his burger and set about chewing slowly like it was beef jerky, giving me a slight grin. He then leaned closer to me, excited, his clear eyes as determined as I'd ever seen them. He rubbed his hands together as if in exhilaration, like all of a sudden he'd been freed from his tortured mind, or he had figured a way to beat them.

He said, "I'll tell you, Sonny. It works out right, this might be the thing that breaks Jim Crow. And believe me, it will put Woodstock on the map … Damn, this is a good hamburger."

Chapter 51

The time had come again for us to part for good. He didn't say anything; I didn't either. His face turned gloomy, and so did mine. But I also knew Doctor Joe wouldn't just say bye and go. He'd have to give me something more. And he did, or tried to:

"We've been through a lot together, huh, Sonny? And not all of it pleasant. But now—"

"Just a second," I interrupted. "Do you have a place to stay tonight? Cause I bet you don't; you're probably going to sleep in this dirty car. Right?"

"Thanks for the thought, but I have somewhere in mind. Sonny, listen to me. I am a danger to be around. You know that better than anyone. I'm here now only because I promised to meet you and to keep you up to snuff. But now it's time to part ways. Seriously, you understand?"

"Your policeman friend. Right? Well, you could stay at my grandmother's. She's a good sport and she lives over on East 14th Street, close to everything."

"That's your Pops's mother, right? How is she?"

"Fine. I was there Sunday. She always makes me up a hot breakfast after my route."

"I'll be okay, someplace where they would never think to look. Don't worry and don't get nosy."

"Well, I hope so. I was wondering, too, how're you going to file your insurance claim for the house, or get your money out of the bank, all that stuff when you have to hide like this. And what about Pearl? Want me to keep her? She can herd my cocker spaniel around."

"Yeah, that would've worked. Wish I'd thought of it. She's at my brother's in Montgomery. That's where I left the Thunderbird. As for all my business, Bill's going to take care of it … Okay, I can read your skepticism. Bill may work for the Attorney General but he's still my brother. I trust him when it comes to family affairs, just not politics. But, thanks for your concern. I mean it."

"Yeah, and everybody knows how thick Southern blood is."

Maybe I was being sarcastic, but it didn't bother him. He just gave me a tight hug around the neck. A farewell hug that I didn't want cause it meant the end.

"It's time for you to go, Sonny. Get on your bike and ride. Go home. Don't ask me where I'm going or what I will be doing.

"One thing you can do. I'm really hoping you'll speak with Herman," he said. "If he will agree to an affidavit, I can move ahead on those Klansmen."

"You bet I'll do it. I'll do anything you want. Look, Joe, I know it's dangerous but I'm dying to be part of this, and I don't like it that you're kicking me out. Like you said, we are part of something big going on and, boy, do I want to be included. Come on, please. I think I have earned the right to decide if I want to help you out."

He wasn't going to budge. "You cannot be involved, Sonny. It's over for you. Now, I'm not going to sit here talking about it any longer. Get out of the car."

He sounded like he was about to get real mad and I didn't think he was just putting on a show.

But I could be a stubborn one too, more stubborn than him.

"But—but, we had plans. We're friends. I've helped you. I'm your go-to guy, remember? I've even gotten myself beat up helping you, turned down three thousand goddamn dollars to keep you out of jail.

You bastard! You can't dump me."

He let out a long sigh and squared himself to face me sitting close on the car's bench seat, his face still chiseled hard. "I'm going to tell you this just once, Sonny. So try to follow me. The friendship you and I had, no matter the strength of it, counts for nothing to what's happening here. I have committed myself to a cause and it cannot include you. Just like there's no place for Jeanne either. Besides the danger you'd face, you would only be a weight on me. Losing you is a sacrifice I have made. You must do that too. So, my good friend, it's goodbye. Get out of this car. Now!"

I got out and slammed the door of the stupid car, hard. I watched him pull out of the station, no wave bye, and move like a Sunday driver out of the drive-in.

Another jalopy that had been parked somewhere I didn't notice pulled out a couple seconds later and went in the same direction. I couldn't tell if there was more than one person inside. But people leave when they're through eating. I let it go.

He was lying.

He was only saying those things to protect me from trouble; he didn't mean any of it. He was lying, lying, lying so I would go home like a good boy and do my school work. He just didn't want to see me get hurt. He didn't know me that well, I guess.

I had an idea what he was up to.

I got on Red and cranked her up then rolled up the cuffs of my jeans and drove. I caught the dirty brown Ford a block down 10th Street. The other old car must have turned. I passed the Ford, gunning the bike. I thought I should tell him one of the taillights was blown. Two blocks later I turned north onto Collins, toward my house, so he would think I was being mindful, doing as he'd said and going straight home. But I pulled over and cut the lights and waited till I saw him go by then followed the Ford out 10th with my headlight off all the way to Ash Town.

I parked a little down the way from Harvey Nixon's house and hid Red in the bushes, then ran along the side of Harvey's house.

You could see inside the dining room. I guess they were gathered for supper. Harvey wasn't at the table but his mother and wife were and one of the daughters, the one that I always saw with her hair pulled tight like two curly horsetails. They weren't talking and the way they hardly moved in their chairs told you how much they still grieved for the boy. That little girl missed her brother. A wave of self-disgust passed through me for staring and I lowered my eyes and went on about my business.

I saw Doctor Joe's car cruise by, slowly, like it was casing the place. I wanted to scream, *Just speed it up a little or stop, for chrissake.* When he kept on moving, I knew he was headed to the house behind Harvey's, to the mulatto woman's whose daddy was the governor of our state.

I jumped the fence and ran through the Nixons' backyard to the alley. I didn't sweat being detected cause I knew they didn't have a dog. I climbed the wire fence again and stood in the upper end of the alley from the mulatto's house till I saw the lights of the coupe turn into the alley.

Doctor Joe pulled right up to a junky car that looked like it'd been parked there since I was in diapers. He didn't have to worry about hiding the coupe cause it fit in just fine out here.

I figured he'd set this up before he went to Montgomery. I could've done it cause I was the one who knew these people. Forget it, I thought.

I moved slowly toward a window that was raised a couple inches, the dining room. Most everybody in Ash gathered in that room because it was larger than the kitchen.

Four or five people milled around. There was no chance of me being heard cause their chatter sounded like a buzz saw. Then came a knock at the door and it turned quiet enough I could hear a woman's light-footed steps making across the wooden floor.

I figured on being there awhile and I tried to get comfortable, but there was no way with the bottom of the window above my head. Standing on tiptoes I could see inside. Harvey Nixon stood taller and bigger than the others. I'd bet Harvey would be giving Doctor Joe the eye and wonder how he might make out in the ring.

The woman who'd opened the door had skin a high bronze color. Waves cascaded down her shoulder-length hair like waves on the seashore. I had never seen a Negro's hair that shiny and wavy, except maybe Little Richard's, although he had small waves where hers flowed.

"Doctor Peach? We're excited you came." There wasn't much drawl in her voice but it still sounded inviting. She added, "I tried hard but could get only three people to come."

"That's a start," Doctor Joe said, encouragingly. No doubt she was nervous having a white man in her home. They all looked nervous, except Harvey. It surprised me a little that they didn't come to the window to see if anyone followed Doctor Joe. Negroes were always on the lookout for troublemakers, always throwing their eyes after dark.

The other man there looked yellow. Maybe he was part Chinese, I thought wickedly. But his color was different, brighter. I would've bet the discoloring came from working with all those poisons at Vulcon Industries. He said his name was Jimmy Winston.

The other woman, Lorraine Cout, said she'd worked the production line there, "ever since I be fifteen, yessah."

Doctor Joe said, "So you've been in the shop about twenty years?"

Lorraine Cout didn't look too healthy either with her skinny frame and saggy skin.

I could hear the tick-tock of the clock when the place grew quiet. My leg muscles began to cramp after about three minutes and I let off for a minute or two.

The bronze woman without the accent said, "I don't carry his name but I s'pect you know who my real father would be."

"Only by word. Thanks for clarifying it," Doctor Joe said. "May I ask, did the governor ever offer you any support?"

The bronze lady spit her next words. "He's a pig. Nothing, not as long as I've lived. That answer that?"

"That answers that. And you're right about him. Kimbrough may be the most regressive governor we've ever had. He proved it again when he kicked the NAACP out of the state earlier this year. I hate to say it, folks, but his defiance of desegregation is what's going to get him reelected."

Their murmur drowned out the clock.

Doctor Joe didn't say anything about his troubles, that his house had been burned down by the KKK, that he'd been beaten, lost his job and license to ever practice again, or that he was a wanted man. All for trying to stick up for people. He only said he worked with the Civil Service Commission and he'd uncovered pollution problems in Ash and that he was here to raise awareness and get the people out here to act.

"Harvey has told you that Vulcon disposes of dangerous waste products in Ash—uh, sorry, I mean Overton. But you know that, right? So let's talk about doing something about it."

The saggy-faced lady named Lorraine said, "It's all right, we call it Ash too. Only when we say it, it come wid a lot moe bitta'ness. And, yessah, Mr. Harvey don tole most folks bout the poison in the ground. But what we gonna do bout it, suh?"

I was on my tiptoes again and watching. But they now sat at the table and obstructed the angle of my view, so I just had to listen.

"There's not a lot we can do to clean up the area, not after thirty-plus years' worth of seepage. The first thing I want to see you all do is get medical checkups. I've made arrangements for lab work for all—everyone—at the Buford Street clinic. You don't have to schedule an appointment; they work on a walk-in basis. It won't cost you anything, just tell them the Peach Group sent you. But someone here tonight needs to get everyone together and send them over there. Not all at once, that'll overwhelm them."

"I do it," said Johnny Winston. "I ain' at work now, gots the time on my hands."

"Good. Next thing. I have asked a chemical researcher I know at the U of A to draw some samples from Leonard's Creek and its surrounding grounds. Someone will need to meet and direct him when he first comes. He's white, wiry, studious-looking. Okay? It will take some time to get those results, however. Now I know that having to ask you to leave your homes is a real hardship on everyone, but you should be preparing yourselves. We'll just need to wait on your lab results and the ground samples. But I'm positive there's pollution at dangerous levels, and you are at risk the longer you stay. Meanwhile don't use the creek water or even drink the tap water. I'm sorry to be the bearer of this news. I hope you all will trust what I'm telling you ... I wish I were equipped to help you relocate."

"Well, it's not going to be that easy, Doctor Peach," the mulatto said. I thought she'd said "Delores" was her name, Delores something, or maybe Harvey had told me that at another time. "I have a job outside the plant but I still wouldn't know where to move. A lot of people out here are in a desperate way. They don't have jobs. Some are just no-accounts, I reckon. But everybody owes the company and ain't nobody here not beholden to the store."

"I understand. There may be a way to get out of that debt. I want you to listen carefully because you are going to have to sell the other residents on what I'm proposing. Everyone in Ash needs to be in on this for it to work."

The clock tick-tocked again, louder it seemed, since they must have stopped breathing to listen.

Doctor Joe said, "What you can do is file a civil case in court against Vulcon. Under federal law, a group of people with a common complaint can sue a company, or township, any entity. It's mostly done by large groups like shareholders of a company or by employees as a group. Sometimes against doctors and hospitals for maltreatments of patients. A government lawyer I spoke to suggested this kind of group lawsuit might work in this case. It's called class action, a class action lawsuit. All of you will act as one."

I could almost feel the fire in his voice. "The lawyer says it's never before been done in a case where a community of color sues a company. There was a case in the last century where a mixed-race group brought a case against a Louisiana railroad company over its segregated train compartment policy. That one unfortunately backfired and ended up creating the Jim Crow laws. But this case is not about segregation, even though it will use racial abuse as its basis. Your case could be a lot broader than just the injustice that Vulcon's been dishing out since your parents' time. A case like this, if it's successful, could be as big as the school integration decision by the Supreme Court—the Brown case. Which *was* a success. It could set a precedent that, just by bringing it and long before it's settled, will greatly benefit the whole Civil Rights Movement."

I hardly breathed. It was a really inspiring idea.

"Yes, well that sounds all highfalutin' and all—" Delores said but abruptly stopped. I guess the huge implication of the life-changing suggestion needed a moment to sink in, cause her voice seemed to brighten when she added, "You really think? …"

I could imagine Doctor Joe showing off his pearled teeth. "If such a suit can make it into federal court, I certainly do. Anyway, you all really don't have much choice. You can't go on living here. If you do your parts, rally your neighbors, you can get this done … Delores, you should be the one collecting signatures. Make sure they all understand what they're agreeing to and that nobody at Vulcon or outside will find out. I'm sure a reputable Atlanta law firm will take the case *pro bono*. If not, the NAACP will."

I wanted to scream in through the window, *Damn right! They'd better.*

"Harvey? Johnny? Lorraine? Delores?" he said, making their names a question. "We can do this thing, you can. This is your opportunity and your obligation. Think of it as revenge, if you want, for all the indignities of your fathers and mothers.

"There may even be compensations. But mainly, a case like this will help the cause, yours and all Negroes."

Things drew real quiet before he spoke again. "I want you to know that if you stand together on this thing, I promise you I'll get you that legal help. And if something happens to me in the meantime, you know to go to the NAACP or any civil rights organization. The evidence is in the books and in the ground under your feet. Okay?"

"He means it!" I blurted, and my voice carried loud. I couldn't help it. I was overtaken, like that time I got the spirit and gave myself to Jesus. Doctor Joe had mesmerized me.

He wasn't a mystery to me anymore. Now I could see who and what he really was. He was strange; he was flawed. But none of that mattered because he had grown way beyond civil concern, way beyond me and even himself. He'd been right, I did not matter, nor did we together; *he*, Doctor Joe, did not matter. It was the cause that moved him, that was him now. He needed to do this more than he needed to love, to live. And that's why he had no fear of the lurking harm ready to wipe him away.

Nobody cared to look out the window. They knew it was only another disciple of Doctor Joe's.

Something rustled behind me but I didn't get turned in time to see how many there were. It came quick, a hard thud that penetrated my skull. Before I hit the ground, I was floating in the deepest reaches of space, up there in the starry night where I liked to daydream of being.

Chapter 52

I could not open my eyes.

The ringing in my head was so disorienting I could've been on a floor or floating in water. Or hanging from a clothesline. I tried again to wedge open my eyes but couldn't manage it; maybe I was just too afraid of what I'd see.

I wanted to reach out but my arms were locked down. There was some kind of sound breaking through the ringing, a voice, voices.

I pushed myself to one side. My head banged against something stiff that gave more than metal. Glass, a car window? Was I in a moving car? I knew my hands were tied behind me but I had no feeling in the arms. The pain in my head was no worse than if a cherry bomb had exploded inside it.

I banged my head again. It was a car window with a metal strip separating panes. I put all my effort into opening an eye and it paid off with a little glimpse of my lap. Then I gave in, opened the other one and looked up.

The light was blinding. It rushed my thoughts as fast as the vision of fire just there, beyond the car window.

A giant wooden cross blazed in the windless night. The cross stood in someone's yard. I didn't count them but there were probably fifteen Klansmen in a semi-circle, still as cardboard cutouts, arms akimbo, waiting for something. Their white robes fluttered only from a wind stirred by the flames.

My eyes frantically searched for Doctor Joe. I turned suddenly to my other side, but nobody was there, nobody in the car but me. I sat back. Where was I?

The car was old, like the one Doctor Joe used last, a confining coupe. The binding on my wrists was tight, constricting like a straightjacket. I felt panicky. Except for the window, I could've been in a coffin.

I pressed my mouth against the glass and screamed; I could have been some lunatic at Thornton House slobbering and biting on the glass to get out.

Stop it!

You can see what your mind wants you to see or you can see what's there, what's real. I looked now beyond the burning cross and saw Delores's house, and the side window where I'd been watching. I saw all four of them on the porch, Delores, Lorraine, Johnny and, with his arm around the three, Harvey Nixon. Delores and Lorraine under one arm and Johnny held in the other. He was the only one of them who didn't look stiff with fear, just controlled hatred etched on his face. But maybe that's what I wanted to see. I would see the fear if it were his family under his arms.

I had gone nowhere, only to the street.

A Klansman stepped up to the porch and pushed the women back against the door. He studied Harvey Nixon then grabbed his biceps, squeezing the arm like he was evaluating the fitness of a slave on the block.

I could hear him when he spoke. "You a scrapper, nigger? Ever been in the ring?"

Harvey didn't nod or shake his big head. He didn't even move an eye to look at the man. The man talking sounded and looked a lot like Sergeant Dutch Roach, like he would look with a hood covering up his head. It had to be him. If I hadn't been so goddamn nervous and fearful for those four black people, I'd be finding delight in this moment. The

Kluxer wanted to fight a man he didn't know was a professional boxer. And Harvey wanted to fight him; he'd told me so, talking about the reach on the man being shorter than his.

And that's what happened. The other Klansmen made another circle away from the flame and three of them pushed Harvey inside the circle. The fire was going good, the whole thing in a strong flame. A coating of sweat gleamed on Harvey Nixon's muscular chest.

"Let's go, boy, show me what you got," the man said, provoking him with jabs in the kidneys and nose. I thought it was pretty dumb wearing a hood with two holes punched in it for your view; he couldn't even see an uppercut coming and had to adjust it after every punch. But it stayed on.

Harvey wouldn't put up his dukes. The man said, "You refusin' me? Alright, then."

He slugged Harvey hard with a bare fist square in the jaw and the big black head just snapped back a couple of inches, like it was a blow from a kid like me. I could see his eyes water up, though. It got him to put up his dukes, but just halfway. Nothing like a real boxer, like Sugar Ray, starting a round with the dance, some rapid body punches, all full of vim and vigor. Harvey brought his fists up to about chest level and the hooded man jabbed his jaw again, hard. But it didn't seem to faze the black man or even tilt him. One of the things Harvey impressed on me was the importance of taking punishment, that if you couldn't you weren't a boxer and you would lose. It was a matter of bracing yourself for the blows and the pain and to shake it off and go back for more punishment. I thought of it as head-butting a bull. I could not see doing it for any reason but to save yourself. I thought getting knocked around for its own sake was stupid, even as a contest. And in a rumble, what did beatings prove? What could be settled or righted? Herman Brown could take it, and he did, usually with guys bigger than him. That always confused and irked me about him, I mean that he would take a beating even when he was going to lose the girlfriend anyway.

The Klansmen in the circle started mumbling, getting restless. A man said, "You ain't gonna whoop him, let me at 'im, Dutch, goddamnit."

"Shut your mouth, Kenny," the fighter said.

Turned out it was Roach. He then took off the hood. That could have been what Harvey had been waiting for, cause I saw the spark come to his eyes when the hood slipped off. He knew the cop as the redhead who'd given him the ticket at Richards Street and 4th, the man who had started the whole mess. He was also the man that got Harvey interested in putting a stop to always being stepped on. Harvey badly wanted payback for his son, too. Harvey's fists lifted just a little and he looked lighter on his feet, leaning forward.

Roach cracked a nasty grin and went after him, full wild swings that seemed amateurish even to me, and Harvey ducked and dodged them all. It excited the crowd. They were getting boisterous now and I thought this wasn't going to lead to anything good for Harvey or the others. He would know that too, but he had to have something. If I could possibly think like him, a black man in a white man's evil world, I would know that tonight I am a dead man, regardless. Here is this minute opportunity and you have to go for some little thing, pride, revenge, your own prejudice or hatred, retribution in God's name. Call it what you like.

Roach kept his guard high, making useless chin jabs that Harvey merely slipped sideways and dipped avoiding. And then it happened, Roach dropped his left so slightly an amateur would never notice and the blow arrived full force against his ear and down he went, as fast as that. Flat on his back. It was boxing art, a beautiful display of the real sport. I felt myself smile with so much secret cheer for Harvey I could have forgotten everything else that was happening. And maybe I did for just that moment.

Now it was time to pay. Harvey dropped his guard and let Roach pound his face and throw punches to the ribs until, finally, Roach's arms gave out. The other Klansmen seemed to have grown weary as well, watching but not participating in the familiar beating of another black man.

The flames of the burning cross licked at the sky and spit ambers on the metal awning of Delores's squat house.

"Get over here, all you fucking people," Roach said, breathing hard. "Right here."

Delores stepped quickly off the porch and helped Harvey stumble closer to the flaming cross. He was a bloody mess; a hive of wasps might have attacked his face with all the knots around his eyes and lips. But he was standing. The four gathered and huddled in the yard, all too aware their fate was closing in.

Others from the neighborhood would have been watching all the while and some may even have been bold enough to call the police, knowing it would certainly mean a beating or going to jail or worse. If someone had, it made no difference. No patrol cars showed up.

The scene was quiet now, the loudest noise being the popping and sizzling of burning pine.

Most of the Klansmen sucked on half-pint bottles of moonshine or bonded liquor they'd occasionally bring out of their robes. Most of the bottles were drained by now, tossed in about the same spot at the foot of the fire, as if that kind of orderliness came from regimental training. They wanted to see a lynching tonight, you could tell by the increased chatter, and arguing.

I twisted around and looked up the alley for Doctor Joe's old coupe. It wasn't in sight. Very close behind me was a pickup truck that I recognized from the firebombing at Doctor Joe's house. There was another car behind the pickup. I peered into the darkness to the next house, searched that yard, searched the street and the other side as far as I could see. No human beings, nor even any lights in neighboring houses.

There was no one to help.

But where was Doctor Joe? This was once I didn't want to guess. But I had to and it wasn't good. It was possible they couldn't wait, their bile ran so fervent and uncontrolled that they'd already beat the life out of him, and now in the boring aftermath, the boys needed to have a little fun. After all, it did take some effort getting everyone together and dressed in the White Knights of the Ku Klux Klan regalia, constructing and hauling that giant cross, caravanning to the west side. Someone had to get the hooch.

And me? I was a bonus for Roach. For hitting him in the nuts, for one, and for not being one of them, was another.

What was next, what did they have in store for these poor folks?

For me?

One of them swayed drunkenly over to Delores and squeezed her waist in both hands. It caught her by surprise. I watched her recoil but she didn't do anything dumb like slap the man. He laughed and pushed himself against her, pinning her to the porch wall.

"Now, you just take her easy, honey pie ... This ain' gonna take long. Come on to daddy, now."

Her hand then came up to hit him when almost invisibly Johnny stopped the hand with an arm. I didn't think the drunk Kluxer noticed.

He was a real hick. "You are one fine-looking woman to be a goddamn nigger. You one of them half-breeds, ain't you, what they call 'high colored?'" The man took his hood off. He had a long hatchet face that showed nothing but meanness. I thought it might go better for him if he had left the hood on.

"Cecil, cover your damn face," Roach said, who hadn't put his hood back on. "Get your ass on over here."

Roach held onto a long stick, like a shepherd's staff or like Moses carried around in the movie. He must have used it to keep the others straight. Maybe the bastard was the supreme wizard, or whatever they called the High One.

When Cecil got close enough Roach popped him behind the knee with the rod. "What'd I tell you, huh? ... You're drunk."

He swatted him again, obviously disgusted.

"Okay, people, we got choices here," Roach said. He was talking to the Negroes, not the boozed-up Klansmen. "And those choices all depend on you. We can take the two nigger men with us and be gone, you like. You won't never be bothered by them again, least not here on this earth. Or we take all y'all on a nice ride. Your families can moan and weep and forever hold a dark secret they can tell they kids all about down the line. So, it's up to you, heroes or life."

"Aw, come on, man. Let's get on with it," someone slurred.

Roach approached the man and slipped the stick between his legs and pushed him down. "Now you shut your goddamn mouth, Earl. I'm talking ... Okay, sister. What do you say, huh? We ain't got all night." He pointed his staff at Delores. "There another choice you can think of?"

She stood tall and spoke clearly. "I know this won't do no good for us, but it could give you something else to think about. The governor of the state of Alabama is and will always be my daddy. You know of him, don't y'all? Governor Kimbrough, call him 'Moose?' He don't like me, never did, and he don't want to have nothing to do with me, but he is who he is and so am I. I only say this so you might think about what happens here. It might get to him."

The Klansmen, as if by some natural sober instinct, backed away, like they could get a dreaded disease from the half-white Negress.

"Don't mean shit, woman," Roach said. "But you got brass telling me. You got that … So, I tell you what we gonna do. You know how word gets to us every time some nigger starts talking things they ort not to? Huh? Believe me, people, we hear everything that's so much as whispered in Ash Town. How you think we knew to get them awnings hung on your houses and about that troublemaker coming out here tonight? Just for example. And also, don't forget that other queer that disappeared from right here in good old Ash Town two years back; that for example too.

"I'm gonna tell you what. I think you can keep your fucking mouths shut about this night, us coming here not to bother you folks. I just know you like the choice I'm giving you. Huh? Let's see some heads shaking then."

Everyone there who was black nodded big. Delores said, "Yes, yes, we can keep quiet. We don't have no good business wid them white folk. We just trying to get on with our lives, not cause no trouble."

Johnny said, "Quiet as a mouse, yes-suh."

The wisp of a woman, Lorraine, and Harvey, both of them nodded silently. You just know they all meant it.

"I get wind of anything contrary we'll come back and put knives in your heads. All four you niggers. Do hope you appreciate that … Pack 'em up, boys. Let's get outta here," Roach said. "Just let that thing burn, Kenny. Be their little souvenir to remind them a little longer that they is one bunch of lucky niggers. Do you good to remember we're the only justice in this town. Now all y'all get your asses on inside that house. And you pray to God and thank Him for His saving graces here tonight.

He done seen fit to spare your useless lives this night!"

The Klansmen piled into the three cars and we took off, double shifting, getting rubber. It was something Herman would do.

The two guys that got in the backseat pinned me against the side panel. Three men piled in the front. They talked, started cheering and hooting, working themselves into a regular party mood.

"Giv' that shine up here, Lonnie," the guy riding front shotgun said to the man next to me. Lonnie's hand came out from under the seat with a pint of white. Before opening it and taking a swig, he slapped the bottom of the bottle and watched under the roof light for the thin bead of foam to form at the head, which it did. Which meant it was cheap, dollar-and-a-half stuff you got in Ash. He chugged it and shivered. "Whoa-ee, that is raunchy shit. Take it, Cec."

Roach drove. He drove fast. I would've been tossed all over the back with my hands tied if two guys hadn't been there to keep me in place. Nobody else noticed or cared about his recklessness, like they wanted to come as close as possible to crashing.

Honky tonk blared from the tinny speaker, right then Hank Williams giving us "Mind Your Own Business." It would've been good to listen to that one another time.

"Where is he?" I bellowed to the man in front of me, Roach. "What'd you do with Doctor Peach? Please."

A quick hand suddenly caught me across the nose and it didn't wait any time to start dripping blood down my lips and into my lap. I just let it go and breathed through my mouth and tried not to swallow.

The guy that hit me said, "Shut the fuck up, queer boy." He sat in the middle of the front seat. He didn't even turn to look at me. "Just count your blessings you ain't dead too."

With that my lower lip began tremble uncontrollably and my eyes leaked tears. I tried to keep the sniveling down so they wouldn't notice. I knew the man next to me, Lonnie, could feel the shaking in my body and hear my gasps, but he didn't tease me. I must have been getting blood on him too. He didn't seemed to mind that either.

The bottle went all around and by the time it got back to Lonnie, the one who opened it, the pint was empty. He found another one from the same place and they did the same thing again. I wondered how much of this cheap hooch they could drink before it ate their stomachs up and killed them. If they weren't good and drunk already, then they were working hard at it, and I wondered what that would mean when they got wherever they were going.
   I clamped my eyes shut and tried to vanish into that dark starry place again; I just couldn't believe Doctor Joe could be gone, dead.
   I heard a tiny, insignificant voice that I thought was mine. "Where are we going?"

Chapter 53

"You!"

Someone tried to grab my hair and pull my head up so I could see something. But there wasn't enough hair to get hold of, so they gave up and I stayed slumped over.

A Zippo lighter snapped open close to my face and struck flint, a sound as recognizable as the pipes on a Harley Davidson. Stuart used a Zippo when he was out on the streets with the Dukes, acting tough, lighting his and gang members' cigarettes.

I managed to crack an eyelid, barely. Held a foot away, the yellow flame burned my eye. I looked off but it still got me.

"You a niggerlover, right? Well, get a load of this."

I didn't recognize the voice or the man.

He lifted my head by the chin so I could see what he had to show. I looked. I jerked back like my nose had touched the flame.

The man—it could've been a cadaver—was black as soot with white flecks on a mouth without lips. It was eyeless, it seemed, with a face of meatless charred skin.

Impossibly it moved. Real slow, like someone manipulating a puppet to entertain me. But I was right to think it wasn't a puppet or a cadaver.

The splotched flesh on its cheeks and those thin lips shifted as if the creature was about to feed itself. I had this wild thought it might be a grin. There were no teeth you could see inside the mouth, just space and tongue. Orbs in the eye sockets rotated behind eyelids so thin I could make out the pupils as they shifted.

"Speak to Leroy, niggerlover. Confederate Negro 9th Cav Regiment. He seen the elephant more 'an once. Right, Leroy? You kilt you some yankee troops, right? True Rebel patriot, our Leroy."

Behind the skeletal cadaver was the dried-up remnant of a dried-up old, old man. I couldn't see anymore of him than the face; a blanket covered the rest, a motionless, sunken body in a wooden wheelchair. But that face was plenty. His face was level to mine and it made me figure I was on a bed or a couch. Leroy looked that old, like he really could be from the Civil War.

"I's a officer—" Leroy whispered.

A stench came from him like some dead animal that had been turned with a stick.

"He's a honest-to-God nigger Johnny Reb, boy. We keep him here so's we can reflect on what niggers are good for. Which ain't nothing, not a got-damn thing. We—"

A door opened. "Leon, shut your trap. You talk too much." I recognized the voice as Curt's, the big detective. His frame in the door took most of the light from another room but I got a quick look at my surroundings. A large Confederate flag was pinned on the wall with framed photographs surrounding it. The human figures in the pictures were dull but they wore uniforms. The pictures seemed old. I got a quick glimpse of a couch or bed under the Rebel flag before the light went back out.

Curt didn't say anything else. The door shut and it was once again down to the Zippo's waning flame. The lighter must have been getting hot to hold by now.

"Somethin' ain't he? A hundert-ten years old." Leon Legget said. He snapped the lighter shut and shook it, like that would cool it down.

I knew the punk. From the Legget clan, Kenny Legget's boy. The Leggets were the baddest Klansmen in Woodstock. Everybody knew their reputation for getting away with their abuse of blacks, even lynchings. Two summers ago, in the woods outside of town, I saw Leon put the noose around William Earl Johnson's head. He never even started high school. He would have been in the same grade as me.

I was in the belly of a notorious Klan lair with no way out.

My hands were still tied behind my back and the feeling in both was gone.

"Leon, please loosen my hands. They're going to rot."

"Shit, I know you, punk." The Zippo came back on. "What the hell you doin' here?"

"Please, Leon. I can't feel a damn thing in either hand."

"I'll have to ask."

When he left my eyes took to the couch under the big flag. I could barely make out a body, turned to the wall. It wasn't moving. The body was clothed in the brown jacket and soft-yellow pants that Doctor Joe had worn at the Hitchin Post and still wore at Delores's house just before he disappeared. Nice clothes.

"Sir, is he alive, that man over there on the couch?" I squeaked the words excitedly, trying to keep my voice way down.

He moved like molasses in winter, but he moved. I saw a bony elbow lift, a hand on the wheel of the contraption holding him up and then he suddenly whipped out of view.

I tried to stand. I couldn't. Had they tied me down or was I so weak I couldn't stand up? I rolled to my side and tried to slide myself off the bed. My knees touched the floor.

"Yes suh, he breathin'."

I could barely hear the wisp of a voice. But those were beautiful words.

"Joe, it's me, Sonny? Can you hear me?"

The body didn't move.

"He heah," the wizen man sighed. "He alive!" And his voice rose on the word "alive," holding for him a special meaning, no doubt.

"Are you a prisoner here, sir?" I asked, low and close to his ear. "Holding you against your will?"

He shook his head but I didn't know what that meant. What the hell kind of question was that for me to be asking him anyway, an ancient and frail Negro in captivity by the Ku Klux Klan? Of course he was a prisoner. So was I. So was Doctor Joe.

I could make out some objects with the little light leaking in around the door. I stared at Doctor Joe; he didn't move at all. Maybe the old Negro was wrong.

"You sure he's breathing?" I said from my knees on the floor. They hadn't tied me to the bed; it was just my hands bound up so tight I could hardly think of anything besides getting them free.

The old man grunted; he didn't like me questioning him. I guess Doctor Joe was out cold or asleep. At least he didn't seem to be in pain.

"Sir, can you untie my hands? If I can get in front of you?"

I practically tried to sit backwards on his frail legs but he couldn't get his hands to find the ends of the rope. If it was rope; it could have been metal cuffs like Roach would use or something plastic. I felt him fumbling without an ounce of strength in his bony fingers. I stood off him before my weight broke his fragile bones or something, and worked my way back to the bed.

"Thanks anyway … What will they do with you, Leroy?"

"Ain't got nobody. Not one soul. Don't care."

His head slumped and that was all I would get from him.

I held my breath and listened, trying to hear Doctor Joe breathe. His breath came so light, I couldn't tell that he was even getting oxygen; he usually took deep breaths. I could hear nothing coming from the couch but I could now hear voices in another room.

I made my legs hold me up, a big feat at the moment that actually made me proud. I managed to walk to the door where I put an ear against it. The door was shut and I didn't think I could even feel the doorknob with my numb fingers, much less open it. So I listened.

The spinning inside my head told me I was about to take a fall, so I pressed my weight against the door and spread my feet and took deep breaths. I didn't fall and in a moment the dizziness passed. And once again I felt a little proud of myself.

The voices were mostly mumbles but I made out them talking about something going to happen later, maybe tomorrow or the next day. Something that stirred them up. I could not make out whose voices I heard.

The door suddenly pushed in on me and I did tumble.

"What's this here?" a man said, trying to sound funny. "You through suckin on that old nigger's cock and now wanna know what's up? ... Well, don't just lay there, come on in."

He grabbed my shirt collar and I trudged along with him into a huge brightly-lit room with enough smoke hanging in the air it could've been the West Tenth Pool Hall.

A man said, "It's nearly six. Get that other one in here too."

There may have been twenty men in the room. From the other room it hadn't sounded like nearly that many, which meant there were a lot of followers. I saw chairs that faced up front where this little podium stood. The Roach man stood by it, casually, like he hadn't called order yet. I got the idea they had something planned for me and Doctor Joe. There was a circular illustration, kind of a plaque, stuck on the front of the podium that showed a Kluxer in white robes holding an American flag and standing in front of a burning cross with the words, THE KU KLUX KLAN IN PROPHECY. On the wall was the Rebel flag and next to it was a Nazi swastika emblem on a flag twice as big as the Confederate one. What was that supposed to mean, I wondered, but it made me feel a lot sicker seeing the emblem that had created the Holocaust. These were serious and deranged people.

There seemed to be a lax formality about what it was they were doing. Roach moved behind the podium, squaring himself in front of the big swastika. When he started talking some of the men listened, while others still softly jabbered. Curt leaned against the backdoor of the place, close to where Roach stood. He wore a shorter black robe like a sergeant at arms, which I guess he was because of his size.

Doctor Joe couldn't walk on his own. Two of the bigger guys had him under the arms and his feet never took any of his weight that I could see; they just drug along behind. He was a mess and I tried not to look at him, but I was so thrilled he wasn't dead I couldn't help it. He had taken a bad one this time. His eye had swelled seemingly beyond any reason why it shouldn't burst open. If someone touched it, it would, I was sure. It needed more than ice. His mouth didn't look any better. No way could he have talked. I wondered how he could even breathe with all the swelling on his head. Some part of him had died, you could see. That big friendly smile would probably never come back on his face. He had lost some of his perfect picket teeth, too. His nose was moved under an eye, pressed away from the grapefruit eye. But as they drug him toward a chair, as he passed by me, he lifted his head, just slightly, and I knew that was a sign only for me. *Goddamn*, I thought, *he's faking it*. He was there, inside, the Doctor Joe who never gave up on anything and he was telling me, *Don't do anything stupid, kid. I'll get us out*.

I could imagine, couldn't I? What else was there to keep me going.

Everyone watched them drag him across the room, and you could sense their collective bile rise as he passed them. If it were left to them, they would have torn Doctor Joe's head off. They hated him as much as they hated Martin Luther King. Maybe more. They hated him like their Nazis idols hated Jews. More. And why? Because of the caustic, stupid rumors out on him and because he wanted to help out black people. Like Stuart and so many other people I knew personally, they hated him because he wasn't like them; Doctor Joe didn't have hate. He was a *divine* person, like his spiritual leader, Gandhi, and he was pure. He had nothing but good feelings for them all, Negroes, yankees, Nat King Cole. The Klan knew that and it made their hatred for him even more visceral. It hurt me to think what they still had in store for him, with all that bitterness roiling and rising from their ignorance, the putrid leftover of a backed-up century of hate ready to spew all over the peacefulness Doctor Joe felt for those unlike himself. Oh, did they have it in for him.

I was afraid they were going to finish him off right now, so I shouted, loudly, "You've got to loosen my hands! Please."

Leon Legget said, "Oh, yeah. His hands is gonna rot off. They been tied a long time."

Someone talked to Roach and he gave him a key and the man came over to me, twisted me around and popped off a pair of cuffs. I heard the rasping sound but still couldn't feel anything at the ends of my arms. I brought the dangling flesh to my sides. I didn't want to see them, afraid of what would be there, but I looked. They weren't as ugly as in my mind. Blue, swollen, but not oozing with gangrene. I still thought they may not function. But slowly the wonderful feeling of shooting needles pricked at the fingers and soon shot up my arms and I knew they were good.

"Thanks," I said, rubbing my hands. I plopped down in a chair a little closer to Doctor Joe, who lay on the floor where they dropped him.

Roach was keen to me. His sleepy-eyed grin told me he knew I had something up my sleeve. "Put the cuffs back on, in the front this time."

The man did but loose, allowing some wiggle room. I was grateful and whispered just for him, "'preciate that."

"Now listen up, people," Roach said to his small audience, "we're splitting up in the next hour and heading out. I want to make sure every last one of you clowns has got it down what you're job is. Lonnie, did you get the bottles put together?"

"Yeah, did."

"How many?"

"'bout six."

"Well, make it a fuckin dozen. That would be twelve, shitforbrains. I keep telling you, you got to be prepared. Those things don't work half the time. Now get on it, and don't let them blow up on you. That's our whole arsenal, understand?"

"Yes sir."

"Gooba, Cecil. I want you to get there early and park your cars on either side of the entrance—that's so nobody gets in our way. Make sure you don't run out of gas, nothing stupid. Now get going."

Hatchet face and another guy picked themselves up. On his way out Cecil, or Hatchet face, the one who groped at Delores on the front porch of her home, stepped close to me and lifted his hand like he wanted to shake mine, then pulled the hand away, shot me a bird and laughed going out. He didn't grin, frown, nothing.

Daylight streamed through the door like a fireball; I almost turned to see if these vampires would burst into flames. Out there was a lovely spring morning. I heard a mockingbird that was happy, not angry.

"All you other guys know your roles, right? Huh?"

Some soft mumbling sounding like this undisciplined group might have doubts, like they weren't too sure the earth wasn't square.

"Earl, goddamnit, how many robes did you put in your car?"

"Sir? Uh, I think about fifteen."

"Earl, how many people you think are in this room? *Were* in this room a minute ago?"

"Sir? Uh, I guess there's bout ten."

"Wrong. There's eighteen of us and we got these two cherries."

"They don't need no robes, do they?"

Roach made a sound like a sigh, except gravelly. I thought he threw something from under the podium at Earl but he just faked it. I took it they liked to kid around in their meetings.

"Just put more outfits in your car, Earl. We want everybody fully attired the whole time. There's some more over in that side closet."

"Uh, yes sir. We ain't going in no woods today, are we, sir?"

I watched the Roach man sigh. "Prob'ly not. But you can bet we are going to have a blast. This could be our finest moment; these maggots'll remember us, that's for sure ... Well, what're you waiting on, Earl? Get choppin'."

"Yes sir. Got it, Sir."

"I want all you people to drive orderly today. No drag racing. Don't get rowdy. Lay off the booze till after. I don't want no state troopers handing out tickets. Harley, you and Butch get on out to the state line. You got that Walkie Talkie I gave you? Huh?"

One of the two said, "You bet, boss. Got it right here. We're gone."

"And if there is a delay or if the Georgia SP is leading them, I want you to call immediately and lay back. You got that, Harley? Tell me you're on the same page with me, cause we don't need no Georgia Patrol interfering."

"They won't interfere. They don't have no jurisdiction in Alabama."

"You just call if there is anything out of the ordinary. You've got brains; that's why I'm putting you on this. Look for big dark-colored cars following them, for instance. Or leading. They're Secret Service. Keep your eyes open for every possibility, any eventuality. There could be some local yokels from Georgia wanting in on the action. We don't want that cause you know how dimwitted those crackers are and they'll just screw up the operation. Right?"

"Hell, they wouldn't care if they did. They're civilians. They can go wherever they want."

"Long as they ain't niggers!"

There was a burst of laughter that sounded like cattle getting slaughtered.

"Goddamn, you're a smart cookie, Harley. How come you're not a damn detective like Curt here, instead of a dump truck driver? Huh!"

"Gotcha."

"Any questions people? Huh? Oh, and Harley, God speed."

Leon Legget said, "I got a question. How do we know for sure that they'll be comin through Woodstock? I mean what if we get all dressed up and they chicken out, or go another way?"

"Damn, Leon. That's a good fucking question. Curt, you want to talk to this idgit."

"Son," Curt said dryly, swelling a little, "Who do you think's running this show? The Attorney General of the State of Alabama, that's who. And right here in Woodstock the chief has got a red phone inside his desk, just like Premiere Khrushchev and our president has, and Bulldog sits there and waits for the Attorney General's calls. Well, the Attorney General called the chief on the red phone yesterday. He told him they're going to be here at one o'clock this afternoon, to get his men prepared. So, that's how we know they'll be here, the big man on the hill with the red phone says so.

"But it won't be his troopers who'll be waiting; he don't want no blood on his hands, so to speak. It'll be us. We're the lucky ones get to do the Alabama Attorney General's work. We're gonna do him proud, aren't we?"

Chapter 54

By now I had figured out what was happening and I hoped it wouldn't be those same college students from the roller rink coming to town again; they'd done enough, I thought. Doctor Joe had told me a little about it at the Hitchin Post and these men just confirmed it.

In a while they crammed us side by side in the back of the same coupe that Lonnie passed around the shine in after their little victory celebration in Ash for capturing Doctor Joe and shaking up some Negroes. They were just a band of cowards. It was my guess they celebrated after every cross burning, after every time they got the chance to dress up in their ghoulish outfits, whether they hang someone or not.

Nobody had yet wiped the blood from my busted nose off the car seat and still didn't. There were five people crammed in there with Roach driving again. Leon Legget sat in front. Another man I had seen only on that terrible night two years ago had squeezed in on the other side of Doctor Joe. He was a man as mean looking as they came. His face had long pointy bones covered by oily pockmarked skin. His hands were calloused, as you would expect of a grease monkey. I knew him even if I'd never met him; his hard stance on segregation was well known all over the South. It was posted on the pumps of the Leggets' filling stations: *Only whites served here. Nigger beware.* He was one of those brothers, the one Roach had called Kenny. Kenny Legget, Leon's old man.

He glared at me. I thought he might be trying to figure something out about me. He didn't say anything.

Doctor Joe sat in a lump, breathing only in tiny rasps. Legget had helped drag him into the car and didn't show any mercy doing it. His head banged on the door rim getting in and then he fell hard on the hump in the back floorboard. I tried to butt my way close so I could help lift his limp body into the seat, but they forced me to get in on the other side.

My hands were still cuffed in front but I could move them freely. They didn't put cuffs on Doctor Joe. It wouldn't make much difference even if they had when he was beat to a bloody pulp and could not even open his eyes, not when he was more than half dead..

The crusting in my nose had broken loose from bumping into the doorframe when someone pushed me. Again, I just let it bleed.

We bounced along a half-dirt and gravel road throwing up dust. Flickers of sunlight constantly hit on the windshield as we pushed fast through the red oak woods. Flowering dogwood marked springtime, which they like to say officially starts on Easter but the cotton-white blooms were always earlier than that. It was mid-morning. I suspected that their hideout, where we'd been, was on the north side of Woodstock because that was where you found the thicker, taller timber that we were in; south was flatter and not so thick. Not far from here was a waterfalls called Haley's Falls where us boys would skip school to come and slide thirty feet down mossy boulders into a deep cold pool. In the springtime it was deeper. I went there four or five times before getting caught. I guess it was a serious offense cause they sent me to the top dog, the principal himself. For some reason Blue Nose Dobbs gave me a choice—go to detention after school every day until I learned this poem he picked or it's a week of suspension. He didn't give the others an option for some reason, just me. The others got suspended. I said I'd do the poem, why not. But I should've asked first what poetry he had in mind, cause I had to learn and recite in full, in one standing, "The Raven" by Edgar Allan Poe. Maybe he did it cause he thought I might have been related to the writer, but I was pretty sure I wasn't; my father was German and came from too far South. It took me three weeks to finally learn the whole thing, my goal being one verse every afternoon and two or three more on Saturday and Sunday. That was in eighth grade and I wondered vaguely if I could still recite the whole thing. Probably not. I wasn't going to try right now even though it would've taken my mind off my grim situation. I knew what the poem meant, though, even if I couldn't get through it again; it meant that God couldn't do anything to ease your suffering when you lost someone you loved. And you only got taunted for not muscling up and getting over it. Like I wasn't over Harvey Nixon Junior.

The clunker in front of us churned up dust and threw it in our windows like it had been sucked in. Why the hell didn't Roach fall back a little, I wondered. Cause I knew he wasn't going to roll up his window and have no place to spit the juice from his Beech Nut. I could hardly breathe.

I kept my eye on Doctor Joe for a sign. I felt as sorry for him as a human being could; I couldn't stand looking at his face and not being able to wash some of the blood away and hold some ice on the big ugly lumps around his eyes. His hair was matted in sweat and blood and dirt. His head lolled on the curves and he would've fallen over if there hadn't been the man on his other side. Kenny Legget didn't talk; he didn't even move. He just sat there breathing dust as if it was the same as air. The quiet ones, like him, like Sugarman Cole, were the ones you had to watch out for.

Roach turned dials on his Walkie Talkie and made it squeal. "Dutch here. Stopping for gas. Is everybody okay on gas? Over."

Two separate voices responded, said, "A-OK," and "Ay, ay, boss."

We pulled up to a pump at an Esso. We were on the outskirts of town now.

A man came out of the shop and waved. "Hey, Dutch. What you doing way out here?"

"Just don't go asking no foolish questions, Ricky, and give me some gas."

"Okay. Fill 'er?"

Legget suddenly leaned forward and spoke to Roach in a low flat voice. "What's a matter you can't get to my station?"

They say Klansmen planned their lynchings at the Leggets' gas stations; they'd gather the loyal brothers in the garage and go late at night figuring out the details and get going sometime after midnight. All three brothers, I'd heard, had been taken in for terrorizing Negroes' homes, burning crosses, beating blacks and taking men away, and sometimes, like with William Earl Johnson, making them disappear. But when a Legget got accused of those things, he always had an alibi that held up in the local courts. The wife would say he was snoring his fool head off, worse than ever, and kept her awake the whole night that night or there'd be five men testifying he was playing poker at the station. Prosecution was a half-hearted effort; nobody cared because the mindset around here was the victims were Negroes, who no doubt got what they deserved. Hardly ever did an accusation make it to trial. The Legget brothers had wives and children and steady work at their gas stations and could have been regular folk, nice human beings going about their lives trying to give their children better than they had, pass along some meaningful legacy. But hate was their legacy; it consumed them.

I guess they didn't plan all their business at the garage. They had a headquarters too.

I never wanted to be anywhere near a Legget, but I was in a car with two of them now. I figured they wanted their biggest and meanest Klansman in the car with the two hundred pound dentist, in case he came alive and started something.

Roach said to Legget about using his filling station, "Not convenient right now, Kenny. Live with it."

"No problem. But look-it there," he said, nodding outside the store. "You won't see no useless coons sittin' around any of my stations."

Roach shook his head. "You gonna get your action soon enough. Just cool it, man … You and Leon keep your eye on these two for a second. I gotta get me some Beech Nut. Damn if I ain't slap out again."

Kenny Legget lit a cigarette and fixed his gaze past us to the old man out front that leaned lazily against the big window, probably thinking up some awful torture he would like to inflict on him.

Roach disappeared inside.

The Negro was in a wicker chair, his eyes closed, doing nothing but slightly rocking. He didn't seem to have a worry in the world. They say ignorance is bliss, but I don't know; seemed to me it's just restricting. There was a checkerboard on the low table next to him but there weren't any checkers on it. And no one was near the other chair. I watched him a second. A good look showed me something else. He was sad, lost. His checker partner was never coming back, and he was trying to live with that idea.

If there was a chance to break loose it was now. My mind raced. My heart started pounding. I could flip the front seat up and scramble out the front door and be gone into the woods behind the station before the older Legget could get out of the car. I wasn't too worried about the kid Leon. It was risky; what if the seat didn't flip forward, or the door handle was too far forward to quickly reach? I checked. I could reach it but would have to flip the seat all the way forward. If I could get away, I might could save Doctor Joe. But how? I was sure they were headed for the bus terminal in town, but how was I going to get the cops there in time? And who would I call? Which cop would help against the Woodstock Klan? I didn't know Doctor Joe's officer friend's name or phone number. Could he do anything even if I got him?

I looked at Doctor Joe and leaned against him.

I waited till a car came in making a little noise and then I whispered as quietly as I could, "If you can hear me who's the good cop? What's his number?"

His head accommodated my whisper by leaning over on me. It was slow and subtle and I knew he was with me. I knew it!

I could see his better eye crack open just a slit. I saw his upper lip trying desperately to lift, like he wanted to give me that smile.

"The number."

Legget leaned forward till he had me in his eye. He wanted to make sure I could see his dead-serious grin. His lip didn't lift; I didn't know how you could grin without lifting something on your face, but he did it. I saw the pistol ease out from his far side. He laid it, casually, on Doctor Joe's leg, a finger inside the trigger guard and aimed straight at me.

"You better get those thoughts out of your head, boy. I'll shoot you soon as look at you, you try anything stupid. I'll shoot him for nothing. Right now."

"Yes sir." I sat back and did what he said, stopped thinking about running. But I knew Doctor Joe was aware. He was with me and just waiting for the right moment. Goosebumps popped out on my arms.

Chapter 55

Roach turned in the alley between Freemont and 8th Street and parked the coupe in the shadow of Woolworth's bland backside in front of a metal rear door that I went through practically every school day to get chocolate. We were across the alley from the bus terminal.

The terminal building was a squat redbrick structure about the size of two buses side by side. Small. It was on Dixon, the next street south of Mason. Half the emblem of a skinny gray dog in the middle of a sprint hung over the side driveway and a Trailways sign was painted above the double swinging door on the same driveway side. That narrow driveway, with an overhang for weather, was where buses loaded and unloaded passengers; that was probably where the Freedom Riders bus would pull in. The flat side of Raymond Bros. Printing Co. closed in the entrance. The overhang made the entrance even narrower and darker, almost like a tunnel. I doubt I could've driven Big Red down either side when there was a commercial bus in there. It would have been claustrophobic as hell if you were on a bus, and especially if you were student Freedom Riders expecting something bad to happen on your first stop in Alabama.

I didn't know if they would all be students, but I did know they were all crazy as bats to bring their protest into the crater of the worst Klan sect there was in the entire nation. I would have bet none of them were from around here, so they wouldn't have any idea what they were getting themselves into. One thing I knew, they didn't comprehend how bad to the bone Alabama's Klan was, that Klansmen here were on a lifelong mission to keep the Negro cage and in a cotton field. Bad as the vicious Nazis they praised. If the Freedom Riders knew that, then they had death wishes and were categorically crazy, pure and simple.

Maybe a highway patrolman or an armed federal marshal was on board to look out for them, cause I knew, as devotees of Martin Luther King Jr., they weren't going to fight when they got attacked. They were here to protest, without violence, and that wasn't a fight at all. They'd been trained to resist when they got hit with baseball bats and iron chains and cut with knives and spit on and called terrible anti-American names. They could take a lesson from Harvey Nixon on taking pain.

Right now it was quiet; there were no buses at all and no traffic, not even a delivery truck entering the alley. The sun was bright and warm. Cotton candy roamed across the heavens, like that "lucky ole sun" of the song. Mother's Day was Sunday. It wasn't any day to hurt people. It was a day to celebrate life and the new spring, a day to spend with your family, go to the park and pitch a ball around.

I looked at Doctor Joe and I would've burst into tears except that there wasn't time for such foolishness. I had to put all my thinking into how I could help us get free and help those bus travelers.

They had something special planned for Doctor Joe or else they would have just shot him or strung him up last night, been done with him. My best guess was they wanted to somehow use him to show the world what happens to niggerlovers who mess with Alabamians. I didn't know what the plan was but everything I could come up with had a terrible conclusion, meaning Doctor Joe would die in some horrible, public way. They might want to burn him alive along with all the others on the bus. That could explain Roach wanting more bottled bombs than was necessary. My guess was they would wait for the bus to stop in the narrow entry then seal it off with their cars and throw Doctor Joe inside the bus then firebomb it and cheer while the people burned alive.

Then I thought, *Was that my fate too?*

The alley was awfully quiet for lunchtime on a weekday. None of the upstairs windows on the back of Woolworth's were open. It seemed clear the cops knew about the raid; they'd been ordered by Chief Bradley to alter traffic away, hold everyone back but the boys in white. Let them do the Attorney General's rotten work, taking care of the out-of-town troublemakers before the law shows up. Spread the word so those boys will know they are safe to beat, maim, kill and they won't be interfered with. They got the chief's word on it.

The *Woodstock Star* building was a half block down the street and it occurred to me that Herman probably forgot to tell the Oldham kid to deliver my papers this afternoon. Here I was, going to die in a little while, worried about the customers on my paper route. I sure wished I could get over there and pick them up myself, fool around shooting the shit with the other paperboys. I never thought I'd miss it.

Cars began to pull through the alley, driving so slow they could only have been Klansmen. I could tell too because they were dirty, beat-to-hell vehicles, just like their owners. It had to be after noon by now, though I didn't think it was one o'clock yet. You could see the City Hall clock tower from here. It showed 12:10, but of course that was useless time from a useless city hall.

Once they'd parked and the men had come around, Roach spit out the name of everyone, and then saluted and gave them God's blessings. In his name, like he was God. Crazy bastard.

Roach leaned in the car window, speaking to Kenny Legget. "Did you notice if Cec and Gooba got the cars parked in front?"

"That's them comin'," Legget said and pointed to the two men moseying toward our car from the front of the terminal. They looked proud and satisfied, like they'd just eaten a big Sunday meal. "Gooba." Some name, I thought, but it fit the guy; he looked like a Goober, stringy and unkempt, walking with a limp, a misshaped spine. He probably got one of those diseases when he was a rug rat from eating scraps off the floor.

Gooba and Cecil nodded at Roach, meaning the cars were in position, and walked on around to the back of our car and joined the others.

I watched them through the back window. They all lit up, giggling, poking each other like schoolboys, boys younger than me.

"There's Earl, our very last swinging dick," Roach said, speaking to Leon and Kenny Legget in the car. "C'mon, let's go."

When the two of them were out of the car, I leaned quickly against Doctor Joe. "Can you hear me, Joe? I know you can, nod or squeeze my hand, something."

He squeezed my hand without much strength, but he did it.

"*I knew it!* Please, I need the officer's number."

"No good," he spit, and some blood flew over his lips. He seemed hardly able to hold up his head. His mouth was so busted up inside that he couldn't talk around the engorged tongue. "Sonny ... Sonny, I wanted to tell you long before ..."

I gripped his arm and held tight, so close I smelled his broken, dying scent. "What, Joe, what?"

"There's you, Sonny. I love ..."

His battered head lolled and smacked the window.

I cringed and welled inside. "Joe! I hear you; it's the way I've felt all along. I love you too, Joe ... Joe, you've got to tell me what to do. Please ... Is there something wrong inside you? How bad is it?"

He came back for a second, teary in his good eye. He couldn't seem to look up, so I bent to let him see me. Our eyes met and in both it was another goodbye. Another; I couldn't bear it.

He whispered, "I'm sorry, Son ..."

I thought that would be all I could get from him now. Was he saving his strength? Or was he dying right now as I held onto his arm?

My feelings were all over the place; but I could not think about that now. It was not the time to feel. I had to do something. My hands started shaking.

Earl walked by the car window carrying a huge box he could barely get his arms around. But here he came with it. He couldn't see where he was going and tripped but didn't stumble enough to lose the box or fall. The others just stood there watching him, laughing, making no effort to help out. Roach opened the trunk and Earl put the box inside. They all dug into it and came out with robes and hoods and began dressing right there, turning into a bunch of sinister clowns. In the center of the white gown was that hypnotizing insignia that looked like a .45 record disk with an X and a drop of blood in its center. They tied linen belts, then top their outfit off with the tall, pointy cone that didn't stand up straight but tipped over and hung crooked. Becoming Ku Klux Klansmen.

Leon came around to the passenger-side car door and crawled in. His cone bent even more bumping the roof. He was elected to keep tabs on us, I guess. But the hat kept twisting sideways and making it so he couldn't see.

"Take the damn thing off, Leon. Nobody's going to see your face in the car," I said. I could say anything I wanted now, what did it matter?

"Oh, yeah," he said. I just sighed.

Doctor Joe was still in a slump. I made sure his head didn't strike the window frame, putting my hand between him and the glass. He moaned.

I could think of nothing to do for him. I just hoped that his insides weren't busted up too bad from the beating that he was hemorrhaging somewhere, right now bleeding to death.

A sense of total helplessness swept over me in a torrent of panic and shame and grief. The feeling was a lot like that day the football toughs tried to draw and quarter me, giving me a equal sense now of futility, of finality. I felt so lost I almost prayed to God for help.

I pushed myself even closer against Doctor Joe hoping his strength or spirituality or whatever it was that gave him such bullheaded determination would assimilate into me and help stop me from falling apart. It was him who needed me now, not the other way around.

The rest of their cars, four of them, were parked at the far end of the alley, lined up behind each other for a fast departure onto 11th Street, which was only a block from the wider 10th Street and an easy getaway through the west side out of town. Back to their headquarters hidden deep in the woods. My heart sped up thinking about them returning to their compound afterwards. It would be only minutes before things started to happen, and where would we be then, Doctor Joe and me?

I watched Lonnie hoist an apple box from the trunk of his dusty Plymouth onto his shoulder and walk toward us. He had a slow lanky gait, like a boy on a country road heading nowhere in particular. And that's probably all that he was, just a bumpkin heading nowhere outside his own muddled mind, a person with no ambition, no vision, not even any freedom. He was a slave, the way I saw it, to the narrowest minded beliefs that ever was.

He sat the box down on the hood of the coupe and Roach inspected the contents.

"Kenny, come here," he said.

Leon stayed inside with us. They were all in robes now and gathered for instructions. Fully robed and standing right out in the open, like they were getting a lesson in fly-fishing. Not a worry in the world when their usual murderous acts were carried out under cover of darkness when righteous people were peacefully dreaming of their children's future.

The men watched like attentive pupils, standing straight and still, as Roach demonstrated how to hold the pop bottle Molotov; you'd think they would already have gone through this drill. I heard him explaining which end of the wick you had to light. I couldn't believe it, there was only one end of the rag coming out of the hole in the bottle. There was no other end to light, but he instructed them anyway.

"You hold your lighter away from you to strike it, then bring the flame to the end of the wick that's hanging outside the bottle. Make sure the flame has caught good. Wait two seconds longer, when it's starting to smoke, then toss it. It's just that simple, people," he growled. "You all got lighters that work?"

Heads nodded.

"Good. Let me see them work."

About five men pulled out Zippos and tried to light them. I didn't think there was a breeze but four of the men had trouble getting or keeping their lighters lit. They had probably forgotten to put fluid in them before coming today. Some band of terrorists. How could this group of buffoons be the meanest Klan in all the South?

"Okay, you numbskulls. Kenny, get the lighter fluid."

The fluid container was in the dash of the coupe. Leon Legget handed it to him.

He demonstrated as Roach explained the process. Roach watched each man strip his Zippo or Ronson and saturate the inside cotton with fluid and then try again to light them. This time they over-flamed, burning the hands of three of the men. They dropped the lighters and stomped them on the asphalt.

"Alright. Now they work. Let's get strack."

The Klansmen lined up in arm-length formation, again like a slick paramilitary unit, and stood at attention. I didn't see any weapons on the men but they surely had concealed bats and tire tools under the robes and I knew Kenny Legget had a gun.

Roach looked inside the coupe and then motioned Leon out of the car and Leon jumped, knocking off his hood. He galloped to the end of the line and fell in.

"Okay, all y'all know your roles? … Hold it, what's that?"

The group grew dead silent.

They all looked at one end of the alley.

"It's here!" Roach said. "Get in position. Now, you idgiots!"

Men scattered, white blurs crisscrossing the black asphalt, some running for the terminal and some to the side of the alley and the rest to the far side of the bus station, and then they just seemed to vanish into the walls.

Curt appeared from nowhere. He was not in a robe and hood. He'd just gotten there, I suppose. He looked in and saw Doctor Joe motionless and me shivering, holding Doctor Joe by an arm. He frowned and stood back out, then went behind the car and donned white garb. Then he opened the door to the coupe.

"Get out," he hollered at me. "Can he move?"

"No, he can't, he's beat all to hell," I said viciously. "Can't you leave him be? He's dying!"

He laughed in my face and drug me out, pushing me to the asphalt. I thought he was going to pull his sap on me. Roach came over, looked quickly in the car.

We all turned to see the bus slowly pull in, a big gush of airbrakes hissing. A Greyhound, huge, its chrome glinting in the sunshine.

Everyone watched solemnly, like seeing a funeral procession coming through.

It was just me and Roach and Curt at the car now, with Doctor Joe still inside. The rest of the Klansmen including Kenny Legget stood somewhere in the shadows, not moving, watching the slow-motion bus creep in. Then the Klansmen stepped out into the sunlight. Those on the bus couldn't miss the sudden gauntlet of glory suits; it had to have been a surprise to them.

I looked at Doctor Joe through the dusty car window and he looked up and our eyes meet. I could suddenly see through his one bloodshot, swollen eye all the way to his heart. He was telling me to stay strong, keep my wit. I knew then it was time to die.

The bus never hesitated. It crept under the overhang, into that tunnel of no escape. The big airbrakes hissed again, so loudly you'd have thought the pressure line broke. When he saw all these Klansmen, the bus driver must have given at least a thought to crashing through Gooba and Cecil's cars that blocked the exit, but of course he wouldn't do that cause he was white and probably belonged to the Knights himself. Or maybe he was the new guy, on the bottom of the totem, so they stuck him with the assignment of hauling the mixed-race Freedom Riders through Alabama. And he would be going *Why me?* but would still do it; it was his new job.

"One false move from you and you are dead," Curt said, his eyes burning into mine. I took it he had a gun too, concealed under the robe.

I made myself small as I could, slumping, my mind swirling in desperation for some kind of break, or a sign.

He and Roach together pulled Doctor Joe out by his arms. He immediately collapsed. If he was faking it, he did a convincing job cause I thought I heard his head thump against the asphalt.

"Goddamnit, take it easy on him. *Please.*"

I got smacked for that. It tore my nose back open and I blew blood at Curt.

I could see what was going to happen, what their plan was and I said, "You can't do this! They're trapped in there."

I stood back an arm's length. They ignored me and hefted Doctor Joe's dead weight. It took all the two had to get him moving; so neither could swat at me.

"Stay put and shut your damn mouth," Roach said.

I didn't shut up. I said, raising my voice to a scream, "What're you going to do with him?"

I didn't expect an answer and they didn't give one. They were going to haul him into the bus before they threw all those Molotovs, intending to kill every last person on that bus, even if some of them might be innocent passengers just traveling from Atlanta to Birmingham or somewhere in between, to visit a loved one on Mother's Day.

I screamed again, "There could be just passengers in there. Let them go, please."

The bus door suddenly opened on a much softer hiss and a long moment passed when nothing happened, nobody came out or even looked out. They may have thought they would get blown away. Then someone got brave enough to show part of his face, then all of it. Fat guy in a hard-brim bus driver's hat. He didn't look scared. Maybe the guy had been in Korea or World War II and had been shot at and he had been in a flashback moment, like Nookie's old man, because he stepped out into the open, casually stretched his back. Not a care in the world; he had seen a lot worse than this. Then he nodded to the closest Klansman like he knew him despite the hood and I got it. He was no survivor from the war. He was just another one of them, a useless redneck hick. He disappeared through the swinging silver-glass door into the terminal.

There wasn't only no lawman in sight. There were no civilians, no traffic, nobody besides white-sheeted men. Not a soul to help these people, except me and I was handcuffed and brain-dead for a way to stop the catastrophe from happening. I swallowed hard. I had not thought of anything I could do.

The white robes moved quickly toward the back of the bus now.

Lonnie went to one side of the bus, working with an RC Cola bottle, adjusting the wick. He pushed it deeper into the bottleneck, then pulled the wick back out some and pushed it back in some, then turned it upside down to get the rag wick good and soaked. Another Klansman was doing the same with another soda bottle at the rear of the bus. They seemed to be in synch; they would be lighting the firebombs when a window got knocked out, I figured. The people on board had been smart enough to close the windows.

Another Klansman just then pulled a tire iron from under the robe and swung it against the back window of the bus, striking it until it finally shattered. He continued to hit the window till he'd knocked a large enough hole in the glass for a cola bottle to easily fit through. Another man was pounding a side window with a baseball bat. Space constricted his swing and it took a bunch of tries before the glass shattered. Two others were at the front tires cutting valves.

I moved closer to count heads inside. Nobody seemed to notice me. There were twelve people, about half were white and half were black, less than half women. Except for the seats where windows were being smashed, nobody inside moved much, a few glances outside but mostly they stayed very still in their seats. Docile, cardboard-like figures. Maybe they weren't people at all but manikins and the trick was on the Klan and the bus driver had played his part well and hightailed it inside and out the other door, free to live. It was a fanciful thought but I knew that's all it was. The people inside the bus were real as me.

A sudden rumbling noise came from the 11th Street end of the alley. I turned and looked. Some Klansmen did too and saw a crowd of people heading this way. Civilians. Talking loud, excited, moving faster toward us, their voices menacing, like hoodlums working up to a rumble. They weren't here to help the people stuck on the bus or for Doctor Joe or me.

They'd come to cheerlead for the Klan. Here to see these yankee troublemakers get their due. They wanted to see firsthand their Klansmen pour out the vengeance, like watching the hangman at the gallows. They wanted to see these Freedom Riders die.

They're going to get what they want, I thought.

There wasn't a marshal to protect the people on the bus or he would have come out by now. From where I was you couldn't see anyone standing in the aisle. The people were trapped. What would be going through their minds? Were they praying, preparing to die, I wondered.

I fell in with the advancing crowd and moved closer, trying to make myself invisible. I stopped when the crowd stopped.

Out of the chattering crowd popped a short man with a box camera strapped to his neck and held in both his hands. He wore a fedora and a leather jacket with his tie loosened. I caught Roach staring at him. The man's presence frustrated him, particularly with his hands full dragging Doctor Joe to the bus. He and Curt were at the rear of the bus now and he put his attention on his task.

Seeing with terrible clarity the death warrant now on the brink for Doctor Joe made me suddenly sick. I heaved but nothing came up but blistering bile. I caught the little cameraman taking a picture of me.

Kenny Legget had moved on ahead, a heavy chain in his hand, to join the muscle crew pounding the bus. No one was watching me right then; this was my chance. Just on instinct I searched for some kind of weapon, a brick or piece of wood, even a rock. Wide-eyed, I looked all around. A dumpster was parked just feet away.

The next few moments became a single instant in my mind, even though it wasn't. I didn't think, I just moved, unexcited and with no feeling, just moving like a robot.

I threw the dumpster lip back and lifted up and over the edge. Inside were a couple of wooden crates, for tomatoes. Too flimsy to do any good. A shattered wooden lift platform was under some trash. I dug and yanked using my cuffed hands as one to lift a broken plank. It came loose from the nails, a solid, two-foot piece of splintered fresh wood. The stake you'd drive into Dracula's heart.

Incredibly, nobody noticed me climbing in or out of the dumpster. Their attention was on the man snapping pictures; they didn't want photographs of this scene. Pictures would show the world the Klan in action.

Kenny Legget noticed me then and ran full throttle toward me, swinging his chain. Then he saw the splintered wedge and he dropped the chain and reached behind his back. He kept coming closer, fast; I did not forget for a second his threat to shoot me. I'd seen the gun he laid across Doctor Joe's lap.

Roach suddenly screamed at him, "Get that camera guy, Kenny!" distracting Legget for just a moment. Roach apparently hadn't noticed me.

That moment was enough to set the stake against my inner arm and charge him, Legget. I ran hard as I could. I had always been fast; now

I ran like a leopard. Before his gun came around, the stake ran through his gut, maybe his heart. It went all the way through him. His hood flew off. I let go the stake with a little push that took him backwards, falling against the asphalt with a sickening spew of blood from his mouth, and a grunt I would never forget.

I looked for his gun, desperate now since I was certain Roach or Curt or both would start shooting. It was too far back; he'd dropped it coming after me.

That single moment in time had passed now, and now came a moment of extreme anxiety. It was a terrible sense of impending pain, of death, leaving the earth to the dark void. I dropped to the ground and waited for the bullet to hit. But no gun fired, no bullet hit me or around me. I rolled close to the dying and gasping Kenny Legget. I looked at him, into a face of incomprehensibility; he didn't seem to understand what his eyes saw. Maybe they saw nothing; maybe he was already dead and his body was in its dying reflexes.

He lay helpless as a new baby. His arms wouldn't work for him. I thought this because his hands seemed to grope for the splintered stake in his heart. The speaking parts of him didn't work either but his mouth whistled, sucking air. His eyes bulged out, closed and the last of his breath hissed through his teeth.

I got up and ran behind the dumpster. Still no bullets came my way. It could only mean that Roach had been ordered to lay off any gunplay. That would be an order from the white citizens' council that had trickled down from the state confederation. Or maybe from the governor himself, cause if it had been left to the Klan, statewide or local, guns would be blazing. These boys much preferred violence that's lethal.

A Klansman lying dead and bloody on the ground seemed also to freeze the thrill-seeking crowd. For some strange and miraculous reason they didn't turn on me. If there was a God, He'd just shown Himself to me.

I spotted the photographer dipping and dashing as agile and swift as a sparrow. One look at the fury on Roach's face, I thought he or Curt might break with those orders and shoot the man taking all these damning pictures. I thought they were trying to decide if they could let go Doctor Joe long enough to get a bead on him.

They ended up leaving him alone. Their plan to get Doctor Joe on that bus, I guess, was more important. They would run the photographer down afterwards, take his film. Doctor Joe still appeared to be dead weight, and their struggling so far hadn't yet gotten them to the back of the bus.

Up till now the Klansmen performed pretty smoothly for a bunch of "idgiots," as Roach had called his crew. They seemed only to be waiting for the command to fire up their Molotovs, pitch them through the smashed bus windows. But seeing their fiercest brother impaled and lying in an incredibly large pool of his own blood that had soaked and stained much of his full-body white robe, his soul now flying around hell with his comrade Knights, they would've been discombobulated, unsure of themselves or what to do now. Roach and Curt were taking too long getting Doctor Joe on the bus, which also threw things off, I figured.

A Klansman at the back of the bus all of a sudden took it upon himself to light his firebomb. Maybe he just wanted to get the ball rolling; his hands were unsteady holding the bottle. His lighter wasn't working right and another man had to light it for him. They stood there with the dark smoke coming off the saturated wick, as if not sure when to throw it. They looked to Roach who had the Klansman to his back.

But Lonnie saw the burning Molotov and lit the fuse on his own bottle. He lit it with ease and held it up as if proud of the accomplishment. A small plume of black smoke drifted by the bus.

"Goddamnit, Lonnie!" Roach screamed, the smoke catching his nostril. "We need him on the bus and *then* you light the goddamn thing, remember? Fuckin idgiot. How long you got before it blows?"

"Uh—I—I dunno, maybe a couple minutes. That is, unless it pops."

Roach just shook his head and looked away. Discouraged, Lonnie seemed to lose the air that held up the shoulders of his Klansman's robe. He lowered the bottle, and it just then flamed up, catching fire to his long sleeve and racing up his arm.

At that instant, the present, the future of everyone around and inside the bus, all changed. For the trapped, frightened Freedom Riders, it would mean life instead of a fiery death. They would suffer only from smoke choking their lungs. They would get over the trauma of knowing, up to this final moment, that they were going to burn to death, burn alive. It would be a victory for CORE, too, and a landmark victory for the Civil Rights Movement. It would be a humiliating defeat for the KKK, Woodstock and the state of Alabama.

In that instant, Doctor Joe came to life. As if Zeus or the phoenix or my new God Himself had whirled a bolt of life into him.

I saw it all from behind him. He grew a foot taller; his arms shot out and took Roach and Curt both into headlocks that kneeled them over. They didn't anticipate his strength and quickness. I didn't think Doctor Joe could open either one of his eyes, but he could see well enough to locate the flaming cola bottle in Lonnie's hand, and just as Lonnie dropped it, Doctor Joe kicked the bottle so precisely that it spun end-over-end in a smoky flame through the air about seven feet high and came right back to him, to Doctor Joe.

I heard a muffled gunshot and knew Curt, or maybe Roach, had put a bullet in him. He didn't move an inch. Doctor Joe had an All-American football player's willpower to resist pain, to gather strength. Another muffled and awful shot went off and Doctor Joe then stumbled backwards but never let go his grip on either man and never went down.

The RC Cola bottle hit Doctor Joe in the breast and fell to the asphalt where it exploded into a fireball at the shoes of the three men, sending up an initial wave of yellow and white flames that enveloped them all. The explosion would have knocked them all flat on their backs but for Doctor Joe's great force against it; it nearly knocked me down and I was several yards behind. He held the Klansmen tight and kept his arms locked on their necks; then he bent over into the hot flames with their heads pinned in against his bullet-riddled ribs.

The first sound you heard after that was screaming, then the whooshing sound of flaming fiber and hair. It seemed their clothes went very fast in one big fireball. Then came the terrible sizzling. And then it turned nauseatingly quiet but for burning gasoline sucking the oxygen from the air. It took little time for the flesh to weld and then molt and begin to melt; that's when I heard the awfulest sound I would ever hear, the bubbling and popping from under the surface of human skin that burst like water in hot oil. I threw hands to my ears and turned away. Tall flames rose into the sky in a dark plume that drifted toward the broken-clock tower at City Hall.

The little man with the box camera darted about, the only person on the asphalt to move. Every one of the white-robed Klansmen I could see stood limp and still, like so many boards in a broken picket fence. The group of cheering civilians had stopped cheering and for the moment also seemed paralyzed. Then, like a pack of wolves, they began in unison to retreat. I had to back away, too. I could not bear looking at that heap of bodies, which now had formed into one hideous mound of burning rubbish.

The Klansman who lit the first firebomb had tossed it inside the bus and smoke began billowing out through busted windows. Riders, hesitating at first, finally streamed out. They were orderly, probably from their training—*When they move on you, you* must *remain calm.* I doubt they would have left the bus if the fire and smoke hadn't forced them out. They moved away from the burning vehicle, most of them going to their knees, coughing violently. But all of them looked upon the heap of burning flesh with a sense of awe and, it seemed to me, reverence.

The interior of the bus suddenly burst into flames, billowing through windows in fingers of yellow flames that climbed up and around the top of the bus. If fire trucks didn't show soon, the overhang was going to force the flames into the terminal building. The building attached to the terminal would go up next and there were other stores on the block, all connected by shared walls. I was hoping the trucks would not show up for a while, just as they had taken their sweet time getting to Doctor Joe's torched home. A greater fire, a city block say, would create much more spectacular pictures for tomorrow's papers, and with it, greater attention to the South's racial hatred.

I remember Doctor Joe saying just two days ago, hardly able to restrain his excitement, that this thing was going to put Woodstock on the national map. It was going to also put him in the history books as the man whose self-sacrifice to save the lives of a dozen people opened the nation's eyes to the depraved conditions of our black citizens in

Alabama. So that now we could get on the road toward equalizing civil rights across the South and on to all of America.

The way I saw it the sum of Doctor Joe's worth, the beauty of his being, came from an absolute refusal to ever give up trying to do good for people who needed help. He didn't care what color they were.

Woodstock police didn't have much choice but to forfeit all authority to the FBI. The FBI didn't charge me with a crime, nothing. Three agents scoffed at the lone one who said while interviewing me, "But the kid *killed* the guy, tilted that fucker like Lancelot. Gentlemen, isn't that a crime?"

Killing Kenny Legget was a crime alright, but they weren't going to prosecute me for it. A good lawyer would prove it was self-defense, that I had saved lives; the man I killed meant to commit mass murder. But as evil as Kenny Legget was, did I do wrong? Doctor Joe would lecture me that nonviolence is the better way to bring civility and peace to a given condition, or some other words meaning the same. But at the time, I knew he was aware of what was happening and what I'd done and I want to believe and I hope I always will believe that he was proud of me for taking that action, that it might even have been the okay that let him sacrifice along with himself those two monsters Roach and Curt. This town, this world was going to be a lot better off without them in it. I realize my crime and Doctor Joe's, too, are a slap in the face to Gandhi and the Dalai Lama and to Martin Luther King and the whole Civil Rights Movement. It went completely against Doctor Joe's disciplined morality. But because of his final deed, the violence in it, I don't have any choice but to believe he did not disapprove mine before he left me.

I have that of him. It helps.

I think this, too, that killing Kenny Legget like I did helped ease me through my first sanctioned killing a few years later in I Corp. The lynching in the Alabama woods that awakened me to the haunting epiphany that I could never shoot another human being, well, that got trampled down to a good laugh. I am not proud of it.

ABOUT THE AUTHOR

Ron Argo is an award-winning journalist and a decorated Vietnam veteran. His first novel, *Year of the Monkey* (published by Simon & Schuster), has been hailed as one of the seminal novels of the Vietnam generation, ranking him alongside America's best war novelists—Mailer, Stephen Crane, Jones and Dos Passos.

Growing up in Alabama at the time of the events in *The Sum of His Worth,* Argo will not deny the novel is semi-autobiographical, as some of the events were real and some of the characters in the story are based on people he knew back then, including "Doctor Joe."

Argo is also the author of *The Courage to Kill,* a murder mystery, first in the Ray Myers series. Second in the series is the forthcoming *Baby Love,* a story pitting Myers against a bumbling but ruthless gang of international baby smugglers.

Argo lives with his second wife and Aussie cattle dog in San Diego. Visit his website at ronargo.com.